SC
O A
GAME

Raghav Chandra has master's degrees from Delhi University and Harvard University, and is a permanent civil servant. He has lived, for a large part of his life, around the beautiful forests and bewitching tiger reserves of Central India. He has closely observed and is passionately moved by the conflicts that are critically endangering our ecosystem and wildlife, particularly the tiger.

SCENT OF A GAME

Raghav Chandra

RUPA

Published by
Rupa Publications India Pvt. Ltd 2014
7/16, Ansari Road, Daryaganj
New Delhi 110002

Sales centres:
Allahabad Bengaluru Chennai
Hyderabad Jaipur Kathmandu
Kolkata Mumbai

This is a work of fiction. Names, characters, places and incidents are either the product of the author's imagination or are used fictitiously, and any resemblance to any actual persons, living or dead, events or locales is entirely coincidental.

ISBN: 978-81-291-3111-9

Second impression 2014

10 9 8 7 6 5 4 3 2

Printed at Gopsons Papers Ltd, Noida

CONTENTS

TIGER'S SKIN

The tiger skin shone brilliantly in the pre-lunch Jabalpur sun. Of the two men who spread it in front of the chai-shop, Ramchandra Prasad—the older one with a shaved head and gentle, hesitating hands, had a natural poise establishing his higher position in life. That he had come from the United States was evident from his elegant, though creased, Hilfiger jacket and the airline-tag on the Hartmann bag by his side. Jugnu Pardhi, the younger man with gaudy sunglasses, and tight-fitting jeans that did little to conceal the bulge of a fat wallet, displayed the confidence of a local.

The gleaming skin on the bench also cast its spell on the chaiwallah, who begged to feel it. He turned down the radio and quickly jumped off his shop on stilts before Ram could say a word.

'Tiger is truly king of the jungle,' he said admiringly, looking at the others. He poured chai into glass mugs from his aluminum kettle, wiped his hands thoroughly against his shirt and caressed the gold and black skin. 'Sheer velvet...Burree Maada must have been at least ten or twelve feet big when she ruled the jungles of Kanha. What say you, Jugnu?'

Burree Maada was the famous Royal Bengal tigress that had vanished recently from Kanha Tiger Reserve despite camera traps in the core area and a radio-collar around her neck. No evidence of territorial fights between felines had been detected. No carcasses of dead tigers, let alone of this mature tigress, had been found. The matter had attracted instant local and even international media attention because of the massive ongoing national conservation program. Quite expectedly, the government had been hauled over the coals by the opposition for this failure.

'Good skin,' Jugnu said. He pushed his sunglasses over his forehead and remained lost in thought for a few moments, before extracting two multiple-folded dollar bills from his leather wallet. He straightened them carefully before pressing them into Ram's hands, saying authoritatively, 'Good two hundred dollars for Jabalpur!'

Jabalpur, on the banks of the mighty central Indian river Narmada, and an entry-point to key Tiger Reserves—Kanha, Bandhavgarh and Pench, is a busy city. Its life revolves around several ordnance production factories, a vibrant military command and its many regimental centers, a rambling railway establishment, a huge Electricity Board, a bustling High Court and a large educational fraternity. And well before lunchtime, a large number of those employed in these establishments throng the streets to shop for knick-knacks from street-vendors and impromptu bazaars—to strike mean bargains, light up a cigarette or just soak in the gossip.

The tiger skin was attracting hordes of curious bystanders who quickly made their way towards the chai-shop. They commented about the tiger and its unique attributes—its natural ferocity and speed, how it attacked and bit the throat of its prey until it died of strangulation, how a diminutive tiger could win against even a mighty elephant by attacking its cumbersome behind, and how tiger bone dipped in Darjeeling tea worked wonders for flagging manhood. Another piped up with a story of the warrior-goddess Durga, who fought her battles against vicious demons of the netherworld astride a huge tiger. While yet another related the story of the Hindu god Shiva who sat on a tiger skin whilst he meditated.

'This is a James Wilson skin,' Ram said to Jugnu, sipping his tea, subduing his surprise at the different responses.

'Okay, good, three-hundred dollars,' Jugnu said conclusively, with a sigh. He put his hand on Ram's shoulder and whispered conspiratorially, 'Boss, this offer is the best in the market. It will solve your problem of carrying it around. The Forest Department people are big idiots. Even when you return to the States, their questions will continue to chase you.' And then, as if guided by some sixth sense, he whispered urgently, 'Hurry!'

Ram stared hypnotized by the lustrous skin, the dollar bills and the huge crowd around him. He seemed to realize the value of this tiger skin, as he faltered and asked Jugnu inconsequentially, 'Really?'

'Yes, Boss,' said Jugnu, and nudged Ram for a hint of confirmation.

'I must go,' said Ram apologetically, pushing the dollar bills back to Jugnu. He was stuffing the tiger skin nervously into his bag when he felt the weight of a heavy hand on his shoulder and turned around to find it was a policeman. He dropped the bag in fright, wincing in distress, but the grip only hardened.

'You have to come to the station,' announced the policeman authoritatively.

'Why?'

'For Burree Maada, the Royal Bengal tigress killed by poachers in Kanha Tiger Reserve last week,' the policeman replied.

'But this is an old skin,' protested Ram. He recalled Jaya, his wife, reading out a report about a missing tigress in India and how wild tigers were on the brink of becoming extinct. There was something about China as well; and she had mentioned Burree Maada, the Big Female.

'Then show me the the Wildlife Protection Act Registration Certificate for this skin.'

Ram fumbled in his pockets wildly before admitting, 'I am sorry. I can't find the papers. But I am a famous global citizen... like Sabir Bhatia, like Laxmi Mittal.' He fidgeted, trying to relieve the grip.

The policeman looked uncertain for a moment as he gauged the people around him. There was excited chatter—some accusations and many taunting sneers from the spectators. Just then a nerdy-looking cadet dressed in the olive uniform of the Forest Department surfaced and shouted angrily, 'Global citizen, my bloody foot!'

'I am Ramachandra Prasad, NRI...from Silicon Valley,' Ram retorted, wary about naming his company, given its current controversial status. But, as a non-resident Indian, or NRI, he could enjoy the privileges bestowed by a government keen to attract remittances from its citizens abroad. Surely everybody would look at him differently now.

'No, you are a global smuggler taking away our Burree Maada,' the cadet shouted. 'The Forest Department gets a bad name because of greedy people like you. You lure poachers to kill tigers for aphrodisiacs. You want them to adorn your mansion. Wait till your photograph is published in *Time* and *Newsweek* as a poacher.'

'Run, you NRI idiot, get lost!' Jugnu shouted urgently, jabbing a dazed Ram in the ribs, and snatching the Hartmann bag with the skin. He set off at a good pace, wriggling deftly through the crowd that had collected, but barely made thirty yards before a whistle blew. He decided to run, prompting another man in khakis to run after him.

'Catch him! Catch the poacher!' the cadet screamed. The crowd roared its approval.

Jugnu seemed to be an old hand at this game. He had almost turned the bend before the policeman caught up with him, swinging his baton menacingly. He grabbed Jugnu with one hand and the bag with the other and dragged him back towards the chai-shop amongst cheers from the swelling crowd.

Ram seemed to be stuck to the ground with shock. He managed a look at Jugnu who seemed to be faring no better. A Maruti jeep drew up and screeched to a halt and within moments they were hustled into it. Strong policemen held them physically while one of them clung to Ram's bag with the tiger skin as if it were gold.

The jeep lurched forward. But journalists—the other stakeholders in the drama, wanted a bit of the excitement too. They pursued on motor cycles and sputtering scooters and halted their vehicles in front of the jeep. Flashing their press cards they converged towards the rear of the jeep. 'We just want photos,' they shouted.

The policemen, filled with importance, laid down the law. As per convention, no photographs were to be taken. But there was enough in their manner to convey that the press could milk this Jabalpur Police environment-related-success-story as much as it liked. Ram attempted to hide his face with his hands, but it was too late. Jugnu seemed more hardened; he stared brazenly at the photographers as the cameras clicked.

A siren hooted discordantly. The jeep sped off at top speed with its prized catch and halted outside a plain-looking building with unkempt lawns.

Ram and Jugnu were ordered out of the jeep and directed to stand on the cemented central platform of the police station. Far more than his body, Ram's mind ached; he was unable to comprehend why Jugnu seemed unfazed.

The policeman on duty opened a red, hard-cover register and glared at the ashen-faced Ram, and asked, 'Father's name, and where you belong to?'

'Ramachandra Prasad, NRI,' said Ram. 'I live in the United States of America and had come to see my father, Professor Ananda Prasad who lived in Amarkantak. This skin was gifted to him. It is of a man-eating tiger that had been shot decades ago by the famous English hunter James Wilson, a contemporary of Jim Corbett. I was simply bringing the skin to fulfil my duty to have it deposited with the Conservation Department.'

'Wilson?' mumbled the policeman, nodding understandingly. Ram sighed with relief.

The policeman clicked a ball-point pen and rolled it inside his ear thoughtfully. Next he pulled it out and studied the nib curiously before scraping it against an old newspaper and commenced to write. Meanwhile, the policeman who had arrested Ram leaned against the iron-bars of the lock-up. A rat clambered down one of the rusted bars and scurried for cover inside the cell, toppling an empty steel glass. He chuckled, 'Burree Maada! Who killed her? Jugnu Pardhi? Or perhaps it was Corbett, or was it Wilson?'

'I don't know anything about Burree Maada,' Ram replied piteously.

'Burree Maada was killed near Jabalpur in Kanha and since then the government's mother is getting screwed,' the policeman said with a dour look, tapping his pen against the table noisefully. 'Okay, how much did you buy Burree Maada for?'

'Three-hundred American dollars plus other foreign exchange recovered from Jugnu Pardhi. Price of Burree Maada,' announced the other policeman. He took out a small packet wrapped in newspaper and tied with rubber bungs from the Hartmann bag and tore off the wrapping to produce the dollars and other currency bills that had been seized from Jugnu. He also produced a handwritten evidence-voucher written in Hindi, along with its smudged carbon duplicate mentioning the event and the objects—especially the tiger skin and the money that had been recovered from the arrested duo. At the bottom of the page were the names and addresses of witnesses and their signatures.

'This is ridiculous!' protested Ram. 'This tiger skin has been with my father for so many years. In fact, it is, now it is mine.'

'Sir, indeed it is yours, and now you are ours,' the policeman sniggered poetically. 'Educated people never feel the need to admit their crime.' He glared at Jugnu and continued, 'of course, Jugnu

Pardhi is a history-sheeter, a poacher of wildlife. He has been inside seventeen times. Even if he speaks, be cannot be believed. So Sir, tell us the truth and go free. Wildlife poaching is a heinous crime.'

'I have nothing to tell...nothing to hide,' Ram groaned, trying to suppress the chilling numbness that was overtaking him.

'Very well then, Mr Ramachandra Prasad and Jugnu Pardhi...'

'Allow me to prove the heritage status of this skin,' Ram pleaded breathlessly. His spirits fell as he caught a glimpse of the police lock-up.

'Sir, you will have all your life to defend yourself in court,' said the policeman with empathy tempered with realism. 'We have only done our pious duty.'

The iron door of the lock-up made a grating sound as it was dragged open and Ram and Jugnu shown inside. It was a bare cell, without furniture, lit only by a naked yellow bulb and a fan whose blades were laden with dirt and cast eerie shadows on the floor. The door was closed with a loud clanging sound and the bolt drawn before a lock was turned.

Ram stared at the iron bars, stunned. How could this be happening to him—to one of the brightest young executives in Silicon Valley; the Forbes 'savvy business leader of tomorrow'? Suddenly, in one surreal swoop, time and space had been snuffed out of his life. 'You know Jugnu that I did not buy any animal-skin, let alone that of a tiger,' he said, hoping to elicit sympathy. 'For no fault of mine I'm embroiled in this Burree Maada matter and you did not speak,' moaned Ram shaking Jugnu violently.

After a deafening silence, Jugnu spoke, 'These bastards only believe the opposite of what we say.' And then he added philosophically, 'sometimes we fall not because we are bad, but because we pay for the actions of other damned fools.' He looked indolently at Ram, and kicked a cigarette butt till it rolled out of the cell.

Ram was flabbergasted! Jugnu actually had the audacity to blame their current state upon him; and now he was propounding a deeper insight into life!

On the other hand in a moment of reflection, was he, Ram, paying for his past actions, or was he paying for somebody else's actions, or inaction? James Wilson, the English hunter of man-eating tigers and Burree Maada, the missing tigress of Kanha, were suddenly the most overpowering mysteries of his life. Something deep within him knew that he needed to introspect if he had to discover why he had fallen. He fell on his knees and reflected on the events of the past week, ever since Jaya and he had talked about tigers in their cozy home in Cupertino.

'Pan Therapeuticals of China will be hitching-up with Zentigris of India and producing in Silicon Valley, the cute little…'

Ram smiled at Jaya curiously, 'What?'

'Pan-the-ra Ti-gris,' she drawled. 'You could have kept that name for your JV. It's also the scientific name for the magnificent Asian tiger which is a hot topic these days,' Jaya's red lips curved into a sardonic smile that lit her full and voluptuous face.

He gawked, marveling at the coincidental conjunction that emerged from the names; what a pity he hadn't thought of it. 'That's interesting,' he remarked, sipping some sherry.

'Unlike Zentigris which is a priapic bull on NASDAQ, the Asian-tigris is unfortunately getting buggered royally.'

'Has something unusual happened today?'

'It is tectonic, and all over the media,' Jaya announced. 'I just read an incisive HT feature out of Central India. Half of the Project Tiger Reserves—Sariska, Panna, Melghat—have no tigers left. The swan song all over Asia.'

His mind drifted lazily to India. Even though Jaya's roots

were Indian, she rarely missed an opportunity to highlight bad news about the country. He often wondered if it was because she had been born in the States and had lived most of her life in the protected academic environment of Cambridge. Her newfound interest in tigers surprised him. He cast his mind on laid-back India and the state of tiger reserves. 'I feel sorry,' he mumbled.

'You know, a popular Royal Bengal tigress called "Burree Maada", the Big Female, disappeared recently from the Kanha Tiger Reserve, and hardly a head rolled,' said Jaya.

'The tigress was possibly killed and buried there.'

'Why bury a carcass when there is demand for tiger parts? I believe there's quite an appetite for tigers in China.'

Ram jerked up his head, surprised. He had heard of Tiger Balm, Tiger Air, Tiger Beer and other products that had exploited the brand value of the tiger name. But tigers were meant to be observed in a zoo or during a safari. Perhaps to be admired in a picture. Never to be consumed. 'That seems most unlikely,' he said.

'How do you think China has the world's largest population? Tiger wine, tiger sprays; all performance enhancers for that extra T.'

'Really?'

'Yes! Viagra's only a recent, very multinational-corporation-thing,' said Jaya. 'By the way, how do you think it got its name?'

'Roman god of passion? Greek goddess of love?'

'Neither! In Sanskrit, the tiger is called Vy-aghra. And now the natural Vy-aghra is getting screwed.'

'Queering the pitch for the artificial Viagra!' Ram was amused. After some thought he said, 'But Jaya, poaching of elephants, tigers and wildlife has always been commonplace in developing countries. What's new?'

'Ram, the tiger is the head of the biotic pyramid,' she said. 'Political sidekicks get bumped off...not presidents.'

'Point! But why should you care when there's so much else

that is getting screwed.'

'The Prime Minister should just make an honest confession from the Red Fort. My beloved Indians, I may have let Paki terrorists off the hook, but I've successfully nuked tigers.'

'You're wicked,' said he, switching off the Sufi-ballads. He removed his Lanvin python strap loafers and put his feet on the coffee table. Loosening his shirt, he continued, 'In any case, I doubt if people like us will ever have any truck with tigers in our lifetime.'

'Let's keep our fingers crossed,' Jaya said. 'Tigers are such a huge mystery. Anyway, now that we're on tigers, if there is one thing that I ever want from India, it has to be that tiger skin your father uses as a prayer mat. For my yoga,' she said, pleadingly.

'You actually want that ancient tiger skin?' he asked aloud, startled by her demand. He fixed his gaze at the glittering chain of her Fendi bag unseeingly, wondering what had got into her.

'I love antiques,' she said, with a mischievous smile.

He nodded. Jaya was deeply involved in her current project with a professor of Art History at Stanford University. A few decades older than her, he was scripting her documentary on the nature-worship similarities amongst Mayan, Inca and other ancient civilizations. He smiled sarcastically and said, 'That I know…some antiques are undeservedly lucky. They are sought relentlessly by quirky collectors.'

'Ram, if only you could understand,' she said pulling herself comfortably against the sofa. 'That tiger skin is chic. It has cachet that Prada and Louis Vuitton don't. The skin of a man-eating tiger, shot by a brave English hunter in the dense jungles of tropical India; who sailed away on a ship laden with priceless wildlife trophies, and was finally attacked and sunk by pirates off the Cape of Good Hope! Romance and mystique!'

'Anything for my Jaya,' he said smiling, extending his hands to her. He thanked his stars for having held back from saying,

'My femme fatale!' But noticing her seriousness he quickly added, 'Strangely, I can't understand why the old man's so touchy about that damned thing.'

'He'll relent if he knows I want it,' she said, chuckling. 'Didn't you say he is likely to kick the bucket soon?'

'Come on, I hope otherwise,' he said, suddenly stung by her remark, but taking care not to show his indignance. 'But yes, for all his yoga and mathematical puzzles, I agree that it's a downhill spin for him now.'

He visualized his father sitting in the padmasana or lotus-posture on his tiger rug, eyes closed, meditating in his tiny home, redolent with incense. How assiduously he had preserved that skin gifted to him by his good friend Wilson, the legendary English hunter of man-eating tigers who had become famous in the sub-continent, much like Jim Corbett. And then suddenly one day, again pretty much like Corbett, this hunter had disappeared quietly, perhaps to lead a reclusive life in England or Africa. There had been no Tree-Tops-like feature about him, although somebody had mentioned that a biopic was being planned about his adventures. Or were they misadventures?

He looked at Jaya across the antique Laotian tea-table—he loved this corner of their home in beautiful Cupertino. He held the crisp, silver-edged card that was the invitation for the 'Wedding', as the grand gala commemorating the much-publicized partnership of Zentigris with the Chinese company was referred to in jest. The word ZENTIGRIS dazzled on the front leaf above the company crest—a silver tiger encased in the black of the yin-yang circle. At the bottom of the card were the words: 'Driven by Instinct, Powered by Passion'.

He reflected on his life. He worked for fiercely-ambitious first-generation entrepreneurs who had ruthlessly built their business to a point where they commanded recognition from the highest echelons of American corporate society. He had kept up the pace and been supremely pushy, often skittering beyond the limits of correctness, with no regret about giving up his coveted but prosaic job with the famous consulting firm McKinsey.

'The Rajas have finally promised me a Board-level position,' he announced proudly. She was always egging him on to achieve new heights. It fired his imagination and spurred him to work harder. He parsed his Egyptian cotton shirt and ran his hands over his athletic chest. It gave him unusual happiness to have soared beyond his humble roots to become the ultimate immigrant dreamboat. She patted him and smiled complacently. Her blood-red nails complimented her alabaster skin and her pool-deep eyes added to her unfettered beauty when she smiled. But was a beautiful face enough to comfort an anxious mind? He picked up his glass and looked at her again. A cool breeze with the fragrance of prunes and apricots wafted across the terrace from the direction of the golf resort, assuaging his misgivings.

Jaya downed her sherry and announced excitedly as she got up to refill their glasses, 'I'm looking forward to my gaucho trip. It will be fun. I strongly recommend that you take a break after this...do that Classical Greece tour. Or better still, just go to India and check out the tigers, before they become history like the cheetahs that have become completely extinct. I remember reading that there were thousands of cheetahs a century ago until they were all hunted down by the locals. Go ahead and unleash your mojo and maybe I'll join you later.'

'I'd love to do Mycenae and Corinth. But I've some important submissions. Besides, I have to finalize the work to be done on the Manhattan Apartment.'

'Yes, the interiors, especially the woodwork. That's sooo sooo important!'

He pronounced loudly as if laying down the last word, 'History,

India, tigers... All have to wait for now!'

'Your choice,' said Jaya, shrugging her shoulders. She placed his glass aside and gently rubbed his face with her hands, kissing him on the forehead. 'G'nite honey,' she said. 'Get some sleep to look fresh.'

He watched her as she sashayed out seductively. Like an Andean gazelle? He perused the colourful brochures of her forthcoming tour. All of them had exciting pictures of prehistoric relics, gushing waterfalls and florid parakeets. He was about to put down the stack of brochures, visualizing her in khakis with a camera in tow, trekking across ancient hills shrouded by forest, when another pamphlet caught his eye. The front page had the title *Chihuahua* while the last page had the caption *La Barranca del Cobre, Sierra Madre Occidental*. There was a picture of a glistening copper-coloured stone monolith with a breath-taking vertical face.

Pena del Gigante. A solitary man was rappelling down a huge, sharp hill, bagpack on back. The golden caption, written in minute print, barely discernible, read: 'Fall of joy'.

Fall! He suddenly missed a heartbeat. As he laid down the brochure, something else caught his attention. There were two short articles out of India in the newspaper that lay in front of him—one about Burree Maada, the missing tigress of Kanha and the other about Bandhavgarh Tiger Reserve. He picked it up and read:

Two Britons in Jungle Fall

> Stewart Mackenzie, twenty-two, and Clark Macmillan, twenty-five, from Edinburgh, Scotland, fell off a steep cliff in the jungles of Bandhavgarh in Central India where the two had gone to study tigers, the British Foreign Office said. Their bodies have not yet been located, despite a search having been launched by the local authorities

> immediately after their fall. Bandhavgarh is one of the sanctuaries of the endangered Royal Bengal tiger and it is feared that the two were chased by a ferocious tiger.

Tiger! Fall!

The frightening words used by his father! Jaya and he had spent a wonderful weekend on a friend's yacht off the Caribbean coast. Just as they were about to set sail, he had received an unexpected call from his father, causing him to suddenly drop his Blackberry. The old man's voice was quivering, ancient as the hills.

'Ram,' his father's tone was anxious. 'Are you okay?'

'Yes, of course Da,' Ram said, relieved. 'We are both on a wonderful holiday. Why?'

'My son, I had a strange dream last night. I'm very disturbed.'

'Da, you probably saw me with an even more sensational woman,' he said with a sly wink at Jaya who was plastered with suntan lotion and dressed in a tiny bikini and Armani sunglasses. He had received a rap on his butt for that irreverent remark.

'I saw you fall…from a great height…into a cage.'

'A silly dream, Da,' scoffed Ram. 'There are no high cliffs here…only sun, sea and sand.' He had always described his father to his friends as a spiritual man who had never hurt a fly and, in fact, levitated in respectable deprivation. Perhaps that last word would now have to be substituted by delusion.

His father went on, refusing to be pacified, his words disconcerting, 'Inside the cage…a snarling tiger crouched nearby… ready to pounce.'

'Utter madness!' Ram had reacted vehemently. He whispered into Jaya's ear, 'You're right…the old man has lost it.' Jaya kissed him, reminding him of her interest in the tiger skin.

'Listen, my son,' his father's voice boomed back after a brief pause. 'I have something very, very important to disclose…'

And then, the line went completely dead as they had left the shore. They had reflected on the absurdity of his father's dream and laughed heartily for several minutes, before diving inside for their mojitos and margaritas. But even as he stared at the creamy surf and the clean blue sea ahead, a startling thought crossed Ram's mind—had the enigmatic Mr Wilson surfaced?

Even before the clattering of the rotor blades had died down, Ram tossed away his father's surreal premonition and concentrated on the spectacular 'wedding' before him. A man in his fifties, dressed elegantly in a grey Nehru jacket and black trousers, stepped out of the helicopter, and walked briskly towards the waiting party.

Ram rushed forward to greet him with a respectful namaskar, laying aside a promotional feature that detailed the alliance between Zentigris from India, a software company and Pan Therapeuticals, a bio-genetics company from China. It explained how the joint venture would tap the extraordinary genome sequencing requirements of the future with increasing convergence between the real and the virtual worlds.

Taruneswar Raja, the Vice Chairman of Zentigris, handed the dignitary a bouquet of red roses, large enough to be carted, as a photographer clicked dutifully. A redesigned golf cart whisked them off to the red-carpeted entry point where rose petals were showered and Jaipur essence sprinkled from silver dispensers. Narasimhan Raja, Chairman of Zentigris, limped forward to embrace his old friend Perumalan, the Chief Minister of Karnataka and former Mayor of his beloved city Mysore.

Perumalan looked at the Raja brothers and beamed, 'So, now the world will see our flag rise even higher.' He looked like a midwife holding a healthy child as he reminisced, 'It seems only yesterday when I had allocated land for the Zentigris IT Park in Mysore.'

Cameras converged as Perumalan breezed past the guests and foreign dignitaries to be introduced to the Mayor of Kunming. Perumalan collected the Raja brothers and their Chinese partners around him in a circle and proposed a toast, 'To the Asian Century!'

Loud applause interspersed with sizzling sounds succeeded in drawing everyone's attention to the heavens. The evening sky was splashed in turquoise as intersecting lasers began to scissor and scythe each other, making the steel and glass buildings of the Zentigris Knowledge Park sparkle in blue and green. A crisp silhouette of a silver tiger lit up the sky. It pranced gingerly, followed by another laser silhouette of a golden panda, and the two images waltzed to a musical fusion of James Bond and Pink Panther. Soon the tiger shook paws with the panda and embraced it, and both creatures bowed to the audience. Champagne popped amidst strains of Carnatic classical music in fusion with Dvorak's New World Symphony.

Colourful fountains erupted and flags of all the thirty-three countries where Zentigris had its offices came under the spotlight. The master-of-ceremonies announced a stage performance and Ram happily watched the satins, silks and taffetas swirl around him.

His gaze fell on an attractive brunette in towering Louboutins, weighed down with diamonds, and encased in fur. She seemed to be riveted by a cheetah mounted in the center of the room. 'Oooooh…Tres jolie,' she gushed, pink with excitement as she moved closer to caress it, when Perumalan moved forward and clasped her hand, 'Madam, many, many years ago, I had shot such a wild beast.'

'Yes?'

'A tiger, Madam! It was much bigger and far more powerful, more ferocious than this cheetah.' He waited for her to evince interest and was not disappointed that she was all ears, digging her sharp nails seductively into his hand, egging him on.

'It had taken my hunting party many days to track the beast through very thick jungle near the Kabini River, west of what is now the Nagarhole National Park,' he bragged. 'Finally, when the rest of my hunting party had given up hope, I heard a crunching sound from some bushes close by. The beast had attacked silently, almost killing this young man, raking his chest and belly with his razor sharp claws, dragging him by the neck... I have never seen so much blood. But I went after it, even as it tried to hypnotize me with its blazing yellow eyes. When it let out an earth-shattering roar, it was so terrifying that the others in my party ran for cover. And then, just as it prepared to charge at me, I managed a shot at its chest, rescuing the young man's life. Of course, I was mentally prepared to fight with my bare hands like our great warrior Tipu Sultan, the Maharaja of Mysore. Madam, you cannot even begin to imagine how suspenseful and dangerous it was.'

The woman was fawning all over Perumalan, 'Danger tests and illumines beauty, Monsieur.' Her face conveyed admiration for such a valiant feat as well as the hope of participation in a similarly exciting expedition. The gallant hunter in Perumalan permitting, she would have hitched along with him for any wild game.

Choosing wildlife as a theme had been Ram's idea. All the female ushers and staff wore Tibetan silk chubas with trims and sashes that drew heavily on tiger stripes and leopard-spots. The Raja brothers had been hesitant to part with their exquisite collection of wildlife artifacts. It had taken Ram's extraordinary persuasive powers to have them agree to lend a few trophies of African giraffes, zebras and leopards. Ram was particularly keen on the beautifully stuffed and imposing, twelve feet long Royal Bengal tiger with its jaws wide open and the fangs showing. When the Raja brothers finally agreed to exhibit some of their trophies, their emphatic caveat had been, 'These are priceless pieces of art by Rowland Ward of London's Piccadilly, the amazing Edward

Gerrards and the great artists in taxidermy, the Vin Diesels...be extremely careful.' The Chinese partners agreed to bring in two stuffed giant pandas and the Persian cheetah from their personal collection in Kunming.

Something caused Ram to freeze and drop his champagne goblet. Why the hell was the earth shaking? Was it an earthquake? He looked around. It was his mobile buzzing in its vibratory mode. All that was currently important in his life was here. This was his moment! He tried to ignore the call but the vibration persisted. In disgust, he whipped out his cellphone. The screen displayed: 'Unknown Number'.

He was about to turn off the phone, when a terrifying thought crossed his mind and he took the call.

The voice was of that one person in the world who would transmit the news that he dreaded to hear—Atma Ram Bishnoi, better known as Guruji, his father's neighbor. His father led a reclusive life in Amarkantak, the source of the holy river Narmada, deep in the jungles of Central India. Guruji's voice was clinical in its intensity.

'Ram...' A long pause before he acknowledged. Then the voice asked, 'How have you been?'.

'Guruji, we are well...how are you?' Ram shouted spiritedly, hoping to elicit some joyful remarks. There was a bottomless pause at the other end. He shouted again, 'Tell me, how is Da?'

His worst suspicions were stoked by Guruji's morbid tone, 'He's been asking for you.'

'How is he?'

'He is going,' pronounced Guruji. 'Perhaps forty-eight hours.'

'I propose a toast...' said Narasimhan Raja, raising his glass.

'Honoured to be with our best friends,' said the Chinese

partners, raising their glasses.

The Chinese partners Tong Choo and Jin Fung, and the Raja brothers, Narasimhan and Taruneswar, better known by their childhood nicknames Leo and Taurus, now retreated into a private corner of the celebration tent. They loosened their collars. The guests had left and it was their turn to chat and enjoy the evening, Asian style. Ram noticed the stack of beautifully wrapped boxes in a corner.

'Please fetch our gifts!' Tong and Jin directed their aide. A handsomely wrapped box with a crimson velvet cover was brought forth and its contents displayed. A green-leather bound book with the title written across it in gold.

'Ben Cao Gang Mu! We present a condensed English version of the centuries-old original that was found in the historic tombs of the Ming Dynasty,' Jin announced.

'Materia Medica. The compendium of traditional Chinese medicine handed down from generation to generation, incorporating the work of the great Master Li Shizhen,' Tong echoed.

'It preaches the amazing efficacy of our traditional cures, how pervasive they are,' said Jin. 'Modern allopathy and multinational pharma solutions are far too expensive. It is a pity that modern literature on TCM has deleted several important recommendations.'

Leo held it respectfully. He passed it on to Ram who quickly turned the pages. Something about four natures, five flavors and yin and yang caught his attention. There were elaborate diagrams of herbs—ginseng, mushroom and ginger; sketches of musk-deer and sea-horse and mention of a pig's epiglottis, a buffalo's nose and porcupine urine.

A flatter and larger box was being brought in dramatically by the aide. Exquisite silk wraps in myriad colours emerged—mauve and beige, blue and turquoise... Leo and Taurus maintained a discreet silence, while Ram admired them. If only he could take a few of these silks to Jaya, he thought, her happiness would know no bounds. Only then would she acknowledge the advantage of partnering with the Chinese.

And then, just as it seemed that the box was empty, Tong plunged his hand in to pull out a larger wrap. It was pressed crisply, gold in colour with the dark stripes of a jungle cat and dazzled brightly against the light.

Tong proudly presented it to Leo who was captivated.

It was Taurus who reacted exclaiming, 'Chinese silk, from the Silk Route...intricate Chinese workmanship...Wow!'

Leo continued to caress the lustrous velvet lovingly. 'It feels like tiger skin!'

'Indeed this is tiger skin!' said Jin beaming. 'It is not woven like traditional Chinese silk rugs in some sweat shop in Suzhou but organically derived from our own tiger farm in Guangxi.'

Leo could barely conceal his amazement, 'Natural...no different from those in the wild.'

'We have a few hundred tigers now and they are multiplying faster than we had imagined,' announced Tong. 'Unfortunately, some countries obstruct our captive-farming policy.' He contorted his face, 'India also opposes our CITES submission to relax the ban on trade of tiger parts from our farms. It is scandalous—especially when it is failing miserably to protect wild tigers even inside special tiger reserves!'

'That's another issue we should raise with Perumalan when we meet him tomorrow for breakfast,' Leo said to Taurus. 'We need to sensitize him about the next CITES meeting of ministers and brief him of our investment in these farms.'

Ram had been asked by Leo to urgently research the latest developments in CITES. The Convention on International Trade in Endangered Species of Wild Fauna and Flora was an international agreement between governments, supported by the United Nations, based out of Geneva. The aim of this extremely obscure inter-governmental protocol was to ensure that international trade in specimens of wild animals and plants did not threaten their survival. Leo had been particularly interested in learning about India's stand on matters connected to the tiger. Ram was curious about the reasons for this interest, considering tigers were vanishing in India.

The one point that had stood out was that while China wanted trade in tiger parts, or derivatives as they were called, to be permitted, India and several other countries were against it. The apex forum for policy-making was in the Conference of Parties that took place at the ministerial level of member countries. The next CoP was to be held at The Hague in Netherlands in June 2007, less than a year away.

'Our brand consultants have confirmed that there is indeed a huge and untapped demand in the States and in Europe for niche tiger artifacts,' Leo said. 'Gift shops and jewellers love to keep paws and teeth as pendants. Quirky but trendy!'

'It will be a pity to let our break-through advances in genomics and molecular evolution go waste,' said Jin. 'We have to get the tiger farms legalized. Collective pressure and focused strategy is needed.'

'My wife has been after me to get her an old tiger skin,' said Ram, recalling Jaya's obsession with his father's tiger rug and also her mention of the uses to which a tiger could be put.

'Indeed, now you can roar like a tiger and she will purr for you like a pussycat in bed,' Tong smiled mischievously and winked. He clapped his hands, as if calling out to a waiting genie. A female usher materialized and he pointed to her chuba that had a tiger skin-like silk trim, 'See how elegant they look. It is tiresome that the "Wolf in Monk's Clothes" has issued an edict forbidding his people from wearing animal skins.'

'Wolf?' Ram asked.

'The devil hides in the hills of India,' Tong said, 'Better known as the Dalai Lama, his supporters have lit bonfires of animal skins, desecrating thousands of years of Tibetan-Chinese tradition.'

Another cardboard box was opened and yet another lot of silk wraps displayed before Jin pulled out a fuzz-coated bottle shaped like a tiger, without a label, inside royal-blue velvet casing. It could well have been carrying cognac or perfume. Jin hailed for wine glasses, and poured from the tiger's mouth into five flutes.

'From Guilin, this elixir is fit for the gods of love,' Jin said. 'Top quality tiger bone wine—it can sell for a hundred dollars a bottle if marketed properly!'

Leo and Taurus proposed a toast. 'The Black Goddess,' they said in unison, and the Chinese partners followed suit.

Ram wondered what they meant by the Black Goddess? Was this wine fit for the Black Goddess of Love? There had been many women in black cocktail gowns at the party. Some had been provocative and voluptuous, but not the kind you would worship, except perhaps in bed.

And then he asked himself—could this be a reference to the Goddess Kali?

Kali, the dark and hypnotic destroyer of evil, the Hindu goddess of tantrik power and eternal energy, bearing a staff decorated with a garland of skulls, with her tongue lolling out fearfully, her eyes red with the intoxication of battle. She was depicted as piercing the snout of a demon, amidst a gory fountain of blood.

It struck him suddenly—a place of communion!

Kali-Mata? Kalimantan?

Suddenly it made sense. Last year, November. It was on a business trip with Leo to the Far East. Seoul. Tokyo. Kuala Lumpur. And then again east to Borneo!

Leo had been making several unsuccessful calls to someone and was visibly irritated on the flight to Tokyo. Upon landing, he resumed calling the reticent number. Leo Raja was not used to being ignored by anyone; he had become abusive.

Finally when he had turned on the speakerphone to conference with Headquarters, Leo had received another call, causing the conference to be called off abruptly. Ram remembered the voice of the caller—muffled—perhaps some disturbance on the line. The caller was laconic but Leo looked relieved. The relief of a drug addict assured of his next fix.

All through their next stop Kuala Lumpur, Leo gleefully repeated what his 'dear friend' had conveyed: 'The Goddess can be worshipped'.

Assuaging Ram's curiosity, Leo merely said that it was a personal invite by his friend to a private safari in a wildlife Park in East Borneo. Ram could also accompany him to go leopard spotting.

They had caught a Malaysian Airlines flight to Kota Kinabalu in Sabah, the speediest way possible. And then by chopper to Kalimantan, in Borneo.

Leo seemed to be in love with Borneo, acclaiming it as the Riviera of tropical Southeast Asia.

Ram picked a brochure on Kalimantan idly and read: 'Straddled by three different countries—Brunei, Malaysia and Indonesia—the landscape and wildlife are diverse and include high mountains and rugged coastlines. Think jungle and wildlife and you could think of this amazing island.'

Leo waxed eloquent, 'A Hindu friend of ours believes that much like the tourist paradise Bali, named after a character in the Hindu epic Ramayana, Kalimantan too has a connection with

Hindu mythology. It derives its name from Goddess Kali, Durga's exterminator manifestation, in sublime manthan or meditation. It could describe the periodic volcanic eruptions, followed by long spells of blissful inactivity.'

Ram nodded and began to read aloud from the brochure: 'Borneo's tropical rainforests have some of the richest biodiversity on earth. Borneo has nearly eleven thousand species of flowering plants. Kalimantan is inhabited by ten primate species, over three hundred and fifty bird species, and one hundred and fifty reptiles and amphibian species.'

'Most impressive,' said a fascinated Ram. 'Apparently there are plants that eat insects and frogs! Scientists have recently discovered a large cat-fox mammal in Borneo's rainforest; of course the undisputed king of all is the clouded leopard! Have you ever seen it?'

'Indeed,' said Leo. 'It is a beautiful creature!'

Ram continued to read: 'Clouded leopards are some of the best climbers in the cat family. Several adaptations give clouded leopards amazing arboreal skills. They can climb tree branches upside down and hang from their hind feet.'

Leo announced proudly, 'This friend of mine is fantastic…he seems to be omnipresent. He has data about leopard locations, received through camera-traps set up along the paths frequented by wildlife. When a clouded leopard or other animal crosses the sensor, the image is chronicled digitally in a control room which my friend can access in real time. He has used his contacts to organize an expedition to hunt the Borneo gibbon and the humble jungle cat. Spotting the clouded leopard would be an added attraction. Of course he has taken care to be on the right side of the Indonesian Department of Forestry, Directorate-General for Forest Protection and Nature Conservation, the PHKA.'

'And the damages?' asked Ram.

Leo grinned dismissively, 'Value for money!'

🐾

Deep inside the tropical rainforest, the cacophony of the world receded as the mesmerizing sounds and beauty of nature gained precedence. It was indeed an experience of a lifetime. Ram feasted his eyes on the pristine beauty of this wildlife sanctuary. As a child he had visited Achanakmar, and been proud of its abundance, but the forests here were no less treasure-troves of bio-diversity. It had rained heavily the previous day. Water and sweat irritatingly flooded their gumboots and they emitted an anguished squelch. But, the distant growl of a jungle cat seemed to inject fresh energy in Leo. Ram, armed with a hip-flask and water bottle, was to follow at a discreet pace behind Leo, at least a hundred metres away, to avoid any disturbance. He was to realize that the distance also made it woefully impossible to save a man's life.

They trekked deep into the jungle and were rewarded when they spotted a family of jungle cats. They watched the breathtaking sight patiently, Leo resting his gun against a trunk, under a beautiful canopy of branches interlocked with each other. A pair of macaque monkeys groomed each other high up in the trees as a small animal, a cross between an ET and a Gollum stared at them.

Leo was about to take aim and shoot the leader of the pack of jungle cats when his attention was distracted by what he would later refer to as a turning point in his life.

Two clouded leopards hung upside down, suspended against the limb of a yellow meranti, thirty feet above the ground, barely twenty meters away. It could have been an exquisite porcelain creation of Lladro on the mantelpiece of a luxurious home. Tails hanging in full glory, they lay impervious to the world and the threat looming around them.

Leo felt captivated by their beauty. But, as he watched them he debated whether to focus on the clouded leopards or to go after the jungle cats. His friend's warning had been explicit—Guns are prohibited but a special dispensation has been made for you. However, killing a big cat meant saying goodbye to Borneo forever.

He held his breath and inched closer, ignoring the jungle cats, with concentration acquired over years of sport in the jungles. Within meters of the clouded leopard, Leo focused and took aim to squeeze the trigger, when a sudden sound distracted him.

A flying squirrel jumped across from the overhang, grazing his left hand, in his line of sight of the leopards drenching him with a shower of water. And in that instant, though dressed in breeches, and gum boots, Leo felt a leech up his thigh. He rubbed one leg with the other, trying to squeeze and kill the leech, pulling the trigger.

The lapse in concentration took its toll. He missed the leopards narrowly, instead hitting the branch from which they hung. It swayed under the impact as the clouded leopards dropped down like ripe fruit. Unlike porcelain, they fell with a thud on the richly cushioned vegetation.

Leo hurriedly wiped the sweat from his face with his elbow and bit his lips to ignore the leech which seemed to be headed for his groin. He could not see the leopards, but using his instinct, breathlessly inched closer, his rifle cocked. Water drenched him, upto his ankles, soaking his shoes, giving him the feel of being stuck in a swamp.

Suddenly, as he raised his hands to avoid a low branch, Leo tripped against a broken stump and slipped backwards, still clinging to his rifle. The clouded leopards snarled in unison as Leo tried to scramble to his feet, his face smothered by a mangle of black orchids. The bigger leopard charged and pounced on his chest, pinning him to the ground. As his rifle fell it began to pull Leo by his feet, his head and body tearing against the wet undergrowth. With an incredible instinct for survival, Leo screamed, his terrified voice piercing the stillness of the jungle. It was the final call of a hunter, now the hunted!

Almost instantaneously, just as the leopard grabbed his windpipe, there was a dazzling flash of light. A shot rang out like a whipcrack. Both Leo and the leopard collapsed to the ground.

Ram saw the flash and heard the gunshot. He raced frantically forward, fearing the worst. Leo had either been killed by the leopard or shot by a stranger's bullet. Just then he heard a rapid volley of Mandarin as two Chinese men with hunting rifles rushed towards Leo's body. He was quickly hoisted onto a makeshift scaffold by several local men dressed in khaki and olive and rushed into intensive care in a private hospital. Ram, stunned and tense, wanted to arrange for an air-taxi to fly Leo to a bigger and better medical facility, but the Chinese advised against it.

Tong and Jin, the two Chinese, arranged for the surgery and necessary medical treatment. Both seemed to know the territory rather well, apart from being acquainted with Leo's special friend, who was opening the required doors, cautioning them to avoid any paper-work lest it became a medico-legal case. Finally, Ram and Taurus took charge. Leo would live, but his left leg had been chewed into and he would take years to recover.

Tong Choo and Jin Fung, though originally from Taiwan, had settled in Kunming. This incident was the start of a long and fruitful association between the Raja brothers and Tong and Jin. With time Leo limped back to normal, and as good friends, they made joint expeditions for animal-spotting, visiting many exotic places all over the world.

'Just as we hunted for wild cats in the dense jungles of Southeast Asia, we will make a killing in the wild markets of the USA,' they vowed.

'This great man will arrange for our visit to the most enthralling game in India,' said Leo beaming with anticipation. It was well past midnight; they had wrapped up the festivities and were about to retire for the night. 'You will forget Bouba N'Djida, Niassa and Quirimbas when you visit the Indian tiger reserves. They are just bulging with wild life,' he announced with his hands thrown open as if laden with heavy objects. 'Indians don't even know what to do with so much fruit.'

Tong smirked, 'Then it is our pious duty to teach Indians what to do!'

Everybody burst out laughing.

'It's been some years since we visited India,' said Tong. 'We had gone to Calcutta and Sanders Bay the last time. I remember the amazing mangrove swamps. It was dusk when I followed an enormous Royal Bengal tiger in a boat and it just kept swimming for a mile along the bank. I nailed it as it was about to leap to the shore, but was almost swept away in the bargain when the boat turned because of the recoil.'

'Sunderbans in the Bay of Bengal, not Sanders Bay,' Ram corrected. 'It's still rich in tigers.'

'Are you sure visiting the tiger reserves won't be a big issue?' Jin asked.

Leo was confident, 'This missing tigress story, like other such stories, is dying a natural death. In fact, I can get tigers to perform Kamasutra 69 for you in India.' He guffawed raunchily and everybody joined in the infectious laughter.

Ram rose slightly and then winced as Leo gripped his arm tightly. 'All right,' he whispered.

'Ram will go ahead of us,' Leo announced, 'Like Mirza in Islamabad, his family is well-connected. He will make all the arrangements for Bandhavgarh or Kanha...guns, gear, the works. I will revert to you all with the exact dates.'

The Chinese guests raised their glasses, 'To Mother Nature.'

Ram stood paralysed. This was going to be Indian soil, close to somber Amarkantak, the holy town of priests, prayers and pilgrims, where temple bells never stopped ringing. Minutes away from his father's deathbed, would he be arranging an adventurous safari?

Leo whispered conspiratorially, 'Just pretend you will be doing it! Actually, Tusker will be doing the needful.' Who was this Tusker? Was he the friend with the haughty sneer and deep voice, the one who had arranged the hunt in Kalimantan? He seemed to have the resources to penetrate the highest echelons of the Indonesian government's Department of Wildlife and Forestry and now would he do so in India as well?

Ram closed his eyes momentarily and visualized the rustle of the forest, the sudden gusts of cold breeze and the sound of the drizzling rain as it pattered incessantly on the asbestos rooftop of his father's dwelling. Along with the brass bells suddenly he could hear the deafening sounds of gunshots and the blood-chilling roar of tigers as they leapt into the air—the shrieks of the hunted and the blood-cry of the hunter.

'Welcome to the Maharaja Lounge and the special Raj Exhibition this week,' said the pretty girl at the reception counter. Ram smiled, glancing at the plump, red-and-yellow bent Maharaja with a sharpened moustache. He was reminded of a mix of Porky Pig and Santa Claus and laughed to himself.

An empty corner with a padded sofa beckoned him. He dumped his jacket on it and wedged his bag between the sofa and an adjoining chair. Taking a deep yogic breath he laid aside the available newspapers to glance at some of the books on the table:

PORTRAITS OF BRITISH INDIA; PLAIN TALES FROM THE RAJ; THE MEN WHO RULED INDIA; AN ANTHOLOGY OF HUMOUROUS AND OTHER WRITINGS PERPETRATED BY THE BRITISH IN INDIA

He dived for up a bottle of Perrier and began to look at the Indian art in the lounge. He recalled Jaya at art exhibitions—traipsing around thoughtfully, appraising with an upturned nose, never commenting, not spending too much time on any particular piece.

On the mantelpiece were Indian idols and mythological sculptures. The front wall was a huge map that showed the extent of the British Empire, including present day Pakistan, Bangladesh, Myanmar and Sri Lanka along with India. There were smaller maps alongside. One depicted the stretch of the Indian Railway network, claiming it to be the fourth largest in the world at that time.

Gayatri Devi, the stunning Maharani of Jaipur, stood out in a sepia photograph. The young bride-to-be of the Nizam of Hyderabad, photographed by the inimitable Margaret Bourke-White looked captivating in yet another period picture. Another picture depicted preparations afoot at the Agra Fort for the visit of the Prince of Wales to the Taj Mahal.

An interesting picture showed Lord and Lady Curzon after a tiger hunt in the Deccan, with a pair of dead tigers at their feet, against the backdrop of a sprawling banyan tree and a fancy camping tent. The caption read: 'Their Excellencies Lord and Lady Curzon with the first day's bag, 1902'.

Yet another picture depicted a massive elephant howdah, the caption reading: 'Elephant Carriage of the Maharaja of Rewa, Delhi Darbar, 1903'. To its right, a photograph of an enormous dead tiger with an inscription: 'Shikar Party Amarkantak, 1914'. Ram looked at it carefully, recalling the dense forests and wildlife of Achanakmar near Amarkantak, which he had visited several times with his father. So Amarkantak where his father lived was more than a place of pilgrimage. It was actually once a famous shikar destination!

'You seem to have considerable interest in India,' the voice rang out and Ram jerked back in surprise as a warm hand rested on his shoulders. A fair and handsome stranger with brown eyes that had a hint of grey and could make a woman go weak in the knees towered above him flashing a winsome smile. Dressed in a designer khaki suit and white cotton shirt, a sky-blue cravat and matching lapel-kerchief, he sported a diamond stud in his left ear. His bon-vivant, about-the-world style was infectious and Ram felt elevated just being spoken to. He could have been an Italian playboy or a French aristocrat. He looked familiar. Where had Ram seen him before—perhaps a film? Or was it on television?

'Yes,' said Ram, a trifle apologetically, 'I love India.'

'India throws up endless possibilities,' said the stranger cryptically. The accent was English; the diction of a BBC commentator—clear, resounding, elegantly modulated. And yet, there was an enigma about his Gatsbian charisma.

'In fact, I have a few very crazy American friends who think no end of India's wildlife,' said Ram.

'The woods are lovely dark and deep...and we have promises to keep,' quoted the stranger mysteriously, as he waved his hands lyrically. 'India offers vivid diversity—you can trek on foot, ski on snowy slopes, travel on elephant-howdahs through exotic forests, and much more.'

'Hunting?'

'Thankfully shikar is a closed book,' he said, seemingly alarmed by Ram's question. He paused before adding, 'Just as well. Only crazy Texans hunt when there is so much nature to admire.'

'I agree,' said Ram, succumbing to the man's charm.

'By the way, I am Abhimanyu Singh,' the stranger smiled

disarmingly and shook Ram's hand. Though his hands were soft, the grip was rock-solid, like that of a tennis star.

'Hello,' said Ram, shaking his hand firmly. 'Ramachandra Prasad. I work in Silicon Valley. I'm going to India briefly...do you live in England?'

'Nah, I am an Indian too,' he said with a sly wink and a reckless wave of his hand, 'But a little on the wild side, as James Bond would say, with a nasty habit of surviving.' He paused to absorb the surprise on Ram's face and added, 'Actually, I am just returning from Canada. I had gone to finalize a deal for my films on the Royal Bengal Tiger and the Barasingha—I make films on wildlife.'

'I am saddened to learn that Asian tigers are getting knocked out like nine pins.'

'I'm afraid that is reality,' said Abhimanyu, his voice dropping to emphasise the gravity of his feeling. 'Unscrupulous people are out to destroy the tiger story.'

'You must've heard of Jim Corbett,' Ram said, 'And another famous English hunter that my father knew as a youth—Jim... James Wilson. He shot the biggest tiger of his time.'

'Colonel Edward James 'Jim' Corbett of Kaladhungi, Nainital,' pronounced Abhimanyu as his chest heaved forward. His voice resonated as if he was reading out a scroll of honour. 'What a hunter! He is one of my role models. A true wildlife lover, widely respected in India for saving poor villagers from man-eating tigers. We're planning to restore his old cottage and turn it into a museum.'

'And Wilson?' Ram's heart had begun to beat faster.

'Actually, because of Corbett's popularity, many small hunters became his clones. He was the one who was reported and written about extensively. I haven't heard of a Wilson. But then, I was probably not born then,' he shrugged his shoulders expressively.

Ram admired his elegance and dapper sophistication. Abhimanyu opened his colonial-brown Globe-Trotter briefcase and rested it on a table to pull out a green crocodile-leather visiting card holder. He snapped it open and handed Ram his visiting card. The paper was thick and along with embossed gold-leaf elephants and the peacock, with a subtle wisp of saffron in one corner imparted a scent of royalty. It read:

His Highness Abhimanyu Pratap Singh
Maharaja of Baikunthpur

Conservationist, Explorer, Wildlife Film Producer and International Polo Player

Baikunthpur Palace
PO: 497335
India

Ram decided to stroll towards the duty free shops. What should he pick for his father, and the un-put-downable Guruji?

He went into a Burberry shop and picked out two neck scarves, bargaining charmingly with a pretty salesgirl, who melted and favoured him with a discount several days before it was applicable on being told that his old folks needed protection in the Himalayan cold. He whisked out his Titanium Citibank Visa Card and paid for the purchase.

The listing of his flight had vanished completely from the electronic display board...much like that tigress of Kanha, Ram mused. Shrugging, he took off his shoes and spread out on the sofa, covering his face with a copy of the WSJ, and tried to get some sleep. He had already asked the receptionist to check with Air India to let him know when he had to proceed for his flight. He reached out for some additional cushions and sprawled his legs over the arm of the sofa in an effort to make himself more comfortable. But his mind kept drifting to Jaya's insistence on giving this trip to India a miss.

They had a tiff when he asked her to accompany him to India. She was abrupt, 'I have this South American trek. But you go to your father and humour his bad dreams.' Ram was hurt; she was adamant on her trip even though he had related his father's premonition and extreme ill-health. It was more than a call of duty for him—a desire to repay his father's love at this critical moment—with physical presence and touch. So what if Jaya wasn't coming; Jaya, the bewitching, Jaya the sorceress—heartless and unremitting in her decisiveness!

Well, probably it was better that she was not accompanying him. It would give him time and space to fulfill his commitment to Leo for the special task assigned to him. Amarkantak was close to at least five world-class wildlife parks—Achanakmar, Bandhavgarh, Kanha, Panna, and Pench; all brimming with tigers, leopards, nilgai, wild boar and much more. But Leo had also cautioned him with an article in a foreign journal reporting that Naxalites controlled as many as seven tiger reserves! The Red Corridor of communist extremists stretched from Nepal and Bangladesh in the northeast to East and Central India. Ram's job was to also ensure safety.

'We're getting late for our flights, let's go!' Jaya called. Their domestic flights were about the same time and so they had shared a taxi-sedan holding hands. Ram looked at the manicured lawns, admiring their elegant beauty. Just then he noticed a black cat crossing the driveway making him wonder aloud if it was a bad omen.

'Silly! In this day and age, how can one have bandwidth for omens,' Jaya rubbished him.

'I agree,' he said, though praying silently. It was only after he had boarded the plane at JFK, and downed two glasses of South African white wine that his mind relaxed.

He had barely turned on the video screen when the pilot made an announcement, 'The plane has hit an air pocket, please fasten your seatbelts and remain calm.' The plane shuddered as if it were a beanstalk being shaken by a giant. Ram pushed up the window flap but it was pitch dark outside. He was finally lulled to sleep by the horrible rumbling sound of the plane tearing aimlessly through the darkness.

He must have been asleep for an indeterminate period before he was jolted awake by another announcement. They had just crossed the Atlantic safely, but their plane had developed a technical snag, a failure of the weather radar. They would be making an unscheduled landing to address the issue.

'Please remain calm, and keep your seat belts fastened,' the pilot said. 'All should be okay in a while. Upon landing, there will be an emergency desk. Our ground staff will pull out all stops to take care of the passengers.'

There was a hushed silence as the plane descended. The delay in his reaching Amarkantak was depressing for Ram. But then such things happened in life. He reconciled himself philosophically to spending several hours in the Maharaja Lounge at Heathrow. After all, it was an active airport.

The landing was smooth. Sirens blared and police lights flashed, but luckily there was no blaze or mishap. A security cordon and cold wind with a little rain greeted them before they were enveloped in the commotion of Heathrow.

He must have dozed for a couple of hours in the lounge before he realized that the cute girl gently shaking him awake had apparently been calling for him for some time. She was in charge of the lounge and had good news; his flight would leave in two hours.

Feeling grimy and disoriented, he decided to take a shower.

He laid his Hilfiger jacket and Hermes tie on the sofa, concealing his bag and watch under it. He stacked the gifts he had purchased on top in their duty-free packing and then removed his wallet and added it to the heap. Finally, he spread a newspaper over his belongings, as if to mark his territory.

Ram ran the shower at full force, experiencing the feel of a tropical waterfall, until he was absolved of fatigue. Changing into fresh Tommy Hilfiger undergarments with a dab of traveller's Armani helped him balance the crushed shirt and crumpled trousers.

The girl at the counter waved cheerfully, 'Sir, you ought to rush towards Gate 47.'

The lounge had just been cleaned and the chefs had brought in fresh food from the kitchens. He looked away, telling himself resolutely that he could eat on the flight and collected his belongings, placing his boarding card in his coat pocket. He stopped only to get a caramel cappuccino on his way to the aircraft.

As soon as he settled into his seat, he stretched his legs and turned on the audio-visual, picking up a copy of the NYT. There was mention of the release of Al Gore's *An Inconvenient Truth* at the Sundance Film Festival and its reception by enraptured audiences.

He was just about to lay the paper aside when his eye caught a report that made him miss several heartbeats:

> 21 June 2006: Software Firm's Investments under Government Scrutiny
>
> Following a lead, the SEC, in tandem with a Federal investigation agency is examining the accounting practice of the software firm Zentigris, listed on the NASDAQ. It is believed to have issued notices to key promoters and top executives seeking details about certain cross-border transactions the company has concealed from its accounts.

Ram was stunned. He was vaguely aware that some trouble had been brewing. He had been privy to Leo speaking in hushed tones to Taurus one day, 'I am trying to trace the leak. Besides, the investment is only five million dollars and in the name of bio-forestry.'

Even the whisper of a Federal investigation was damning. A delayed flight was disturbing enough. And now, this report about his employers seemed to be deflating.

'Mr Charming, doesn't it feel good to be home?' Abhimanyu Singh, the Raja of Baikunthpur asked as they stepped off the plane at Mumbai Airport.

'Feels bloody good to be here!' said Ram confidently, his chest swelling with pride and happiness.

The Indian heat embraced Ram with motherly warmth; it hissed lovingly through chinks in the aerobridge and smothered him. And even though it arrested his swagger, he was relieved to have touched ground after such a long and tiresome journey. But how did it matter as long as he was home? India was the ultimate home!

He quickened his pace to the crowded immigration check to make an early exit. The sombre-looking officials tossed passports in the air with the panache of a celebrity chef flipping omelettes before an audience.

When one is exhausted, the most immediate anxieties take precedence over the others. For once, Ram simply did not know how it all started to unravel.

He took out his Blackberry Pearl and switched it on. There was no backlight. He tried once again but the phone remained comatose. He tried every trick as the screen remained stubbornly blank. Surely the battery couldn't have run out—he had hardly used the phone, choosing to switch it off at Heathrow to save battery life. There was obviously a bigger problem. He cursed his luck.

The luggage was yet to arrive. Tired and angry passengers milled around the carousel, 'This delay occurs only in Indian airports and only with Air India,' somebody shouted. Ram could have told them they were wrong, but he chose to keep quiet. Other flights had arrived a few minutes earlier and their luggage was strewn all over. Enthusiastic relatives who had managed to enter the arrival area were loudly exchanging bear-hugs with those who had come from abroad. Some travellers dived into the duty free shops to buy liquor and perfumes. Thanks to the Green Channel, customs officers appeared to be unemployed.

Ram decided to go over to the foreign exchange counter. He had to have enough Indian currency to pay for his onward journey and decided to change two thousand dollars into Indian rupees as there was no certainty that his credit cards would work in Jabalpur. The exchange rates were listed on a flashy signboard that rivalled the signs outside a nightclub. A long line seemed to have formed as the man at the counter took his time, counting notes and remaking bundles with the help of thin red rubber-bands.

The dollar was worth forty-four Indian rupees. This meant, he calculated swiftly, about eighty-eight thousand Indian rupees. It was enough to last his time in India.

'Your turn, Sir', the agent said.

Ram smiled as his hand reached for his hip to pull out his wallet.

'Sir, please hurry up,' the agent was clearly irritated by his sloppiness.

Ram broke into a sweat as he fumbled for his wallet. He could have sworn he had it on the flight, the bulge, the simmering heat of calf-leather against human flesh. He felt inside his coat pockets. Where on earth was it? Then he remembered that when he had gone to shower at Heathrow, he had left the wallet on the couch.

Could it have slipped inside the comforting warmth of the Burberry mufflers? He stretched out the mufflers. No such luck! Where was his wallet? He couldn't have lost it!

A gnawing fear overtook him. He left the counter and sat on a plastic bucket-chair along the walls of the airport lounge. All his credit cards were inside the wallet. He couldn't afford to lose them at this moment. All his cash, largely in dollars and a few hundred Euros, was in there too. Without money, and without an active mobile phone, he was completely helpless. His stomach churned.

He had to keep his cool and retrieve the telephone diary that was his standby for all his contact numbers. It was inside his suitcase. The luggage had begun to arrive in spurts and spasms. Tired travellers were thronging the belts heaving and hawing and there was a celebratory exclamation and patting of backs each time someone recovered all their bags. Within minutes, Ram's worst fears came true as he realized that almost everybody had collected their bags, except for him. He could not spot his Hartmann Stratum black suitcase and bag anywhere around the carousel. A First Class passenger! Yet, no sign of his bags!!

Everyone else seemed to be moving on. The Raja of Baikunthpur was wheeling his luggage with confidence through the Green Channel. Ram looked around for an Air India executive. A lady-officer ordered a steward attached to her to hasten the search for Ram's bags. One of the boys lifted the black leather flaps of the carousel and ducked inside the narrow passage, vanishing from sight. As Ram tried to control his anger, the steward re-appeared and rushed to another corner where some suitcases were stacked, trying to match the baggage slip numbers. Ram knew it was a futile exercise.

After what seemed an eternity of discussion and searching, the officer escorted Ram to the Airport Manager's room. A call was booked to the Station Manager for Air India in London and a global search launched for his bags. After about twenty minutes the call from London brought relief to their faces, 'By mistake, Sir, your bags weren't put back by the SOCA after they were segregated for random narco-surveillance... Their fault.'

His bags were safe! But they would come in only after two days. Meanwhile, the airline offered him a hundred and twenty five dollars per day as an allowance till his bags arrived. He opened his bag and took out his laptop to check all the numbers that he had saved by synchronizing his Blackberry. There was the familiar sound of it booting—the light indicated that current was ebbing through the system before the light faded and died. He booted it again. This time the light did not even come on. He repeated the procedure knowing full well that it was a lost cause. His laptop was dead.

Ram counted his money. He had less than four hundred dollars, including the two hundred and fifty given to him by Air India. He changed the dollars into rupees; just about eighteen thousand. He had to be careful now. In the past he would have cruised into the Taj or the Oberoi and checked into one of their executive suites overlooking the sea. But he could not do that without his credit card. What were his options now?

He buried his face in his hands, lost to the world, when he heard a voice, 'Prince Charming, you seem to be distraught. Can I help?'

Even before he looked up, Ram recognized the deep and resonant voice. It was Abhimanyu Singh, His Highness the Maharaja of Baikunthpur. He exuded compassion in a generous kind of way—like a feudal lord concerned for his vassals. Ram stood up and quickly narrated his woes; his missing wallet and the misplaced luggage.

Abhimanyu chuckled sympathetically, 'Come on, every hunter has to become the hunted sometime!'

'This is absolutely extraordinary,' Ram moaned. 'I am royally screwed!'

'Collect yourself buddy, it isn't the end of the world,' Abhimanyu consoled, 'I have a tiny transit pad which is hardly ever used. Even now I won't be staying there, though I could drop dead for a week...go ahead and use it for a day or two.'

'But I can't possibly inconvenience you this way.'

'No issue man,' Abhimanyu said. 'A friend in need is a friend indeed.'

'That is extremely kind of you, Highness,' Ram stared at him. How generous people could be! He'd not have been able to trust a stranger that way. 'I don't know how to thank you. Are you certain you weren't headed home?'

'Nah, I've been requisitioned by the forest authorities to advise them. I have to drive all day to reach there. A bloody man-eating leopard has created havoc in villages near the Tadoba-Andhari Tiger Reserve in Maharashtra. Villagers are scared to venture out. And listen, just cut out the formality and call me Abhimanyu. If it weren't for this we could have...can I loan you some money?'

Ram said, 'No, thanks, I can manage for now. By the way, where you're going, will you be shooting with a gun or a camera?'

Abhimanyu spoke matter-of-factly, 'It's terrible...the insensitivity with which wild animals are treated...so what if they have been forced to become man-eaters...I like to shoot strictly with my camera, to chronicle how such a situation is being addressed...essentially to keep a check over these irresponsible Forest Department guys.'

❧

Abhimanyu's flat was a lavish penthouse on top of Hiranandani Gardens; anything but the 'tiny transit pad' he seemed to call it. The colony itself was impressive, resembling the pastry-shaped and candy-floss coloured towers in Disneyworld, with a St Petersburg onion castle as the central icon. Abhimanyu's housekeeper was on leave, but the keys were with his neighbour.

He did not expect to see any news about Zentigris. He was proved wrong. Zentigris was all over CNN. In a major swoop, the promoter directors of the company had been arrested for accounting fraud after the SEC gave out a statement that the accounts were deliberately manipulated and made a criminal referral to the US Attorney's office. There was a picture of the Raja brothers, looking shocked and haggard. The report said Zentigris had concealed its retention of money in offshore accounts and opening of a new company under the dubious guise of bio-forestry. One talk-show organizer, displaying a cartoon depicting a silver tiger caught in an iron trap and roaring with pain, argued sarcastically, 'The silver tiger, like other tigers in the wild in India, is very sick.'

Soon Interpol or FBI would want him as the most visible face of Zentigris. The relationship between Perumalan and Zentigris could charge the matter politically. He spotted a phone next to the bookshelves. There were dusty brochures and books on tiger conservation and wildlife protection. The Mumbai edition of a Sunday newspaper carried an interview of Abhimanyu Singh, the renowned naturalist and film-maker, in which he said that conservation was an obsession with him and he advocated its inclusion in the academic curriculum of schools.

Was Abhimanyu married? There were many framed pictures and hand drawn portraits of remarkably beautiful women—some decidedly European, while others were Asian. But all had svelte figures and intensely passionate looks. Perhaps he was also an artist. The pictures did nothing to suggest that he was married. Besides, his house was in bachelorly disorder and had a carefree air. That spring in his gait…it came from detachment. You could, in Abhimanyu's words, travel the world at free will and do your own thing—climb mountains, trek deserts, live in forests and dive deep into oceans. And of course, be a high-flier. Abhimanyu seemed to epitomise the freedom of the single man.

Ram called Enquiries for the numbers of the credit card companies and tried them one by one. Not a single number was correct. He spotted the Yellow Pages. Stacked inside were brochures of French and Italian manufacturers of yachts, satellite phones and other luxury goods. There were business class boarding cards of trips to Hong Kong. He chanced upon a number for Citibank Customer Relations. The auto-response facility led him on a wild goose chase; just as he was about to give up exhausted, he was asked for his card number. He did not remember it! He called afresh hoping to talk to a customer relations executive, but the line went dead.

Finally he decided to write to the credit card companies to block his cards against likely misuse and stuck a yellow slip for Abhimanyu requesting him to follow-up on his behalf with the card companies. Just then he saw several DVDs stacked neatly. Apart from some old classics, there were several of a series called Earth Games and another called Planet of the Apes. Perhaps they were social anthropology, like *The Ascent of Man* or *Civilization*. He selected one on impulse. The jacket read: *'Deer Hunter'*. He had bumped into Robert de Niro once at a private Hollywood party; the actor had asked him if he had seen that film…

Deep inside a thick forest flanked with undulating hills, and plants and ferns of myriad hues, two men and two women stood against the breathtaking landscape. Smeared in camouflage-paint and earth plastered on their bodies, dressed in sheepskin thongs like primitive hunters, they stalked a herd of antelopes. The men held spears while the women carried crossbows with quivers of arrows slung across their shoulders. As they approached the herd, they ran swiftly, leaping across bushes like Olympic steeple-chase sprinters, pursuing the antelopes which bounded away. One of the woman hunters slipped and fell, shrieking in pain, but the leading hunter continued onwards climbing on to a high ledge. He perched himself strategically on his haunches atop a mushroom-shaped boulder for a vantage view of the herd. A close-up in slow-motion showed him crouching and taking aim with his spear as the herd galloped below him. The spear could be seen flying in the air, before it honed in to pierce an antelope. The man raised his arms and sprinted towards the injured animal dislodging earth and stone pebbles. With all its strength, the bleeding animal tried to get to its feet but the spear pinned it down. It writhed in pain before collapsing finally. And then the hunter stood with his leg over the animal like Tarzan: the Apeman and ululated loudly. The shrill cry rang through the forest, echoed by the other hunters. Was it a signal of victory or a call for a feast?

Advertisements for Barnett Demon and Excalibur crossbows punctuated the film. He forwarded to one of the women hunters bagging a small antelope with an accurately placed arrow from her crossbow and a whoop of joy. The hunters, done with bloodsport, were now plunging daggers and carving two antelopes with a carnal lust that Ram had never seen before. Blood was splattered over them and they seemed to revel in it, even tasting it like they were participants in a Tomatino festival in Valencia. A fire was lit in a primeval way, with stones rubbed against each other to generate friction. Thick chunks of fleshy meat were impaled on skewers and barbecued while they sniffed the pleasurable roast in the air with satisfaction.

His heart began to pound heavily. The hunters were laughing as the background music changed to hard rock. It seemed familiar… the kind of music that played in the IIT at the end of the semester examinations when everybody was high on alcohol or weed. One of the woman hunters was on the run, like the antelopes. The others pursued her, and caught her after a rugged chase through the thick forest. She struggled and screamed as they dragged her back. Suddenly, her sheepskin was torn away as the others pounced on her like animals. The next moment their naked bodies intertwined, silhouetted vividly against the smoldering fire…

The landline phone rang harshly jerking Ram out of this fantasy. He deliberated whether to ignore it, before switching off the television and answering the call.

It was a foreign accent, American perhaps, or was it Australian? The caller was on a long-distance line, female.

'Helloo,' she said in an accented drawl, difficult to understand, 'A. P. E. S?'

APES? That was a strange name. Ram answered, 'I am…'

She interrupted to continue rapidly. 'I wanted to check about that leopard.'

Ram broke in, 'I am sorry, Abhimanyu is away.'

There was a sharp click as she disconnected the line leaving Ram bewildered. He made one last abortive call to the credit card companies and after writing a note of thanks to Abhimanyu rushed to the CST station to board the train to Jabalpur, the closest station to Amarkantak.

The Chhatrapati Shivaji Terminal in Mumbai was hot, poorly lit and overcrowded. Ram was there in time and read the citation about its history. This historic Gothic monument was now a UNESCO heritage site, first named Victoria Terminus in honor of the Queen Victoria as it was inaugurated on the date of her Golden Jubilee in 1887.

Winding his way through throngs of people and tonnes of cargo strewn all over the platform, the smell of unopened wooden crates of fish from Calcutta and twig baskets stuffed with mangoes was overpowering. He bought a ticket and boarded the unreserved compartment on the train. It was without berths; just the floor to squat upon with fellow passengers. He jostled his way to a grubby corner littered with monkey-nut shells and slippery banana skins. Within twelve hours he had slithered from first class to cattle-class!

🐾

The train ride to Jabalpur was a body trap as he was jostled about like popcorn inside a micro wave oven. People spilled all over; struggling for space and gasping for breath, touching and brushing against each other. Suddenly he remembered a similar scene from pop art.

He folded his Hilfiger jacket and stuffed it inside his bag. How could he avoid drawing a comparison between this trip and the earlier one, as a first-class, Maharaja class traveller? The smudgy stains on his trousers reminded him dramatically of the towelettes drenched in cologne that the air-hostess had laid out for him. He had been offered champagne and caviar and an array of Italian and Mughlai cuisine with the accompaniment of French and South African wines.

How stupid of him to have left untouched, with such contemptuous flourish, the accompanying exotic cheese platter and choice of Belgian chocolates. Had he known misfortune was round the corner, he would have stuffed some in his handbag—they would have served him now.

The train rumbled through narrow tunnels and past exotic locales that he had almost forgotten existed in India. The dark and dank Deccan plateau gave way to lush greenery drenched in rain, to miles of exquisite teak forests and then deep valleys and wooded hills thundered away behind him. The Satpuras rose in the backdrop and the tin roofs of small houses glinted intermittently in the sun. Villages rolled by, nestling happily in the foothills, amidst the birds and the animals and the bridges and the unbreakable culverts that British engineers had built centuries ago.

He recalled his last visit to the Marble Rocks. How huge and magnificent everything had looked, with the monumental waterfall and the boat ride made interesting by Ramesh the rapper-boatman. He had recounted the history of Narmada and the cult of suicide and the many epics filmed here, while rowing the boat through the breathtaking gorge with jagged marble cliffs, tinted a dull rose-red in the fading sunlight before they turned silver with moonlight.

When the train finally trundled into Jabalpur, he was surprised to find that the station had hardly changed in a decade. It was still swarming with faceless men, impossible to recognize. Though some people were in a tearing hurry, others had nonchalantly spread out in the open corridors along with their sacks and hold-alls. He deftly wriggled free of an anorexic tout with pierced ears, and an irritating pre-pubescent nasal voice, 'Bhedaghat…Bargi… Madan Mahal.'

Ram staggered out to ask the black-and-yellow Ambassador taxi-drivers if they would ferry him to Amarkantak, the source of the great river Narmada. None of them seemed to have the necessary license to go there. MP Tourism ran an air-conditioned coach all the way to Amarkantak, but the next coach would leave the following day. It was time to touch base with Guruji. A public booth with a coin-a-minute facility beckoned him and he looked around in vain for somebody to change his money.

He ran towards the parking lot, narrowly avoiding being hit by a maroon Volkswagen Cabriolet racing towards him with furious intensity, its bulbous, old-fashioned bicycle-horn positioned unabashedly. A slim, white-skinned girl jumped out apologetically, her weight poised gingerly on her toes, her pony-tail swinging lightly, exposing a long neck and flawless skin on a sensuous face. She wore khaki half-pants and a white cotton shirt with its sleeves rolled, revealing the faintest hint of cleavage. Her legs were strong and her jogging shoes seemed to have seen better days. She looked surprisingly fit and fresh, distinctly more athletic than any foreign tourist he had seen around. Ram stared at her. She faced him squarely, 'Sorry, I didn't mean to hit you.'

He stared at her, admiring her beauty. Perhaps Jabalpur would turn out to be more interesting than he had expected. He shook himself from the momentary trance and pulled out a hundred rupee note and waving it said, 'I'm okay. But I need help desperately.'

The fleet-footed girl giggled before asking in a lilting voice, 'Sure, we all need help. Don't we?'

'Listen Madam,' he said. 'Will you change me please?'

She glanced curiously at this harried, English-speaking man in a smart Hilfiger jacket and Harmann bag; Jabalpur was mainly populated by the armed services, the legal community and Anglo-Indians who still conversed publicly in English. But this man had an American accent! She winked mischievously, a twinkle in her eyes, 'Sir, it is difficult for me to change myself; how can I possibly change you?'

'Actually, I need to change very urgently…to speak on the phone.'

'Since when have our phone booths prescribed a dress code?' she asked. Suddenly they both burst into laughter. She added teasingly, 'I thought our telephones were quite secular when it came to attire.'

Ram was taken by her repartee and her ability to stand out in such dull surroundings. She was decidedly pretty and her youthful cheer endearing. Grinning shyly, he handed her the note as she obligingly pulled out some change.

He stretched out his hand; a mite embarrassed that it was not as clean as he would have liked it to be. 'Ramachandra Prasad,' he said. 'Glad to meet you. I am visiting my father in Amarkantak. Just came in from the States.'

'Sherry Pinto,' she said, shaking his hand with a firm but

light grasp. 'Glad to meet you too. I work for a local newspaper. Pleased to be of help. Take care.'

'Thanks, you've been ever so helpful,' he said, continuing to hold her hand.

The girl stared at him before jerking her hand free and rushing away. He had a strange feeling of having seen her picture in a magazine or album. And then he remembered. The feature on the missing tigress Burree Maada in the daily newspaper was written by her.

He waited in the queue for an eternity to make his call. The phone kept ringing for a long time before a voice at the other end, out-of-breath and rushed, answered. It was not his father but Guruji, his father's neighbour and best friend for the last fifty years. Ram did not need to introduce himself.

'Ram...where are you? We expected you yesterday.'

'How is Da?' Ram asked nervously.

'Bad news,' Guruji's voice was matter-of-fact. 'He is no more.'

'No more?' Ram dropped his bag.

'When I told him that you were delayed, he sighed sadly, and then he was gone,' Guruji said.

Tears rolled down Ram's face. He had come all the way from Silicon Valley to be with his father and had lost him, when he was barely a few hours away. His father's foreboding resonated hauntingly in his mind.

'I am going to be there in the next few hours,' Ram shouted loudly. Guruji explained that he would lay the body on a slab of ice until Ram arrived. Meanwhile, he would organize Akhand Path, the twenty-four hour relay of prayers, conducted with the support of neighbors, pundits and friends who would continuously recite verses from Hindu scriptures.

The tout with the nasal voice cornered him once again, this time offering bear bile and a deer skin at a hefty discount. Ram asked if he could arrange to have him ferried to Amarkantak immediately for his father's funeral. To his credit, the tout sobered down and whipped out his cell phone. He chatted excitedly with several people before nodding his head with the rhapsodic joy of a composer who had created a new symphony. A truck was leaving for Anooppur in half-an-hour! If Ram was ready to pay the full price of a bus ticket he could travel in it.

They hurried to the parcel yard where an old truck was waiting. The tout collected two hundred rupees from Ram and gave half to the conductor before helping him on to the truck to join a dozen goats tethered to a huge iron hook with ropes. Some of them were branded with green, blue and red markings, while the others had numbers and colourful satin ribbons tied to their ears. Fortunately, he could raise himself onto a ledge and look beyond the goats at the countryside.

'Where are you taking these goats?' Ram asked the goat herd, perched in a corner.

'They are for sale!'

'Why sell them? Don't you need them for milk?'

'They are going to rich sahibs in the colliery areas of Anooppur, Baikunthpur, Bilaspur and Shahdol. They will be prepared for the sacrifice festival.'

Ram blinked. The goats were timid—and even as they bleated, belched and farted, he pitied them. They would be feted and fed for the next few weeks. And then on the appointed day they would be dressed and killed in ceremony, before the full family; amidst the chanting of prayers by a family priest. This killing and bloodshed would be sanctified by the strength of legend and tradition. He looked at the goats, finding in their soulful eyes kindred spirits. Born for slaughter; ready for slaughter. The truck ambled along the narrow road, past forests and the tribal belt of Shahpura, Kundam, onwards to Dindori. The earth became darker, more red-ochre. The houses were small, made of mud and wood, entwined with bloated green and yellow legumes and other fruit bearing creepers. He spotted the occasional yellow gourd hanging perilously or a blood-red tomato. There was the odd cow or goat tethered to a stake and a flock of clucking hens, flitting from one end to the other under the watchful eye of a doddering old man on a wooden cot. The homes were more artistic than those of the city folk, orderly with sloping roofs and beautiful pictures painted on the front walls. The designs on the walls were simple; the symbolism lucid. My Planet! My Animals! My Family! To a troubled mind this was trivial; but to an evolved mind, evocative.

He woke up with a start. He had been dreaming of work and the imperceptible intrigues in Cupertino, when the back of the truck was thrown open and the goatherd rushed to contain the goats as they readied to jump out. A rapid volley signified to Ram that he was to descend. The goats looked dolefully at him, envying his freedom, though Ram looked quite lost. And then he saw a tiny signboard in blue ink on white marking his location.

This was the historic Kabir Chabutara where the great Sufi saint Kabir had performed austerities and achieved spiritual powers, spawning the Kabir Panth sect. Drawn from amongst Hindus, Muslims and other religious groups, these followers believed in the goodness of all human beings and animals. It was at this very place that Kabir and Guru Nanak, the founder of the Sikh religion, had met and provided inspiration for the ballads that are sung passionately as Gurubani by Sikh singers. And then he remembered one of Kabir's famous couplets, the one he had tried to remember in vain when he was in the company of the goats—it was a reprimand to those who pretended to be religious by fasting ritually in the day, but killed animals at night for a meal.

He looked around. There were colourful signboards for Kapildhara where the Narmada descended steeply as a waterfall. Another sign was for the Narmada Kund, the heart of Amarkantak. This was where his father lived in a small dwelling, his sanyasgrih or abode of renunciation. And Guruji, his intellectual companion and life-long friend lived in a similar fashion next door. One a widower; the other, a sworn bachelor. He could not spot any vehicles and so he walked up the long and lonely path, treading slowly, gently absorbing the beautiful sights and sounds of Amarkantak.

As he climbed, silhouetted against the horizon, and illuminated by a solitary sodium light he noticed a tall man standing still as the night. And as Ram drew close, he recognized Guruji dressed in his customary white dhoti-kurta, head tonsured, expressionless and sombre; almost as if he had been waiting for several hours.

Guruji hugged him. They held each other silently for several minutes as a timeless bonding bridged their common grief. Ram began to cry. After a few moments, Guruji lifted the pallu of his cotton dhoti and wiped the tears from Ram's eyes. 'For your father, it is liberation from his human bondage.'

'I am shocked at my luck…I was so close to meeting him.'

Guruji led Ram to the small room where his father sat for hours and read the scriptures or solved his mathematical problems. The room bore the scent of agarbattis and herbs. Resting on a large slab of ice was a body, embalmed with sandalwood paste, cold but recognizable. The head was visible through the white cotton sheets. It was his father.

He quickly bent down and placed his head against his father's feet. After a few minutes he touched them with his hands and brought them against his forehead, saying the few words of prayer he remembered. Guruji watched intently and said, 'His last words were: "I must go and answer for my actions".'

There was an undeniable aura on his father's face. 'His face has natural lustre. He has the tranquil look of a yogi, perhaps because he never did anything even remotely wrong in his life,' observed Ram.

In the opaque gloom of the room, as he tried to recall his father's uneventful life, against the flickering light of the butter-lamp, a glint of brightness caught his eye. It was like a sheet of beaten gold. He held his breath and walked up to it.

In the corner of the puja-room lay the lovely tiger skin his father had always used as a prayer mat. It was the skin given to him by the famous white hunter…Wilson, James Wilson. Jaya had wanted this skin for a long time now, as if this was the only thing worth bringing back from India. He would now be able to give it to her!

Guruji followed his gaze. 'This tiger skin had been gifted to him,' he said. 'James Wilson used to hunt man-eating tigers along with Jim Corbett and the Maharaja of Baikunthpur. He gave it as a token of his gratitude and friendship to your father just before he left for England. It had been Da's most prized possession, his seat for meditation, and an inseparable part of his life. Unfortunately he didn't have a photograph of this great hunter.'

Ram was drawn to the tiger skin. He stroked it gently, it was crisp and clean with a satin border and the skin glowed magically, as if the tiger was alive.

How old was the skin? It looked fresh, as if the tiger had been stalking the jungles of Kanha or Achanakmar only yesterday. How could an old skin look so good? It was difficult to maintain old paintings because the varnish darkened by oxidisation, or the canvas dried out and tore or the frame disintegrated. But then, the centuries-old works of Rennaisance Masters looked so true inside famous art galleries and museums only because they were well-preserved and kept away from glaring sunlight. Preservation and restoration had reached new heights with modern technology and techniques. In this particular case, Amarkantak's cool and dry climate may have helped.

Ram inhaled the fragrance exuding from the skin. It was redolent with the scent of piety infused with the more earthly fragrances like incense, jasmine, rose and ashwagandha. He casually lifted one end of the rug to see if Mr Wilson had left a signature, or something else to convey the legend of this historic tiger shoot. As his fingers felt the crisp base of the rug, they fumbled upon a wispy label. His heart beat faster as he quickly unfurled the onion-skinned label, purplish-pink with age. The letters were faint with age, an element of mystery about them. He turned the label and managed to read:

Van-Ingen and Van-Ingen, Mysore,
Artists in Taxidermy,
January 1949

'Ram, we must prepare for the funeral without delay,' Guruji's urgency betrayed his mood; sad, but firm. 'I expected Gangavardhan to come…it seems he is caught up with something.' Gangavardhan Aranyaprem Bishnoi, several years younger than Ram, was Guruji's nephew and only living relative. Literally translated, his name meant Protector of the Ganges and Lover of Forests. Quite aptly, he worked for the Forest Department of Madhya Pradesh and was currently posted as Deputy Field Director of the Kanha Tiger Reserve, one of the Project Tiger sanctuaries. His nickname Ganga was bestowed by service colleagues at the National Forest Academy—the mighty river worshipped by Hindus. Ram wondered what he was like; they had never met.

'What do we do with his body?'

Guruji explained, 'We will follow all the Hindu traditions. The cremation on a pyre of sandalwood and mango logs is an invocation of the Fire-God Agni. Your father held that we mirror the cycle of destruction and creation that defines our larger universe. He was emphatic that complete obliteration of the remains was an essential prerequisite to fresh creation.'

Ram baulked at the spiritual drivel. 'Fine…and I'll carry the tiger skin to the States!'

'You cannot!'

'What? You mean we have to burn it with his body?'

'No! We cannot!'

Ram stared at him, bewildered. Did Guruji want the tiger skin for himself? He knew Jaya would never spare him if he failed to carry it for her. He asked reasonably, 'What are we to do with it?'

'Your father was adamant. The tiger rug must only go to a conservation museum.'

'Really?'

'That was his wish! Purify yourself quickly!'

Ram protested, 'Antiquated rituals!'

'Yes, but as you will realize one day, they help absolve ancestral sins!'

The old barber could have defeated both Rip Van Winkle and Benjamin Button in a wrinkles competition. He made Ram sit on the sidewalk and confront a cracked mirror placed on a stack of bricks, resting against a neem tree trunk. Next he took out a primitive cut-throat razor that looked dangerous enough to slash a throat. Ram panicked, insisting that he procure a new razor—he could charge more. The barber sheared Ram's hair to a crew-cut with his rusty scissors, creating more noise than a pair of skeletons making love on a tin-roof. Then, beginning imperceptibly with the forehead, in swift homicidal strokes, he scraped off Ram's hair, heartlessly throwing crisp-black strips to his lap and exposing stark-silver furrows on his skull. It was in a moment of hairless-nirvana that Ram saw a headline in the small four-page Hindi newspaper, lying by his side:

> Man-eating leopard of Tadoba-Andhari hunted down. A notorious leopard that had been injured in a village-poacher's trap and turned man-eater was finally tracked and hunted down after an operation that lasted for several hours in the night. An award has been announced by the Conservator of Forests to the alert staff and the visiting expert who had rescued the villagers from this menace.

Hadn't Abhimanyu Singh, the Raja of Baikunthpur gone to Tadoba-Andhari sanctuary to render advice to the authorities about a man-eating leopard?

'Hair offering is complete', the old barber pronounced tersely, making Ram perk up and quickly run his hands over his head. It felt velvety smooth except for the tiny pigtail that remained, sticking out like a retractable antenna—as if in astral communication with the powers above. What did he look like now? At first he could hardly recognize the man he saw. Then realization struck—he looked like a monk!

At the cremation site, the solemnity was all-pervasive. A mild breeze blew as they looked down at the valley more than a thousand meters below them. In the distance the densely wooded Vindhyas, the Satpuras and the Maikal range of mountains, for which Amarkantak was the meeting point, stood in stoic and respectful silence.

The body was eased onto a pyre made of wood from mango and sandal trees. A red tilak was put on his father's forehead by the pundit, attired in a clean, linen dhoti, with no upper garment except for the ceremonial holy thread with the ends of the dhoti slung around his shoulders. His father's body, draped in white linen, was covered with flowers. Sesame seeds were fed into his mouth and Ram, guided by the pundit, circumambulated the body three times, poured water and drew three lines to represent Yama the Lord of Death, Kala the Lord of Time and Death itself. At this stage he was handed a wooden stick for the most important ritual to be performed by a son, the Kapal Kriya. He touched the stick symbolically to the skull to initiate the liberation of his father's soul for its passage into the next world.

Sticks of camphor were dropped into the pyre and cow-ghee poured onto it. Ram lit the funeral pyre, and instantly, hungry flames shot out, as if awaiting this promised feast. The pundit chanted religious hymns—invocations for absolution from this life and acceptance into a higher order.

Within an hour, amidst prayers and folded hands, and more prayers and disconsolate looks, the body of his father was summarily reduced to ashes. They bowed in respect and quietly returned to the house. Guruji looked at Ram and said, 'In a few hours we shall go to to disperse the ashes which Punditji will give us in an urn. And we light a lamp for his soul at the Narmada Kund.'

'Isn't it necessary for us to disperse the ashes in the Ganges, as devout Hindus?' Ram had heard that Haridwar, Allahabad and Benares, on the banks of the Ganges, were the favoured destinations for this ritual. 'Which is a more holy river, the Ganges or the Narmada?' he asked.

'There is a pervasive belief in these parts that whoever dies at Amarkantak, the source of the Narmada River, is assured of a place in heaven,' explained Guruji. 'Narmada is Shiva's daughter, born from a drop of nectar from his head. She is the only river that survives the transitions of Kalpas or the transcendental time-cycles of Brahma, wherein the earth is totally destroyed and recreated afresh. When Yudhisthira, the Pandava king, of the famous epic Mahabharata, asked this question of the immortal Rishi Markandeya, he was told that when water would cover the world, marking its end, only Narmada would be left. It derives its name verily from Na-mrata, Sanskrit for that which never dies—the immortal!'

'Then why is there no Kumbh here, the congregation of millions of people to take a holy dip here, as it happens at the confluence of the Yamuna with the Ganges once every twelve years?' Ram asked.

'According to another story,' said Guruji, 'Ganga and Yamuna, Narmada's sisters, were blessed by Shiva to be revered by all; bathing in their waters would cleanse people of their sins. Narmada was enraged by this favouritism. To placate her, Shiva blessed her too; and while one has to bathe in the Ganges and the Yamuna to be free of sins, simply sighting the Narmada gives absolution.'

'And you believe in that?' Ram asked incredulously, fascinated by his endless repertoire of mythological stories.

'Of course,' said Guruji.

Ram stepped into the dimly lit study room, which also doubled up for prayer, his head reeling from the religious kitsch. Framed pictures of Hindu gods and their tiny idols in brass and coloured clay were assembled around a translucent shivalinga. The air bore the scent of incense.

An overpowering emptiness gripped him. Suddenly the States seemed so distant and futile; inside he felt the urge to remain in Amarkantak. He could sense his father's enigmatic presence in the black-and-white portrait reposed on the corner table. Once again, in the flickering light of the oil-lamp, he saw and felt drawn towards the tiger skin on the floor. It was so perfect! Ram picked it up.

It felt smooth and loveable; like holding a tiger cub in his arms. He rolled it over once again and his eyes fell on another label diagonally opposite; it had clung to the skin, almost becoming a part of it. It read:

> Careful attention is required to keep this specimen in good; brush at least once a week as the accumulation of dust neutralizes the action of the preservative applied to the hair. Do not use turpentine or kerosene oil. Keep away from strong light and the sun.
>
> Van Ingen and Van Ingen, Mysore

Van Ingen? Where had he heard this name?

It came to him in a flash. Leo Raja had mentioned Rowland Ward and Edward Gerrard and Vin Diesel when Ram was coaxing him to lend a few trophies for the gala 'wedding'. He had mistakenly referred to Van Ingen as Vin Diesel, the actor in the *Chronicles of Riddick* and *The Fast and Furious*.

Ram deliberated about the rest of his father's possessions. Apart from the spirituality bric-a-brac, his father was a recluse; he hardly had anything worthwhile. The tiger skin, although in immaculate shape, was anachronistic in its presence, a classic reminder of a bygone age. Its length must have been at least ten feet and the width about one-and-a-half feet. Where had Wilson shot this tiger? Was it Kanha, Pench or Achanakmar? Or was it somewhere in the south? Was there any book written by Wilson in his father's collection? He looked around but couldn't spot any.

Something else puzzled Ram. Why had his father retained the skin of a dead tiger all these years? Why was he bound to this skin? Guruji answered the puzzle.

'Da believed it to be his connection with the Goddess Durga. And a reminder of the pledges he had made to her. After prayers he would roll it up with his own hands and put it back into the cupboard. He would brush it himself, very carefully. Nobody was allowed to touch it.'

'Yes, the skin is a piece of art. So much energy pulsates through it,' Ram said. 'By the way, did Da ever get to meet Mr Wilson again?'

'I don't think Wilson ever looked back after he left India. I only know that he was from Bombay and was also known to the Maharaja of Baikunthpur, whom your father knew. In fact, so profound was Wilson's influence on Da, that he often uttered his name in his sleep.'

'And he never thought of giving the skin away?' asked Ram.

'Strangely, he did seem to waver when a wandering sadhu asked for it one day. But when he spotted the sadhu smoking weed, he made up his mind to leave it to a conservation museum. He mentioned writing this down in his diary. I've looked around, but I can't seem to find it. Anyway, it can be given over to the State Forest Research Institute on Narmada Road in Jabalpur.'

Ram rummaged his father's cupboard. There were a few hundred rupees. Not enough to run this house, even in deprivation, perhaps for more than a fortnight. His bank pass-book revealed withdrawals that were larger than his pension. Then he remembered what Guruji had said—his father had become insanely charitable in his last few months and had donated blindly to schools and temples in and around Amarkantak. Ram was now down to the last thousand rupees after paying the pundit for his services and procuring the materials for the cremation. There was still no news of his luggage. Meanwhile some Brahmins had to be fed and final prayers offered on the thirteenth day of the death. For the first time in more than a decade, money was an issue!

A visit to Jabalpur would be necessary to deposit the tiger skin with the conservation authorities. He could ask Guruji for some money; except that his financial position appeared no less pitiable than that of his father; abnegation had been etched equally in both friends.

He strolled across to the marketplace to check for an internet kiosk or cyber café. He was not very surprised to find that such facilities were yet to reach Amarkantak. The world still worked on smoke signals in this town. The local post office would have accepted telegrams which sometimes preceded letters, but it happened to be a holiday. Guruji's voice shook him from his reverie, 'Let's go to Chakratirth with the ashes and diperse them.'

They walked to the circular temple built near a quiet pond, non descript and tranquil. A few trees lined the outer edges. There were smaller temples, honouring various ancient Hindu gods. Ram held the urn carefully, pausing to absorb the finality of the moment. With moist eyes and trembling hands, he sprinkled the remains into the holy waters. Guruji stood behind the pundit as they chanted mantras and showered flower petals which floated in whirls and circles, before becoming one with the river. The temple shadows fell upon them and bells tolled in the distance. A cool breeze flushed their cheeks as a feeling of timelessness descended upon them.

They walked to the the tiny, twenty-edged water tank that was the fount of the great Narmada—gurgling silently out of the ground, forming a small pool. They lit an oil lamp and placing it on the parapet went inside the thousand-year-old Narmada temple where the black basalt idol reigned supreme and rang the gong. The flame of the lamp began to flicker rapidly. Was Ram's father communicating with them?

They huddled together, tired and grieving, as they contemplated the source of the river and the view beyond the bee-infested plateau.

Suddenly, these waters would fall a thousand meters, in the form of the vibrant Kapildhara waterfall, onto rugged and inaccessible tract, between rocky banks of basalt and granite. They would then descend onto fertile lands in Mandla district, before passing through forest and hill country, where deer, antelopes and tigers lived in harmony. They would cascade down in gorgeous abundance into the reservoir in Bargi, and in the temple towns of Hoshangabad and Omkareshwar where the temple bells chimed incessantly, and into the fort city of Maheshwar, the famed seat of the Queen Ahilya Devi Holkar. And then the waters would traverse to Gujarat where the people were destined to pray to this river goddess for benediction. It would finally end its long and hard journey and find cathartic liberation by merging with the Arabian Sea.

The day's newspaper lay unclaimed on the damp floor. He was about to lay it aside when he spotted some disturbing news:

> Burree Maada's death followed by that of yet another tiger
>
> Bandhavgarh: Within days of the disappearance of the famous tigress Burree Maada from Kanha Tiger Reserve, a three-year old tigress was found dead on the road to Tala in Bandhavgarh. Necropsy revealed that she suffered severe internal injuries including a ruptured liver, leading to rushing of blood into the abdomen. It is surmised that she had been hit at least twice by a blunt object. Tyre marks of a jeep were visible for a long stretch on the muddy earth shouldering the road. A nature activist is reported to have questioned whether the assailing vehicle belonged to a relative of a powerful politician of Madhya Pradesh, considering at that time of the night (9.45 p.m.), all other vehicles had already left. This vehicle, along with

> the Director's vehicle, were the only ones left inside the Park in the Garhi beat of the Tala Range where the tigress was hit. A demand has also been raised by the activist that both tourist and VIP vehicles ought to be restricted inside the Core area.

Ram gasped. Bandhavgarh Tiger Reserve was one of the sanctuaries mentioned by Leo Raja in his conversation with the Chinese partners. But Leo was in jail, and the Chinese could not have come all the way by themselves. Besides, he too had been out of action.

He still had his father's tiger skin in his possession. He needed to deliver the tiger skin to a secure home without delay; otherwise, he could land in trouble for no fault of his.

Guruji walked in as he was carefully rolling the tiger rug into a tidy packet to stuff it into his Hartmann bag. Ram said, 'I feel orphaned in more ways than one.'

Guruji looked at him quizzically, his bushy white eyebrows raised, a slight crease on his otherwise unlined face. His silver mane made him look very much the ancient sage from an Ayurveda tonic advertisement.

Ram recounted the disturbing incidents of the past few days. Guruji was receptive, absorbing each nuance, encouraging him to tell his tale.

'How could this have happened to me?' asked Ram. 'I travelled first class which literally means Emperor Class. Yet, I lost my luggage in transit. Of all the passengers, I was the only one whose mobile was discharged which meant I couldn't talk to you as soon as I landed. I was the only one whose computer crashed. And my wallet, with a considerable amount of money and all my credit cards, was stolen, leaving me broke. Above all, the company I served so diligently has suddenly been discredited and the directors arrested. I reached Amarkantak, to find that my father, for whom I travelled half the circumference of the earth, was already dead.' Tears rolled down Ram's cheeks; the dam of emotions had burst now.

Guruji merely shook his head, as if to say that such things did happen once in a while to everybody. He fetched Ram a glass of water from a clay pot kept in the corner of the room.

'Guruji, please explain, why me?'

Guruji walked across towards the window and gazed at the wooded mountains silhouetted against the horizon, as if seeking an answer from them.

After a while he spoke, almost inaudibly. 'At best, you are merely the front-end of a larger game. What has happened to you is indeed extraordinary,' he said. 'It is the inverse of a destitute hitting the jackpot in a hundred-million dollar raffle. Strange things happen even in nature, like the five solar eclipses in 1935. Your location had something to do with the intensity of the event. It is like being at the epicenter of an earthquake...or being on that beach struck by a tsunami wave...like being in Hiroshima or Nagasaki on that fateful day when the nuclear bomb was dropped. Thankfully, you are still in the game!'

Ram shivered. It was late November 2004, barely a few weeks before the tsunami, when he was in Phuket. While swimming in the lovely turquoise blue waters of Phang Nga Bay, he had suddenly experienced a high swell that had lifted him several hundred meters into the sea in micro-seconds. It was almost as if the Indian Ocean had been rehearsing the tsunami that was to destroy so many lives the next month. There had not been time to scream. Fortunately the same wave that had carried him into the jowls of the ocean deposited him back to the shore, almost apologetically.

'Da called to warn you,' Guruji said. 'He maintained a diary as I told you. Surprisingly I can't find it.'

How could he forget that horrifying call from his father warning him of an impending 'Fall into the Cage' and the 'Snarling Tiger' ready to pounce! They had laughed it off as a manifestation of his father's senility, luxuriating in their Caribbean cruise. What would his father have written in his diary?

Suddenly the lights went out and a deafening silence descended all around.

There was a torch at hand. Guruji went into the kitchen and came back with a conventional butter-lamp, already lit. He was about to leave when he remembered something, 'By the way, I got a call from a Miss Pinto, a journalist from Jabalpur, she writes for *Hindustan Time*. She is very keen to interview you. She was to come here, but when I told her that you would be going to Jabalpur, she requested you to spare a few minutes for her.'

Guruji got up and left. He heard the clanging of the metal hook as it was laid in place on the gate separating Guruji's identical home next door. Now he was all alone in the house. The moon was shining brightly. A sudden gust made the lamplight dance, casting queer shadows against the walls.

The silence was broken by the distant howling of a dog. Ram went into his father's bedroom and lay down on the wooden takht. His eyes closed and he soon fell asleep. In a distant battlefield, a bloody war was being fought. Goddess Durga sat on her tiger in the fighting stance, hacking and killing endless numbers of blood thirsty demons with her magical trident even as they kept reappearing. The tiger snarled and pounced on the vehicles of the demons—buffaloes of the evil world, dark and shaggy. Sticky red blood gushed out in a hundred fountains as dead bodies lay littered like confetti.

And then the tiger turned towards him with its bloody fangs, roaring, pouncing at him. Ram screamed.

❦

He got up before the cock next door and stepped onto the small grassy patch with the glistening green kali-haldi growing in the corner. The early rays of the sun fell on the dew drops, forming tiny rainbows, bathing them translucent. Several striped tiger butterflies perched happily on the wild zinnia flowers growing in merry profusion. A whiff of smoke brought with it the smell of burning dung cakes and bells chimed.

He noticed a tiny clay statue of the dancing Nataraj embedded into a recess in the wall, a miniature replica of one he had seen in Geneva at CERN, and another of Durga astride a tiger. Were they meant to convey any message to him? Perhaps Nataraj represented the cycle of creation and destruction and Durga retribution.

The bus to Jabalpur would leave at 10 a.m. Guruji was awake, standing next door with two glasses of chai in his hands. They sipped their chai and gazed affectionately at each other for a few moments. Ram reflected on the conversation of the previous evening and asked, 'Guruji, how could I, several thousand miles away, be convinced in a thirty-second long conversation about another person's dream? I naturally took it to mean the emotional upheaval of an old man wanting the return of his only son.'

Guruji stood up and said, 'Because you were destined to go through this, your mental predisposition was to disbelieve what was being communicated.'

'But how does one analyze unscientific predictions?' Ram asked.

'That is precisely the point.' Guruji pronounced, his lips twisting. 'Is modern science able to predict a tsunami? Unlike two-dimensional space which has only two axes, the universal space has multiple dimensions. There is some method to that madness.'

Ram's heart beat faster; the Zentigris logo typified the yin and the yang. He said, 'The good part is that after things fall apart they automatically correct themselves like the swing of a pendulum, don't they?'

'In fact, they can get worse,' retorted Guruji. 'Imagine being bitten by a snake in a snakes-and-ladders game at 99—down you go all the way. A single tsunami is only a warning of the many to come.'

Guruji's voice rang out, sending a chill through his spine, demoralizing him. Ram contemplated the silver hair, the aquiline features and the clear penetrating eyes. He had just lost a major part of what mattered in his life, and here was this man propounding some half-baked science and asserting that he was right! Was he fatherly or just demoniac? It was strange how he could twist every argument to prove his point. Perhaps he was actually a hoax, a charlatan? Had his father been a source of bitterness by outperforming him in solving some complex mathematical conundrum? Suddenly, disturbing questions arose in Ram's mind.

Perhaps he would be safer in Jabalpur, away from the clutches of this sinister man. There was also no point in borrowing money from him and being in his debt.

The honk of the bus stirred him into action. Ram assured himself that the tiger skin was in his bag and rushed out.

He alighted outside the Forest Research Institute and addressed one of the guards who lorded over the gate, 'I want to meet the Director of the Department of Conservation of Wildlife.'

'Sir, the Director is away on tour,' the guard said. 'Do you have an appointment with him?'

'I believe that there is a museum here,' said Ram. 'I have a skin to deposit.'

The guard appraised Ram's tonsured head and analyzed him sceptically. 'Sir, you have already given your hair somewhere, and now you wish to give your skin. What will be left of you?'

A young man stood by, smoking a cigarette indolently. He was athletic-looking, dressed in tight-fitting jeans and Nike running shoes, with a packet of Marlboros in his hand. He stamped out his cigarette and asked, 'So you are American?'

Ram realized that his accent and bag were dead giveaways. 'I am an Indian, living in the US. I am visiting Amarkantak.' He left out the Zentigris piece, fearing it would provoke the wrong kind of questions.

The guard and the man in jeans exchanged glances and nudged each other. 'That explains the firanghi accent,' they agreed.

'Sir, are you a consultant?' the man in jeans asked, offering Ram a cigarette.

'No my friend,' Ram said, recalling with a sense of regret the day he had decided to look beyond his successful Mckinsey career to pursue the faster track to riches. 'I wish I had remained a consultant.'

The man in jeans tried to look into the bag, but Ram moved it away from him. He asked, 'what skin?'

'A tiger skin,' Ram said.

'Tiger skin! Fantastic!' the man exclaimed, as he screwed up his eyes, trying to catch a glimpse of what lay inside the bag. 'Animal skins are my business.'

'What do you do here?' Ram asked him.

'I am an exporter of carpets and rugs.' The man seemed extremely confident, perhaps haughty.

'Listen,' said Ram innocently, 'I have an extremely well-preserved tiger skin. I have to entrust it to this museum in deference with my father's last wishes. Who should I speak to?'

There was a sudden change in the expression and mannerism of the man. He offered his hand, 'Sir, I am Jugnu Pardhi. Welcome to Jabalpur. May I please have a word with you privately?'

Ram sized him up quickly. He seemed a jolly fellow, making

light of his name Jugnu, which meant firefly, saying that he was like a jungle fire. Ram remembered his own experience with a firefly that he had snuffed out when it had the temerity to enter his mosquito net in the IIT hostel. He had jokingly referred to it as a horny female mosquito searching him out desperately in the dark with the help of a helmet-lamp. Ram grinned. After his experiences of the last few days, he was glad to meet somebody with a sense of humour.

Jugnu pointed towards a bustling chai-shop on the other side of the road. Ram nodded in agreement.

They walked along for about thirty meters. The rickety chai-shop had a narrow wooden bench for clients to sit on. The shop itself stood on stilts, under the shade of a leafy neem tree. The chai-wallah looked at them curiously. He appeared to know Jugnu well for he immediately asked, 'What's so exciting? Looks like you've laid your hands on something precious once again.'

'Two chais please,' Jugnu ordered, and lit a cigarette off a knotted string that hung smoldering, like a snake's tail from a branch of the tree.

Ram lowered the bag containing the skin onto the bench, unsure of what to do next. Meanwhile Jugnu eyed the bag intently, as if determined not to let it slip out of his sight. He whispered into Ram's ears, 'Sir, incidentally I am a noted expert on animal skins and trophies. I will give you a receipt for the skin as proof that you donated it to a museum. Show me the skin please.'

As he hesitated, Jugnu opened the bag impatiently. 'Come Sir, you can trust me,' he said. 'Buying and selling skins is an ancestral pastime in our family.' He put his hand over Ram's shoulder to relax him.

'Remember, it is not for sale,' Ram said, even though a part of him wished he could get something for it.

'Come on, come on Sir, show it to me. Nobody knows about

tigers and tiger skins as much as I do,' Jugnu said, fixing him with a hypnotic look.

Still hesitating, Ram pulled out the tiger skin. Jungu grabbed it excitedly and unfolded the skin, placing his own bag at one end of the bench to support it. The head of the skin lay on the bench, while the tail rested under the bag. The tiger skin looked formidable, the golden glow resplendent.

Ram woke from his reverie to look angrily at Jugnu curled into a bundle in the lock-up corner, facing a wall. He was both exhausted and drowsy, but the circumstances of the past few hours had kept him from falling asleep.

Suddenly, a girl shouted somewhere close by and was answered back by an equally aggressive and abusive repartee. He peered through the iron-bars. An amazingly beautiful girl was being paraded into the police station by a lady constable. She was dressed in faded blue jeans and a tight-fitting white t-shirt that accentuated her alluring figure prominently. She was clearly livid and her face flushed a becoming pink.

It was hardly the kind of spectacle that one would associate with a dreary police station in dismal Central India. The lady constable began her report to the clerk who started writing it up in his thick register.

'Sheer mistake,' the girl shouted. 'Haven't you heard of Lara Pinto of Grey Goose? I am her niece. My grand-uncle used to be the Deputy Commissioner of Jabalpur. If this could happen to me, then what would be the lot of the common man? The items seized from my house never ever belonged to me!'

'No Madam,' the lady constable said in a matter-of-fact way, 'We don't make such mistakes.'

Ram stared at the girl. She seemed so familiar. Was she not the girl who had helped him with change when he was in a rush to reach Amarkantak? She had punned on the word change and made him laugh. Could she also be a case of mistaken identity on the part of the police? If so, that would be an extraordinary coincidence!

Just then she looked towards him and they stared at each other. He suddenly felt attracted to her. He had an urge to talk to her, ask her what had gone wrong, to touch her. But, he only managed to croak, 'Hi!'

The door of her cell clanged shut and a plastic curtain was drawn, sealing her from external gaze. Ram remembered her name...Sheryl? Sherry? Cherry? She was certainly a terrific looking girl, hardly the kind to make enemies. Hardly the kind who should have done anything wrong. Was she as astounded as he was, at the dramatic turn of events that had culminated so unexpectedly in police custody? What could she be thinking?

Sherry responded with a faint greeting. She was, as Ram correctly surmised, totally flabbergasted by the events that had enfolded her. The lady constable drew aside the curtain to hand her a glass of tea. She could see Ram staring at her, eager to talk. She felt like a caged tigress—fiery and frustrated. She dragged a tin chair from the corner and sank into it to reflect on the events of the past week.

In just a matter of days, strange things had transpired. It had all started that fateful day when she had gone to meet Ganga Bishnoi, the ebullient Deputy Field Director of Kanha Tiger Reserve to discuss the curious case of Burree Maada, the missing tigress of Kanha Tiger Reserve. No doubt her decision to suddenly call on him on a Sunday morning had been somewhat unusual, but after all she was a journalist. Her tribe did worse things—snooping and hacking. And yet, none of her recent actions had been wacky enough to justify her being in police custody. What had been her failing? Was she atoning for somebody else's actions?

MISSING TIGRESS

Sherry Pinto stopped by to interview the Deputy Director of Kanha Tiger Reserve (KTR) on an impulse. Returning from Kanha, she realized that he was the only person who could shed light about Burree Maada, the missing tigress. Her suspicions were aroused when she discerned that the KTR management seemed to be trying very hard to keep the matter under wraps. Sunday morning was an inappropriate time to disturb a senior official at home, but she could always try her luck. In the past she had rarely failed in such endeavours, especially when it came to men.

She parked her maroon Volkswagen Cabriolet and walked towards the small government bungalow. As she opened the gate and strolled towards the porch, past the small lawn and the cabbage and cauliflower patch, Bhaloo the khansama came running and offered to fetch his sahib to meet her. Idly, she visualized Bhaloo rehearsing the announcement he would make—for a change, not about what he had planned to cook, but about the young English memsahib who had unexpectedly appeared on their porch.

She was right. Bhaloo could not help but reflect on the lovely English memsahib outside and inhaled deeply before lifting the curtains of his sahib's living room nervously. But as he tip-toed inside he froze. Sahib, who had been enjoying a program on the television moments ago, was now swatting flies with uncharacteristic vehemence, ranting, and now glaring accusingly at him! What was wrong?

Bhaloo sensed, with the experience gained from years spent with direct-recruit Forest Officers, even though he could not read, that this drastic chill had something to do with the scroll running at the bottom of the television screen. It screamed obscenely: 'Jungle Tsunami! No Tigers in Sariska, Panna! Wild Tigers Unsafe!'

That scroll had indeed blown the sahib's mind. He felt as if he had been slapped by a friend, as he recalled his private discussion with his superior, the Director of KTR, the previous evening. They had debated about the fate of Burree Maada, the Royal Bengal tigress, the pride of Kanha's natural gene-pool, which had simply vanished. And the freshly recruited Forest Guard. The Director had only been suggestive, but Ganga had stupidly volunteered to keep the matter under wraps, 'How far can Burree Maada go? We can't let anyone think she has been poached—we can't allow KTR to be labelled Sariska!' And now his bravado seemed to be turning into a colossal misjudgement.

After a cautious pause, Bhaloo pointed towards the front lawn and stammered in a mix of his native Korku and Hindi, 'Baiii... Inglis...'

'Bai! Dai! Mai! Ya tai! Kuchh Nahi!' Ganga shouted, but even the high decibels did not fully convey the extent of his anger at the breach of his Sunday inviolability especially when coupled with his growing concern over the Burree Maada affair.

Bhaloo pursed his mouth and quickly melted into a corner to avoid abuse. Sahib—called Ganga by Forest Department colleagues was much like the mighty river he had been named after, quite unpredictable.

Ganga had begun that sunny Sunday morning with a six-kilometer jog along the rim of the KTR-Core at dawn. After a cold shower and an hour of yoga he sat down to skim through a pile of unread travel and leisure magazines, pleasurably imagining himself scuba-diving amidst marine iguanas in the Galapagos and marvelling at orangutans playing around Indonesian rain-forests. He had switched on the television to catch the last day's play of the British Open Golf, copying the players each time they teed off. He glanced at his watch as he licked the salt at the rim of his characterless nimbu-paani, wondering if he could start on the sizzling-chimlet that he had promised himself with a hot biryani brunch. But 10 a.m. was early, even for him! And then, that devastating scroll had begun to glide rapidly across the screen, like an impudent circus clown with a pair of drums given a free run across the show.

In the corner, a sulking Bhaloo cringed, like a snubbed pug. Ganga watched him through the corner of his eyes for a few minutes before wiping his hands free of salt against the green towel resting against the antique chair that had been part of the KTR furniture for several decades—low slung, wood and rattan, the aaraam-kursee had retractable oblong hands that protruded forwards rakishly. He had been wallowing in its ampleness, relishing his leisure. Suddenly, with an impatient jerk, he extricated himself from its luxury and straightening his cotton t-shirt, swung outwards to summarily dispose of the white Bai that had captured the ebony-skinned Bhaloo's colonized imagination.

Ganga swaggered out, his head held high, his multi-pocket olive-green Bermudas flapping along his muscled thighs like elephant ears and his thonged-leather sandals slapping the Kota stone floor as he bounded down the stairs. His eye caught the sand-bag hanging from a hook in the ceiling of the portico and he delivered a rapid volley of boxing punches into it. The bag surged ahead, narrowly missing a fair, athletic girl with dazzling eyes, dressed in sepal-green jeans and a white cotton shirt, seemingly straight out of a women's magazine. Ganga quickly rested the sand-bag as he stared disbelievingly at her.

'Hello Sir,' she said, looking up respectfully. 'Sorry for barging in like this. I am Sherry Pinto.' She stretched out her hand. He took it indifferently, but was surprised by its steadiness.

'Madam, I just don't meet people at home,' he said abruptly;

adding in the next breath, 'How may I help you?'

'Sir, I need your help in several ways,' she said, smiling. 'In fact, I need it urgently in connection with a feature for my newspaper, *Hindustan Time*.' She blinked, momentarily distracted by the birthmark on his forehead—it was a vertical knife-gash. The tattoo on his left arm in dark-blue ink caught her eye next—a religious symbol was not something one expected to see on the body of an officer of the Indian Forest Service. But then she couldn't complain about tattoos; sometimes you were just born with them.

He looked at her, rather surprised, 'What is it about?'

'Sir, perhaps you should be concerned that Kanha is going the Sariska way,' she said.

He stared at her—she was unlike the pallid, withered foreign tourists who visited Kanha in swarms. He replied dourly, 'That's impossible.'

'No Sir, I am convinced,' she said. 'I just need a few facts for my story.'

'Sorry, Madam, we're not in the business of story-telling,' Ganga said, twinkling, happy to have caught her on the wrong foot. 'Kanha's glory isn't just another story!'

'Tigers, you will agree Sir, are to wildlife what humans are to nature,' she said.

'Sure, we are in tiger territory,' he interrupted

'Tiger mafia territory,' she corrected and glanced disapprovingly at the distended hedge, where a blood-red hibiscus lurched with a lascivious tongue.

He followed her gaze to the hedge and protested instantly, 'I can't speak for Sariska or Panna. This is Kanha.' He looked uncomfortable now.

She looked towards the blue sky and he followed her eyes curiously. It was a clear day and the sun streamed down, gently buffered by the glossy foliage and tangled branches of the banyan tree they stood under. Half-eaten blossoms and scarlet fruit lay all about them. She noted a rose-ringed parakeet perched on a leafy branch, with appreciation. With an enticing flicker of eyelashes, breathless with excitement, she said, 'You know Sir, I was at your Forest Rest House yesterday, thanks to a reservation for our Editor. What a panoramic view! And as I was sipping chai, I was fortunate to see this magnificent tiger barely fifty yards away, stalking a sambhar. It attacked like a monarch right before my eyes. What an unforgettable sight! I witnessed the hunt! The scent and the action, that powerful drama still keeps drumming in my ears!'

'So chill and say cheers!' said Ganga encouragingly. 'Tourists stay for days on end and don't even spot the tiger, let alone witness a kill.'

'What a spectator-box you have there,' she said, pointing in the direction of the Forest Rest House. 'Chital gambolling in herds, feeding-distance away from me when I woke up in the morning. Not surprising that the Gandhis and Ambanis visit Kanha regularly. Of course you have to be a powerful celebrity to see mating tigers.' Ganga stiffened, before saying abruptly, 'No skating, dating, mating here.'

'You were not here then,' she said with a wicked smile, refusing to give up.

He looked away and scratched his arm; his eyes searched impatiently for Bhaloo.

She pointed appraisingly towards his tattooed arm. 'You know Sir, the tiger intrigues me. It is an article of faith in Hindu and Chinese mythology…and yet we have Java, Bali…Sariska, Panna, and now?' He twisted his body away from her, thumping his sandals angrily. She did not want to lose the thread of her contention; it was now or never. She raised herself on her toes, stared at him pointblank and asked forcefully, 'Surely RT-9 should ring a bell?'

His jaw dropped. The knife-edge birthmark suddenly dissected the center of his forehead as his eyes pinked. Only a handful of senior forest officials—the KTR Director, Sanskar Shekhar Singh, Ganga himself, and two other officers, both Assistant Directors, were aware about the missing tigress with the Collar-ID Code RT-9. It was true that with public outcry about the endangered tiger, the government had set up camera traps in the core area and begun collaring tigers, linking them with tracking facilities, so that their movements could be recorded. This had been an exceptional case. A fully mature, seven-year-old Royal Bengal tigress Sita, fondly called Burree Maada, or The Big Female, was under observation by Control Center in Kanha and its radio collar signals were being chronicled and documented. Just the day before, in the early hours of dawn, she had hunted and killed. Then the location changed rapidly. She had fed on the kill and was spotted by KTR staff and the mahout on elephant back. Photographs were taken, she had looked perfectly healthy. Three tiger cubs had been seen with her.

The next day, Burree Maada, with the Collar-ID Code RT-9, just vanished. Without a shred of evidence! There was no recorded mortality signal from the radio-collar. Territorial fights between felines could not have been the reason as no injuries had been spotted on any of the other cats. No unconsumed kill had been detected. No carcasses of dead tigers, let alone that of the missing tigress had been found. Worse, a new KTR Recruit was also missing. And like a fool, he had fallen into the trap of voicing his opinion to keep the matter under wraps for a few days.

'Are you insinuating something?' Ganga asked disbelievingly, staring at her.

Kanha was globally recognized as the holy grail of tiger conservation efforts and was the most prestigious of the Project Tiger Reserves. Burree Maada was perhaps the most photographed tiger in the world. Her fight with a bison double her size had been the subject of wildlife folklore. Ganga realized that a missing tigress was a story that the rest of her journalistic tribe were bound to copiously write about. Vidhan Sabha, the Legislative Council's next session was around the corner. Although normally a poached tigress would not attract serious attention, in the currently turbulent political climate, it would give the opposition an opportunity to bay for scalps.

'Burree Maada had cubs—still quite dependent on her,' she continued, almost accusingly. 'They will be orphaned; soon they too could die unnoticed.'

'How can you infer that she is dead?' Ganga asked, his eyes burning holes into her.

'I always think ahead,' she said, trying to match his skill at rhyming words.

Ganga thought of what the KTR Director had said—he was to avoid speaking to the outside world about this affair, especially to some of the nosey tabloid-journalists, they were so difficult. Although coveted, a posting in Kanha came with unexpected administrative challenges.

'Kanha is so damned huge, and policing it is so bloody difficult. And recently we've been ordered to add Phen, another zone, to the KTR Core,' Ganga defended. Orders to expand the operational core area of the KTR had just devolved from headquarters in Bhopal, perhaps on extraneous considerations, without a process of recommendations from the field. 'Where are the matching resources?'

'That's an excuse Sir,' she retorted. 'The problem is that there are chinks in your core.'

Her remarks seared him! Chinks?

What rubbish! True, the KTR staff had guns, but they weren't gangsters. He searched his mind to consider the various people he had met in the three months he had spent as Deputy Director of the Kanha Tiger Reserve. The only significant person from the outside world he had met had been the man with a voice as smooth as silk.

🐾

Ganga's entire office had seemed energized by Feroze Goenka's presence, like the effect of cool breeze after a drought. Or, as a junior official Bisnu described it: like rain to parched soil. His choice of an elegantly tailored linen suit, neat moccasins, crisp white cotton shirt and illustrated book on Romantic Getaways which he presented to Ganga, proclaimed his civility. He boasted politely that he had been the biggest donor to the national Tiger Conservation Program because of his genuine belief that unless you protected nature it would not protect you. Besides, he claimed personal acquaintance with most Forest Department stalwarts over the last twenty years and of still being in touch with several iconic figures.

'Salim Jafri Sahib, Mr Barretto and Dr George Chatterjee... many others—they still visit me in Katni, whenever they are passing by,' Goenka said. 'Sir, I have a passion for the tiger. That is why I am planning a resort near Mukki, the southern part of KTR, adjoining Balaghat. It will be the best in the world. And for that I will need your blessings.'

'Do you have suitable land for your resort?' Most of the land in that area was classified as forest land or it was owned by tribals; private transactions were therefore, few and far between.

'Sir, with great foresight I picked up an abandoned bungalow, Bagheera Cottage, many years ago from an English family from Bombay. It is named after the panther in Rudyard Kipling's famous Jungle Books,' Goenka said. 'The Englishman once owned the Bharweli manganese mines, but when his fortunes changed, he could not afford to maintain the place. I got it for a pittance, considering the rich sal trees on its grounds. I have already thought of a name—The Crouching Tiger Resort. I am trying to tie-up with Kruger of South Africa to run world-class safari tours...it should contribute immensely to tiger awareness.'

'Good...but, I am totally against resorts in Core areas,' said Ganga tersely. And then he warned, 'I hope your land is out of the Core?'

Goenka seemed to flinch, but recovered to laugh composedly. 'Sir, thankfully only a tiny part of my land falls in the Core, the rest is in the Buffer area, which is marked by low tree-density,' he said. 'But for obtaining statutory approvals, I will need your help. You are the Law and the Lord here and your word is final. We will do whatever you decide.'

'I appreciate it,' said Ganga.

'By the way Sir, my resorts in Thailand and Nepal are highly praised by Conde Nast and Lonely Planet,' Goenka said proudly. 'So far, out of all my resorts, only the one in Sariska failed. But I am not to blame. How can you run a successful resort when there are no tigers left to be spotted?'

'An empty tiger sanctuary is a dirty joke,' Ganga admitted.

'Absolutely Sir!' Goenka said loudly. He opened a map that had red circles to mark the geographical regions from where tigers had become extinct. And then he slid his finger back to India and further up to a region beyond the Himalayas, beyond India's northeast.

'What? Where?' Ganga stared at Goenka's finger, not clear where this was leading.

'China,' Goenka said in a measured way, gently sizing Ganga's appetite for the subject. 'In frustration, we have now commissioned our own exclusive tiger park there.'

'China?' Ganga screamed. 'China!' He was yet to visit the country, even though it was next door. Almost every tiny thing that he liked came from that enormous country. He had read about the 1962 Indo-China War; one of his uncles had died fighting it.

He had not quite understood how India had lost that war. And now he had the uneasy feeling that India had pretty much lost the war again!

'Yes Sir, China is India's best hope for the future,' Goenka said. 'India should collaborate rather than distrust China. We should copy the China model. It is so practical. Then the dragon and the elephant can tango to save the tiger. We can set-up tiger parks and resorts as joint ventures in the buffer zones and leave the core areas of our wildlife parks sterile and undisturbed.'

'Tiger parks?' Ganga asked with extreme disbelief. He had read about the Chinese fad for free Trade Zones, Special Economic Zones and Industrial Parks. But not for animal parks! 'You suggest doing this on a commercial scale?'

'Sir, you must have heard of the Sriracha Tiger Zoo near Pattaya in Thailand. I tell you, captive farms with speed-breeding techniques, and use of bio technology are the best way of conserving the tiger,' Goenka explained. 'Tourists succeed in seeing tigers. Later dead tigers can also be used for traditional Chinese medicine for which there is huge demand. Sir, it is also good business. Even Sariska can be turned around. We will form a company...you could invest in the name of your mother or relative; it will give you an extra source of income for the rest of your life.'

Ganga stared at him, taken aback by his suggestion, 'Hmm. I'm not sure if that is workable.'

'Sir, our experiment for captive breeding of long-tailed macaques in Vietnam has been a success,' Goenka said. 'Most of our produce goes to the States for bio medical research, and now we are planning medicine farms for that scaly anteater...the pangolin.' Goenka flashed a big smile.

'Yes, but why have unnatural captive parks like zoos when you can preserve diversity in the real wild?' Ganga asked. He recalled reading a feature about captive breeding farms where animals were divorced from their natural habitat.

'Even in the United States, Sir,' said Goenka, 'Department of Agriculture permits rearing tigers privately. Similarly, in India you policy-makers have to rise above narrow thinking. The Indian government cannot be solely responsible for conservation—it has its hands full.' He shook his head and looked at Ganga wearily, pointing to the day's newspaper that carried yet another stormy story about farmer suicides due to drought. 'India has bigger problems...plague, poverty...Pakistan!'

Ganga was silent. He stared at Goenka who seemed so confident about everything.

'Sir, let the private sector participate in conservation,' Goenka suggested ingratiatingly. 'China is so easy for business—only single window! India? North versus South, Left versus Right! India has more windows than Microsoft!' Goenka sniggered. He laid an arm on Ganga's shoulder patronizingly and said, 'You should visit China Sir. Just come till Kathmandu and leave the rest to me. I will show you Shanghai and Shenzen, where the future is!' Then he had added with complicit warmth and a lavish spread of his hands and a suggestive wink, 'Work goes on...there are so many beautiful and pretty things in China!'

Ganga recalled that the KTR Director had just returned from an official trip to China, loaded with branded Swiss watches for his family, and a brand-new Callaway golf set that would have cost a fortune in Mumbai or Delhi. China was a dream destination. Curiously, even Sherry had a tiger embossed on her shirt with some complex Chinese signs beneath. Had she visited China?

He had kept Goenka's visiting card carefully in the top-drawer of his study-table, just in case he had to go to China, or some place nearby; then this friendly businessman could be useful for that extra bit of entertainment that a government allowance could not accommodate. Businessmen wanted to be friendly with Forest officials—they needed protection not only from wild animals but wilder officialdom. After all, inside the forests, the officials had authority to register offences under the myriad provisions of the Indian Forest Act, the Forest Conservation Act, the Wildlife Protection Act and the Environmental Protection Act.

Who else had he met in KTR? Yes, the KTR Director's cousin, the Maharaja of Baikunthpur, a Principality to the east of Katni and south of the Vindhyas. Tall and handsome, this globe-trotting epitome of royalty was elegant and unassuming. The Director had described him as the David Attenborough of India, adddressing him respectfully as *Raja Sahib* or *Darbar*, meaning King, with the honorific *Hukum*, the Dispenser of Royal Justice whose wishes were to be obeyed like commands. Ganga had been taken by his scholarly and in-depth knowledge of wildlife and in particular of KTR. There had been spontaneous body chemistry between the two and they had chatted like long-lost brothers about nature films. Ganga recognized instantly that this would be his long term ally in the game for conservation. In fact, it was Darbar who had recommended strongly, 'You shouldn't be deterred by the expenses involved in installing modern systems of electronic surveillance. Radio-collaring of tigers is definitely the way to go.'

There was Melanie Gardner, the attractive, though somewhat enigmatic English widow who ran Wildflower Camp fastidiously. She was seen mostly in the company of foreign tourists and researchers. They preferred her low-carbon-footprint, mud-thatched-roof huts with hammocks, and her large library of wildlife and travel books, to other resorts with the regular trappings of jazzy concrete-brick-and-mortar structures with glitzy bars, fluorescent lighting and noisy cable televisions. Salacious stories had been spread about her by other jealous resort owners that she travelled abroad frequently to trade in animal skins. But to Ganga she had come across as harmless, even if somewhat quirky.

She hunted unsparingly with her pen and wrote regularly about wildlife mismanagement. Not surprisingly, her biggest critics were from the Forest Department, whose officers were mostly at the receiving end. She had rung up his office for an appointment, but he had deferred calling her back till Monday.

And finally, there was the staff at KTR. There was the Field Director, the Deputy Field Director (Ganga himself), and two Assistant Field Directors who had about twenty-five years of service each, assisted by more than two hundred junior staff including forest guards who patrolled the various beats of KTR on foot and reported any untoward incidents of injuries to tigers or damage to the forests.

Ganga also kept a watch on the Gond and Baiga aboriginal tribes who lived in the villages surrounding Kanha and contributed hugely to the KTR work force. They were quiet and submissive. The other group were the impoverished Pardhis who lived on the fringe of the Core area in constant threat of being arrested on suspicion of poaching. There was as much convergence of interests between them and the Forest Department as there was bonhomie between snakes and mongooses. Barely a few days ago, two of them, Chirag, a headman, and Jugnu, a youngster, had met him. They had complained against the atrocities of KTR Guards when their little ones had been apprehended with a dead chital and a few rabbits that they had hunted with primitive bows and arrows. But Pardhis, for all their legendary cunning could hardly pass off for mafia.

No guns. No fast cars. No cigars. No oomph.

Sherry looked at Ganga critically. He was of average height, muscular, well-tanned with a tattoo on both his arms. Although he had a square, masculine jawline, most women would describe him as ugly, perhaps even brutish. He was crudely dressed with an air of abandon—clearly a man with a low elegance-quotient. Yet, luckily for him, there was this fiery edge to his demeanour—it shone out of his smouldering dark eyes, causing a frisson of raw energy to pulsate from him. Her instant thought was that it gave his quirkiness an exceptional character, making him likeable.

She noted the various bags, nets, and target-practice boards attached to trees all around crafting his house into an outdoor boxing and shooting ring. Suddenly she felt the urge to tease him out of his comfort-zone. 'Quite a joyful playground, this place,' she said, pointing to the nets.

'Why should life be a rat race?' Ganga responded, running his fingers through his thick tangle of brown-black hair.

She pointed towards the rusted golf-wedges, leaning against a lemon tree. Next to them was a pile of muddied golf balls. Though her Aunt Lara had been an avid golfer, she had found it more capricious than anything else she loved. A freak birdie had been the lone highlight of her distressing tryst with this game. She smiled and asked tauntingly, 'Playing the Runaway Tigress golf course?'

Ganga winced before turning it into a chuckle, 'no such luck… just trying to stay in touch for the Civil Services Cup. I have all the time and space to practice my short game…'

'And no dearth of ball-pickers…'

'Unusual caddies…'

'Village youth?'

'Crows! They often pick up balls.'

'Flying caddies!'

'And so I end up playing from the rough.'

'If you can master the rough, that's half the job done,' Sherry said. 'My golfer aunt used to say she was good with the woods, but had difficulty in getting out of them.'

'I'm pretty well out, thanks,' said Ganga sardonically.

Sherry grinned, surveying the modest government bungalow with its quaint grass-patch and tree-laden yard. The tangy aroma of vegetable stew wafted languidly across from the kitchen. She inhaled deeply, selecting like piano keys, the local herbs used in her mind—curry leaves, ginger, cinnamon, cloves, cardamom, lemon-grass… She picked up a jamun from the ground, wiped it against her pants and popped it into her mouth.

'You should always wash fallen fruit,' he advised spontaneously.

'I have fallen enough and am naturally immune,' she said slowly with a smile, as she savoured the pulpy but slightly dry jamun. 'By the way, this is a nice cuckoo's-nest you have here, though it's a pity that it lacks old-world charm—like when the English worked the Forest Department.'

Ganga inhaled and held his breath back to calm himself. He had seen the majestic residence of the Commissioner of Jabalpur—it looked like a palace and had an entrance big enough for an elephant to enter. The Collector Mandla too had a rambling mansion that overlooked the mighty Narmada River; it had its own jetty and ferryboat. He tried to visualize a long drive-in and a convertible jeep and liveried orderlies with crisply-ironed caps and gleaming sashes, bowing obsequiously, unlike his own plainly-outfitted Bhaloo in torn rubber slippers, the pest! But he was happy; he loved this small house and its nondescript informality. So what if it was unimaginatively Public Works Department—painted shitty-yellow and built like a kindergarten crayon drawing. He focused proudly on the piece de resistance—the ancient banyan tree—it was jungle-green and earthy-brown, fecund and overflowing rhapsodically in all directions. Wasn't this a billion-dollar artistic feature? Besides, it was a free gift from nature! And it was far more original and pleasing to the eye than any expensive monstrosity installed in Paris, London or New York by modern sculptors—pigmented steel, PVC and glass shards and tubes that orbitted asymmetrically into the sky like mangled intestines.

'Why can't you just let us do our Project Tiger work?'

'What I don't understand,' she said, with matching sincerity, 'Is this Project Tiger or Object Tiger?'

'Subject Tiger!' he retorted, his hand to his chest. 'Have a heart! I have been here for only three months.'

'Listen, when I mentioned Kanha, I was only mirroring the situation prevailing in the Project Tiger Reserves at large,' said Sherry. 'Do you have any idea how many tigers have gone missing in the last five years from Panna, Bandhavgarh and Kanha?' she paused dramatically.

'Statistics was never my strong point,' he shrugged his shoulders.

'The floodgates for tiger genocide seem to have opened! A tiger a day! India—the graveyard of the Royal Bengal Tiger!'

'Bad press,' said Ganga.

'Press?' she arched her eyes. 'If I may take the liberty of saying so, then it is bad and sad that the Khejri Bishnoi gene is mutant!'

'What?'

Sherry rubbed her eyes and sighed. She noticed a woodpecker that had begun tapping the soft and porous branch of the banyan tree, desperately seeking insect quarry. She eased her tone and said, 'Our own precursor to Wangari Maathai, Amrita Devi, would have raised hell.'

'How?'

'When the Maharaja of Jodhpur's army began to cut trees from Khejri's own nistari forest for his Palace she stood up firmly against it. I love the lines: "Better to lay down your life for your environment than to live in indignity".'

Ganga realized that this meeting was a point of inflexion in his graph of continuous invulnerability. He recalled how his mother would narrate stories from the ancient Panchatantra and the Jataka tales of Buddha; about the importance of natural balance. An earthy smile flickered across his face and revealed well-structured teeth. His chest heaved with pride and he said, 'While my father retired from government service in this part of the country, Amrita-Maa, who lived near Jaipur, was one of my great grand-aunts.'

'Both my aunt Lara Pinto and my grandmother worked with the Bombay Natural History Society. They had accurately chronicled the gradual extinction of cheetahs in this sub-continent. I'm terribly afraid tigers are going the same way.'

'By the way Sherry, don't you have something going on in Hasdeo near Baikunthpur?'

'Yes,' said Sherry excitedly. 'I've drummed up local support for an elephant sanctuary there...and made powerful enemies because I've opposed the Goenka's coal-mining project. I've also got the villagers of Karopani to donate their land for a black buck sanctuary. It's a template for involving village communities in conservation.'

'Great initiative!' he said admiringly. There was something else that was related to her, he tried to recall. And as he began to walk away from her, he remembered the Director's cryptic, rather wicked description of somebody who matched her description: White Bitch with Great Piece. Perhaps he referred to Greenpeace, the environment movement. She had begun to feed a crumb of arrowroot biscuit to a bushy squirrel and looked up, inviting him to do the same. His eyes inadvertently fell on her cleavage as she fell on her knees and stretched her hands. Suddenly she appeared very vulnerable, very lovely.

'Sir, I have a personal request,' she pleaded, with wide eyes. 'Please, find Burree Maada's cubs before it is too late. And, by the way, my story about the missing tigress is pretty much done.'

Even as he stood transfixed, she got up and handed him a piece of paper with a phone number scribbled behind it:

Sherry Pinto
Reporter, Hindustan Time
Naturally Obsessed, Compulsively Inquisitive
Lara Pinto's: Grey Goose
Cobra Ground, Jabalpur Cantonment

He stared quizzically at the card. Cobra Ground was the military parade area in the heart of the Army Cantonment. How was she a resident in such a prohibited area? But, before he could ask, she set off at a brisk pace towards the road. Bhaloo emerged barefoot from the shadows and lunged forward to open the low wooden gate. Ganga traced her furtively with his eyes—her body was elegantly proportioned, and she was minimalist in her attire, an attribute unusual among young women these days. And yet she looked appealing. Bhaloo closed the gate, unobtrusively noting Ganga's observations, before smiling to himself and racing towards the kitchen. Ganga continued to stare at the gate and noticed a blue-jay as it descended on the red-brick pillar to which the gate was creakingly hinged.

He felt the sweat as it trickled down from the deep furrows on his forehead. What did she mean by saying her story about the missing tigress was pretty much ready. He swore to himself. That was a threat!

He went inside, punching the sandbags as he passed them. A program on the lost river Saraswati and the descent of the Aryans into mainland India was on television. He watched it for a few moments before switching it off abruptly and reaching for the unfinished nimbu paani. He spread a map of the Kanha Tiger Reserve on the table. He pored closely over the topography of the area where Burree Maada was last spotted and glanced at the antique clock placed over the rickety cupboard—10.25 a.m., well before noon. He pondered over the possibility of a search operation.

The trek would lead him deep into the steamy entrails of the Kanha Tiger Reserve. Subordinates would curse him for ruining their holiday. They would call him a killjoy, even a freak—but that they probably did in any case. The Director would feel cheated; so what? He was screwing up his own Sunday too!

Besides, he was posted in Kanha. It was still Kanha!

'River Ganga is in spate,' was the general refrain when the Kanha officials were informed of the sudden trek. As a rule they were less concerned about losing wildlife than about Ganga losing his temper. Ganga was in full flow; oscillating furiously from being sarcastic one moment to being crude and obscene the next. A man possessed.

The word had spread like jungle fire that Ganga was tooth-combing the entire area in which Burree Maada had disappeared. His rasping commands and imperious marching-call were a warning to forest staff to cut short all other activities and head back to their formal positions in the KTR. If found missing, they stood the risk of being served the dreaded Chargesheet, a product which required more creative writing skills than exactitude. So even though it was a holiday, since Ganga was commanding inspection of the *mauka-e-vaardat*, officialese in Urdu, for scene of crime, they scrambled into full battle gear.

Kanha was back-of-beyond, far from the seat of government. Here the word of the cranky superior was final and binding.

As he shouldered his backpack, Ganga felt all-powerful. Tourists had been recalled for the day. Tour operators desperately tried to contact him; he was incommunicado. He gloated over the vistas of his kingdom and imagined himself as the Lord-Protector of Kanha. He remembered contemptuously the great Maharaja of Vijaynagram, nicknamed Vizzy by his English friends, who had shot about thirty tigers (of the three hundred that he shot in his lifetime) in Kanha alone (even though this was not part of his kingdom) and commented, 'He should have been called Krizzy instead!'

He prided himself on his tiger connection! It was in 1973, the year of his birth, that the nature-loving Prime Minister Indira Gandhi had launched the Project Tiger scheme. And then, much ahead of his batch mates in the service he had got the hugely coveted job of Deputy Director of Kanha Tiger Reserve.

Kanha was divided into two protection zones—a sterile area of a thousand square kilometers as a Core Zone, free from biotic interferences, and a Buffer Zone around it, the multiple use area, that had villages like Mocha and Khatia, where the hundred odd tourist resorts and small hotels were located. Ganga's personal belief was that sustainable tiger conservation could only be achieved by policing the forests and cutting out all tourist activities from the Core area, even though official thinking was that it was better to widen the stakeholder participation and integrate the landscapes of the Core and Buffer Zones, so that elements of the natural equation could be balanced.

While he had enjoyed trekking in the forest ever since he had arrived in Kanha with large teams of personnel—these treks had been useful for sharing ideas, finding shortcomings in the staff and for punishing the incompetent, he was sure of one thing. This trek would be different. It would establish his credentials as a tough officer and enlarge his sphere of influence amongst the rank and file. That would sustain his long innings in Kanha.

The two Assistant Field Directors, moon-faced Manmohan Gopal, a. k. a. Mango, and parrot-nosed Karua Lal Neema, a. k. a. Karela, were next only to Ganga in KTR hierarchy. Mango's leukoderma'd lips, and consequently ever-smiling face was in sharp contrast with the poker-faced Karela, whose disposition was pungent like the bitter gourd grown on village vines after which he had been nicknamed.

Ganga had not batted an eyelid while directing them on his walkie-talkie to reach Kisli, abruptly ending their relaxed family-brunches. Pulled out of their Sunday somnolence, they were grumpy and inactive.

'Sir, this trek will entail climbing rocks, wading across reptile infested waters and holding slippery vines hanging from ancient trees,' Mango said.

'We have to do the inspection!' Ganga retorted.

As he peered into the detailed 'topo-sheet' of Kanha, with the myriad contour lines and elevation points describing the height and formation of each significant feature, they sensed his drift and switched tack. He chose the direct and more vertical route and not the 'kuchha pagdandi' path, which forest staff normally used to go to Bamni Dadar when they were not driving up. Someone suggested timidly that they drive to the top first. Ganga promptly snubbed him as a 'bloody shirker and coward'.

'Bamni Dadar is the highest point of KTR,' Karela said. 'It used to have an airstrip at one time for the British RAF pilots to land their planes before embarking on shikar. But those were the real days, days of fun.'

'Days of shikar,' said Ganga curtly. Karela continued to engage and humour Ganga, but drew a dark blank.

It was Mango's turn next, 'Water oozes out of mysterious rocky fissures and causes moss-laden boulders to be dislodged, leading to unsuspected land falls.'

'But the jungle calls,' said Ganga dryly.

Mango continued, 'Sir, two Irishmen who displayed rare courage were chased by a female bison in heat. Both jumped off the cliff.'

'I get the drift.'

'One died and the other recounted the real-life drama from the confines of a hospital. He swore never to return.'

'Our trek we will not adjourn! Look, look at those foolish bastards!' Ganga clapped his hands and shouted suddenly, pointing towards a couple walking a few hundred yards away, armed with cameras, with a Maruti Gypsy trailing behind them. The moment they saw the forest staff they jumped into the Gypsy which began to rapidly change course. They seemed to have emerged out of nowhere.

'Strange, Sir,' said Mango, a little shamefacedly.

'What's this? Haven't we recalled all tours?' Ganga asked Mango, accusingly.

'Yes Sir, this is a breach...sorry Sir,' stammered a shivering Mango as his eyelids fluttered guiltily and he signalled a silent message to a subordinate with his hands.

A Ranger set off at full speed in another Gypsy, leaving behind a cloud of dust. Within moments an apologetic tour guide and an apologetic couple were presented before Ganga, much like prisoners-of-war. The man was strongly built and wore khaki cargoes and a checked shirt. He practically had an entire photography station strapped around him and held what looked like a bazooka in his hands. The woman was pretty and fragile and wore a colourful gypsy scarf. She had a gaping mouth and round, wondrous eyes and a smaller camera hung around her neck. Cowering behind them was their guide-cum-driver in a green golf cap with a tiger embossed on it in gold; a wimpy youngster with more bluster than bravado. Ganga beckoned and he came forward reluctantly, his knees bent and his head slung low.

'You know the danger of being on foot, you son-of-a-bitch!' Ganga shouted at the guide. 'It is because of irresponsible bastards like you that I am convinced that the Kanha Core should be free of tourists.'

'Sir, sorry Sir,' the guide said, shivering before the mute audience. 'I should not have...' But even before he could complete his defense, Ganga broke the silence and slapped him powerfully on his face. It was a solid blow, like a whipcrack. The guide staggered and fell back, his golf cap flying and tears welled in his eyes. Ganga raised his arm to slap him again when he saw the woman-tourist trembling; he suddenly restrained himself.

'Jay walking in these jungles is prohibited,' said Ganga.

'We're from Kentucky,' she said, stepping in bravely between Ganga and the guide. Her lips quivered as she pleaded, 'We come to Kanha every year. We are friends of Nawab Sir Ali Beg of Dhaka who knows the Maharaja of Baikunthpur. He put us in touch with the Director of the Tiger Reserve; it was he who had instructed this gentleman to help us.' She pointed towards Mango who flinched as Ganga glared at him. She continued, 'Our guide told us that a tiger had been sighted in this area. But, we've waited for an hour and apart from a fox, wild-dogs and the usual chital, sambhar and nilgai, we haven't been able to spot a single tiger yet. So when we spotted a herd of sambhar racing away, we presumed that they were being chased by the famous Burree Maada and stepped down to try and film the hunt if we could.'

Ganga winced at the mention of Burree Maada. Were they simply innocent and perhaps over-zealous tourists? Could they be private sleuths hired to ferret the truth for an investigative magazine or wildlife body? He looked first in the direction they had come from and then at Mango and Karela. Both looked ashamed. 'Madam, a few weeks ago, a wildlife-worshipping Canadian couple gave their guide the slip and disappeared into the jungle, armed only with their SLRs and water bottles,' Ganga said. 'We spotted them from a distance, excitedly shooting pictures of wildlife, until suddenly...' He infused the right amount of suspense; the woman-tourist's eyes widened, 'Until they vanished! Some days later their bodies were found impaled in a bamboo grove, dismembered and mutilated.'

'Oh,' the woman looked frightened. She stared at Ganga who was glaring at the driver.

Mango's eyes also grilled holes into the driver-cum-guide who sensed danger and froze.

'Pack your tourists away this very moment you bastard or I will kill you,' Ganga commanded as he held the collar of the guide and hustled him administering another slap for good measure. An attentive guard managed to arrest the fall. Within moments the tourists were bundled into the jeep and whisked towards the entrance of KTR.

Ganga was intoxicated by the posse of khaki-uniformed forest staff trailing him with a mission in mind. He felt like an Army Captain, leading his commando sortie for a behind-the-lines guerilla attack. Holding a bamboo cane and a sickle in his hands, he forged ahead of the others through the clinging undergrowth and the bushes. He stopped at every little crest that he ascended and paused to review the lush forest around him with a feeling of exhilaration, marveling as much at the majesty of nature as his command over it.

The rich forest cover consisted of tall sal and saja trees from which birds and monkeys and langurs gawked at them curiously, their tails swinging aimlessly as they chirped and chatted. Then, beginning to feel outnumbered, they bounded away, shrieking loudly to alert the jungle about the advancing human army.

Though the ground was soft in places, Ganga was disappointed not to find pug marks anywhere. Meanwhile, parakeets and jungle fowl on leafy trees added to the variety of the rich foliage. Once again he reveled in the utility of his education in the Forest Academy. He recalled his Professor, nicknamed Snowy Egret because of the shaggy mane of white hair that imparted to his character the fashionable loftiness and drift of that bird. The

Professor conducted a test once on Indian trees and their taxonomy, which Ganga had topped. He then invited Ganga to his modest kitchenette and presented him a hand-bound version of Robert Scott Troup's monumental work in three volumes: *The Silviculture of Indian Trees*.

The troop crossed a thick bamboo grove to arrive at Shravan Tal, a large pond, encircled by tall sal and jamun tree-covered hills. A herd of sambhar, with dark chestnut marks highlighting their beige rumps, slurped nonchalantly. One of the females stood inside the water, with only its head bobbing out aerobically, antlers balanced gracefully like a tiara in the center of slowly dying concentric ripples.

'Tourists love to shoot here,' Mango said absent-mindedly.

Shoot? Shadows from the jagged crags and swaying trees created shifting patterns on the jade green water, he recalled his school mythology and the story of Shravan Kumar after whom the pond had been named. Kanha, apart from being another name for Krishna, the Hindu god of love, was also connected to the sad story of Dashrath, the father of Ram who was the hero of the epic Ramayana. According to legend, Dashrath, King of Ayodhya, was hunting in this forest, when he heard what he perceived to be an animal drinking water. He used his 'shabda-vedi', or the guided-by-sound technique that he had perfected, to shoot an arrow into what he assumed was a deer. He discovered to his horror upon hearing a shriek of pain, that it was not an animal that he had shot. He had fatally injured Shravan Kumar, the epitome of filial obedience, who was carrying drinking water for his blind and aged parents. The resultant curse of Shravan Kumar's distraught parents was the cause for Dashrath's son Ram to be banished from his rightful kingdom for fourteen years, barely moments after being appointed as the crown prince of Ayodhya. Dashrath, without the fortitude to bear this loss, died heart broken immediately thereafter.

🐾

The strain of the ascent showed on their faces. The forest was denser and the tree variety more diverse. The climbers had begun to sweat and looked visibly tired. Ganga wondered how to relieve the monotony and keep them motivated. Should he start with a text book discourse to build the ground or start challenging everybody with questions?

'Seventy-five percent of the forests in Kanha are sal,' Ganga said after some thought. 'Which famous personality is associated with sal?'

'Sal is the tree under which Buddha was born in Lumbini, in what is now Nepal at the foothills of the Himalayas and is sacred to Buddhists,' Karela answered promptly.

'Ok, now who will tell me what tree is held sacred by our own Gond tribals?' Ganga wagged his finger, refraining two junior rangers from the Gond tribe from answering. Of the two, he was particularly fond of Bisnu, who was good at electronics and worked closely with Ganga.

Karela raised his hand to speak, a haughty smirk on his face. 'Saja, terminalia alata, the abode of Burradev, the God of the Gonds.'

'Correct!' Ganga smiled at him appreciatively and bent down suddenly. 'And here I pay my humble respects.' He stooped in front of a saja tree. It was old and straight, about ninety feet tall with a formidable girth, the crocodile-skinned bark gleaming in the sunlight, very true to its depiction in paintings by tribal artists. He closed his eyes in silent prayer, and touched its trunk in reverence.

Mahadeo and Bisnu, followed by the other forest staff also prostrated in front of the tree, foreheads touching the ground above the roots, hands out in supplication. Perfect yogic postures, making them look artistic against the verdant surroundings.

'Sir, I want to ask: what is the significance of Boswell's Errata?' asked Mango, suddenly inspired by the question and answer session.

'Boswellia Serrata,' corrected Ganga, amused at the slip.

'The salai, it supplies us with an aromatic resin,' said Karela. The excitement of trivia was helping to maintain the pace of the trek.

'Fantastic! We can form a trivia team for ecology,' suggested Ganga appreciatively, energized at the knowledge base that was available, as he walked beneath a beautiful palas tree, the Flame of the Forest, its flowers velvet-like, coloured vivid orange and red.

'The salai is also used in tribal rituals,' added Karela.

'Keep moving, keep the pace. Keep your eyes open for any pug marks, scats or other signs of Burree Maada or any other dead animal. Talk while you walk!' Ganga commanded, slashing against a thick clump of tiger grass that was almost waist high. He stepped out into a clearing, and shouted loudly, 'Is there any person here who is not fond of our good old pet, vassia latifolia—so genial, and the giver of much pleasure?' They were beneath a huge mahua tree, its deep yellow flowers strewn all over the ground. He held a mahua flower, crushing the petals and releasing a sweet fragrance much like dried grapes, encouraging him to comment, 'Almost a joint.'

Everybody laughed.

'Sir, what a pity you haven't tried mahua liquor as yet,' Karela said.

'Oh, I'm an old sinner! We will certainly drink and dance like the devil to celebrate our trek!' Ganga did a quick gig, imagining a tribal family brewing their own liquor by boiling mahua flowers in clay vats over a fire. He would spend a night with the Baiga tribes, learning about their customs and bonding with them over mahua wine.

They had now reached a point which was surrounded by caves

in the hill and a massive grove of assorted trees on one side when something caught his eye in the mosaic of shadows, It was nothing distinctive, yet Ganga froze, more by instinct than by vision. The others stopped dead behind him as he continued to stare fixedly where his eyes had fancied movement; within moments he was rewarded by a flicker of gold and the burning eyes of a leopard several meters away, its spotted hide concealed intermittently by the rich foliage. It stared at him, its eyes penetrating, inscrutable. Would it come at them? Mango raised his gun, but Ganga brushed it aside! There was a slight whisk of tail before the beautiful animal turned and disappeared quickly from view.

As always, he was inspired by the scenery. This was a Jurassic Park without the dinosaurs. Even the usually argumentative staff was now under its spell.

Mango leaned against an aamla tree. Karela and the rest began to lose steam too. Handkerchieves and cotton gamchas were used unceasingly to wipe sweat.

'No resting,' Ganga barked. 'We need to move on!' He surged ahead and the rest followed obediently. He pulled himself up over sharp-edged rocks, narrowly missing a family of cobras. The rocks were full of etchings, done with primitive tools or perhaps with bare hands.

'Pictographs,' said Ganga. 'They carry mysteries of our past.'

The drawings depicted deer, bison, and men riding horses, and the organic colours used were red and ochre, browned with the passage of time by seeping water and insects. Ganga stepped inside one dark cave to explore further. He hoped to find a carcass if he was lucky. A deep rumbling sound greeted him as the leaves of the neighboring saja and sal trees rustled. He stepped back hurriedly and turned to look skywards. Was a storm brewing? Maybe they would have to seek shelter in the cave.

'Reechh!'

A guard screamed. Ganga heard the warning in the nick of time and flew out of the cave like a speck ejected from a plane. A snarling sloth bear charged out furiously, kicking and dislodging pebbles and clumps of grass, its jaws wide open in a terrifying grimace, flashing scary long teeth. Ganga stumbled backwards into Mango, who in turn, fell onto a panting Karela. The guards were just behind and raised their guns, poised to shoot the bear, while Ganga froze like a statue.

The bear sniffed and stared, standing immobile for a moment, before it growled and scratching its shaggy fur with its huge claws, disappeared into the cave.

Ganga stopped to look around. On one side of the caves was a thick, almost impenetrable coppice of sal trees with a dense eruption of bamboos in between. It was almost as if nature were supervising a fertility competition. He wiped his brow and face with the cotton gamcha he had slung around his neck and sat on the mangled roots of a sprawling banyan tree. A slight breeze cooled the air, providing momentary relief as a covey of peacocks preened past.

Mango and Karela exchanged sullen glances to convey that it was about time they turned back. They searched for an excuse to prove that their operation was futile; they had to prevail on Ganga to call it off.

Ganga sensed the unease, but he was unwilling to turn back. He racked his brains trying to figure out new ways of breaking the monotony, when he noticed something gleaming under a karonda bush some yards away from him.

At first he ignored it, presuming it to be a lemon-emigrant butterfly. Or, perhaps it was a white feather reflecting the sun.

But, when a gust of breeze failed to dislodge it, he awarded it a more penetrating stare.

As the sun unshackled itself from the clouds, the shimmer became even more pronounced. He broke a ber twig and tried to drag the shining object towards himself from beneath the karonda bush. It was heavy; probably entangled with something. So he pushed it hard in the opposite direction until it rolled into a kachnar thicket, mixing with its sweet-smelling blossoms resembling azaleas. He descended towards the flowers and groped with his hands while the others watched him.

Flowers were entwined with colourful butterflies lost in lustful frolic. He felt cautiously till his hands hit something heavy; it had a metallic feel. He wrenched it out quickly. A metal plate, beveled at the edges and made of brass was attached to an orange strap about two feet long and two inches wide, with a buckle and holes. The buckle was intact and locked with the strap passing through it. He stared at it closely, missing a heartbeat. The strap had been sliced apart. The cut was not a tear—it was made with a series of fluent strokes with a knife.

The buckle had an engraving: RT-9.

'This is the collar-ID of Burree Maada, the missing tigress,' Ganga said. He flipped the object and announced, 'The radio telemetry collar has the name of the manufacturer, RadoTel Corporation inscribed over it!'

'How can we be sure it is Burree Maada's? What about the antenna?' asked one of the rangers, as they all huddled around him, holding their breath, the implications of the find dawning upon all of them.

'We have to find the pugmarks,' ordered Ganga, 'the tiger must have come here, there have to be pugmarks.'

A small team under Mango's command began the search for pugmarks along the damp forest track. It did not take them long to locate the pad and four-toe marks.

'Sir, we have got the pugmarks,' announced Mango excitedly. 'Burree Maada did make it upto this spot, the marks are there.'

'Ok, get the PML and PMB,' ordered Ganga, as he ran to the spot where the pugmarks were visible, though somewhat smudged.

A ranger bent to lay down a flat glass over a pugmark and placed his eyes at a ninety degree angle to sketch the imprint with the tracer—a black felt pen. Every tiger left its own unique pugmark. PML or pugmark length was the distance beween the end of the longest toe and the base of the pad, and PMB or pugmark breath was the distance between the outer edges of the two toes on the sides.

'Yes indeed, the tiger was here,' Ganga confirmed, after examining the sketch. 'Now we have to confirm that this was Burree Maada's current radio-collar and not one that may have been discarded earlier.'

Bisnu who was conversant with collaring methodology pointed to the orange bar below the numeric code. 'Had to be Burree Mada,' he said. 'She was one of those whose collars had an orange colour-code, the colour we received recently from RadoTel. Sir, the antennas are secured inside the collars,' he explained.

Karela added, 'The radio-collars consist of two layers of butyl and one of urethane laid over them.'

'Bastard poachers forgot that collars do not degrade. The biologically inert material can survive high temperatures,' Ganga ranted.

Shadows lengthened around them and the foliage started thickening. Ganga had half a mind to return—but he knew that he had to persevere if he wished to make a discovery. The others were also more amenable, sensing the possibility of some success now.

'Ok. Let us have some chai,' said Ganga. His offer was greeted with smiles and applause.

He sat down on a huge boulder while a ranger spread a bamboo mat and opened a canvas bag that contained flattened purees, aaloo-bhaji and pickled lemon. It was a simple snack and they quickly consumed it, draining it down with the hot masala chai carried in a thermos flask.

'Sir deep in the heart of this jungle, on empty and stressed stomachs, even this simple food tastes heavenly,' Mango observed, wiping his pickle-stained hands against his trousers.

Just then the wireless set crackled.

'KTR Control to DD Patrol. Report signal. Over.'

'DD Patrol to KTR Control. Loud and clear. Carry on.'

'Director Sahib wants to know location and report of DD Patrol. Over.'

Ganga motioned him not to respond, to ignore the message. But it was too late. Mango, standing close to the ranger operating the wireless set, promptly revealed their location, while Karela hung his head as if he had been caught red-handed breaking the law.

The instructions from base were loud and clear.

'Director KTR to Patrol Mobile: Return base immediately for important meeting. Over.'

The party was over. Mango and Karela exchanged glances as if they had expected this to happen. They quickly sidled up to Ganga to seek his decision to turn back.

On instinct, Ganga turned to look back at the phalanx that had started lagging behind. 'I am the man on the spot!' he screamed. 'If anybody turns back before we find Burree Maada, I will screw them!'

The insouciance vanished. Ganga wished Sherry could see his firm sense of commitment.

🐾

As he slid down a rock, Ganga accidentally stepped into a hollow pit, bustling with snakes, their skins camouflaged naturally against the stone. He was pulled out in time by an attentive guard.

'Sir this trek might be fine for a thick and furry-skinned animal, but not for a human,' Mango said. His khaki uniform had been scratched in places and was honourably adorned with clawy leaves and thorns.

'Keep together and keep moving!' Ganga commanded forcefully.

They reached a level area, ideal for halting. Hardly had they stopped when Bisnu came running out of a dense grove, screaming excitedly.

'Sir, Burree Maada!' he shouted. 'I have found Burree Maada.'

'Where?' asked Ganga.

Everybody turned around and ran in the direction of the discovery. They could only see vultures hovering in the sky above. Bisnu pointed towards a mound.

'They killed her. She is lying there in a khud,' pointed Bisnu.

Beyond the mound, in a depression in the hillside, were smudged marks of animal movements and droppings. A dead crow lay in the khud with its feathers around it. Close to it was an assortment of branches and twigs, piled into a huge stack, in an artistic pattern. From a distance, there was no chance of noticing it.

'Has to be the handiwork of trained humans,' Karela said. 'The mud has human footmarks.'

Everybody gathered around the stack, tension writ large on their faces, while Ganga ordered the stack to be undone in the manner of a coroner ordering a grave to be exhumed.

'At last we know what happened to Burree Maada,' said Ganga. 'She is still with us. The bastards have hidden it here, hoping to carry away when they were ready.'

The forest guards began to pull away the twigs and branches rapidly when a strange smell caused them to block their noses instinctively. And then they stepped back, gasping in shock.

The stony-eyed body of a young tribal boy lay before them, dressed in the khaki uniform of the KTR Guards. The face was drained of all colour and the mouth and lips were bloated. There was no bullet wound.

'Open his shirt!' Ganga ordered. 'Tear it!'

As the guards bent to unbutton his shirt, Karela rushed forward and pulled them back. He studied the corpse closely. There was no visible mark.

'Clothes are intact,' Karela said. 'No struggle. Taken by surprise and knocked out clean.'

'How can that be?' Ganga was confident there had to be some tell-tale sign.

'It is so, Sir,' said Karela as he peered again. 'There is no mark of injury.'

Everyone surrounded the body and examined the dead man. 'Look for a stab wound,' ordered Ganga.

'There is no wound,' said Mango.

'Look at this,' said Ganga, pointing towards a crimson latitudinal mark, running along the dead man's neck.

The silence was deafening as the team comprehended the situation.

Ganga announced, 'He has been strangled.'

'Sir, here lies Burree Maada!'

Mahadeo panted, pointing to another stack, concealed by bushes in another direction. It was identical in arrangement to the other, also arranged as a lattice. They rushed there as guards threw out the logs of wood and twigs and peered inside.

Mormon butterflies flew out devilishly in a dark swarm from a corner of the stack. All shapes of ugly worms—long and short, slender and fat, in iridescent blue and orange, white and red, insects with wings and jungle ants with bulging heads, wriggled and squirmed over each other in ceaseless orgy. But inside the stack was no carcass of a Royal Bengal tigress. Instead, it was the half-consumed and decomposing body of a chital.

Ganga stared at the rotting carcass, trying to work out the puzzle. It intrigued him that the lovely, lyre-shaped antlers of the chital had been left untouched!

Meanwhile, the big question remained: Where was Burree Maada?

The forest staff raved and ranted as they crowded around the wrenching discovery. The riot of worms, disturbed from feasting upon the putrefying chital carcass crawled out menacingly towards them.

Mango made loud gurgling sounds in his mouth and then ejaculated the phlegm with repugnance. Others held out their gamchas and handkerchiefs to wipe the sweat and block their noses. The smell assailed Ganga too, but he forebore from reacting. He stooped to dilate the chital's eyes with his fingers. The luminosity had long since vanished; the eye fluids had dried as rigor mortis set in.

'This chital was killed at least twenty-four hours ago,' Ganga commented diagnostically, recalling with regret that though he had thought of a search, he had not insisted for it earlier.

'Chemical poisoning?' inquired Mango, pointing to the dark innards.

'Possible,' Ganga looked down at the carcass with revulsion.

His eyes fell on the battered rear end. 'Look at these claw marks. The skin here has been ruptured with powerful claws. Tigers start from the rump...'

'If Burree Maada was poisoned, the hunters obviously tracked her for some time,' conjectured Karela. 'No city person would have that much time or patience. It was probably the Gonds.'

'No,' Ganga was emphatic, 'Primitive tribes like the Baigas and even the Gonds do not kill tigers unless it is a matter of survival. They have a symbiotic relationship with them. Haven't you observed their paintings?'

'But Sir, why would the hunters leave the antlers?' Mango asked.

'It is the handiwork of a trained hunter who knows the science of tracking tigers,' said Ganga. 'The tigress consumed parts of the chital...roughage for digestion, but would have no appetite for horns. Pardhis will carry away something only when they have hunted it themselves. Only then is it an offering to their goddess. In the olden days they used to feed opium to the bait so that the tiger would be slow in its reflexes after the kill, making it an easy shikar.'

'Furadone is being used by farmers to keep wildlife out of crops. We have found many Pardhis with something like it,' Karela said.

Ganga waited until Mango and Karela huddled around to hear his verdict. Then, with a somber expression he pronounced, 'The bastards killed Burree Maada.'

'Sir, perhaps we should go further,' Mango suggested.

'No point now. Why would anybody hide the carcass of a half-eaten chital? By now the carcass would have been taken...'

'The dead tigress would have reached Jabalpur,' Mango filled in promptly.

'Maybe Kolkata,' said Karela. 'Cleaned, chemically treated, and pressed sheet-thin, like acrylic on canvas by Ping-Pong Leathers on Sun Yat Sen Street.'

'Chinatown?' It was Mango.

'A little bit of China is embedded in India too,' said Ganga philosophically, staring at the blue sky. 'The Chinese came to Calcutta before the Opium War. It used to be an opium auctioning centre for secretly routing supplies to China. Then it became the center for the leather business when East India Company officers needed high-quality leather belts and shoes. Leather was first a hobby, then handicraft, and later a cottage industry,' Ganga expounded proudly.

He remembered how they had splurged on Chinese cuisine in the course of his mandatory Bharat-darshan after joining the Forest Service. Chinese food had been the preferred choice—cheap, tangy and perfectly delightful. At the end of their trip, after a reality check of a few dozen Chinese restaurants in different cities—from the premier five-star hotels in Delhi's Lutyens zone to the modest offerings of the Tibetan Monastery in North Delhi and the cheap restaurants in Kolkata's Chinatown, they had arrived at one intriguing conclusion: to the traditional Indian palette, spoilt by pickles, spices and chillies—the tastefulness of Chinese cuisine in India was inversely proportionate to the sterility of the kitchens in which it was cooked.

Bisnu bounded up, panting, his hair and clothes laden with leaves and dust. He pointed beyond the stack to several bamboo sticks that were lying on the ground. Ganga picked up one and examined it closely. Golden fibres were stuck to it. He picked up the other bamboo pieces.

'Tiger hair is intertwined with the cellulose fibre,' Ganga said, picking out strands of lustrous golden hair with his fingers.

'This means that the tigress has been,' Mango gasped.

'It seems that the tigress, like the guard, has been done neat, without bullets or poison!' Ganga continued. 'With one of her legs stuck in the iron trap, probably they paralysed her by stuffing an iron spear into her roaring mouth. And then she must have been thrashed with sticks and beaten to death.'

Mango picked up a crumpled piece of paper from the ground.

'What is that?' asked Ganga.

'A train ticket from Katni to Jabalpur...dated two days ago.'

'That doesn't prove anything. But this is a criminal case. We should inform the police,' Ganga said bluntly.

'Sir, let the body of the Forest Guard remain buried for some more time. First, please consult with the KTR Field Director. He will tell you how to handle this serious matter,' Mango suggested.

'No. We will take the body with us,' thundered Ganga. 'We will get a post-mortem done and send the viscera to the forensic lab.'

'But, how did the poachers track the tigress?' Mango wondered aloud.

'Not possible without intelligent support,' Ganga said. He looked down towards Kisli. The trail of smoke from a cow-dung fire made zig-zag spirals in the air leaving behind the smell of wood.

There were innumerable messages ordering them to see the Field Director immediately. Ganga wasted no time and headed straight for the Director's Camp Office. The lights were on and the brass plate with the Field Director's name gleamed brightly even from a distance. An old orderly in uniform stood outside.

Sanskar Shekhar Singh was expecting Ganga. But surprisingly, he asked Mango and Karela to also come in for the meeting. Ganga squirmed, but concealed his hurt.

The teak-panelled room was furnished with thick coir matting, while clay pots filled with coleuses and crotons gave it colour. A norman-window shaped incumbency board carried the names of Singh and his predecessors. The wooden table had a tiny brass bust of Mahatma Gandhi and the Indian tricolour flag pegged to a small metal stand. The walls had large pictures of tigers and barasingha and coloured charts that painted a rosy picture of conservation in Kanha.

Ganga walked in, saluted and greeted Singh who maintained an expressionless face.

Suddenly Singh burst into speech, 'Darwin's missing link! I suppose you want to be rewarded for solving the biggest mystery of this century!'

Ganga sat squarely in front of Singh, opposite the Gandhi brass statuette. Mango and Karela had sidled in and sat in armless chairs with their backs erect against the rear wall, below the huge forest map of Central India. The expressions on their faces were similar to those of an accused who knew that the verdict would be adverse. 'We should send the dead animal's viscera for a forensic examination, and lodge an FIR to report the death of the guard,' Ganga said. 'We also need to send out an alert to apprehend the poachers.'

Singh ignored Ganga and raising his eyebrows, glared at Mango and Karela, who cowered in the corner, their shoulders hanging. His voice was theatrical, penetrating. 'Like little school boys, all of you seem to be excited about a missing tigress?'

'Sir, but we couldn't have delayed the search for Burree Maada! Such things can't,' Ganga was about to say 'be kept hidden', but controlled himself enough to say, 'remain hidden.'

'What made you conclude that Burree Maada has been poached?' Singh sneered.

Ganga fumbled for words.

'Direct impact of your impetuosity?' Singh looked viciously

at Mango and Karela, continuing to ignore Ganga and stormed, 'Central funds for Kanha and other Tiger Reserves will be blocked! An MLA will ask in the Assembly: What action will government take against those responsible for the mismanagement of KTR? When it comes to international trainings and conferences, who do you think will be sent? Not experts, but other forest officers. Principle of equity! He goes with his family, salutes the Statue of Liberty and makes photo albums.'

Ganga turned to look at Mango and Karela. They sat like two Humpty-Dumptys, their faces forlorn. They nodded their heads in unison every time the Director looked at them, almost as if to say that they were always against the idea of a search in the first place, but were forced into it.

Sanskar Shekhar Singh continued as though Ganga did not exist, 'How are we supposed to survive with bamboo sticks and clunky World War II muskets? Resources are scarce and yet...an offer from the World Bank for assistance in tiger conservation is spurned. Our brilliant colleagues in government advocate as usual that we in India know best—after all we have a rich history of conservation, going back to the Indus Valley Civilization...five thousand years of accumulated knowledge.'

'Of course, Sir, we do need resources,' Ganga pitched in, trying to assuage him. He could well have been speaking to himself.

'Beat a Pardhi who has been caught killing wildlife and the Human Rights Commission fucks you. Why not just do away with tiger reserves and simply have captive farms—fat and healthy tigers like they do in China?' his voice boomed, as if he was blowing into a saxophone.

'What do I get instead? A new law giving property rights to all encroachers on forest land. We now have to rehabilitate those very people we chased away from the Core Zone all our lives. The forests of India are forever fucked.'

Just then the Director's phone rang. He lifted the receiver and studied Ganga closely. Suddenly his tone changed and he seemed to stop just short of standing up to perform a royal taslim. 'Darbar! Hukum Darbar! I'll call you back in a few moments.'

Ganga got up to leave. 'We'll come back in a while Sir,' he said.

The Director laid down the law, 'My instructions are clear. We keep the police and the press away from this case until we are completedly satisfied with our own investigations!'

Ganga punched the boxing bags for several minutes till sweat trickled down his face and his shirt was soaked. He went to the basin and splashed some water on his face. That relaxed him. The phone rang.

'Mr Bishnoi?'

'Yes, who is it?' Ganga asked anxiously.

'Sir…I am your brother,' the speaker said. 'I am your well-wisher.'

'Sorry, but I can't seem to place you,' Ganga said. Where had he heard this sing-song accent? Oh yes! It was Feroze Goenka, the businessman who had visited him in his first days at KTR, and invited him to China. The voice was unforgettable, smooth as China-silk.

Goenka's tone was honeyed, 'Sir, I am very proud of you and your sincere approach to your work. Everybody is full of praise for you.'

'Thank you,' Ganga swore under his breath. Why was he being so patronizing?

Goenka lowered his voice into a conspiratorial whisper and said, 'Unfortunately, the KTR Director is unhappy with you. I have learnt that you are likely to be transferred out soon.'

'That is impossible! I have been in KTR for barely three

months!' Ganga snapped. 'How can I be transferred so soon? It is against convention!'

'Listen brother, this is India,' said Goenka. 'Government is emotionless. I want to intercede on your behalf with the Forest Minister, who is my intimate friend. I have no personal motive, it is just my nature to help good officers in their career. Mr Barretto was in trouble once—a shikar case connected with his brother, but I helped him. He still thanks me. A posting as Deputy Director KTR is not to be given away on hit-wicket. I know for a fact that several senior officers would offer their right hand for it. One day you can be Director-General Wildlife.'

Ganga was speechless. Should he accept Goenka's support or ignore him? He stared at the phone mindlessly hearing Goenka at the other end. Finally, he placed down the receiver carefully and began to massage the deep furrow on his forehead.

Ganga took out his old laptop and started typing frenetically, summarising his trek and the findings. Surely, this would force the Director to order a forensic inquiry. He gave a brief background and divided his report into two main sections: Administrative Lapses and Technical Lapses. He concentrated on one particular paragraph for the latter section:

> There are no standard operating procedures (SOPs) for radio-collaring. Modern poachers can easily map the topography of Kanha and crack the security procedures. In this case, it is likely that the poachers had been tracking the tigress for days, possibly with a parallel receiver system. After triangulating the tigress they set a trap. The murder of a Guard demonstrates their ruthlessness. In all likelihood, the poachers killed Burree Maada before

carrying away her carcass for skinning.

Forensic examination of the viscera of the dead chital in the Central Forensic Science Laboratory, Sagar, or the Indian Veterinary Research Institute in Bareilly is a must. It will serve to conclusively reveal the turn of events leading to the disappearance of Burree Maada and the murder of the Forest Guard.

Ganga had barely entered his house after what he considered a revitalizing jog when the phone rang. It was Sherry Pinto. He held the receiver, pondering if he should talk to her, lest it was viewed that he was leaking facts to the media. On an impulse, he decided to take her call.

'Mr Bishnoi, this is Sherry Pinto. Remember me?' her enticing voice seemed to hold a subtle taunt.

'I do,' said Ganga cautiously.

'Sir, can you confirm that you did not find Burree Maada or her carcass, and that you found a dead chital instead, with the antlers intact?' Sherry asked.

'Yes, what you have just stated is factually true,' said Ganga. 'But how did you...'

'Thanks Mr Bishnoi,' Sherry said curtly. 'I hope you will see my story in the HT.'

There was a sharp click and she was gone.

His steno-typist was on leave. The computer station was still out of action—the mother board needed repair. The printer's cartridge was dry. He carried his report on a pen drive and went to the Director's secretary, requesting her to print his report.

The *Hindustan Time* reached at 10.30 a.m. by the first bus from Jabalpur. He anxiously scanned the pages, fearing the worst. Sherry's report was on the last page. It left him dumbfounded.

The Mystery of the Missing Tigress:

It does not require the intellectual felicity of a Sherlock Holmes or the ingenuity of a Hercule Poirot to solve the mystery of Burree Maada, the missing tigress of Kanha. A search organized by Gangavardhan Aranyaprem Bishnoi, the Deputy Director of the KTR uncovered facts that would have remained hidden. With the discovery of a neatly concealed carcass of a half-eaten chital, in the course of a rigorous combing operation, and the failure to trace the missing tigress, it is now abundantly clear that Burree Maada is missing forever. Despite KTR being an extremely prestigious Project Tiger Reserve and under the close watch of the Prime Minister's office, it has been possible for ruthless poachers to track and capture a tigress! Unfortunately, several tigers have been missing from Kanha in the past few weeks.

It may be recalled that poachers were able to kill more than thirty-five tigers in Sariska last year, causing the complete decimation of tigers from that great sanctuary. The magnitude of the catastrophe ensured that it attracted nation-wide attention and now it seems that Kanha is also going the Sariska way!

It is shocking that the viscera of the dead animal have not yet been sent for analysis to the Central Forensic Science Laboratory. The results would have helped to retrace the sequence of events, such as the last meal of the ill fated tigress and most importantly the modus-operandi of the poachers. Where is the carcass of the tigress? Why have no

> raids been conducted upon known recipients of poached animals and the tiger mafia?
>
> Can we conclude that Burree Maada has been killed for her skin and body parts? Or should we surmise that she has perhaps been shanghaied out, lock-stock and barrel? Could it be that the DNA of Burree Maada, the purest of the pure amongst the Royal Bengal Tigress species is of special interest to those who are in the business of genome sequencing—cloning tigers in captive farms to the northeast of India!
>
> Not many in India would have heard of an obscure UN body, the Convention on International Trade in Endangered Species of Wild Fauna, also known as CITES, which sets protocols to save endangered species like the tiger. The tiger is currently on the prohibited list of CITES. Despite huge accumulated surpluses from captive tiger farms, and insatiable demand, Chinese investors in tiger captive-farms are frustrated because of their inability to sell tiger parts and derivatives legally.
>
> Illicit trade in animal parts is, it must be remembered, the third largest illegal business in the world after arms and drugs.

Next to the written article were three photographs with captions below them. The first showed a huge tiger titled, Burree Maada; the second was of a tourist on elephant back with the label, Kanha, displayed on the howdah; while the third was of dead tigers sloshed against ice, like cocktail olives titled, Tiger carcasses accumulating outside tiger farm in China.

The old office orderly stood outside like a faceless sentinel; his red sash displayed a round brass plaque with the emblem of the state government. He ushered Ganga respectfully to the waiting room with a cane sofa and red cushions meant for guests and fetched a glass of water. Mrs Nair, the middle-aged secretary, dressed in a magenta Chanderi sari that made no effort to conceal her ample bosom, was fond of Ganga because of his youthfulness. She smiled warmly as he waited for the Field Director to see him and handed him a printout of his report, whispering, 'Director is busy on the phone talking to higher-ups in Bhopal. He is very angry after he read…'

'My report?' asked an alarmed Ganga.

'Report in *Hindustan Time*,' she whispered.

Ganga bit his lips. He decided to wait there, staring at the colourful photographs of the birds of Kanha. He wondered what the Director and his friend were twittering about. The call-bell sounded harshly, causing Mrs Nair to rush in.

'Field Director cannot meet you just now…perhaps you could try later,' she advised on her return.

Ganga was just about to thank her and leave when a guttural sound stopped him. It was the fax machine spewing out paper, the printed part curling backwards in a defiant roll. She rushed to retrieve the fax and tore it out in one jerky action, her breasts bobbing wildly; one glance at it and her face dropped like her pallu. She turned around and hesitated briefly before reading out the substantive part:

> Pending further inquiry into lapses relating to the Tiger Conservation Program, Government hereby appoints Gangavardhan Aranyaprem Bishnoi, IFS, 1999, Deputy Field Director Kanha Tiger Reserve, as Divisional Forest Officer Working Plan, Balaghat, vide existing vacancy. Assistant Park Director, Manmohan Gopal will hold

> charge of the post of Deputy Field Director, KTR, until further notice.

Ganga peered disbelievingly at the fax. Such travesties never occurred to his ilk—the hallowed, steel-frame civil servants. And yet, the earth seemed to move under his feet. Mrs Nair made sympathetic noises as the orderly fetched him another glass of water. She muttered incoherently about the importance of keeping cool.

'Date of order is yesterday,' she whispered breathlessly.

The order had been deliberately backdated to predate it to his report! The orderly commented sympathetically, 'George Schaller Sahib lived here for many years... Only then could he write about Kanha wildlife.'

Suddenly the door opened and the Director loomed into view. Ganga stood up at attention and saluted him. The Director's usually relaxed look had morphed into a stony one and he avoided eye-contact. He asked Mrs Nair curtly if there was a message from Headquarters. She promptly handed him the fax. He grabbed it and returned to his room without closing the door.

The call-bell rang long and stridently. Once again, Mrs Nair rushed in and came out almost instantly.

She returned to her position behind the computer and looked helplessly at Ganga.

'Yes, Mrs Nair?' he almost had it in his heart to pity her.

'Director has asked me to serve the transfer order upon you, here...now,' she said apologetically. She showed him the order. The Director had written on it in red ink, underlining and circling for extra emphasis: 'Most Urgent—For Immediate Compliance'.

Ganga took the order and signed an acknowledgement into a Dak Register. His stomach churned as he trudged back home. He felt a decade older.

Bhaloo was nowhere in sight. Ganga directed a series of

punches at the hanging sandbags till they swung rapidly in all directions, colliding against each other with dusty thuds. He carried a bottle of gin into the kitchen and poured out a generous measure before dropping several ice cubes into it. Next, he squeezed a lemon viciously into it, extracting every single drop. He plastered salt on the rim of the glass and using a twisted green chilli, stirred the cocktail swiftly before dropping it in. He downed a large swig of the chimlet hoping it would relax him. Back in the living room, he put up his legs and settled down to crunch the chili and savour his drink. He got up and made another chimlet, much stronger this time, crunched more chilli before he switched on the television.

The warmth helped to diffuse the events of the past hour. MTV was playing the pulsating Summer Mania at Ibiza. Attractive bikini clad girls danced erotically. He sat back and stared at the gyrating pelvises and the jingling breasts, and even bobbed his head in rhythm. But his mind throbbed with the shock of being deceived.

His transfer order lay before him. He stared at it. He believed he had served the government scrupulously. And yet they had had no compunction about transferring him as if he was an inanimate object. They would rationalize by saying that it wasn't a punishment. But his psyche had been hurt. His dream of writing a book on Kanha rudely shattered.

He banged his fists on the table. Why did he have to suffer this fate? Suddenly he got up and tossed the glass against the wall. It smashed instantly with a bang and the pieces flew and careened across the floor in all directions. He began to pace the room and shouted loudly, 'Bastards! Bloody Bastards!'

🐾

Sherry remained abreast about the developments in Kanha post-Ganga. She learnt about Mango's party, just a few days after his coronation, attended by the rank and file of KTR, with a cameo appearance by the Director. It would not have been worth a mention, but for Bisnu's gaffe. As somebody whose career had followed the same trajectory as Ganga over the last three postings, Bisnu had remarked undiplomatically that had Ganga stayed on longer, 'He would have substantially changed the face of wildlife conservation in Kanha.'

'He would have been a disaster!' Karela rebuked, 'How can you praise a maniac?'

Two days later, following the footsteps of his mentor Ganga, Bisnu too had received a transfer order. He had to report to the Statistics Section in the office of the Conservator of Forests in Jabalpur.

Sherry surfaced a few days after Ganga departed from smouldering Kanha. She was pleasantly surprised when Shekhar Singh promptly gave her an appointment. She noted that he appeared bright and cheerful. His handsome kshatriya features and large, puffed eyes lent gravitas to his position.

'Sir, the Kanha brand owes much to you,' Sherry said flatteringly, her face a picture of appreciation. 'Were it not for you, it would have lagged far behind Ranthambore and Bandhavgarh.'

'It hasn't been easy,' Singh said, acknowledging her comments gracefully, without showing that he was pleased. 'We have learnt to live with unusual challenges.'

'I wish this Burree Maada incident had not occurred though,' Sherry said softly.

'Miss Pinto,' he said cautiously, 'I do not wish to discuss this matter until we have a complete report.'

'But a chital carcass has been found,' Sherry said. 'And a Forest Guard has been brutally murdered.'

'Sorry, no comments at this stage,' Singh said with finality. 'You can discuss anything else about KTR other than Burree Maada or matters connected with her!'

What else was there to discuss that she couldn't pick up from a website? Would it help if she wrote about his recalcitrant attitude? Perhaps not! She seemed to be up against an official stonewall! However she persisted, 'I have one last question. Why did you transfer Mr Bishnoi so suddenly?'

'I didn't!' Singh objected, glaring at her. 'Government has exercised that power, in its supreme wisdom!'

'But Sir, Bishnoi had only been here for three months,' Sherry argued. 'How can you show any results in such a short period of time?'

Singh lowered his voice confidentially and began to spin a multi-coloured glass paperweight on the glass surface of his office table. It spun like a top and he managed to hold it back from rolling away at the edge. 'Well, transfers are just an occupational hazard. Did you know Bishnoi before he was posted here?' Sherry shook her head in negation. 'Frankly, I must say he belongs to a breed of blustering officers—technically savvy, but unable to absorb the larger view,' he said. 'Did you know that I had to practically force him to conduct a search operation?'

Sherry dropped her shoulders and sighed. As she rose to leave, he asked casually, 'Miss Pinto, have you congratulated him?'

'Who?'

'Darbar.'

'Pardon me...I don't get you.'

He smiled provocatively. 'Surely you remember?'

She raised her eyebrows and stared at him, 'I am sorry...'

'Our Darbar, His Highness the Maharaja of Baikunthpur,' Singh announced deferentially.

'You mean Abhimanyu Singh?' Sherry's face flushed pink as she bit her tongue.

'Indeed!' Singh said, absorbing every nuance on her face.

'Has he been awarded his PhD?' she asked, infusing the right degree of interest.

'No!' Singh sounded impatient; he dismissed such a probability as an impossibility. 'It's in all the magazines.' He pulled out a copy of India Today.

'I don't get the time to read magazines,' Sherry said apologetically.

'Darbar's film on Barasingha Conservation has won an award at the International Wildlife Society Films Festival in Montana,' he said. He showed her the box item which mentioned Abhimanyu Singh and carried his photograph.

'Great!'

'Did you know that he shot it in Kanha?'

'Fantastic! It's the equivalent of an Oscar! Admirable!' she said appreciatively. It was unnerving to have Sanskar Shekhar Singh dissect her. She added, 'I will definitely congratulate him if I meet him!'

'Yes,' continued Singh, 'I've asked him to make a pitch for the Whitley Award as well. I wish I had half his hunger for wildlife.'

Hunger for wildlife? She recalled that Abhimanyu had once bragged about his powerful cousin, S-Cubed, who had been posted as Field Director of the Panna Tiger Reserve. Then later, he had chosen to demolish him, 'He is quite a screwball, happiest when engaged in building and feathering his private cottage near the Bori Sanctuary. Frankly he is incapable of protecting any jungle from shikar, let alone Panna. I wish he had more hunger for wildlife.' She had begun to admire Abhimanyu for being so frank and honest. It was then that she had whispered lovingly into his ear, 'I can love a man, only when he is able to command my respect.'

🐾

Sherry rose early, and was startled to notice the dark circles below her eyes. She had been missing her cycling routine in the morning for some time and her early evening round of tennis at the Narmada Club had also taken a back seat of late. She needed to keep fit. After gulping her usual mix of honey and lemon, she performed the surya namaskar yoga-asana in the Cuckoo Room. This room with teak flooring, her personal favourite, overlooked the distended oval garden and had also been Auntie Lara's earthing place. She absorbed the breathtaking view of wild roses, lime and jamun trees that grew wild at the rear of the house, guided by some unknown force. A pair of orphaned pigeons cooed as she scattered their daily feed of bajra and bread crumbs, before Riki-Tiki-Tawi, her pet mongoose, hopped jealously onto her lap.

After checking her e-group on the net, she decided to step out. Clad in half-pants that she had trimmed from her overused Levi's and a cotton tee-shirt, she slapped sunscreen lotion on her face and hands and retrieved her ancient Dior sunglasses. Her hair was pulled into a pigtail with the help of thick red bungs. She took out the old war-horse—her historic red BSA cycle, a trifle scratched, not too feminine, but extremely efficient. She carried her iPod—music was her unfailing elixir. It promised to be a clear day and although the sun was out, a pleasant breeze was blowing down from the Dumna hills.

As she left Grey Goose, she was glad there were no prurient schoolboys hanging around to catch a glimpse of her. She passed the stray dogs and the jawans in their crisp uniforms marching in formation on the road adjoining the Cobra Ground. She remembered that in a few days the Chief of Army Staff would be visiting Jabalpur; the whole cantonment was abuzz with preparations. After all, Jabalpur was the geographical heart of India and the safest station for various Corps to have their regimental centers, the EME, JAK Rifles, Signals among others, besides being the Sub-Area Command for Central India and the home of the College of Materials Management.

Military equipment gleamed reassuringly all along the way. She cycled as usual to the top of the Dumna Ridge, past the CMM Museum, with its antique cannons and artillery guns displayed outside. She noticed the long turrets of the 155mm Bofors Howitzer (that, she rued, cost an environment-loving Indian Prime Minister his job) stare brazenly at her. She soaked in the lush landscape and the Satpura hills beyond. The fragrance of jasmine and menthol filled her senses as she pedalled easily, before stopping briefly near the Khandari Reservoir.

She perched on a rounded boulder embraced by a clump of red and white bougainvilleas overlooking the tranquil water body with its crumbling Victorian relics which peered out stoically from amidst the dense tangle of trees and shrubs. She admired the abundant canvas of natural beauty, and allowed her senses to rest, soaking in the beauty of nature and the joy of freedom. A kingfisher swooped down to hunt for fish and she marvelled at the ease with which it soared back into the sky. Could she ever do that with her own life?

After a while she turned around and walked back slowly to her cycle. She pedalled lazily; it had been an invigorating though tough uphill trek, but downhill would be much easier. She spotted a flock of Monarch butterflies, tawny-orange and black, speeding ahead of her along the road. She pedalled faster now, deciding to outdo them. The bike obeyed her command and she just about managed to sail past the butterflies, whooping with joy, as they flew higher, swerved in perfect formation and vanished to her left.

Ahead of her lay the point from where the slope of the ridge forked, with one end going towards Mandla and beyond to Kanha, and the dog-leg into Ridge Road towards the Cobra Ground.

She cut the pedaling, allowing the cycle to freewheel. Keeping her hands on the hand-brakes, she allowed the cycle to zip down in cruise mode, gaining speed and momentum as it descended, whistling past the wooded hills. She enjoyed the exhilaration of freefall as the cool wind hit her face, making her skin tingle. Her iPod was playing her all-time favourites; music had always been an expression of her soul and it was now on top of the world!

Pink Floyd was followed by John Denver and the Beatles. And then Bono and the Corrs sang the evergreen Summer Wine. She could see the tri-junction below where the three roads forked. She sang along the words loudly, as loudly as she could:

Strawberries, cherries and an angel's kiss in spring,
My summer wine is really made from all these things…
Take off your silver spurs and help me pass the time,
And I will give to you summer wine…

How lucky she was to be able to live life on her own terms. She had almost cracked the Burree Maada mystery. Just then she saw somebody standing at the tri-junction. He seemed to be waving like the pointsman for a race…very soldier-like in olive greens. She waved at him.

Was it a bust tyre or had she dropped something? As she coursed past the soldier, instinct prompted her to look back. Not one, but two soldiers were running after her with oblong objects in their hands. Something was wrong! Why should they be running after her? What did they have in their hands? Grenades?

But in turning to look back, she missed the tractor-trolley carrying hay and goats, chugging caterpillar-like towards her, in the centre of the road. The driver, talking to his mate and puffing at his bidi, also failed to spot the cycle zipping down the slope like a bolt of lightning. A heavy crash was followed by a series of quick explosions.

The cycle rammed headlong into the tractor and Sherry was catapulted high into the air before landing miraculously into the hay. Panic-stricken goats muzzled her, bleating loudly. As she struggled to sit up, the soldiers hurled the objects towards her. One missed her completely, landing on the driver of the tractor. There was a flash and a hiss as the glass broke and the driver screamed in pain as the contents ripped his face, shredding his skin to bits. Fumes shot out as the other object landed on the hay and it started simmering. Nudged by the angry goats, she rolled out and fell to the ground. The hay caught fire and connected with the fuel and soon enveloped the tractor and the trolley in one large orange ball of heat and fire.

There was complete mayhem as the bleating goats were grilled in the fire. Vehicles coming from both directions screeched to a halt and a huge crowd collected around the scene of the tragedy.

She lay stunned, staring at the sky, hearing sirens blaring in the distance. Suddenly the reality of what had happened struck her. She had been attacked with acid! Acid was used for the pickling of raw leather and animal skins. It was available in the four ordnance factories and the many foundry units in Jabalpur. A few days ago, a young bride who had complained against her in-laws for torturing her with demands for dowry, had her pretty face scarred forever with concentrated sulphuric acid. The police had not yet charged the assailants.

A part of the crowd gravitated towards her. Nobody attempted to lift her, even though many exclaimed in recognition. It was only when an army patrol arrived that she was lifted up and rushed to the Military Hospital.

She woke up in hospital with a start when somebody brought her phone. It was her Editor. He sounded extremely concerned and advised tersely, 'Please Sherry, be careful. Dainik Bhaskar has reported that you are intent on exposing the Forest Department. If you have to stay with us, please understand we are a conservative paper and need the government's support. No more fucking controversy!'

🐾

She looked at the prize-winning photograph taken by her father, Ralph Arnold, when he had first come to India as a nineteen-year-old boy in 1947; around the same time India had became independent. It had been a turning point in his life when he set off on a whirlwind photography tour of Indian wildlife and royalty. It was of three baby elephants splattering themselves with muddy water in a kind of a head-to-toe spa. That picture, perhaps taken in the Nilgiris, had evoked numerous emotions—joy, love, pride and sport, and after earning him global recognition by winning a prize from Life magazine, had gone on to becoming the mascot for a famous baby soap company. Why couldn't she do something as simple and memorable?

She had a camera but seldom used it. She had started on a pictorial book based on the mythology of the River Narmada, for which her photographer friend Robin had already shot a thousand photographs, while she was yet to complete the text. What would she gain by exposing the wildlife mafia? Perhaps she needed to step back; a trekking holiday would do her good. Her father, after several twists in his life, had become the Chief Spokesman for the Dalai Lama's Government in Exile, and lived in Dharamsala at the foothills of the Himalayas. She yearned to spend time with him. An old school friend in Leh who had commenced trekking tours connecting the various monasteries that dotted that part of the Zanskar and Karakoram Himalayan ranges had also extended an invitation.

Just then her phone rang. It was a voice she recognized instantly; it was her friend in Panna.

'Hello Robin, how are you?'

Robin, a Swiss expatriate, ran 'Turquoise Trunk: The River Camp', on the banks of the Ken River on the outskirts of the Panna Tiger Reserve. It was reputed to be quaint, with log-wood terraces and tree houses that jutted precipitously into the meandering river, famous for the long-snouted crocodile or Indian gharial and the marsh crocodile or maggar.

'Sherry! We're so glad you are safe. Both of us were so shocked. Just dump Jabalpur and go incognito for a few months. Get away from those thugs, move away from it all. Why don't you visit us in Panna?'

The Panna Tiger Reserve was practically the other end of the tiger spectrum; unlike Kanha, it had, like Sariska, dramatically hit rock bottom. There were reports that more than fifty tigers had been poached in the last three years. Perhaps, she would also get some insight into what had happened to Burree Maada. It didn't take her long to decide on a trip to Panna.

She was clear, though, that she preferred the independence of the local Government Rest House even though there was an apocryphal story that this it was haunted by ghosts. She was advised by Robin to, 'Keep the door bolted and not to open it in the night.' She was amused. Would a ghost knock and seek entry?

The advantage of the Rest House was that it was opposite the main entrance to the Park. Sherry could manage to be a part of all the activity, albeit from the sidelines. She prepared to operate the tiny kitchen and cook for herself with the desultory help of the rest-house cook, who seemed to have laid aside all pretences of meeting the requirements of his job. Sherry was about to take a bath when Robin drove over in his safari-jeep to meet her in the late evening. Dressed in a bathrobe, she sat in the covered verandah and chatted with him over masala chai.

'Sherry, I hope you are enjoying this luxurious new den of yours?' Robin asked sarcastically, peering at the cracked walls and torn dhurrie.

'Well, it's quite elevating to live in a suite which has a bathtub and fittings dating back to the time of Queen Victoria,' said Sherry. 'I daresay it leaks! In all probability I will hear eerie sounds in the night, and I will definitely have the surreal experience of donating blood to vampire mosquitoes. And then, I may meet a ghost too! I happen to think it is worth it.'

'And if the ghost turns out to be a handsome prince?'

They laughed.

'I am closer to the tiger reserve here,' said Sherry. 'But on a more serious note, how is it that the Panna brand has suddenly lost its sheen? Where have you sent all the tigers? And now even Kanha seems to be affected by the Panna virus!'

Robin looked away before he commented, 'I've heard about Burree Maada. It's been a regular feature here...a dead tiger practically every week! We are being forced to look at non-tiger sources of tourism. Thankfully, Khajuraho with its temples is next door.'

'Panna has therefore graduated as a destination holiday for art-loving Indian youth from being a holiday for the more adventurous ones,' Sherry said cynically. Khajuraho, barely an hour from Panna, had tenth century temples dedicated to various gods in the Hindu pantheon depicting in a surprisingly unabashed way, detailed acts of coitus; perhaps as an expression of how sex was a part of the overall cycle of life.

'Anyway, crazy as it may sound, I've bought some land there and plan to build a resort.'

'I doubt if you can make it economically viable.'

'I wanted to build a tiger resort there. But...'

'Yes?'

'Now I plan to call it The Kamasutra Golf Club, Resort and Spa.'

'And how do you position it?'

'All the greens will be styled after different positions in the

Kamasutra. How's the idea?'

Sherry laughed. 'You'll be hard pressed to select the most popular eighteen!'

'Yes, I have to get my designs right.'

'Check out the golf stars...some of the great ones can have exceptional designs!'

'Diamonds add mystique to this place,' Robin said. 'Besides there is an ancient fort and the breathtaking Pandava Falls where the legendary brothers from the epic Mahabharata are believed to have stayed during their exile. Once I spotted three pairs of leopards there. But with all the negative dead tiger stories, it is a miracle that we still manage to get tourists!'

'Great!' said Sherry, clapping her hands in support. 'You know, I'm puzzled about the sudden hype around the vanishing tiger story. One moment this place is awarded for superlative conservation and the fact that it has more than fifty tigers and the next moment it is completely bereft of them...I wonder...'

Robin looked thoughtful. 'You know, just a few days after they declared PTR was bereft of tigers, I thought I saw Saraswati with her beautiful white mutant stripe. Of course nobody believed me!'

Sherry bent down and picked a fallen twig of neem and began to chew the leaves as they strolled across to the PTR gate.

'You're a ruminant!'

'Merely an earthly shield against inter galactic intrusions,' she said, dusting off a rapacious mosquito from her neck.

The PTR gates opened at 6.00 a.m. Sherry was there by 5.30 a.m. She had engaged a Gypsy jeep for the next few days and had decided to go around the PTR, familiarising herself with its layout. Accompanying the bare-as-bones and open-to-sky Gypsy was a tour guide—a young school dropout, masquerading as a naturalist, carrying a colourful and bilingual book on Indian birds. The driver had his face wrapped in a checked angavastram, which Sherry felt, made him look like a failed Chambal dacoit.

She traversed the length and breadth of PTR, taking a different route each time, until she was fully conversant with its topography. She visited the villages around the Park and talked at length to the villagers, who seemed friendly enough except when the talk turned to the missing tigers. She began to hang around them and gave large tips and eclairs to the little children. She lazed in the sun on a charpoy and shared their food of makka-roti and tuar-lentil with amla-chutney and salt, and even their mahua wine while sharing their sorrows and joys.

Not surprisingly, she soon became a welcome sight. As soon as her jeep approached, the villagers gathered to talk to her and the young boys and girls ran alongside as she went on foot into the forests. One day somebody addressed her as 'Safed-Sherni', or White Tigress. She accepted that proudly. The albino she was being compared to had a splendid white coat caused by a freak genetic makeup; it turned up only once in every ten thousand births. She smiled. She too was a freak; albeit for different reasons!

Her phone rang. It was an excited Robin.

'Sherry!'

'Hey, Robin! Wazzup!'

'You don't know? It's raining manna from heaven. The god of the Forest Department is descending on PTR. The Minister of Forests is landing...'

She rushed to the function spot. There were posters and celebratory buntings everywhere and she could hear patriotic songs. The Minister had just landed in an old MI-8. He was a handsome man in his early fortys, wearing white linen trousers and a starched white shirt with a Burberry-check motif near the collar possessing the youthful zest of an Indian film-star. He was whisked into a Toyota Innova with its air conditioning running in advance to receive him, maintaining the cold chain of comfort till the venue, some hundred yards away.

There were about a thousand people, mostly villagers who had gathered to hear the Minister and observe the proceedings. Many others were bored tourists who had given up hope of spotting a tiger, and were quite happy to be seeing some sort of action at least. All the young leaders of that area were in attendance, all aspiring to follow the Minister's glorious footsteps to enjoy a life of patronage, glamour and power. At least fifty cars of different hues were parked recklessly around the site. Sherry walked in and sat in a corner; nobody took notice of her.

The stage was makeshift, festooned with garlands of marigold flowers and mango leaves. A huge banner of the Save our Wildlife campaign served as a backdrop.

After endless presentation of bouquets, the Director PTR made a flowery speech recalling how the Minister's ancestors had the royal privilege to hunt for wildlife and although the Minister used to own several forests, he had surrendered them to the service of the people and was now a passionate protector of wildlife.

The Minister came to the podium. He folded his hands in a namaskar, bowed and said, 'My beloved people, the government is deeply concerned at the speed with which tigers are disappearing. Recently, Burree Maada, the most famous tigress of Kanha, was killed by Pardhi poachers. I recognize that it is important to protect the biotic pyramid and conserve our wildlife, but it is a question of allocation of resources. It is perhaps in our interest to consider new models for conservation. Henceforth, Public-Private Participation, PPP, the buzzword for infrastructure development, will be extended for conservation of wildlife as well. A donation to the Save our Wildlife Fund of a million rupees would win a businessman the title of Friend of Wildlife. So, does anybody here volunteer to be a Friend of Wildlife?'

Many hands shot up. However, most seemed to have risen without thought; they fell down with equal speed. But one hand had shot up very decisively and stood the test of time. Sherry craned her neck to see past the pedestal fans and the looming security guards. It was a handsome, well-dressed man in his early fifties who was being beckoned to the stage by the Minister. She had seen this man somewhere! Then it struck her. It was Feroze Goenka.

The Minister gestured for him to be led to the dais. Escorted by two smart forest officials Goenka walked up, his hands folded in reverence, and went to the mike to announce in a smooth and silky voice, 'From the House of Goenkas, for the protection of our beloved wildlife, I would like to present an ambulance.'

His announcement of an ambulance for wildlife was quickly followed by a significant pow-wow with the Minister, after which he added laconically, 'Save our Wildlife Fund: Rupees ten lakh.'

Amidst overwhelming applause the Minister came to the mike and said, 'Goenkaji, we are proud of you. What a sincere tiger conservationist you are. That is how model businessmen should be—combining business with social responsibility!'

Another hand went up from the crowd. This was a tall man; once again the Minister prompted him to ascend the stage. He walked up the aisle with a royal swagger. There was awestruck silence as the Minister whispered something into the announcer's ears, prompting him to address this personality as 'Darbar.' In a booming voice, befitting that of an Emperor, he came to the mike and pledged, 'From the Kingdom of Baikunthpur, we donate a fire tender for PTR. It is our bounden duty to save our wildlife.'

This pronouncement drew a huge bear-hug from the Minister

who escorted this philanthropist to the edge of the stage. Sherry kept quiet, biting her lips. Abhimanyu had once again attempted to go up in her esteem.

The Minister and his entourage departed with as much fanfare as had accompanied his arrival – much like a marauding army that had conquered successfully and was retreating with the spoils of war. The pandal and the stage were pulled down within seconds of his departure, as if they were a tin-foil film-set. The SUVs vanished leaving behind them a mushroom cloud of dust and PTR was back to where it was. As if nothing had transpired.

An hour later her phone rang. It was Robin once again.

'Hey, Sherry! Did you get to meet the Minister?'

'No,' she said.

'You didn't go there?'

'I did,' she said curtly.

'I believe he's launched a new initiative for conservation.'

'Yes. Pillage and Plunder in Partnership. They call them PPP in this part of the world!'

On most occasions when she was driving inside PTR, Sherry entered from the Madla village, on the main highway and then drove along the Ken River which meandered through the Park. She passed through open savannah-style grasslands and thick, closed canopy forests of teak and kardhai on the rocky Hinouta Plateau interspersed with acacia catechu plants.

This day, Sherry decided to try the other entrance to the park from Talgaon in the south towards Khamaria. There was an unusual nip that morning, as they drove on the road that was at best pot-holed and terribly dusty. She sneezed several times and wondered if she could be developing a sinus problem.

She passed herds of sambhar and chital sauntering at a

leisurely pace through the dry forest comprising of khair, tendu and amla trees. She left the jeep in places and trekked on the dusty track keeping the jeep well behind her. The guide pointed out cormorants, red-headed vultures, sandgrouse and darters. At one place she spied a paradise flycatcher and managed a wonderful photograph.

She travelled tirelessly for the better part of the day. Her face was flushed pink by the time the blazing sun began to lose its steam. On instinct, she asked for the jeep to stop at a wayside tribal village that was technically inside the Core area of the Reserve. She was greeted warmly by the sarpanch and ate millet bread and boiled gourd with salt. Despite his reluctance, she insisted that he accept payment for her meal. It was warm and languorous and not a leaf stirred. She decided to lie down on an empty charpoy. In front of her was a forest yard, stacked with teak logs, piled high. A few children came and sat next to her, and she told them fairy tales. The filtered rays of the sun came down gently through the thick foliage and fell around her, relaxing her, and increasing the sense of torpor. Just the seductive smell of the bright yellow mahua flowers was intoxicating.

She must have been dozing, when a sharp nudge with a crude twig startled her. She opened her eyes to find the sarpanch's daughter pointing towards the dense lantana thicket to their left, under a patchwork of sunlight. A herd of grazing cattle ran out helter skelter, like a rowdy audience evacuating a cinema hall on fire, their bells jingling and raising clouds of dust. And then she gasped and stared in disbelief.

Following the cattle was a full grown tiger. It emerged out of the bushes majestically, almost lazily, lurching purposefully towards the cattle, as if the prey was a given.

The tiger growled and charged about. Then, just as it seemed ready to leap, it teetered on its haunches and stopped. It snarled angrily but did not spring upon the cattle. Nor did it go after them. Sherry was shocked. It was completely uncharacteristic of a tiger that had decided to go in for the kill, as indeed it must have wanted to. Why else were the cattle so disturbed?

The tiger slowly crossed the dusty pagdandi to disappear into the degraded forest of teak and salai surrounding the village area. Sherry watched with bated breath. The tiger was mature, clearly five or six years old. But there was something else that was disturbing. Why had the tiger not gone after the cattle? There had been something odd about it. It had been limping!

Sherry wanted to run after the tiger with her camera. As it was, she scarcely managed to get one blurred photograph from behind as the tiger disappeared from sight, masked by the forest.

But PTR did not have any tigers. Where had this tiger come from? Why was it limping? And why was there so much hype about Panna being bereft of tigers if indeed there were some left?

Sherry was totally puzzled, intrigued beyond measure.

She decided to keep the tiger sighting a secret for the moment. This would not only make for an internationally acclaimed story but also help her understand the psyche of the Park management. She returned to the jeep and remembered she had picked up a recent research paper, 'Study of Tiger Ecology' by an expert, R. S. Chundawat. It said, 'The distribution of tigers in PTR is closely related to high prey density areas of two species of deer—chital and sambar...'

A few yards from the spot where the tiger had emerged, she had spotted a herd of chital while sambhar stood a short distance away. The tiger must have been desperately hungry for it to have stooped to chase cattle, and not deer. A tiger would pounce on a herd of cattle as a last resort; it had failed to do even that. That would happen only if the tiger was severely injured. Was it on the road to becoming a man-eater? Or, was it being *made* a man-eater?

Early next day, Sherry started off for the village where she had spotted the tiger. It was early evening before a boy from another village arrived on a cycle to claim a reward and tell her that he had spotted a limping tiger. She gave him a bag of toffees and a hundred rupee note. He pointed to the direction in which the tiger was last seen and they set off in the direction of Khamaria, all eyes peeled for the tiger.

They had barely travelled for ten minutes when she saw a buffalo that had evidently been killed by a predatory animal. Its rump bore the signs of the flesh having been gouged out. As she frantically looked around the buffalo, she saw the same tiger she had spotted the earlier day, behind a thicket, sprawled over the grassy land. Its ventral side was exposed to the sky, and there were marks of blood on its skin. Not far, a pack of hungry dholes, barked at it in concert, ready to move in for the attack. With the tiger out of the way, they could feed on the buffalo at leisure. But why was the tiger so still?

Sherry rushed back to the Park frantically and alerted the forest ranger on duty, explaining all that she had seen. 'Sir, I have found an injured tiger. It needs medical treatment urgently and the area needs to be cordoned off, otherwise wild dogs will kill it.'

The forest officer looked incredulously at her and said, 'I cannot believe that a tiger has been spotted.'

Sherry insisted, 'The tiger is in pain. We need to sanitize the area quickly.' The Forest officer appeared to be unmoved. Sherry pleaded with him, 'Please Sir. At least come and see for yourself!' It was in vain. She was up against a wall.

Helpless and anxious, Sherry set off alone with her driver towards the tiger. They quickly reached the once-powerful animal.

They drove the jeep around the body of the tiger and the

buffalo in circles for several minutes, blowing the horn to scare the wild dogs that were almost upon the tiger. The dogs reluctantly retreated into the forest. They stepped down from the jeep. A few villagers including the sarpanch gathered around them, armed with lathis. They poked the tiger with the lathis. It did not budge. Sherry approached the unconscious animal.

There were lacerations on its body and raw flesh hung in tatters on one of its hind legs. It was evident that the tiger had probably been caught in an iron-trap and had fought to extricate itself. In doing so, the powerful animal had torn its leg apart from losing its canine teeth while attacking the iron with its fangs. Thus was the tiger humbled and rendered incompetent to hunt. The wounds were deep, with pus and worm-infested sores. It must have struggled in the trap for at least three or four days, in all probability around the time that PTR was visited by the Minister.

'Look here! The tiger had also been injured by a bullet. See the hole. The other leg has a gaping injury, the skin has blown away where a bullet has possibly gone through.' The tiger was actually incapacitated on two legs! Sherry stared at the bullet wound. It was in the center of an unusually broad and continuous white stripe. It was Saraswati!

With the help of the villagers, Sherry and the driver loaded the tiger onto the back of the jeep. The villagers were surprised by the injured tiger and even more so when they saw it being taken away in a jeep.

Meanwhile, even when the jeep arrived at the administrative complex carrying the injured tiger, the unflappable ranger continued to mutter, 'It is impossible that this creature is a tiger.'

'Sir, whatever the animal, we need to tranquillize it and inject medicine!' Sherry shouted desperately.

'The doctor is on leave. Where do we get medical help? I will put some meat near him and keep him in the dispensary store room and bolt it,' he said.

🐾

They loaded the tiger onto a tarpaulin and left it inside with some buffalo meat and bolted the door. The shadows had lengthened and dusk enveloped the building quickly in a shroud of darkness. The mosquitoes were as big as drones and the air still and funereal. The ranger rudely asked them to leave. Sherry urged to be permitted to keep guard outside. The curt reply: It would be a violation of the Wildlife Protection Act!

Sherry tried to call Robin, 'The forest officials are not ready to accept that a tiger has been found. It is slowly haemorrhaging and ought to be saved at all costs. Robin, help. Help! What a recovery this would be for the Panna brand!'

But Robin was on his way to the Andaman Islands.

Sherry wrung her hands in frustration. But part of her was terribly excited about the existence of a tiger in Panna. It seemed to make up for the missing Burree Maada.

She could hardly sleep. The image of the limping tiger haunted her. What a collapse it was for the King of the Jungle, to be reduced to a sitting duck for rapacious poachers. A cold shiver ran down her spine.

She returned to the Park Director's office at dawn. A small crowd had already collected there. Was she late?

As she came close, she gasped in astonishment. A huge jungle cat with golden fur which had black spots, not stripes in black and white was lying on the ground. It was certainly not a tiger! It was a dead leopard. Much smaller in size than the tiger, but the injuries seemed to be in the same places. It could well have been the injured tiger.

'But where is the injured tiger?' she shouted.

There was pin-drop silence. The official who was on duty the previous evening was nowhere in sight!

'This leopard has died due to old injuries,' said a guard.

Had she been imagining things in her obsession to cover the missing tiger? She rushed to her driver and asked him. He confirmed that what they had seen and carried to the hospital was an injured tiger. At Sherry's insistence the Park officials summoned the village headman.

After an endless wait, one of the village officials appeared, his face hanging low, tears in his eyes. The previous evening, just when the headman was preparing to sleep out on his charpoy, a madman from a neighbouring village assaulted him and he had died.

Sherry recognized him. The village official adjusted his flashy red turban, looking nervously at the Forest Department officials, his eyelids batting as fast as his hands. She beseeched him repeatedly, to admit that they had indeed rescued a tiger. He remained in a trance for a few moments before whispering with a straight face, 'It was a leopard.'

Sherry cursed herself. Suddenly, she thought of Burree Maada and the deceit surrounding her disappearance. This incident was no better. It underlined the chicanery to which officials could descend to cover their backs. Jim Corbett, the famous hunter of man-eating tigers had once said that the tiger was a large-hearted gentleman with boundless courage. It was amply clear to her now: Man was the real animal.

In Balaghat, Ganga had just settled down to listen to Begum Akhtar ghazals after a satisfying dinner when Bhaloo peeped in hesitatingly to say that an old farmer had come a long way to meet him urgently. Village folk, not always literate, had strange complaints and seldom chose their time correctly.

A nondescript, wrinked old man with furrows on his forehead, deep enough to sow paddy, and wearing a soiled turban on his head, limped onto the porch with the help of a wooden stick, and continued to stand, despite Ganga's offer of a seat.

'Baba, have my boys damaged your hut?' Ganga asked. Overzealous forest staff often exceeded their brief and committed atrocities on village folk to prevent the protected forest from encroachment. He was both annoyed and amused with the old man for not stubbing out his bidi when talking to him.

'Sir, I have been told I can trust you. I have some precious information for you,' said the old man.

'Go ahead, let me see how useful your information is,' Ganga said.

'I have come to inform you about timber smugglers.' The old man removed his turban and leaned towards Ganga, looking surprisingly younger and stronger. He whispered, 'Sir, I am from Mukki. You will have to move fast. I have information that the entire protected forest bordering my village is going to be felled tonight.'

Ganga stared at the man in surprise. Mukki, though close to the southern border of the Kanha National Park, fell under his jurisdiction, territorially. It was a few hours away, as the road was terrible and the area reputed to be unsafe. In police terminology, it was Naxalite-infested. It was already past 8 p.m.

He sent Bhaloo hotfoot to summon his next-in-command who lived nearby and to wake up the driver and the other staff. Meanwhile he contacted the Executive Magistrate on the phone and enlisted the services of the village Kotwars and Patwaris. Slowly and assiduously, in the course of the next hour he collected the key staff required for a night patrol. He loaded his team into two jeeps and a tractor belonging to the local agriculture department and started on the journey to Mukki with whatever weapons that could be mustered at short notice—old guns, bamboo poles, sticks and the like!

🐾

Sherry was intrigued by the news that a large cache of animal skins had been recovered by the Forest Department. She would have liked to call Ganga to know if there were any tiger skins or if he had discovered anything new about Burree Maada, but realized that she did not have a phone number. She called the Balaghat Collector's secretary, whose attitude made her feel she was asking for State secrets. By the time she finally secured the phone number, it was a Sunday again.

Nevertheless she called Ganga. She could sense the lack of chemistry—he answered reluctantly, bristled at being disturbed. She visualized him in khaki Bermudas and a crew-neck tee, sweat trickling down his neck onto his six-pack, while he held a cordless phone in one hand and rapidly jabbed at a sandbag with the other.

'Hello, Sir. This is Sherry Pinto. We met in Kanha! Remember me?'

He was quiet for a few moments, prompting her to repeat her name, before he shouted, 'I remember you alright! It was because of you that I was transferred!'

What surprised her was that he felt so near. It was as though they were sitting across each other in a room. 'I wish to dispel your misunderstanding, Sir,' said Sherry. 'That is why I called you. How are you?'

'I am okay,' said Ganga curtly. 'So what is it that you want *this* time?'

'Call me Sherry, Sir,' she said, trying to be engaging. 'I have much to share.'

'About the Burree Maada affair, I am sure,' Ganga thundered.

'Sir, I happen to be curious, how you do like your new posting?

Not as exciting as Kanha, is it?'

'I am quite happy, thank you,' said Ganga tersely. 'There is enough to do.'

She could sense that he was about to terminate the conversation. 'Sir, I hope you know why you were transferred!' He would shy away from the truth. Balaghat was a traditional forest district, and an important one, dating back to the British times when forestry management and working plans had just been initiated. But she had to needle his ego if she wished to keep him on the line.

'Who bloody cares?' Ganga asked, assuming indifference.

Sherry bit her lips. He would spite his face to save his nose. Was it his indoctrination as a civil servant that made loyalty to his situation so unflinching?

'Do you know what happened to Burree Maada?' Sherry asked.

'The chargesheet against me says that I am responsible for her death. So even I am keen to know what the hell happened to her. But now that I am on a new assignment, somebody else must display the required ardor to locate her carcass.'

Sound logic, but an evasive answer. 'By the way,' Sherry asked, changing tack, 'did you hear about the acid attack?'

'Acid attack?' Ganga raised his voice incredulously, a snigger converted quickly to a display of concern.

Sherry had been waiting for such an opportunity. She quickly recounted how she had escaped the acid attack.

'What? Jabalpur's gone crazy!' He seemed to unbend. 'I hope you reported this to the police?'

'Yes, but I don't expect much,' said Sherry.

'I wonder who wants to hurt you,' Ganga pondered.

'You never believed me Sir, when I came to meet you that morning,' Sherry said.

'I'm sorry...'

'I'm curious about a consignment you recently seized...a cache of animal skins.'

Ganga wondered how she had got wind of their latest catch. When he had rushed with his patrol to Mukki to catch the gang of forest loggers the previous day, they had found a truckload of ancient sal trees already cut without official permission and a transit pass. A search around the village unveiled an electric saw that had been used for cutting the felled trees so that the timber could be easily transported. And then, just by chance, they had stumbled upon a huge cache of animal skins. It had turned out to be a trap from which he had escaped rather fortuitously.

'Yes, about three dozen skins,' Ganga said, a trifle excitedly. 'Mostly leopard skins with some deer and crocodile skins.'

'Tiger skins?'

'None.'

'Did you arrest the poachers?'

'You know I can't be sure which side my chaps are on. They actually let the poachers slip away, although, to be fair, one of them was injured as the poachers were armed with bows and arrows. And what a day it was! We were ambushed by Naxalites on our way to the village.'

'What happened?'

'An informer had come to me with a tip about timber smugglers,' said Ganga. 'That part was correct, except that the felling had been done earlier. It was actually a trap to take us into custody in order to seek the release of other imprisoned Naxalites as a quid-pro-quo.'

'How did you all escape?'

'They had laid an IED at an important intersection. But it failed to activate at the prescribed time,' Ganga said. 'It exploded when the tractor that had been following us went over the spot, killing a few village Kotwars. We were immediately alerted and quickly took position. When the Naxalites sensed a losing battle, they retreated into the forest after firing in the air.'

'You were indeed lucky,' Sherry said. She sensed his readiness to talk now and related the Panna tiger story and the Minister's visit. He laughed. It was his turn now to share stories when her cell phone rang.

She looked at her cell phone impatiently, trying to ignore the interruption but the caller was persistent. She pondered briefly before guilt overtook her and she disconnected Ganga abruptly.

It was her Editor, an unfriendly soul at the best of times. Was he going to terminate her tenuous arrangement with the paper?

'Sherry Pinto! Listen carefully,' the Editor barked.

Her heart sank as she replied, 'Yes, Chief, please go on.'

'You haven't succeeded in cracking the missing tiger mystery,' he said. 'And in the process you are now an endangered species yourself!'

She bristled. What business did he have to discourage her from following the missing tiger story? But she was quick to note the underlying urgency in his voice, 'Have the Forest Department mandarins complained about me?'

'Kind of,' the Editor said briskly. 'The Minister called. He sounded irritated...said that though they are not looking for favourable headlines, they expect objectivity in the reporting at the very least.'

'They all say that!' Sherry had read about trouble in the Vidhan Sabha. All Opposition MLAs had pinned a sticker with a sketch of a dead tiger to their clothes, reading—'Save Our Tigers'.

It was Ganga calling her now.

She promised to call back the Editor in a few minutes and answered Ganga.

'You know the Forest Guard who was strangled in Kanha,' Ganga said. 'He belonged to Balaghat. His parents have been coming to me for assistance; he was the only bread-winner in the family.'

'I hope you've been able to help them,' Sherry said.

'Yes, I've appointed his wife as a storekeeper in our timber depot,' Ganga said. 'But what a tragic loss to that family; he was their only support. Well, at least I could do one good deed here.'

'There is more to Balaghat!'

'Of course there is!' Ganga thundered. 'There is the Pench Sanctuary, whose pristine forests and wildlife inspired Rudyard Kipling to write the Jungle Books, with the legendary characters of Mowgli and Sher Khan. Haven't you been here before?'

'Unfortunately, not yet,' Sherry said. 'I'd love to come armed with my camera and notebook.'

'Pench is just a stone's throw from here,' Ganga said. 'Every day I manage to add pictures of rare birds and butterflies to my collection. Some are worthy of the National Geographic. By the way, the forthcoming issue of the Sanctuary magazine has a short pictorial feature of mine on rare butterfly sightings. I've got amongst others, a Blue Begum, a Queen of Spain and a Painted Courtesan.'

'So you have an eye for pretty things with wings,' Sherry teased.

'Come on,' Ganga said laughing. 'I'm only human...wings, however, are not mandatory.'

Sherry laughed at his quick repartee. 'Remember that Bond film, On Her Majesty's Secret Service?'

'Why?' asked Ganga. 'Don't tell me Bond also hit on butterflies?'

'James Bond only hit on a particular variety of birds!'

'Indeed Majesty?' said Ganga, laughing. 'Frankly, I don't seem to remember.'

'When Bond visits M in the country, and that was before the great Judi Dench...M was played by Bernard Lee. Bond learns that M is a collector of butterflies, a lepidopterist...and they find a fictitious species of butterfly called...poly-nympho or nympho-galore something.'

'May I recommend that you write about the serious work foresters do, like the GIS-based mapping system that we've developed,' Ganga urged. 'It allows for forest fires to be detected by satellite. And also helps us against the timber mafia.'

'Timber mafia?'

'Balaghat is to illicit logging what Panna and Sariska are to poaching,' said Ganga. 'What we unearthed was a bunker full of mature sal trunks, illegally felled, with a regular electric saw as mute witness. And on top of that we have the bloody Naxalites.'

Sherry was aware of the Naxal movement, based on Mao-tse-Tung's philosophy of peasant terrorism, which had spread to different tribal and jungle tracts. What puzzled her was that the country where that ideology had originated had veered towards market economics. Yet there was a long arch of the Maoist Red Belt on the eastern flank of India which was rich in forest cover and wildlife. 'Are you safe?' she asked.

'I think so,' said Ganga. 'As safe as one can be in Panther territory.'

'Panther? Panthera Pardus or Panthera Onca?' Sherry asked, amused at his choice of words. Where was this leading?

'Paneerselvam Thyagaraj, unseen and known to the world only as Tyagiji. A local newspaper carried his photograph—a simple, middle-aged man with a tilak on his forehead, dressed in dhoti-kurta. He could easily pass off as a priest at a Venkateshwara temple and he is supposed to be the commander of Naxalite activities in Central India.'

'You seem to have a knack of moving from one trouble spot to another,' Sherry mused. 'Do you have somebody to look after you?'

'You remember Bhaloo, my Korku help in Kanha? He moved

with me. And he has learnt to honour my regimen, like when to serve me a sizzling chimlet.'

'A red-chilly infused omelette?'

'Wide off the mark,' said Ganga. 'It is hot, green and gin-intensive. A potent gimlet with freshly squeezed lime juice added instead of the standard lime-cordial. Along with a generous helping of fresh green chillies, to be crunched and chewed, to emulate the bitters effect. I like to plaster salt on the rim of the glass. Bhaloo too, has mastered the art of making them as screwy as they come!'

'I'm fascinated by your tequila language,' Sherry said, amused. 'In fact, I could do with a solidly sizzling chimlet myself...oh, but, I'm going off alcohol for a month.'

'Dieting?'

'Just detoxing myself,' Sherry said. 'Meanwhile, I think it is wiser for a forest official to get smashed on a chimlet than to hit on an innocent damsel,' said Sherry. She instantly regretted her remark and pinched herself. Ganga guffawed crudely.

'You'd be surprised,' said Ganga, quite enjoying the turn of conversation. 'Some forest officers stay without families and pick up a tribal woman to work for them—clean, cook and lay the bed...'

'Poor tribals! How tragic for them!'

'You'd be surprised...tribals may be intrinsically guileless, but their women are beguiling, superbly attractive,' Ganga expounded. 'Dusky looks, adorned with dark tattoos and chunky, primitive jewellery to accentuate their slim and athletic bodies...even when balancing pitchers of water on their heads they walk erect, looking more attractive than any FTV model on stilletoes...Halle Berry and Whitney Houston type smoldering looks...'

Sherry broke in, 'I had no idea you were a connoisseur of the feminine form.' She suddenly wondered what Ganga thought of her? Was she too English-accented and too fair...not salty enough for his liking? It was a pity there would be no occasion to display the exotic tattoos on her body. She was also a non-conformist—she shunned jewellery and make-up. Clearly, she had underestimated Ganga; this rustic forester was actually a romantic at heart and a keen follower of cinema and the salacious images it purveyed.

He seemed to be reading her mind. He added quickly, 'What attracts me in a woman is the natural, positive energy she exudes. Talking of tribals, what for us is forbidden fruit is for them so natural...rites of passage. The birds and the bees...they learn all this—not through books and films...but naturally, in arrangements like their ghotuls.'

Ghotuls! She recalled her fleeting visit to a ghotul in Bastar—the tribal community hostels which educated their youth in the subtle demands of adulthood. The moment they reached puberty, boys and girls chose partners and lived there, guided by their elder siblings. There they learnt, in the words of the famous tribal activist, Verrier Elwin, about human love and its physical expression—beautiful, clean and precious. As a result, rape, assault and eve-teasing were unheard of in the consensual tribal society.

'Mr Bishnoi,' Sherry said jocularly, 'You seem to be in danger from more than just the axe of the tree-logger and the bullet of the Naxal.' She laughed—Ganga had a humourous streak, so different from most of the other men she had met in her life.

The connection died abruptly. Her Editor was calling from Bhopal agitatedly, peeved by her lackadaisical response.

'I've been trying to get through for the last half-hour,' he said irritatedly. 'Look Sherry, can you try and understand that I need you to get on to something urgently.'

'What's up?' asked Sherry, losing her cool too.

'I've called you for a special feature—a big, fat story,' said the Editor placatingly, sensing her mood.

'What do you have in mind?'

'Have you heard of Zentigris?'

'Sounds familiar,' said Sherry thinking hard. 'Yep! Got it! When a zebra and a grizzly cross in a Tokyo zoo?'

'Very funny,' said the Editor, pretending to laugh at the weak joke. He paused for a while before resuming, 'Miss Marple, surely you've heard of the regulatory flap around Zentigris, once Indian software's flagship company in Silicon Valley.'

'Chief, I'm in…Lost World…Jurassic Park, not Silicon Valley,' Sherry exclaimed.

'I understand,' the Editor persisted. 'This company has suddenly come under the scanner and the top management arrested. I want you to probe at the Indian angle in the Zentigris matter.'

'But I don't have the foggiest idea about Mint and Wall Street,' Sherry said forcefully. 'Mine is a nature story.'

'Doesn't matter,' he said. 'I want you to hear me through. After that, you can go to fucking hell along with your bandicoots and snakes and…dead tigers.'

'OK, shoot,' Sherry said.

'Keep it confidential,' said the Editor, 'One of the top officials of Zentigris, Ramachandra Prasad, part of the charmed inner circle of deceit, is in Amarkantak, a stone's throw from you, visiting his ailing father. My hunch is that there is more to his Amarkantak visit than meets the eye. You must go immediately and interview him—people drop precious nuggets of information when they are off guard. Listen Sherry, this is a godsend! Go for it, you'll be a rock star…'

'But I had planned to go away for a fortnight. Can't I go to Amarkantak after that?' Sherry said. Himachal would be so much cooler. She would also visit her old school friend who taught in Sanawar.

The Editor offered bait. 'Perhaps you would want me to sponsor you to the Global Elephant Conference in Ko Samui, after this story?'

'Hmmm,' hummed Sherry. She had learnt the hard way that it would do her no good to refuse the HT Editor. His personal indulgence had helped her survive when things went wrong. On the other hand Amarkantak was beyond Kanha with poor road-connectivity. She brightened; perhaps she could pretend to fall sick.

Then she remembered that Amarkantak was also close to the Achanakmar sanctuary, linked to Kanha by the sixty kilometre long Kanha-Achanakmar bio-corridor. It was here, only a few weeks ago, that she had read of several wild animals having been poached at the Kumbhipani waterhole in the Chaparwa range. Perhaps it was a chance to kill two birds with one stone.

'Aye, aye, Chief,' Sherry said emphatically. 'I will do Zentigris.'

She woke up to a clatter. Riki-Tiki-Tawi, having smelt a snake or a rat, was leaving no object unturned to attract her attention. She pulled herself out of bed, opened the door and looked at her watch. It was well past 7 a.m. She had to quickly make plans to interview Ramachandra Prasad, this Indian techie from Silicon Valley. She also needed to connect with Ganga—their conversation had ended abruptly. After the Editor had spoken to her, a quick search on the net had revealed that Ramachandra Prasad was an intelligent though flamboyant man prone to self-aggrandisement. She needed to research Zentigris and scan the WSJ and the NYT for financial news related to the scam. A thud announced the daily newspaper as it was tossed into her compound.

She tore off the rubber bung from the Dainik Bhaskar and smoothened out the creases. The front page story caught her attention. It carried a photograph of a handsome man with his head shaved. He looked familiar. It was a Jabalpur story:

> International Poaching Racket Busted
>
> Jabalpur Police last evening nabbed a wildlife poacher and an NRI who is suspected to have purchased the skin of the missing Kanha tigress Burree Maada from him. They were caught near the Forest Research Insititute with the skin and assorted foreign currency. Ramachandra Prasad, a US-based NRI and Jugnu Pardhi, with a history of poaching of wild animals, are currently in the custody of the Kotwali Police.
>
> The Police have registered a case under Section 49, 51, 52 and 57 of the Wildlife Protection Act 1972 (possession and carrying, sale and purchase of parts of endangered animals from the First Schedule), Section 109B of the Indian Penal Code (criminal conspiracy) and relevant provisions of the Foreign Exchange Management Act against the two. Schedule I offences under the Wildlife Protection Act can earn an offender upto six years in prison.
>
> It is noteworthy that Burree Maada, a Royal Bengal tigress, had been poached inside the highly protected Kanha Tiger Reserve barely a few days ago. Police are convinced that the skin seized from Ramachandra Prasad and his associate is indeed that of Burree Maada.

Riki-Tiki-Tawi was back on her lap. She stroked him gently as she fed him a biscuit which he nibbled hungrily. She loved his personality, the unique silver points to his hair and the jet-black tip at the end of his tail. He had been part of her household for several months now, and knew how to extract his pound of affection from her. He had also mastered the science of keeping cobras at bay from the Grey Goose of Cobra Ground; she wished he had the ability to do so in the human world too.

She examined the photograph carefully. When she had bumped

into him at the Jabalpur Railway Station, he had a nice crop of hair. Now he looked chastened. She recognized the other man as well. He was part of the huge Pardhi gangs of poachers that resided in the lower reaches of the various tiger reserves. Though arrested often, they were never convicted, because neither the police nor the Forest Department could produce adequate evidence. Something mysterious was happening. Was a larger game being played?

A bold knock on the door had made her heart pound. She normally did not have anyone calling other than the ironing maid and the vegetable vendor. And their visits were usually prefaced by a shout or a gentle tap on the door, trying to figure out whether she would be free to receive them. But this knock was loud, persistent. She hurriedly shut down her laptop and opened the door, just as it appeared to cave in.

A tall and handsome police officer stood at the door. He could have easily passed off for a Mumbai film actor. He was accompanied by two police personnel, one of whom appeared to be a female (given the stern look, small breasts and short hair, it could have been a man masquerading as a woman). They were both in uniform, suave and well-mannered. The senior officer almost saluted her before introducing himself politely, 'Madam, I am Sub-Inspector Navneet Pandey from Civil Lines Police Station.'

'Yes Inspector?' Sherry looked up inquiringly. Her expertise on wildlife matters was fairly well recognized. They must want her opinion on the Burree Maada matter. Or perhaps about the tiger skin that had been found in the possession of the NRI caught with the poacher. 'Please come in,' she said. 'I will bring you some tea and we can talk at leisure.'

'Madam, that is not necessary,' the officer stated gently. 'We have instructions to undertake a talaashi. We have to search your premises.'

'What?' Sherry screamed. They were going to search her house! Frightful thoughts came to her mind. Her laptop! Fortunately she had shut it.

She stared at them. She was single, they were three. Could they be perverts, masquerading as policemen, intent on gaining entry into her home? There had been instances when potential rapists included a woman in their group. But this lot was in uniform, their name plaques were evident. Two shining Royal Enfield Bullet motor cycles were parked just outside her gate. 'This is ridiculous! Who has given permission for this?'

'Madam, a confidential complaint has been made at a high level,' the officer said. 'We can't disclose the identity of the informer. Our duty is only to investigate and report facts. There is some urgency to our mission.'

'Sure, go search and see whatever you like.' Sherry pulled aside the curtain. 'I have nothing to hide!' She was certain they would cow down in the face of her self-righteous indignation. The police in India could easily be browbeaten by a beautiful woman, especially when she spoke fluent English.

'Please unlock your garage, Madam. We will begin from there,' said the officer firmly.

'Sure, but my garage is never locked,' she said. 'It is open except for the shutter that keeps out rain water.' It made no sense at all! She could not remember seeing anything objectionable ever kept there. But then she hadn't been inside it for a long time.

'Our instructions are to do a thorough check,' said the officer.

'Please go ahead while I make some tea,' said Sherry.

'I think it would be better for you to accompany us Madam,' said the officer.

'Very well,' said Sherry, marching ahead briskly on the cobbled path, with the officer following closely. The police constables fell in line. Was this just an attempt to harass her? Maybe somebody had complained as a prank. She sensed the teenage boys outside her gate, watching the scene develop. She approached the garage.

Her Volkswagen Cabriolet was parked as usual, outside the garage. She wriggled past the ancient relic to the garage and tugged at the shutter. With one rusty jerk and some clanging, it sprang up half way. The officer stepped in chivalrously to haul it further till it retracted fully and stayed hinged at the top. He held it firmly till he was certain the shutter would hold. She thanked him as they entered the garage.

It had obviously not been opened for a long time, for it was musty with cobwebs all over the place. Sherry turned on the tube-light, and coughed, aghast at the many layers of dust. The light came on reluctantly and the constables started looking around. Cardboard boxes and wooden crates were piled high, undisturbed from Aunt Lara's time. Her golf bag stood in one corner, shrouded in cobwebs and dust, much like an erect mummy in an Egyptian museum. She recognized Aunt Lara's ancient Raleigh bicycle with its twisted handle minus the rubber horn that had been installed in the cabriolet. An old gramophone and a wooden box with some ancient 78 rpm records lay by its side. Tattered kites and a glass-mounted collage of articles written by Auntie Lara and published in various newspapers, including the *Illustrated Weekly* and *Imprint*, about the good life in Jabalpur stood negligently against the walls of the garage.

The constables searched methodically, sneezing and coughing incessantly. They picked up cardboard cartons, emptied the contents callously and then dusted their hands, making loud clapping sounds.

'Found anything?' the officer shouted periodically, standing immobile outside the garage, one eye on Sherry. What was his intention? Sherry felt unsafe. Surely, they could not gang rape her? And, if things did go out of control, whom could she call, considering the police were on the spot?

'Sir, I can feel it...something is wrong...I will discover it,' the male constable said looking suitably whipped.

'Yes, Sir,' the woman constable also chimed in. 'I think so too—something is terribly wrong here...I can sense it.'

Sherry stared at them. Goddammitt! What the bloody hell was wrong? If something was so terribly wrong, then why the hell was it not evident? Perhaps...wishful thought...they would admit their mistake soon and beg leave of her.

Suddenly the male constable pounced on an olive-coloured canvas bag and began to dust it. With its faded colours and the frayed leather straps, it seemed no different from the other hold-alls she had in her house dating back to the 60s, but she felt sure that she had never seen this one before. It was smaller, more like a hand bag, tied up with a thick cotton strap. The policeman dropped it at the feet of the officer, like a pet dog dropping a ball before his trainer.

'Open it!' the officer commanded.

The constable undid the strap and lifted it so that the officer could look inside. The bag shook with a jingling sound. He grunted satisfactorily as if treasure had been discovered.

What could be inside? Sherry had no clue. Old keys? Not likely, considering neither she, nor Auntie Lara, ever locked up anything other than the main door, primarily because there was little that could attract a modern thief, and whatever was actually material, like the Volkswagen Cabriolet and the BSA cycle, bore her stamp distinctly. Had the gardener left some of his old tools in the bag for repair before he died?

The constable extricated a plastic packet tied with thick black rubber bungs. He snapped at the bungs and unwrapped the plastic casing. It contained a large quantity of small, fish-shaped metallic objects, some of which slipped and fell to the ground. They seemed to be made of either brass or copper.

'Live rifle cartridges!' the officer exclaimed, as the constables nodded their heads and stared at her suspiciously.

Sherry trembled!

'I have no cartridges or guns in my house!' Sherry exclaimed, 'I don't know where these have come from. Cannot be mine!'

The male constable started counting. 'There are twenty bullets of a .22 bore rifle, with Jabalpur Ordnance Factory markings. Sir, after all Burree Maada...'

The woman constable had stepped into the garage once again and now emerged with the antlers of a deer in her hands—it had three tines and the beams were forked at the tip. 'Sambhar, Sir,' she announced.

Sherry screamed once again, 'It is not mine! I have absolutely no idea where they have come from.'

And then the realization dawned that it was a set-up. 'Oh my God, this is crazy. Somebody has opened my garage and planted these things to frame me.' Her face drained of colour and her hands started shaking.

'Search thoroughly, it is possible that we may find some weapons too,' the officer said. 'Go inside the house. Check if anything has been buried in the compound. And Madam, I would like to see your arms license.'

Sherry was stunned, numbed by the discovery that she was so alone in this world and that she had made powerful enemies who would go to any length to hurt her.

'But I don't have an arms license. I don't need one—I don't possess any guns,' Sherry pleaded.

In a flash the constables returned and stood before the officer. 'Okay, Madam,' he said. 'My men found no guns... That will be all, Madam.' They turned away from her.

'Thank heavens,' said Sherry. To give him credit, he could not have been more civil; in fact he managed to sound apologetic as he looked away. Sherry heaved a silent sigh of relief. He was a good-looking man, the antithesis of the nasty-looking brutes who manned the various police stations she had visited in her professional life. Even his staff knew that a single woman was to be handled with respect. It had been a frightful mistake on her part to suspect that somebody wanted to frame her. The officer had realized that it was not such a serious matter. He would now leave with his staff and she would overlook this event and move on.

Suddenly he turned around and announced, 'Madam, the complaint we received is proven correct. There is conclusive evidence. Possessing prohibited bore rifle cartridges without a valid license is punishable under Section 25 of the Indian Arms Act, 1959 and possessing sambhar antlers is a violation of Section 44 of the Wildlife Protection Act, 1972. You will have to come to the police station.' He dropped his voice, still maintaining his civility. He could well have been escorting her to an investiture ceremony. And then dropped the bombshell, 'Madam, you are under arrest.'

The announcement tore into Sherry like a sledgehammer and she felt like throwing up.

Inside the police lock-up, Sherry mused over the events of the past week. She put the tin chair back into the corner and sat on the ground surveying her dismal surroundings. The news of her arrest would have spread far and wide.

She was surprised to see Ram behind bars even though she had read about his arrest. Their brief interlude was enough for her to discern that he was not the kind of person who would risk his reputation to buy a prohibited tiger skin at a time when, as the Editor had informed her—so much was stacked against him. In fact he looked a tragic hero, a bit of an intellectual, a little aggressive, but hardly the kind who would risk landing in jail. He had merely come to attend his father's funeral; art or business couldn't have been further on his mind. And yet here he was, in police custody!

She got up and stretched herself. How would an impartial observer analyse her situation? She was opinionated and persistent when it came to ferreting facts about wildlife poaching; she had raked up the Burree Maada issue in a big way, but she was hardly the kind of person who would donate her wicket. To antagonize the law and end up cooling her heels inside a police lock-up was the last thing she wanted or expected. Burree Maada, the missing tigress, the injured tiger of Panna and the acid attack on her would be the biggest mysteries of her life. Clearly there was a plot against her. She was being pushed into a corner, being forced to cool her heels, slow the pace of her life.

If Ram was innocent too, then something deep within told her that their destinies were interlinked. She wondered how.

THE FALL

The low-profile visitor attracted Ram's attention. It was a rat making a cautious attempt to feed on the crumbs left over from the food that had been served to them. Ram watched as Jugnu held his breath and allowed the rat to enter cautiously through the iron bars. It was clearly a healthy rat, having enjoyed the hospitality of the Jabalpur Police for a considerable length of time. Imperceptibly, it scampered towards the crumbs.

Ram looked at Jugnu, intrigued by his ability to simulate a predator—he had practically frozen as the rat nibbled hungrily at the crumbs. It reminded Ram of a golfer focusing on his putting—bending over the ball, aligning it with the left heel and transferring the weight gently. Suddenly in one single soundless movement, Jugnu's right foot stood on top of the crumbs as he beamed with pride. Ram was puzzled and everything seemed normal till Jugnu lifted his foot and displayed it to Ram. It was clean. The rat lay still, flattened out like a pancake.

'Poachers! Smugglers!' the police officer shouted again and again in anger, rapping the knuckles of the arrested pair with a wooden school ruler, causing Ram to whimper in pain.

'It is a huge mistake,' Ram replied tearfully. He narrated his story which fell on deaf ears.

'I ask you once again, how much did you pay for this skin?' A police officer anywhere in the world, merely by virtue of his authority, can look tough and abrasive. But this one in Jabalpur made it a point to stand taller than the rest. Not only was he determined to extract a confession, he was a master in achieving it in a miraculously short time.

He rapped Ram again, changed tack and asked with a twinkle, 'Why were you interested only in a tiger skin?'

Ram could not answer that. Meanwhile, Jugnu looked as innocent as a babe in arms.

'You had a lot of foreign currency!' He fixed Ram with a piercing stare and asked, 'You live near Hollywood. Tell me truthfully, how much would you get for a tiger skin there?'

Ram stared blankly at him. 'I don't know Hollywood, I live quite a distance from it and have no direct touch with the world of cinema,' he said.

'Just tell me this, which film-stars like tiger skins?'

'I don't know.'

'My-Donna? Anjali Robe-ert? Sha-kheera?'

'I have absolutely no idea, Sir,' Ram repeated.

'Hollywood actors snort cocaine and then enjoy naked sex on exotic tiger rugs, don't they?'

'I doubt it,' responded Ram, completely bewildered.

'You have not seen it?'

'I think you have it all wrong.'

'Your wish...we have no option but to produce you all before the magistrate who will send you to proper jail.'

As they were bundled into the police van to be taken to the court, Ram cast a close look at Jugnu Pardhi. Cheerful and boyish, he was probably no more than twenty years of age, but seemed well-travelled. There was a comic streak about him, not the on screen dumbness of a Rowan Atkinson or Steve Martin, but reminiscent of a Jim Carey in Ace Ventura, sharp and mischievous. He seemed to have rubber-like flexibility, the ability to adapt to a new surrounding with cool panache. His sharp hunter-eyes were constantly roving, looking for an opportunity to escape, not so much from the police, whom he seemed to accept as a part of the architecture of his life, as from the confines of the dingy cell.

Jugnu too had been busy sizing up Ram. After a while he spoke, 'Sir, what are your plans about getting out of here? Surely you have strong bonds—family, friends or business associates?'

Ram pondered over Jugnu's question. Strangely, there was nobody in India whom he could call on for help at this time!

On the contrary, Jugnu seemed pretty much at home. He had access to a mobile phone and spoke quite often to somebody called Goose. This Goose sounded like a patron saint, far-removed, invisible—but nevertheless capable of granting succour.

'And you,' Ram asked. 'You seem to know everyone around. Do you belong to Jabalpur?'

'Not really. I am from Supkhar, a small village on the outskirts of Kanha Forest Reserve,' Jugnu said proudly, displaying the tattoo of a noose on his inner-arm. 'My parents live there, along with my wife and child, and other relatives. But I keep coming to Jabalpur as I have many friends here.'

'You look too young to be married,' Ram commented.

'Sir, I got married when I was around fifteen,' said Jugnu seriously. 'We had four children; however the first three did not survive.'

Jugnu pulled out a packet of Marlboro cigarettes and smoked one casually. He shared them easily with the policemen on duty; he offered one to Ram who took it gratefully and smoked. The nicotine helped relieve the tension. Clearly there was something humane and earthy about Jugnu. Ram noticed a bone hanging from his neck. It was embedded in silver.

'Is that ivory, my friend? It looks very mysterious,' Ram asked.

'That is Vyaghnakh, a tiger claw,' Jugnu replied, 'it is my talisman for good luck, for warding off the evil eye. I can get one for you.'

'Yes, I need some luck very badly. I might just go crazy if I am not let off,' Ram said. He narrated his affairs, briefly touching upon USA and his work, while withholding information about the fresh developments at Zentigris.

Jugnu appeared concerned and said, 'It is not easy to get out of jail unless somebody manages your case.'

'You seem to have managed quite easily.'

'Ah, well,' said Jugnu with a boyish grin, 'Only seventeen times.'

'The case against me is so ludicrous, no substance at all... they have to let me out,' said Ram confidently. Jugnu looked at him pityingly.

They were led into the narrow and crowded judicial court room. The Public Prosecutor, vulpine and emaciated, wore a long black coat and a white shirt, both having seen better days. He took the papers from the police and flipped through them hurriedly, a scowl on his face. They stood timidly in the aisle as word spread that it was the NRI case—the one who had been arrested as part of an international wildlife racket. All eyes were riveted on them as if they were sacrifice to some primordial deity. The deity in question perched on the rostrum, the portly Magistrate Kumar, rather hirsute, albeit with a balding pate. He gloated over the swirling commotion around him, lording over the scene with beatific latitude.

Magistrate Kumar remembered something. 'These undertrials do not have legal help. Isn't there a Legal Aid Cell here?' Bedlam ensued; a tiger skin had been seized and the perpetrators should be shown no compassion. Magistrate Kumar expressed a desire to examine the tiger skin that had been seized.

The police opened the bundle with ceremony to reveal the tiger skin, and the spectators played their part, jaws dropping in surprise. Magistrate Kumar asked for it to be spread out on one of the benches in front of him. The bazaar-like flurry in the Court now transformed into judicious pensiveness.

The only person who did not seem to be moved by the spectacle was Ram. He stammered, addressing the Prosecutor, 'This skin dates back to the time of Independence, much before the Wildlife Protection Act was ever conceived. For the past four decades this rug was the seat of my father for prayers and meditation…like Lord Shiva is depicted in pictures.'

The Prosecutor looked obsequiously at the Magistrate and barked sharply at Ram, 'Mister, can you produce your father or Lord Shiva as a witness on your behalf? Remember you are before the Lord himself!'

Ram looked to Jugnu for help. He had assumed a non-committal look. Did he not recognize the skin? Magistrate Kumar smiled benignly as he tried to read the expressions on the faces of this impromptu jury.

This was no time to curse his luck. Ram raised his hands seeking for attention and shouted out loud, startling the gathering into sudden silence, 'Sir, I have been wrongly accused. This skin was kept in the house of my father, the late Professor Ananda Prasad. It is decades old. The tiger was killed by an Englishman, Mr James Wilson, a reputable hunter. Much like Jim Corbett and Kenneth Anderson, he only shot man-eating tigers. He gave the skin to my father when he was leaving for England. My father's last wishes were very clear; the skin had to be donated to a conservation institution. That is why I brought it to Jabalpur.'

Suddenly, the court was abuzz. Everyone had a viewpoint, and all were eager to voice it. The skin was brand new! It was probably a year old! The skin seemed to be of a tiger called Arjun! Nonsense, the skin was not of a tiger at all, it was of a tigress called Machhli! No it was of a leopard! This tigress Tara had lived in the jungles of Panna! No, the tiger had lived its entire life in the jungles of Ranthambore. No, and this was the dominant view, this had to be the great Burree Maada, the missing tigress of Kanha.

Magistrate Kumar straightened up for the important task

ahead. He gazed wisely at Ram and asked, 'What proof do you have that this skin predates the Wildlife Protection Act of 1972?'

'Indeed Sir, I can prove it. It bears the name of Mr Wilson's taxidermists, the Van Ingens of Mysore...the famous taxidermists. You can check the label...there is a date too...1949. Van Ingens were the taxidermists to Her Majesty, the Queen of England.' His chest swelled with renewed hope.

The Prosecutor glared provocatively at the police officer who had accompanied the undertrials. The police officer perked up on cue and refuted Ram strongly. 'No question of it being fifty years old,' he responded knowledgeably. 'This is a brand new skin. It is Burree Maada's. She was poached a few days ago. His Lordship would recall reading about it in the newspapers.'

Magistrate Kumar nodded sagely and directed Ram with a forceful wave of his hands, 'Please show me proof to substantiate the vintage of this skin.'

'Certainly, Sir,' announced Ram, with a gravity borne more out of conviction than fear. 'I can and I will.'

'Let this undertrial handle the tiger's skin,' commanded Magistrate Kumar. The Public Prosecutor disapproved of this, but his lone voice of protest was drowned in the roar of expectation. Ram leapt towards the skin, like a tiger devouring its prey.

He examined it carefully, feeling Jugnu's gaze upon him from the corner of his eyes. Yes, it was the tiger skin—smooth as velvet, crisp, gold. It had a satin border. It was the same size. It shone under the sliver of light from the roshandan. It was clearly the James Wilson skin.

Suddenly something struck him. The skin his father had sat on and prayed upon for the past forty years carried the subtle fragrance of camphor, sandalwood and rose-incense. On the contrary, this skin smelt of ammonia, turmeric and possibly something like vinegar. Perhaps even the wild smell of a live animal inside a zoo?

Had somebody decided to dress it chemically, to make it worthy of presentation before a judge?

'I want to turn the skin!' Ram shouted and the Prosecutor most reluctantly flipped it over. Ram leaned over it and searched anxiously with his eyes and hands for the Van Ingen and Van Ingen label.

The label had vanished! Could his eyes and hands be deceiving him? There were two labels on his tiger rug…one with the name of the taxidermists and the other with the conservation instructions—both were missing. He searched the corners to see if they had been cut off with a blade or a scissor. But there was no sign that a tag had ever been torn or sliced off.

What a peculiar smell! Suddenly it made sense. This was the fresh skin of a recently killed tiger. It had been chemically treated and used to substitute his skin. This was the skin of the poached tigress Burree Maada! The Prosecution had been proved right!

Ram eyes burned; he wanted to cry and his heart pounded madly at the deception. A scream shot out from him, but emerged only as a damp whimper. His hands rose in protest but fell back weakly. He called to Jugnu; but Jugnu was in a trance. Suddenly the court room seemed like a mousetrap. The Magistrate beamed proudly in acknowledgement of his ability to discover the truth while having created some amusement. The lawyers bowed gratefully at his benign patronage.

Magistrate Kumar pronounced his verdict. Ram and Jugnu were to be remanded to judicial custody for having conspired to poach a tigress called Burree Maada from the Kanha Tiger Reserve. A judicial warrant was made requiring the duo to be produced before him for framing of charges in fifteen days' time. The Prosecutor bowed twice, flashing an artificial smile.

🐾

Ram and Jugnu were handcuffed and shoved out of the vehicle into a huge compound past a formidable iron gate, in front of a sprawling brick structure with barred windows. Armed guards waited expectantly to welcome them. The building resembled a cage.

'Name...Father's Name...IPC Sections...Police Station.' The jail clerk blinked and slowly pulled out a ball-point pen from a creaking drawer and began to write into a thick register, pausing every now and then to savour tea from a thick glass. The policemen undid the handcuffs and surrendered them to the jail guards who had been sizing them up with unnerving equanimity.

Ram shivered and sneezed. He dug inside his pockets for a handkerchief. He couldn't find it—it must have dropped somewhere. He sneezed again. As he searched deeper with his fingers, he felt something...a knot, embedded deep inside the silk lined pocket of the trouser. He clawed at it with his nails and unfolded it.

It was a once glossy ticket-stub to the Tony Award winning musical Chicago. It seemed another age that Jaya and he had gone for the performance, although it was merely few weeks ago. Jaya had loved it, though he had found it rather flat and boring. They had celebrated their wedding anniversary the next day and he had swept her off her feet when he bought her a beautiful diamond ring from Harry Winston on 5th Avenue. She in turn, had presented him with a pair of snazzy cufflinks from Bergdorf Goodman. They had dinner at Le Bernardin on 51st Street where Jaya had gorged on the Osetra caviar and Oysters and Lobsters in Lemon Miso Sauce, and the Raspberry Vacherin. It was also the day that they had decided to refurbish their Manhattan apartment in anticipation of more frequent sojourns to New York.

Ram craned his neck to look beyond the blazing lights of Times Square and Disney and The Phantom of the Opera. He felt the chill of the Manhattan night breeze on his cheeks as his mind tingled with excitement. And then suddenly the Broadway billboard blanked for a moment before it announced: 'Jabalpur Central Jail'.

Sherry was sure that she would manage to talk to Ram. But he had been shifted out of the police station before she could get her act together. Had he received a special dispensation? It seemed highly unlikely, but then strange things happened all the time.

She reflected on her own condition. Who could help her get out? Melanie Gardner? But she was travelling abroad to attend an international conference on wildlife. Ganga? But why would he risk his reputation to help her?

The object of Sherry's thoughts was lost in pleasant contemplation of her. As he came in from a cross-country jog, he began reflecting on what she had told him. He reached for a towel to wipe himself and turned on the television idly. The local E-TV ran Madhya Pradesh and Chhatisgarh news. A scroll raced on at the bottom of the screen:

'Jabalpur Socialite Arrested. Socialite Arrested for Violation of Arms Act…Socialite Booked under Wildlife Protection Act'.

Serve these high-society types right, he thought. They were too conceited and manipulative for his liking. He was about to switch off the television when a familiar face flashed on the screen. Sherry? He blinked in amazement. It was Sherry!

The announcement said she had been involved in poaching and that cartridges and antler horns had been seized from her home. He closed his eyes and reflected over his interactions with Sherry. Had she been hoodwinking him? He glanced at the scroll once again, recalling every word of their long chat the other day. Was it a set-up to conceal her secret activities?

Then he remembered her feature just before he had been

transferred and the mysterious acid attack, her trip to Panna, her writings. Some of that had even appeared in the HT. He dialled her mobile. It was only 7 p.m.; yet nobody answered the call. Something was gravely wrong.

Ganga debated whether he should try and help Sherry. Something told him it was the right thing to do. In a trice he decided to go to Jabalpur. He rang the Conservator of Forests in Balaghat and asked him for permission to visit a relative who was admitted to the hospital in Jabalpur. Leave was granted. It was only a few hours' drive away. But it was going to be a tough road ahead; he would be risking his reputation.

As his Bolero jeep zipped across the National Highway-7 from Balaghat to Seoni onto Jabalpur, Ganga wondered how Sherry could have got into trouble. Had she been framed? For a start, he had to locate Sherry. Who could he call for help? Then he remembered that Bisnu had been transferred to Jabalpur. He had called once, requesting Ganga to include him in his Balaghat team. He contacted Bisnu and asked him to locate Sherry and establish contact immediately.

Bisnu asked hesitatingly if Ganga was prepared to risk his reputation for a girl journalist. This kind of situation could seriously backfire on him, leading to a juicy scandal about a senior Forest Officer being entangled with a criminal socialite. It was most undesirable, given that the Kanha mafia was already gunning for him.

'Bisnu, don't be personal!' said Ganga, snubbing his well-wisher.

'Sir, I am intrigued,' said Bisnu. 'You want to help her even though she hasn't approached you for assistance.'

'My hunch is that she is clean,' said Ganga. 'Go and find her. My mobile signal will drop along the hills where there are no telecom towers. Get moving!'

🐾

Ganga continued to try Sherry's number unsuccessfully. Perhaps her phone had been confiscated by the police. He had already crossed Seoni when he received a call from Bisnu. He asked the driver to halt the jeep along the side, to retain the signal's strength.

'I traced her,' screamed Bisnu. 'She is under detention in the police station. All the television stations took bytes and the cops nibbled.'

'It's visual rape,' said Ganga. 'Quick Bisnu, find a way of getting her bail.' He had never realized that he could be concerned about a woman he hardly knew.

Another half-hour passed before Bisnu called, 'I have succeeded! She is on her way to an air-conditioned room in my car!' Bisnu sounded like a school boy who had just won a match.

'What?' Ganga was speechless with surprise. 'How did you pull that off?'

Bisnu was euphoric. 'I took my friend, the District Health Officer, along with me and announced that the Editor of *Hindustan Time* had lodged a complaint that one of their reporters was being tortured in police custody. The doctor checked her pulse and heartbeat and announced that she was suffering from acute cardiac dysrhythmia and would die in custody unless she was moved into an ICU immediately. Though that made them shit bricks, they wanted an ECG done. The machine was in the ambulance, and by the way, that is one of the smart doctor's patent tricks—to be able to show that a normal person is going to suffer a heart attack. By the way Sir, she is indeed very beautiful.'

'Ganga! I'll be damned! What on earth are you doing here?' Sherry had tears in her eyes. Bisnu stood respectfully at the foot of the bed in the Military Hospital, in Forest Department uniform. Ganga had come in from behind, beaming, with a large bunch of assorted pink flowers that brought cheerfulness into the hospital ward.

Sherry recounted the full details of the frame up and the harrowing hours she had spent in the police lock-up; and how they had tried their best to extract a confession out of her. Her mobile had been confiscated and she was not allowed to contact anybody.

'But why the sudden arrest?' Ganga asked; his mind probing, inquisitive – much as usual.

'I have been thinking about it,' said Sherry. 'It is possible that I am being prevented from meeting the team that is coming from Delhi. So whoever is behind this arranged and planted the bullets and the antler horns and the complaint to the ever-so-vigilant police.'

'They have succeeded so far,' said Ganga. 'You can't step out of the hospital till you get bail. I have spoken to a young lawyer who has worked for us. His father is a famous criminal lawyer too. He will move your bail application today. Let's keep our fingers crossed.' Ganga looked in command of the situation.

'But where did the bullets and the sambhar horns came from?' wondered Sherry. 'I don't even own a gun. Auntie Lara had sold her weapon many years ago. So the question of keeping bullets does not even arise. And I had personally looked into the garage about a month ago.'

'Jabalpur has many kabaris or scrap-collectors,' explained Bisnu, a glint in his eyes. 'Some are descended from the thugs rehabilitated by Colonel Sleeman. Initially they worked in the School of Industry, which was attached to the Jabalpur Central Jail, and intended to change the life of the convicts. They learnt to weave rugs and make handicrafts and so on. Later many became full-time scrap-collectors—they go from house to house and collect second-hand-objects. All kinds of antiques—from ammunition shells, antique guns, lamps and works of art, to vintage cars and even stamp-paper dating back to Queen Victoria's time can be bought from them for a suitable price. Later, with the establishment of the ordnance factories, the smuggling of metal waste out of the factories became a lucrative business. Set a thief to catch a thief...I have arranged for a Pardhi to be present in Court!'

'My Lord, my client is a young and single working woman,' announced the young lawyer. 'It is society's duty to encourage and protect such women.' He invited attention towards Sherry whose looks owed nothing to artifice; but then, she never needed anything; she shone naturally like a solitaire in a heap of coke.

Magistrate Kumar perked up and looked at Sherry critically. His initial indifference gave way to curiosity, and then gradually with each passing moment to astonishment as his eyes sought to unravel her mystique, layer by layer. 'Go on,' he directed majestically.

'She is a naturalist who has been exposing corrupt practices in the forests, including the poaching of the tigress Burree Maada, and the trade in endangered species. Her writings have offended both the Forest and the Police Department.' The lawyer handed the magistrate a folder full of published articles and features written by Sherry. 'She has been responsible for the booking of various offenders under the Forest Conservation Act and the Wildlife Protection Act. And now it is a case of the pot calling the kettle black. She is being framed for no fault of hers. You should examine the witnesses yourself Sir.'

'But, My Lord, although this lady professes to have high social-standing,' cut in the Public Prosecutor, 'all that environmentalism is only a façade to camouflage the dark side of her which has hitherto escaped public scrutiny. She is an Anglo-Indian who still lives in the fantasy world of the British Raj long after the British have left and would like to prove that our government is not successful.

My Lord, from her house were seized the antlers of endangered species of deer and bullets that can kill a big animal. Only recently the tigress Burree Maada was poached from Kanha. What more is needed to prove her complicity in this nefarious activity of poaching and killing of endangered animals? A few days ago she was involved in an underworld shootout, in which the poor driver of a tractor-trolley was singed with acid and suffered major burns for no fault of his. She is a threat to civil society.'

Sherry stared at him in indignation and almost raised her hands in protest.

'My time is being wasted,' said Magistrate Kumar, following a predictable drill. 'First of all, I want to know if there was an independent witness.' His eyes came back to stare at the beauty standing in front of him. And then his eyes almost popped out of their sockets as she stretched her hourglass waist and her small breasts heaved and she looked appealingly at him.

The young lawyer had made a case study of the mind of the magistrate. He had also tutored a young Jabalpur Pardhi to stand up as a witness.

'Yes, My Lord, I was standing near her garage,' the Pardhi announced fearlessly.

'Why had you gone there?' Magistrate Kumar's voice boomed at him.

'To survey her house if there was anything worth picking,' said the Pardhi.

Magistrate Kumar frowned at him and asked, 'You stole something?'

'No, my Lord,' said the Pardhi. 'I only wanted to do to see if there was some antique of interest.'

'And,' Magistrate Kumar asked. 'What was going on? Could you see the accused?'

My Lord,' said the Pardhi, 'it would not be appropriate to

reveal such intimate details in this august court.'

Magistrate Kumar shouted loudly, 'No! I command you to tell me everything you saw and heard.' He added something about single women being a cultural oddity and scowled at the Pardhi who seemed to be an interloper between this vagrant beauty and himself.

'My Lord, the witness is too shy and scared to open his mouth in your august presence,' the defence lawyer pleaded.

'Either he will open his mouth or I will open the doors of jail,' Magistrate Kumar said.

'My Lord,' said the Pardhi reluctantly, his eyes lowered in fear, 'I saw these responsible looking policemen interviewing this lady. But I blank out the words; I cannot utter them before your honour.'

'Truth must come out. What were they saying?' Magistrate Kumar leaned forwards precipitously.

'My Lord, the policemen were discussing the physical aspects of this lady,' the Pardhi said. And then he lowered his voice and said conspiratorially, 'It will undermine the exalted dignity of this Court.'

'Oh,' said Magistrate Kumar, 'I see that you are scared of the police and have no compunction about contempt of justice. All policemen are directed to step out of the court.' He began to scrutinize every nuance of Sherry's body much like an explorer would pore over a region on a map. 'You, Pardhi, I command you for the last time to tell me what you heard the policemen say… or I will charge you with contempt…'

'My Lord, I cannot be so indecent before you,' said the Pardhi. 'I would prefer to suffer the wrath of your contempt!'

'Take this insolent man away…I condemn him to three months in jail,' Magistrate Kumar roared in anger, beating down the gavel forcefully.

'My Lord,' the Pardhi said. 'The policemen were talking loudly, very loudly. The conversation included you too, My Lord.'

'Really?' The curiosity of Magistrate Kumar knew no limits now. He commanded, 'It is the direction of the bench! Speak out, man!' He felt supreme, and the divine presence of Sherry helped to bridge the short distance between him and God.

'My Lord, they were saying,' the Pardhi cleared his throat and paused, seemingly unfazed by the looks directed at him. By now, even the Prosecutor was looking encouragingly at him.

'Go on, for God's sake, go on.' Magistrate Kumar was pleading now.

'My Lord, they discussed the size of her,' he brought his hands to his chest and caricatured a well-endowed woman's bust. There was pin drop silence. Eyes turned into forceps, shifting away from the grungy Pardhi. They dissected Sherry with a surgical brazenness that had now been conferred judicial indemnity. 'And then they said more. That you hated women because your first wife had divorced you and the second one was about to do so. That as long as you were the Chief Judicial Magistrate they had nothing to worry about. They were confident that you would scoff at all this modern day gender-sensitivity nonsense and definitely convict her. That they had nothing to worry and needed to make the most of this opportunity before she was forever beyond their reach!'

Jaws dropped as an eerie hush descended upon the court room. Everybody stood stunned by this revelation and its likely implication. Surely Magistrate Kumar would charge the Pardhi for contempt and send Sherry off to a long term in jail now!

Magistrate Kumar went red in the face. It was as if he were considering a dissertation before it was discussed in a viva-voce. Nobody stirred. Sherry looked at Ganga. Both he and Bisnu placed their fingers on their lips unobtrusively, pleading her to keep quiet.

With a straight face, Magistrate Kumar announced his verdict and darted away to his Chamber. The young lawyer whooped with joy.

'He has dismissed the case against her!' Ganga leapt up and embraced first him and then Bisnu.

The lawyer said, 'This is the only case this year where Magistrate Kumar has summarily discharged an accused!'

🐾

Ganga tried to control the urge to meet Sherry. Civil servants certainly did not visit journalists' homes, least of all when they happened to be attractive single women.

But she had been insistent that he join her for a cup of tea at Grey Goose. 'I'm sure you'll like some excellent honey lemon tea,' she had pleaded. It was late evening and the Civil Lines area seemed deserted with hardly any vehicular movement. He had already stuck his neck out. It was probably better to be hanged for a sheep than for a lamb.

He entered the drawing room, instantly feeling happy that he had chosen to come in.

'I'll be back in a minute,' said Sherry, rushing into the kitchen, leaving him in the drawing room.

Ganga stood admiring the period furniture and the huge landscapes of the highlands of Central India. He looked at the portraits of the women in Sherry's life and beyond the glass window at the branches of the trees that swayed gently in the breeze. 'Sherry, this is truly a beautiful place you have,' said Ganga appreciatively. He walked across and stood close to her in the kitchen. 'Who are the women in that photo there?'

'My mother Tara, her sister Lara Pinto and Melanie Gardner of Wildflower Camp, in front of the Bombay Natural History Society. In fact, I have tried to maintain this place just as it was in Auntie Lara's time,' said Sherry, as she wiped her hands against a towel. 'Though it is a little rundown, it is very comfortable. My only contribution has been the set of paintings by tribal artists from the Mandla-Dindori area.'

'What a fabulous place to have in the heart of Civil Lines and the Cantonment? Where are your parents?'

'My mother Tara died in an accident many years ago. My father lives in the hills, in Dharamsala. He works for the Dalai Lama. I was brought up by my aunt, the great Lara Pinto, the original owner of the Grey Goose, and lived with her until she passed away. I really miss her... So does the rest of Jabalpur. I guess I am lucky to have been able to hold on to this... I could have easily been on the road,' she said.

'Ever since you were arrested, I have activated my thinking hat,' said Ganga. He edged closer to her.

Sherry saw him staring intently at her and returned his look. His hair had a luster, unusual for men, while his eyes were intense. The knife-edged birthmark on his forehead captivated her yet again. As if by instinct, she traced it with her fingers. 'There is a bit of Shiva in you,' she said, drawing closer to him, continuing to furrow it with her finger.

Ganga froze under her touch. His pulse throbbed with raw energy as her fingers lingered on his forehead.

She noticed that the top button of his shirt hung loose. 'I'll fix that,' she volunteered.

He blushed and said, 'Thanks.'

Sherry held his hand easily and led him back to the drawing room. She sank into a padded sofa chair with faded velvet upholstery and said, 'I happened to see the press release issued by the police when that NRI Ramchandra Prasad was arrested.' 'It is very unusual that it should refer definitively to a tigress' skin and not to a tiger skin... And to Burree Maada.'

'Nobody can conclude with certainty that the skin found with the NRI is that of a tigress and not that of a tiger,' said Ganga.

'Circumstantially, it can at best be an inspired guess that it was of a tigress,' said Sherry. 'After all Burree Maada is missing. But is it possible to distinguish between the skin of a male and female tiger, unless you are privy to inside information?'

'Not unless you get beneath the skin,' said Ganga.

'And it isn't always easy to get beneath a skin.'

They both laughed.

'Burree Maada is missing. But unless her carcass is found nobody can certify that that skin belonged to her. A DNA test or a stripe-analysis is necessary of the hundred odd stripes. And no two stripes are the same!'

'It is possible that police officials seized a fresh skin and then realized that it was too hot to retain even as a trophy. So they exchanged the older and safer skin with the more objectionable freshly poached one.'

Sherry stepped away briefly to return with an ornately carved white-metal tray. She removed the flowery tea cosy and poured the tea into chipped-at-the-edges ceramic mugs that must have been at least half a century old. A salver held arrowroot biscuits. She offered them to Ganga, nibbling one herself and said, 'I wonder if it is a cover up to make us believe that Burree Maada is dead.'

'Highly unlikely that she is alive,' said Ganga. 'By the way, I'm curious about somebody who is addressed as Darbar around these parts.'

'I can only think of one—Abhimanyu Singh, His Highness the Maharaja of Baikunthpur,' said Sherry cautiously. 'Apart from being royalty, he is a nature and wildlife expert with an extraordinary passion for the jungles and wildlife of Central India. That is also the subject of his unending doctoral research.'

'That's him,' said Ganga. 'Tall, very handsome! Like the protagonist of that classic English film I saw the other day, about chariot racing and Christ.'

'Ben Hur,' chimed in Sherry. 'I love watching old English films.

It was shot in Rome by the famous William Wyler in the late 50s. You're talking of Charlton Heston.'

'I too love watching English films,' said Ganga. 'Yes, he looks like Charlton Heston...or perhaps Robert Redford?'

'Abhimanyu Singh is exceptionally handsome! But personally I'd like to think he is more Ralph Fiennes.'

'The very handsome English Patient?'

'Francis Dolarhyde.'

'Who?'

'The psychopath...The Red Dragon...Fiennes plays that role.'

'You're being very unkind to him,' said Ganga. 'He is anything but a killer, so calm and placid...of course you can kill with looks too.'

'You can even kill with kindness,' Sherry said dismissively; she desperately wanted to change the topic. She pulled out her darning kit and quickly set about fixing Ganga's button while he stood erect, holding his breath and admiring her skill with the needle. 'Some impressions stick. By the way I am intrigued by a sponsored report on the television which underlines global poaching of tigers, and the overwhelming demand from all over the world for tiger parts. Not Greater China, not Asia...the world!'

'The tiger agenda appears to be hijacked. I wonder what is causing CITES to hang up when it should produce trend reports.'

'Lack of funds due to delayed contributions is the common concern of all UN and international bodies—remember, Ted Turner of CNN bailed out the UN once,' Sherry observed.

'Yes...I read that.'

'Besides, tiger protocol is hardly a priority matter for most developing countries.'

'Maybe CITES is under the influence of rich tycoons of Southeast Asia who have invested in captive farms,' said Ganga.

'That can't be ruled out.'

'It is a pity that we don't really have an international tiger strategy.'

'CITES convenes next June at Hague, in Netherlands, that is barely a year away,' said Sherry. 'But the government in Delhi is in deep paralysis—busy granting go or no-go clearances to mega-mining projects! Just recently, Uganda has asked for permission to allocate fifty leopards a year for sport-hunting and trophies—this sort of thing sets off a race to the bottom. Currently, the Chinese are treading cautiously, thanks to the forthcoming Beijing Olympics. But they are bound to make a pitch immediately after the Olympics for permission to sell tiger parts from their captive-farms.'

'But,' said Ganga, 'CITES is an international protocol, and its meetings are attended by senior ministry officials in Delhi. What can we do sitting in the back waters.'

'Can we find Burree Maada?' She paused before continuing, 'Only then can we channelize public sentiment.'

'How could she be smuggled out? Where on earth would they find a place large enough to hide her?'

'The Baikunthpur Palace, and the tykhanas of the Goenkas are large enough to keep elephants,' said Sherry.

'How do you know?' asked Ganga.

'Because it is in my blood to know everything,' Sherry said with a conspiratorial wink. 'If Abhimanyu Singh is the lead actor, then Feroze Goenka has to be a supporting actor.'

Ganga stared at her, surprised and confused. He put his arms on her shoulders and looked piercingly at her, 'Forget Burree Maada...perhaps you should tell me about Abhimanyu Singh.'

Sherry let his arm rest and whispered breathlessly, 'Perhaps it's getting late for you?'

Ganga stared at Sherry. There was no denying that she was extremely attractive both physically and intellectually. Her ingenious temperament and her professed boldness had forced him to keep her at an arms length for the moment. But, there was a vulnerability about her which aroused a different instinct in him. 'Tell me, please.'

'We were together briefly,' said Sherry curtly. 'And I'm glad to be alone now.'

'Really?' asked Ganga. 'What happened?'

'I must tell you this,' announced Sherry, hurriedly changing tack. 'When I was holed up in the Military Hospital, I received some flowers with a get well card from Goenka. This was followed by a call from Abhimanyu Singh, even though we are no longer on speaking terms. Burree Maada may have been executed by foot-soldiers, but there is a bigger game at play. My gut sense screams the words: CITES, Tiger Farm and Clone.'

THE CAGE

Much before the bright rays of the morning sun streamed in and the first shuttle train to Katni had whistled past, Jabalpur Central Jail was pandemonium personified. Ram could hear the beating of sticks and whistles in action—first short blasts and then the bugle calls, shrill and electrifying.

'Bloody bastards,' shouted the jail guards in unison. 'Who hanged Silly-man?'

The deafening commotion and the searing commands managed to jerk up Ram instantaneously. His head ached dully. He groped at his once-white pajamas and open shirt with disbelief. His eyes fell on the number 2699, inscribed crudely on his left hand—the blue-black ink smudged around, branding him. He looked around at the huge cage in which he was locked.

It was set in dormitory style, with a row of bunks at ground-level. The lime and mortar walls were bare except for the graffiti on them while the cement floor was a lifeless grey, with grotesque patches highlighting the places where it had been touched up in the past. A naked bulb swung perilously at the end of a long wire caked with dust, heaved by a sleepy fan that croaked like a tuberculosis patient.

The sound of the guards grew louder. His heart beat faster as he stood still holding on to the bed and his pajamas.

'Move bastards! Move!'

Two stout ward boys strutting like keepers in a zoo undid the locks of the cages. One continued to blow his whistle; the other beat his stick and aped a monkey-master commanding his monkeys to perform to the beat of his drum. The inmates had to assemble for their morning prayers and physical training—and to explain for everything that had gone wrong. Ram staggered forwards with a nervous lurch.

That he would be lodged in JCJ, the formidable Jabalpur Central Jail, seemed to be surreal. He remembered his father's premonition. It had come true to an extent. He had fallen into a cage. Would he now be pounced upon by a tiger…and torn apart?

The prisoners spilled out like termites onto a red clay ground.

'Who is Silly-man?' Ram whispered to no one in particular. He was poked in the ribs, with a nudge towards the tree in front of them. There hung the object of the commotion—a white mongrel hanging from one of the branches, its rear legs tied. It was a tongue-tied assembly as nobody was ready to own up to the deed.

They were partitioned into groups for a cane to be administered brutally on their buttocks. One of the guards climbed up and undid the knot; as the mongrel's body fell with a thud, all the prisoners clapped. It seemed no less than the ceremonial unfurling of the national flag.

'Silly-man?' Ram whispered incredulously to the prisoner standing next to him.

A squeaky voice elaborated. 'Silly-man! He was a heartless English murderer, who hanged our brothers in this fashion. We named the bastard hanging there after him.' Ram turned to look at him. It was a sneaky-looking man, short and rather old, probably a friend of Jugnu; Ram had seen them talking often to each other.

'But why name a mongrel after an Englishman?' Ram was completely bewildered

'That white dog Silly-man lived a hundred and fifty years ago when the English ruled us. He called us thugs and hunted us down,' Jugnu's friend said.

'A hundred and fifty years ago?' repeated Ram. This was a nightmare; he would soon wake up.

'Certain things are difficult to wipe out of memory, like Hitler's Holocaust and the Jallianwalla Bagh Massacre,' said Jugnu, standing nearby. 'Our tribes will always remember Silly-man as a cold-blooded English hunter.'

'Why do you say that?'

'He used to hang his victims in this fashion from trees. Did you know that at one point, each tree between Jabalpur and Katni, a full hundred kilometers, had our brethren hanging from it?'

Ram felt rather than saw a bespectacled and bearded man looking scathingly at him. He had been quiet so far; and now he chose to uncoil himself in the manner of a snake. He was apparently the jail's fount of wisdom; for everybody listened with rapt attention to the Prophet.

'Silly-man symbolizes imperialism,' he observed critically. 'Our laws were made by the English so that they could divide and rule us. Therefore, the dog has been served justice.'

Jugnu hurriedly pulled Ram to face the Prophet. 'Narad Sir is a great mind,' Jugnu explained. 'He has predicted that within a few years there will be no need to have jails, and even if there are any, they would hold only corrupt politicians and officers.'

Ram maintained a calm front. He could literally feel the venom spewing out of Narad towards him.

'We have to crush all imperialists and make our own classless government...of the under-privileged, the ninety-nine percent,' Narad asserted, with a clenched fist. He seemed to be quite at home making fiery statements.

'Thank you Narad Sir,' said Jugnu. 'You will show us the way, won't you?'

'Who else can?' asked Narad scornfully.

'But, why do you talk of the English as if they were evil?' Ram asked, deciding to take a hand in the conversation. 'They also gave us a lot.'

'Yes, Ba-Ba-Black-Sheep and Jack-and-Jill,' Jugnu contributed proudly.

'No, Jugnu, they did other good things—they gave us railways, military and education...they taught us how to protect forests and wildlife, for instance,' Ram argued, refusing to buckle down to Narad.

'Rubbish!' shouted Narad. 'The English made laws so that all wildlife in the jungle remained their exclusive property.'

'And alienated us from our only resource—the forests,' said Jugnu forcefully.

Ram sighed. They were too strongly indoctrinated in their own philosophy; perhaps there was no point entering into an argument with them. He observed that Silly-man's neck had been wrung with a pale-coloured scarf and then the rear feet had been tied to a branch—much like a sirloin in a butcher-shop.

There was an announcement on the PAS: 'Since no one owns up to hanging Silly-man, everybody will do two extra hours of carpet weaving tomorrow, and, no morning chai will be served. That is a collective punishment!'

It was a powerful voice, and though greeted with boos, the verdict of the Jail Superintendent was final.

'Our chai is being diverted to serve the Jail Minister's election rally,' Narad muttered wickedly, with a chuckle.

Ram felt his head spinning. Things just did not make sense. He had admired the English for their language, for their systems and above all for their understated sophistication. To be employed amongst the whites had been the fulfillment of his childhood fantasy. In school he had boasted of his father's friendship with true, blue-chip English officers like Mr Wilson, the benevolent English hunter. Now he was being asked to hate them. Everything was turning topsy-turvy in his world!

As Ram was led back to his cage, his eyes fell on the vegetable patch at the far end of the exercise ground and the football goal-post with bitter gourd entwined around it. He reflected on himself and the other vegetating prisoners and the sea of hopelessness that surrounded them. He seemed to be viewing Van Gogh's Stale Sunflowers in a Vase, where motion had been arrested. He had once made it into a bookmark. On the other side of the bookmark, he had chosen to scribble a verse from the one poem that had clung to him ever since he had memorized it in school—Samuel Taylor Coleridge's Rime of the Ancient Mariner:

Day after day, day after day,
We struck nor breath nor motion;
As idle as a painted ship,
Upon a painted ocean.

Suddenly a thought crossed his mind. His father's tiger skin... was it the albatross around his neck?

They had just finished their morning exercises the next day and were savouring a few moments of leisure when something about Jugnu's friend caught Ram's attention. It consisted of hollow bamboo rods arranged perpendicularly and held in position with cotton rags. Barely visible wires ran inside. It resembled a harp and beeped intermittently. Ram fancied it to be a radio and asked Jugnu what he was hearing.

'It is a special frequency that allows Khandar to communicate with our Goddess Bhawanee,' said Jugnu mischievously.

'He is joking,' said his friend. 'This is a battery-operated receiver for catching radio signals. This gadget has an antenna inside which keeps tabs on the radio signals emitted by a radio collar.'

'And what is the purpose?'

'To track animals that wear radio collars.'

'The jail authorities don't object?' Ram asked.

'In fact, the Jail Superintendent's son will use this for his Physics project at school,' Jugnu replied.

'Who taught you all this science?' Ram asked.

'Darbar,' Jugnu replied.

'Who?'

'Raja Abhimanyu Pratap Singh,' said Jugnu. 'I will introduce you to him one day. He is abroad currently. He is Farishta, the Angel.'

'I think I have met him,' said Ram, recalling the flamboyant Raja at the airport and his spontaneous hospitality in Mumbai. 'He is indeed a farishta! By the way, that yellow thing, was that a scarf around Silly-man's neck?'

'Brilliant! So you did notice it,' said Jugnu appreciatively. 'The scarf hid a collar with a radio transmitter. Since I did not know the collar frequency, we adopted a hit and trial method till we could track Silly-man all the time. When he humped Rani—the jailor's bitch; when he chased Billoo, that fat rat that looked like a pig; till Khandar finally flung the noose around his neck. Meet Khandar bhai.'

Jugnu took inordinate pride in introducing to his world—it was the joyfulness of a midwife undertaking a delivery. Ram had heard of radio telemetry. At the highest level it was used to track satellite dynamics—the basic principles were probably the same. He cast a glance at Khandar—prematurely aged and weathered—white stubble on a dark face, like a photo negative. Ram stretched out his hand. 'Hello. What brings you here?'

'Khandar is a high-flier,' Jugnu said. 'He has left us all behind.'

Ram looked more closely at Khandar. His hands were horribly blistered.

'We are still stuck with animals and peeling animal skins,' Jugnu expounded. 'But Khandar has moved on to bigger things like the temples of India. He can peel an entire monument open. He travels to fancy places I only dream of—Istanbul, London, Paris, thanks to his new profession.'

Khandar acknowledged this citation with serene humility, raising a hand to the sky, as if attributing his skills to some stellar source.

'But why do you need to track animals?' Ram persisted, coming back to the main issue. He knew instinctively that herein lay the answer to why he had landed in jail.

'All jungle animals are slowly being collared. We have to keep pace with the Forest Department. But signals drop when the terrain is rugged—hills or buildings come in between—and that is why we have modified our instrument. Meanwhile, no better place than a jail to practice!'

Ram had been too busy adjusting to the new routine to bother acquainting himself with his cell mates. Jugnu, the old hand, gave him sound advice. Pretend that you are an old prison hand who has been shifted from another prison to avoid exploitation by the older and more vicious inmates—the murderers, the rapists and sodomists and the extortionists—first they befriend you and then threaten you with a syringe tipped with the deadly HIV virus, seeking payments to be delivered outside jail. Despite the subterfuge adopted, some had already begun to make advances towards Ram. But they had not bargained for Jugnu. He organized a meeting with his close group of friends and told Ram, 'My tribesmen will act as your firewall.'

'Mr Ramachandra is a big businessman from Amreeka,' he announced proudly. 'He has done BA many times over. He is very resourceful—he could easily get bail. But he wants to know what life in Indian jails is like for us so that he can write about it in a foreign journal. He has condescended to be with us. We should make him comfortable.'

Mention of his interest in understanding the jail system evoked guffaws of applause and appreciative glances. Jugnu carried weight. Ram's esteem went up in their eyes, almost as if he was the Jail

Reforms Commissioner. He had become socially acceptable.

'Thank you Jugnu.'

Jugnu smiled and put an arm around Khandar and addressed Ram, 'If anybody troubles you now, remember that Khandar who is like P.C. Sorkar, the magician, can make him vanish! He has the artistic ability to make an entire elephant disappear—Haathi ki Safai!'

Ram smiled amidst his woes at the prospect of something so preposterous happening. Others joined in and merriment ruled them temporarily.

'I know India has a lot of temples, we are a religious country,' Ram said, just to show his interest in their conversation.

'Sir, this region is the treasure trove of Kuber,' said Jugnu. 'Khandar lifted the Buddha sitting in Bhumisparshmudra from the Tapsimath Bilhari temple. It was finally auctioned for a fantastic sum in dollars. A rich foreign collector from your Amreeka picked it up. Haven't you recently lifted two more Buddhas?'

'Yes, the Padmasana Buddha and the White Tara, also from the same temple,' Khandar said unabashedly. 'It was always difficult—but now it is risky too.'

'Why?'

'Earlier one had to deal only with the police and the Forest Department,' Khandar said. 'But nowadays after the changes to the Constitution, the village headman also needs a cut. So anyone who tries to act difficult has to be Silly-manned.'

He lurched backwards enacting a strangled man.

'Government must be after you?' Ram asked.

'Our government is best—it governs the least,' Khandar said. 'Besides, what all can the government protect—women, children, tribals? The Archaeology Department tries to keep some degree of control. But only notified temples have some security. Meanwhile there are thousands of unlisted ancient temples and monuments not yet covered under the Archaeology Department.'

'India's history lies in ruins,' said Jugnu philosophically. He added, 'India should be rebuilt from its ruins.'

'How?' Ram was fascinated. There was a surreal method to their madness.

'By forming our own government,' stated Jugnu. 'A government of people...ninety-nine percent India.'

'Won't other more powerful groups come in your way.'

'We will keep Silly-manning all those who cross our path!' Narad suddenly intervened, imitating Jugnu's voice.

'Isn't money required?'

'That can be managed. But we have three important assignments initially. We need your assistance,' Jugnu said conspiratorially.

'And what are these new jobs?' Ram asked.

'The first is to package the complete remains of Narmada Saarus, a dinosaur...the great-great grandfather of the elephant, about thirty feet long, with a trunk as long as the hose pipe of the Fire Department, and the height of a camel. It was found in the Shimla Hills near the Gun Carriage Factory in Jabalpur. The fossils are more than a hundred million years old.'

'But, how can you move a dinosaur even if you've found the remains?'

'Bit by bit...bone by bone. It may take months, but we are old hands,' Khandar said. 'After all, we have lifted temples.'

'And who are your buyers?'

'Big Natural History Museums in the western world,' Jugnu said. 'Their sources have already contacted us.'

'What comes next?'

'We have to smuggle out the skull of the super-ancient Narmada Man, the first man in human history—who lived even before the legendary heroes—Ram and Krishna!'

Ram did not believe a single word. He had little interest in anthropology or history. But he did know that Jabalpur, on the banks of the Narmada River, and the geographical center of India, had always been important—he recalled Jaya mentioning it. 'If I ever come to India it will be to complete my paleontological journey to the cradle of ancient civilization... India was part of Gondwanaland... I hope to combine it with Madagascar.'

Perhaps he could elicit more stories from these men; certainly the monotony of jail was being broken. He could, at some later date, when this nightmare was behind him, write about the treasures that abounded here for foreign journals and win some international sympathy for his situation. Breathless with excitement, he asked, 'And my friends, the third?'

'Thankfully we've accomplished that,' Jugnu said, his chest heaving with pride. 'That was one very, very difficult and tricky assignment.'

'What was it?'

'To get tigress Burree Maada out of Kanha Tiger Reserve.'

'What!' Ram screamed and his entire body trembled. So Jugnu had known about Burree Maada and her whereabouts all along and concealed the truth from him. He flopped down and stared wide-eyed at Jugnu in amazement. All along—from the first time that Ram had shown him the Van Ingen skin opposite the chai-shop, to later in the police lockup and again in the court!

'So the skin in court was of Burree Maada that you all killed?'

'Burree Maada was never killed,' said Jugnu.

'You mean she is alive?' asked Ram incredulously.

'Yes!'

'And nobody obstructed you when you abducted her?'

'Well, just when we had loaded the tigress on a bamboo palki, a Forest Guard appeared out of nowhere and confronted us. Luckily he was unarmed. So while I engaged him in conversation and explained our technique, Firanghee gave him paan to eat and then strangled him. We were able to take Burree Maada out of the Kanha Tiger Reserve, without any serious injury.'

Ram shouted, hoarse with indignation, 'Burree Maada is alive! Then how is it that we have been arrested for killing her?'

'The police can arrest you whenever they want,' said Jugnu complacently.

'How could you do this? How did you do it?'

'We had been tracking Burree Maada, waiting for her to kill a chital,' explained Jugnu warming to his tale. 'Tigers feed continuously for two or three days and then suddenly stop eating. So we had little time. As soon as she went out with the cubs, we laid the metal trap and concealed it in a muddy patch between the chital carcass and the water source. The moment she came back to the meat and went to drink water her leg was stuck. Instead of the usual iron spear, we put a bamboo in her mouth and beat her with sticks till she became unconscious. Of course we had to be very careful because we had clear instructions that she was to be taken alive. Then I gave her a dose of tranquilizer with a jab-stick.'

The biggest mystery of his life was about to be solved. He asked excitedly, 'Where is she now?'

'Our job was only to get her out of Kanha in one piece,' Jugnu said. 'And we did exactly as we were told! We smuggled Burree Maada out in a meat truck till Jabalpur. Someone else must have been entrusted with the next part of the task.'

Ram glared at Jugnu, revolted by the deceit. 'Jugnu, where is my father's skin?' he asked indignantly. 'The police had seized it, but the one produced in court was different.'

'Sir, even I am puzzled,' Jugnu said.

'Please think,' urged Ram. His entire defence would rest on proving that the skin produced in court was not that of Burree Maada. 'With all your experience and knowledge…what is your guess…what exactly do you think happened?'

Jugnu scratched his head, lost in thought for a while.

'Sir, Burree Maada was still alive when we handed her in, so it could not have been her skin,' Jugnu said. 'In fact, I can say with certainty it was not. But it was clearly a brand new skin; I can smell a new skin a mile away. However, I do recall the night that we spent in the police lock-up. The lights were off. You were snoring but I was awake, pretending to be asleep. I overheard the conversation between the Police Inspector and the constable in charge of the Nazarat. The constable was whispering to his boss, "Tiger is king of jungle and Police Inspector is king of police station. " And then he said.'

'What else?'

'Chamdi is chamdi,' Jugnu completed.

Ram pondered a while. Chamdi meant skin in Hindi and usually referred to human skin. In a flash it dawned on him. The chamdi being referred to was an allusion not only to human skin but to another tiger skin. The reason it looked so new was because it was the skin of a freshly poached and skinned tiger, possibly from another Tiger Reserve. Not Burree Maada! Did Jugnu know where that had that come from?

'Where do you think that new skin came from so suddenly?'

'Not from Bandhavgarh or Kanha or Pench,' said Jugnu. 'This was fresh shikar! Maybe a week or two old…I can vouch for that.'

Ram had hit a dead end once again; it would be days before Jugnu would reveal the truth, presuming he knew it. He had to wait patiently and not give up. Sighing, he looked at Khandar. 'And how did somebody as smart as you land in jail? You couldn't possibly have got caught?' Ram asked him.

'Who can catch Khandar?' Jugnu intervened haughtily. Khandar blushed silently, embarrassed.

'Exactly,' said Ram. 'Then how is he here?'

'Sir, I came in voluntarily,' Khandar said politely.

'Why?' Ram asked. Why should anybody sane want to commit hara-kiri?

'So that I can handle operations from this secure place,' said Khandar softly. 'Also it helps me in my future court cases. It helps if I was in jail when some of the smuggling was done.'

'You must be having people in the field who obey you!'

'I only plan from here now,' said Khandar, stretching himself lazily. 'I have trained youth from villages; they help me with village Kotwars.'

He wondered how Jugnu and his mates managed things that were clearly beyond the scope of prisoner entitlements. He braved another question, 'Jugnu, how do you manage to keep the jail authorities on your side?'

'By being obedient servants Sir,' said Jugnu promptly. 'Jailor Sahib wanted me to restore his old sambhar-skin suitcase. I have worked very hard. It looks as good as new now...better than the old Loot-on suitcase I had restored earlier for his boss.'

'Loot-on?'

'Yes. Darbar uses them also...best in the world, I believe. Made in France.'

'Then the jailor should help you to get away,' Ram said, amused at Jugnu's pronunciation.

'Instead I am being tortured by that parasite,' said Jugnu with a heavy sigh. 'His wife wants me to restore a leopard head. She says it should be a perfect job. But when it comes to providing chemicals and equipment they are very miserly. No tweezers and wire cutters, just a knife and scissors, no carbolic acid or turpentine, just lime and turmeric and varnish. How can I do a perfect job? The bastards say they love me. But truth is, they want me to remain here forever.'

🐾

Who was Silly-man? Was he really a murderer? What was his father's dear friend, the Englishman James Wilson, like? Was he also a murderer besides being a hunter? What were the English like in India? What sustained them in hot and grimy India for so long? Narad's snide comments about the English had aroused his curiosity. He wished he could use his time to read and discover Wilson. Not to be able to lay his hands on books and newspapers was frustrating.

It seemed that Narad had sole access to anything remotely readable. Whenever he got hold of any newspapers he would read them voraciously, sometimes taking down notes—and keep smirking to himself, until he had, as Jugnu pronounced, 'Chewed and digested them.' After which the newspapers would almost always be consigned to the dustbins in balls. It was as if he did not want anybody else to acquire knowledge. Perhaps his hold over the others would diminish.

'This stupid jail has no library!' Ram protested aloud one day after their exercises.

'It used to have the best library of Central India at one time,' Narad said, agreeing with Ram for a change. 'But what do you expect from a capitalist government that has more value for currency counting machines. No interest in promoting intellectual thinking!'

'Famous prisoners like Subhash Chandra Bose wrote famous books in the course of their incarceration,' Jugnu said. 'All the books have now been consigned to an old store room which is haunted. Since you can read, you should protest to Jailor Sahib.'

And so when the jail superintendent came on his rounds the next day, they collected behind Ram and Narad. 'We want books—it is a fundamental human right,' Ram pleaded, insinuating that this was a deliberate ploy to keep them ignorant and submissive.

'Fools! You should know that we used to have a very good library, but today it only has Subhash Chandra Bose's ghost living in it!' They were being rebuffed.

'We will face the ghost,' Jugnu, Ram and Narad sang in unison. But it had no impact on the Superintendent. So a scuffle was enacted. The protagonists were Ram and Narad. They started slapping each other's cheeks in full view of their fellow inmates, but were soon silently egged on to make it harder. Within minutes each of them were slapping each other with full force and stopped only when they had swollen cheeks and Narad was spitting blood. The two 'trouble makers' were assigned the 'dirty' task of cleaning up the jail library in a week's time as a compromise solution. Later, 2699 was directed to do the dirty job with the help of Phukat, a young Gond boy who could read a little, a friend of Jugnu. Narad had fallen conveniently sick.

Ram was thrilled to learn that a bail plea had been submitted to the court on his behalf. It was the normal course, part of the legal-aid and justice system. He prayed silently that his ordeal would end. Truth would prevail!

He strode across to the library and focused on the cast-iron padlock. It had the words Tiger and Aligarh engraved on it—perhaps after the company that manufactured these locks, located in Aligarh city. He tried out the keys, one by one from the huge bunch with him. They refused to comply. Then he remembered the Superintendent telling him to look for the most uncommon key. There was one shaped like an elephant's trunk—long body with a hollow inside. He put it into the lock and was surprised when it opened smoothly.

The door creaked open, reminiscent of an Alfred Hitchcock

film. Phukat and he tiptoed in. Inside, the hall smelt musty, like an abandoned warehouse. There were heaps of rubbish laden with cobwebs and dust. A family of huge rats that had been lording over this territory without competition darted out. Several large bats flitted from one end to the other with a vicious flutter of wings. Littered on the ground was a smorgasbord of furniture—broken chairs, a planter's armchair with the hexagonal netting ripped out and several condemned gunny bags packed to the brim, shrouded with insect droppings. Beneath the furniture lay piles of books, smothered in dust. He kicked one bundle out of his way.

The bundle vomited out old prison records. Along the four walls of the room, books were stacked in tall cupboards, almost the height of the walls of the room. Ram took out his handkerchief and masking his mouth from the dust, opened the remaining stoppers. The cupboards were full of leather-bound books—English classics, works of Dante, Gibbons and Milton—the pages yellowing with age and stuck in places. Most of them were on the verge of falling apart; some already scattered on the ground. He picked up one book—it had been published in 1885!

He was invaded with the feeling that the library would end up to be a damp squib. But just as he was going to give up in disappointment, the last cupboard turned out to be a treasure trove of books on nature and the cultural anthropology of the Indian subcontinent. He opened one of the books at random—the pages were torn in places, but the print was still readable. There were vivid descriptions of forests and wildlife in the Central Provinces. He turned the pages to see the names of the authors—mostly anecdotal accounts written by lesser known English soldiers and civil servants of their experiences in India amidst the natives.

Though Jaya was a voracious reader, his own reading had always been unworthy of attention. Now was the time to recover lost ground and return to sanity and the wonderland of literature.

It was like being on a time machine. Ram could feel himself being transported back to a time when the English ruled India.

Another shelf was full of *Gazetteers* and personal diaries of English officers. He picked up a dust-laden book titled: *The Rise and Expansion of the British Dominion in India*, written in 1893 by Alfred Lyall, a career civil servant. Ram began to read out aloud, trying to make sense of the fading print:

> All civilization ceases abruptly as soon as you leave the Ganga Valley. How dreary and stiff the Christmas celebrations in Hoshangabad are compared to those in Agra. I am determined not to stay in Hoshangabad…

But Lyall did stay on much longer. What was it about the Narmada Valley that changed his mind? He picked up another book, brushed aside the cobwebs and started reading:

> Your door was always open, literally and metaphorically to all kinds…including fowls of the air and beasts of the forest…not all visitors were harmless…I should be sorry to say, lest I be thought to exaggerate, how many scorpions and black kraits use the house.

Suddenly the drab jail was transformed into an exotic paradise. Ram looked at Phukat and laughed—how inane the endless debate, consuming several dozens of pages, between two senior civil servants, on how to spell the name Jabalpur? Grigson the Deputy Commissioner was of the view that Jubbulpore was far too long, while his immediate superior Greenfield, the Divisional Commissioner who controlled not just Jabalpore but Mandla, Balaghat, Seoni and Chhindwara, thought this would entail unnecessary revisions in the date-stamps and seals and create problems for the Postal Department and the Railways. Finally good sense prevailed; they compromised by using the spelling of their choice when addressing letters to each other!

Ram browsed through a book by an English officer, Henry Sharp. He seemed to have devoted a portion of his memoirs to his experiences as a hunter:

> Shooting game was not only a most enjoyable sport in the jungles of the Central Provinces...it was better than hunting back home in England, for in India it was inexpensive...there were no limits, no marches—the whole world before you...you wandered as you willed, with none to stop you, for there were no game laws, nor, except in the government forest, any restrictions. In small game shooting there was none of the artificiality that robs the sport in the British Isles of some of its charm.

The Indian sub continent was an area of opportunity—of forests and animals, of leisurely times, of howdahs and machans, of watching snake charmers and mongoose fights. Was this why India had been referred to, fondly or cynically, right through the 50s and 60s as the land of snake charmers? British officers used words like 'ferocious beasts' to describe tigers and wild animals; the jungles were always 'infested' with wild animals. Was India the Jewel in the Crown because it was the perfect playground to hunt in, to recreate the charm of English sportsmanship, without the encumbrances of rules and regulations?

He kept his eyes peeled for a mention of James Wilson and Silly-man. But he was disappointed. Suddenly, in front of him was a book: *Indian Shikar Notes*, written by a James somebody, with the letters 'Wi' showing for the last name. The exact name of the author had been torn off. His heartbeat increased as he breathlessly flipped through the pages of the book to find the name Wilson. As he excitedly searched the pages he discovered that James did have both a middle and a last name. But his full name was not

James Wilson. It was James William Best.

Another book caught his eye. In her *Days and Nights of Shikar*, Mrs W.W. Baillie furnished a detailed but humourous account of shooting a nine and a half feet long tiger, and how she kept shooting at it, unloading almost a dozen cartridges into the animal. Obviously women were as good a shot as the men.

Two books caught his attention. They had illustrations in Urdu and English. The first was *Tuzuk-e-Jehangiri*, or Memoirs of Jahangir, a translation by Alexander Rogers and Henry Beveridge of London's Royal Asiatic Society. The other was *The Springing Tiger, A Study of a Revolutionary* by Hugh Toye, a former British Intelligence Officer. It was a biography of Subhash Chandra Bose, who had reportedly given up a promising career in the Indian Civil Service to rebel against the British during World War II for which he was arrested and imprisoned in the Jabalpur Central Jail. Ram stared at the picture of Bose's military flag. It had a springing tiger embossed in the center. This was the man who had met Adolph Hitler of Germany and Tojo of Japan and was on the brink of changing the course of World War II by assisting the Japanese on the eastern front. And then, just when his fortunes were rapidly on the ascendant, this famous strategist suddenly vanished from the scene, literally into thin air. Mystery shrouded his disappearance. Some said his plane had crashed while others felt that he had been imprisoned by the British or the Russians on an unknown island. There was even an apocryphal story that he had renounced the world and become a hermit.

Bose's flag had a tiger on it. Had it been prophetic for him as well?

He rose with a premonition that this would be his lucky day. And though he pretended not to be excited, he had been up the whole night dwelling on what he would do once he was released from jail.

The news that his bail application had been summarily rejected came just after lunch. It was brought by Jugnu and had the effect of sucking the wind out of him. He dropped to the ground like a felled tree, clutching his head in despair.

'American Brother will remain with us for at least a year,' Narad analysed Ram's situation coldly. 'Charges will be framed and the trial will go on. The evidence is overwhelming. Fresh tiger skin is as bad as heroin. Besides, there is the presence of foreign currency to support the allegation.'

'Perhaps it is time you began praying to Bhawanee for a miracle,' said Khandar mockingly. Five others stood by, and joined in.

'Only a miracle can save you now,' said Phukat. 'Sometimes miracles happen.'

'People have rotted inside jail all their lives and been cremated here,' said another.

'Miracles happen only to the lucky,' yet another wisecrack said.

'I know nobody and there is nobody to perform a miracle for me,' said Ram, feeling worse than ever before at this public analysis of his helplessness. Miracles did not happen in places like prisons which were governed by rigid laws that applied equally to all inmates.

Jugnu had been silent for a while, observing Ram carefully. He stood up and beat his breast loudly. 'Don't worry Ram Sir,' he said. 'There can be a miracle,' he said confidently.

All eyes turned to him. Ram stared at him in disbelief. Could he help? For several days now, a sense of worthlessness had crept into Ram. He had descended from Infinity, the name of his apartment complex in Cupertino—to Ground Zero. And there seemed to be no end to this freefall, it was a bottomless abyss. He was regressing westwards along the x-axis—to the negative values.

'All is not lost,' Jugnu said soothingly. 'I know a miracle man.'

'Who?' Ram asked.

'Patience,' said Jugnu.

Ram looked around helplessly and reflected on the incredible coincidences. The library had a tiger lock on it. Subhash Chandra Bose, the political hero who had been incarcerated in the same prison, had a tiger emblazoned on his flag and failed in his strategy against the English to win India freedom. A tiger skin had been responsible for landing him into jail. It made his head spin. His father's bewildering prophesy came back to haunt him:

'The Fall… The Cage… The Crouching Tiger…'

Would he now have to confront a live tiger? Was he to be torn and shredded to bloody pieces like a condemned gladiator?

There was a flutter as the jail peon pushed someone towards Sherry. '2699… Here you are, Madam.'

Sherry rose to greet the person with this unusual appellation. She had used the influence of her position with *Hindustan Time* to soften the jail superintendent and secure an interview with Ramachandra Prasad, the 'NRI skin-smuggler'. She had asked him mysteriously, 'Do you know that you have somebody involved in an international financial scandal?'

'Is that so? How interesting!' The Superintendent's eyes lit up at his good fortune. Finally in his dull life, he had custody of someone who was of interest to the English-speaking elite of Jabalpur; someone who would also be, in his own words, 'Juicy and succulent—unlike the Pardhis who were too bloody dry.'

The room had two foldable tin chairs. Sherry sat down on one. A guard watched attentively by the door.

Sherry had perceived Ram as flamboyant and physically imposing. She had researched his life, even browsed the WSJ and

Bloomberg for the latest business news—expecting him to spew financial jargon. She had even touched up her face carefully.

But the creature slumped across her was not quite the man she had imagined. Limping into the tin chair in front of her was a shadow of a man, jaded and drained—hardly the Americanized NRI she had encountered at Jabalpur Railway Station, who reportedly owned a home in Cupertino and another in Manhattan. His shoulders sagged and his body movements seemed slow and lethargic. He slurred, as if he was under heavy sedation. His shaved head gave him the look of a long-term resident in a high-security lunatic asylum.

'Hello Mr Ramachandra Prasad, I am Sherry Pinto.' She stuck out her hand.

No response from the man; Sherry let her hand hang for a while before pulling it back.

'Sir, I am a nature lover first and then a journalist. I have been following you in the hope of meeting you.'

Ram looked up, utter disbelief on his face. The few days in here were enough to make him sick of the dismal surroundings, the repulsive odours and the ugly people. How had this diva materialized from thin air, in this most damning and wretched of places? Was he dreaming or had a prayer been answered?

'Hello, Madam,' he responded weakly, shocked beyond measure.

Sherry extended her hands once again, and this time Ram placed his hands into them. Sherry's hands were long and fair and steady. They felt tender and the body warmth that pulsated from them sent an exhilarating shiver through him.

Ram continued to gaze at her. Natural beauty, poised... effortless chic. He tried to recall where he had last seen such a face? Was it a perfume advertisement for Dior? Or was it for Lancome or Estee Lauder? Was it for Graff, the jewelers? Her voice was enticing. Clearly she seemed like manna from heaven.

Sherry held his hands gently, understanding that she conveyed some sense of reassurance and encouragement to him.

For the first time since he had left his house in Cupertino, Ram felt the tiniest frisson of joy. A faint smile flitted across his lips, easing the creases on his forehead, lighting up his entire face, revealing soft-cut, gentle features.

Sherry noticed the smile and the light brown eyes. She was amazed at how intrinsically nice-looking this broken man actually was. She blushed; embarrassed by the effect her presence was having on him.

Ram could not take his eyes off her. Suddenly, despite the sordid surroundings and the fact that she was dressed simply, he felt overwhelmingly convinced that this was the most perfect face he had ever seen in his life. She noticed him staring at her and smiled back gently.

'Mr Prasad, I am convinced that you are not a poacher or a buyer of animal skins.'

'How can you be so sure?' Ram ventured tentatively.

Sherry winked, 'I sense a nefarious game relating to Burree Maada, the missing tigress. Contrary to the perception that is sought to be created, I think Burree Maada has not been killed. And it is sheer bad luck that you've landed in jail.'

'Thank you. That is reassuring.' This woman was exuding warmth of attitude that was endearing; it breathed life into him.

'And I can vouch, with all my understanding of this business, that Mr Ramachandra Prasad, NRI, from Silicon Valley is not directly connected with Burree Maada.'

'I am grateful.' For the first time in many days somebody had spoken decently to him. Though the smile had retracted, his face bore a relieved look.

'Look, I need some information, but I wouldn't like to

compromise your personal interests,' she said, causing him to arch his brow and look at her with surprise.

'I have nothing to offer,' he said.

'I am interested in another tiger. I do not refer to the golden one with black stripes that is becoming extinct in our jungles and because of which you have unwittingly landed here. I want to know about the silver tiger—the one that allied recently with a golden panda.'

Ram froze. His eyes widened as he stared at her, shaken from his reverie, as she pierced him with her eyes. Was she a decoy?

The silver tiger of Zentigris! The golden panda of Pan Therapeuticals!

He held his heart to control the pain. In a searing flash, laser images of the silver tiger emerged out of the black yin-yang circle to the rising crescendo of classical music, like a 007 film casting. It embraced the golden panda and the two waltzed together. The images danced through his mind as he recapitulated the fragrance of a million roses, the pulsating music, the liveried staff, and the pretty ushers in Tibetan chubas with tiger skin trims, the cameras and the lights! Only a few weeks ago he was shaking hands with global dignitaries and sipping champagne with them...

'Please share only what you can,' Sherry said. 'I promise to safeguard your sensitivities and concerns.'

Ram looked at her, bewildered. 'What is there to tell?' he asked plaintively.

'Anything that can help me to write a feature. It may be of no interest to Wall Street or the investigators...we journalists can spin a story out of bland nothings.'

'It is difficult to think, especially at a time like this. Please let me be.'

'Try,' urged Sherry. 'Please.'

He observed her closely. She looked heavenly as she turned

pink with the effort of coaxing him. There was nothing worth telling her that he could imagine. 'Like what? Give me a clue, so that I can think about it.'

'Anything, just anything! As long as it is something unusual... perhaps the promoters' diverse interests. By the way, I'd love to know how they got these gritty nicknames, Leo and Taurus. Your name, on the contrary, has something very pious about it.'

Ram was lost in thought. Could he feign loss of memory? He could plead that matters were under scrutiny and could affect the fate of the company and its promoters? He opened his mouth to speak, but then closed it.

'Oh my God!' Sherry bowed her head and touched it with her right hand. 'My deepest condolences!'

'For my imprisonment?'

'No! The demise of your noble father. As they say, when times get bad, they really do.'

He accepted her condolences graciously. Her grace was soothing. The gentle way she mentioned his late father, with respect in her expression, unlike the cynicism Jaya displayed for the old man. Her intonation had warmth and gravitas.

'It's been a nightmare for me,' confessed Ram.

'I know I am being selfish Sir. But it is important for my continuance as a journalist. Please tell me something about the Raja brothers...I am terribly curious to know why they chose a tiger as their company logo. Is there some symbolism attached to it?'

'Leo is actually Narsimha, which means the lion avatar of Vishnu and Taurus is actually Taruneswar, also a name for Vishnu—the all-powerful Hindu God who sustains creation, and the foil to Shiva the destroyer,' said Ram. 'They hail from Mysore in South India. I have known them not only as employers but also as friends and colleagues. They're wonderful people.'

Sherry nodded. She had researched the Raja brothers and had

noted about their frequent visits to exotic locales which appeared to be unrelated to their business. She raised her eyes to look at Ram, 'Come on Sir, I don't need to know about their mistresses or Swiss bank accounts, please give me some trivia...a personal hobby or a quirky passion that turns them on...I need a human interest story.'

Ram breathed deeply. 'Strange that you should ask,' he said as he went back in time. 'And stranger that I should know!'

'Well, successful people usually have one private hobby they don't publicly reveal!' Sherry said persuasively.

'They are both rather fond of...'

'Betting? Gambling?'

'No...'

'Drugs?'

Ram felt the tease of dilemma. What should he reveal? What should he conceal? Why should he conceal?

'Please Sir...'

He smiled and said, 'Wildlife.'

'Wildlife?' Sherry let out a whistle.

'Yes! They are rugged adventure lovers and have an attraction for forests and wildlife in different parts of the world. They have a fetish for hardship and exotica.'

'Exotic places like?'

'Borneo, Botswana, Belarus, Montenegro, Namibia, Pakistan...'

Sherry bit her tongue. Those were the countries that permitted, or tacitly overlooked game hunting. 'Interesting,' she said breathlessly. 'Have they visited India recently?'

'They were planning to come here soon, very soon to...' Ram paused and scratched his head, wondering where this was leading. After a while he said, 'Tiger Reserves in Central India.'

He stared at Sherry as she jumped up with excitement. She looked like a scientist whose experiment suddenly confirmed his hypothesis and wondered why the subject was of so much interest to her. He sneezed.

Sherry handed him her soft cotton handkerchief. Her stomach wrenched as she connected something. Abhimanyu Singh had mentioned two rich friends in San Francisco—the businessmen with deep pockets—who would call him at absurd times and be prepared to dole out absurd sums of money to procure mementos of shikar and antique trophies from derelict public and private collections in India and abroad for their personal collection.

He held Sherry's handkerchief close many times after Sherry had left. There was a unique smell that could only be of her. Each time it revived his spirits and made him think of her. There was a renewed desire now and to be prepared for a conversation with her on matters that related to Jabalpur, India and her apparent interest in wildlife. As the honorary librarian of the JCJ Library, Ram's reading had begun to open up entirely new vistas of imagination besides bolstering his rapidly flagging self-esteem and getting him exemption from compulsory floor-mopping. He just wished he would find some reference to Silly-man, the villainous Englishman and James Wilson, the famous English hunter.

'I am worried that you might end up here forever,' warned Jugnu one day. 'Nobody wants to get you out of here.'

'I don't worry because I have dear friends like you,' said Ram bravely with a deep sigh.

But he shuddered at the thought of languishing in jail for the rest of his life. Several inmates had been inside the jail for decades, and had either become chronic tuberculosis or heart-disease patients, or become mentally ill. At night several could be heard screaming abuses or wailing uncontrollably until they were silenced by the prison-keepers. Surely he would go mad here.

Something flashed across his mind at the thought of escape. The previous afternoon, just before closing the library, he had found a book that mentioned the word Thugs in several places. The cover as well as several pages had been eaten up. He had kept it aside for reading.

It was late in the afternoon when he entered the library. He rummaged for the book and found it by the window just as he had left it. A quick look through the dog-eared Appendix section and other loose articles kept inside the book revealed the title as *The Rambles and Recollections of an Indian Official* by Major General W. H. Sleeman, KCB. The book had been published in 1844 by J. Hatchard and Son of London's Piccadilly!

So perhaps there was a Silly-man? The white dog! The cruel Englishman!

Was this the same Silly-man who had 'murdered' the Thugs? He brushed aside the cobwebs from the bloated pages against his pajamas till they were legible and began to read. To his enormous surprise Jugnu's tale was not wrong—it was only the perspective that was different.

It was an autobiographical chronicle of a famous English administrator, a former Deputy Commissioner of Jabalpur who had become the Assistant to the Governor-General's Agent for Saugor and Nerbudda territories. There was indeed an anecdotal account of how he eliminated the criminal cult of Thugee in a chapter titled: Thugs and Poisoners.

Between 1826 and 1835, about 1,562 Thugs were caught and tried for the crime of Thuggee. Of whom 1,404 were hanged. Jugnu had correctly mentioned that his forefathers had been hanged from mango and neem trees between Jabalpur and Katni. It meant that Thugs had been hanged like a puppets on a chain, every fifty yards, eyeball-to-eyeball from one another!

It also meant that Jugnu and Khandar, and several others

who were in jail along with them, were indeed the descendants of the legendary Thugs. Over successive generations, they had not been able to overcome the epochal trauma of that personal holocaust, and now hoped to be able to redeem their honor with the help of Narad and his party. Unwittingly, he too had abetted in Sleeman-bashing!

In the midst of Sleeman's rambles was a description of how people sought to propitiate Shiva and seek liberation from mortal life—'throws himself from a perpendicular height of four or five hundred feet, and is dashed to pieces upon the rocks below…'

Was this his path to redemption? He reached for the *Imperial Gazetteer* for Jabalpore in a stack of old leather-bound books titled *Gazeteers* dated 1918. Bheraghat, close to Jabalpur, was known for its shining cliffs of marble rising to a height of four to five hundred feet on both sides, and forming a deep and narrow gorge with the river Narmada flowing in between with a mini-Niagara kind of waterfall at one end. In this beautiful tourist spot was a high point called Bandarkoodini (the monkey jump) from where this form of suicide called Bhrigupat was indulged in to appease the God of Destruction. Thousands of young people perished in this fashion—giving up their lives for the sake of a better one in their next birth. Ram thought of 9/11 and WTC and drew the parallel in his mind with the suicide bombers who were possibly promised a hundred vestal virgins and a life of abundance in Zannat, Paradise.

Ram wanted far less—a return to his earlier normal life. Or at least an end to this misery.

He looked around the prison—was there a place from where he could seek liberation from the mess his life was in. Or should he persevere and just hold on? It was a now or never situation. Suddenly everything seemed to be peaceful and nobody appeared to be taking notice of him.

The shadows had lengthened and a there was silence all around.

He spotted a staircase to the roof which had been sealed with loosely plastered bricks. He could easily knock off some of the bricks and barge through. But it would have to be done suddenly without alerting the guards. He held his breath and tiptoed stealthily towards the staircase. Nobody seemed to be watching. The brick partition needed just one hefty push and it would succumb. Just then the thought crossed his mind. Should he surrender so soon? He had yet to crack the biggest mystery of his life.

A whistle blast! Like a gunshot, it rang out deafeningly.

'Stop you bastard! Stop!'

One of the prison guards leapt towards Ram, swinging his cane, shouting menacingly. Ram froze.

'I was testing my heartbeat. The other day the jail doctor said it was too slow.'

The guard swung his cane at Ram's head. It knocked him off like the loose bricks. He fell to the ground, stunned.

Ram woke with a sore lump on his head. He held his head by placing Sherry's handkerchief over it, wondering about Jugnu and Phukat. How could they have such a devil-may-care attitude, considering they were in prison?

Jugnu and Phukat came rushing to him after the exercise session and pointing to Ram's left arm, promptly burst into laughter. Ram looked too. He was shocked to see that a tattoo had been inscribed on his forearm, similar to the noose tattoed on Jugnu and the others of his clan. Who was responsible for it? Was it Jugnu or was it one of his friends as he lay sedated after the futile suicide bid. They seem to have succeeded in marking him for their own.

'Ram Sir, what happened? These bastards are heartless. They are all descendants of Silly-man. They could have killed you.'

'No, Jugnu it is my fault,' said Ram, unwilling to share his momentary lapse of sanity with Jugnu in the presence of the others. 'I was bored. I simply wanted to climb the roof to look around,' Ram said.

'You should have told me, I would have arranged for it. Do you know they could have killed you? You seem to be giving up hope too soon. That is not like a man!'

'I know, I should have thought it through. Perhaps I was being over-adventurous,' said Ram.

'I would have killed that guard if anything had happened to you.'

'Kill…kill?' Ram repeated unbelievingly, amazed at the ease with which Jugnu could say those words.

'Killing is in our blood.'

'Killing leads to more killing… Why kill?'

'It is the process of life. Somebody has to do the cleaning!'

'I saw you clean that poor rat.'

'The English are the first ones who recognized our talent,' said Jugnu. 'They must have observed the absence of rats around our villages. One day a rat sprang out and tickled the Burra Sahib's Memsahib who was in the bath. She ran out stark naked whilst the men were playing bridge. It was after this incident, at their behest, that we designed the first mousetrap.'

'But today the Pardhis catch bigger mice!' Narad chipped in. He stroked his salt and pepper beard sardonically.

'We were encouraged to graduate to bigger animals as the English grew bolder and shikar grew from fashion to obsession. They encouraged us to devise bigger traps,' Jugnu said.

'The English exploited them!' Narad exclaimed. 'Often the animals would free themselves, sustaining grave injuries in the process, incapable of hunting prey. Consequentially, they would become man-eaters, giving the English hunters the moral justification for shikar of man-eating tigers and leopards.'

'Jim Corbett...James Wilson...Kenneth Anderson...all of them hunted to protect the lives of hapless villagers,' Ram said.

'That is a carefully nurtured myth,' said Narad. 'Most Englishmen were simply looking for an excuse to go out hunting.'

Ram nodded thoughtfully. Only the other day, he had read E.P. Stebbing's: *The Diary of a Sportsman Naturalist in India*, in which the author described shikar in India in the winters as a foretaste of paradise.

'But, why make so much out of shikar?' Jugnu intervened. 'You Naxalites also do shikar... In fact, you all do shikar of human beings!' Jugnu threw away the bidi he was smoking, looking contemptuously at Narad who looked flustered for once.

'We kill for social equality,' Narad bounced back. 'You people kill for money! We don't delete nature, we delete inequality!'

'At the end of the day, blood is blood!' Jugnu retorted.

Ram noticed that Narad was livid. Was it because Jugnu had never answered him back before? Narad suddenly strode across the yard and shouted angrily at Jugnu, 'Your bloody bag stinks!' He lunged and yanked at the jute bag which Jugnu held closely and recoiled with horror as a leopard skin sprang out. A hideous smell filled the air immediately. The skin was fresh. It had not been treated as yet.

Jugnu snatched it back hurriedly and pleaded, 'Narad Bhai, please have pity on me. It belongs to Jailor Sahib's cousin who wants me to treat it and fill up the bullet hole. It came from the Kaimur hills near Bandhavgarh. I have to find a buyer for it too.'

'I am really impressed Jugnu, that you maintain such cordial relations with the Jail Superintendent,' Ram said.

'Ha! Ha!' Jugnu burst out laughing and then turned to Ram. 'I have to for many reasons. Actually he is a friend of God.'

'God?'

'My God is Goa Sahib.'

'Goa!' Ram thought of the tourist resort and retorted, 'Goa, my friend, is a place in western India, full of the best beaches, beer, where sexy women tan themselves naked on the white sun and sand.'

'No, no, Sir. Goenka Sahib. My Sweet Lord Feroze Goenka. He can buy places like Goa.'

'He is the greatest!' echoed Khandar with equal fervor, raising his hands in the air in support.

'Be careful…Goa Sahib is reputed for throwing you out like a used condom. He is the one who wanted Burree Maada!' It was a voice of dissension; a relatively more literate voice.

Unfortunately, he had spoken too loudly. All turned around as Jugnu's bloodshot eyes sought out the rebel. It was Phukat, the young boy whom Ram had patronized and introduced to the jail library. Jugnu charged at him, slapping him hard, again and again.

'You donkey! You bastard!' It was Jugnu's turn to be wild. 'You are a blot on our clan. How can you say that about our God? After all he has done for us?' Jugnu raised his hands again to hit Phukat. Ram shielded him.

'I was only joking,' Phukat clarified, suddenly frightened.

'This is the third time you have transgressed,' shouted Jugnu, whipping out his miniature pickaxe and yellow ruhmal. 'Ungrateful bastard!' He finally withdrew miniature as Ram, Khandar and Narad intervened.

Phukat touched Jugnu's feet and apologized profusely after which they embraced each other and laughed, as if nothing had transpired.

'I feel sorry for Jugnu and his Pardhis,' commented Ram to Narad one day as they crossed each other short of the library. 'They are such simple folk.'

'We should,' said Narad. 'They have suffered injustice over the ages. The Pardhis were notified as criminal by the British in the Criminal Tribes Act of 1871, in the post-Thuggee era. Just being born into one of those tribes made one a criminal and nobody cared to civilize them. My friend, crime may be committed with hands, but it is conceived in the minds of capitalists, of politicians and the police...they are the ones who have made permanent criminals and poachers out of Pardhis.'

Ram reflected about Jugnu and the Pardhis and the safety-cordon they had formed to protect him as he entered the library. They were thugs at best by descent. What an earthy sense of humour and helpfulness they had. And they were never ruffled, except for that one time when Jugnu went for Phukat. But it was a spontaneous reaction; he had cooled down almost immediately and all animosity had dissolved.

He spotted a large heap of books arranged in a lattice formation, piled up like a pyramid. Some books seemed to have dislodged from the top of the heap onto the face of a person who looked as if he had nodded off while reading. Whoever it was obviously had a great fondness for books and for arranging them in a neat pile to be so submerged in an ocean of literature.

But there was something odd. There was no sound of snoring—common with most prisoners, and the chest seemed to be still.

Heart pounding, he jumped up and pushed away the books and nudged the person. It was Phukat. There was no movement. His head rolled loosely, lifeless!

There was no mark of a fierce fight or major injury. Was it a case of depression and suicide—but there was no rope, no gun visible. Had he been stabbed?

And then, as he turned the body again, he spotted the thin crimson line around the neck. The haunting opacity of the eyes confirmed that Phukat had been strangled to death. His body had been dragged to the library and buried deliberately under a pile of historic *Gazetteers*. History seemed to be written afresh. What was the secret message for him?

🐾

Ram had just about reconciled to life in jail when Phukat's murder shook him out of his complacence. This could well be his fate. Perhaps he ought to flatter the Pardhis from time to time.

'Jugnu, I am impressed that you can speak English,' said Ram appreciatively to Jugnu. 'You have even travelled abroad—hadn't you just come from some foreign country when we were picked up by the police?' Ram recollected that Jugnu had been carrying various kinds of foreign currency.

'Yes,' replied Jugnu, beaming. 'Indo-Asia was fun—I was on a mission. This was before the Burree Maada project.'

'What was that?'

'I was asked to kill a tiger and remove each and every bit of its flesh and blood from the site. The Indo-Asian Police still don't know where the tiger has gone. I was given three hundred dollars as reward money which I had in my purse. My father Chirag got another three hundred dollars. I was to go to Burma next, but all this happened.' He looked like a child who had been robbed off his favourite toy.

'That explains why you are a rich man,' said Ram. 'But you must have needed a visa and passport? How do you manage to do all that?'

'All arranged for me by Goa Sahib, otherwise I could not have visited so many countries,' Said Jugnu wistfully.

'I am curious about your Goa Sahib. What does he actually do?' Ram asked.

'Feroze Goenka Sahib has interests everywhere…the old gun

shop, the resorts and the mining business. He lives in Katni from where they started out and in Kolkata where they had a leather industry long ago in Chinatown. Herbal exports and imports are another area of interest. On all Indian matters, his word is final.'

'And how do you know Goa Sahib?' Ram asked.

'I am his little baby,' said Jugnu coyly. 'He entrusts me with all wildlife related tasks.'

'Yes, you are very capable. But how did you get to know a big man like him, considering you spent your life in the forests.'

Jugnu sat down and cleared his throat, warming to begin his tale, 'Many years ago, just before sunset one day in winter, a big olive-green Jonga roared into our village, on the fringe of the Kanha National Park. The elders ran for cover thinking that the Forest Sahibs had come to arrest them for killing prohibited animals. Our mothers cowered behind trees and concealed us. But when no Forest Sahibs emerged, we children ran to the Jonga. A very fair Angrez Sahib, dressed in a khaki safari suit and dark goggles stepped down. He looked very handsome, like a film actor. He was accompanied by three woman friends…they were so tall and beautiful. It was the first time that I saw a woman wearing pants and goggles like a man. Later I learnt they were film actresses from Mumbai… The stranger looked very nervous. He pulled my father Chirag aside and spoke urgently to him. Chirag ran with him to the Jonga and they pulled out a sambhar carcass and some guns and hid them in the leafy pit we used to store our kill. Chirag advised Angrez Sahib to drive away in the direction of Mukki.

'Angrez Sahib was being chased by a Forest Sahib who was strictly against shikar. Another cloud of dust announced Forest Sahib who arrived with a posse of guards with lathis, all looking very fierce. Forest Sahib asked Chirag if a hunter had passed by, which Chirag denied and sent them on a wild goose chase towards Kisli. A little while after the Forest Sahibs left Angrez Sahib returned.

He looked very relaxed now and paid Chirag a lot of money and asked for a bonfire to be lit and the sambhar to be cooked.

'The women accompanying Angrez Sahib had something I had never seen before—a camera. They gave us toffees and chocolates and dressed us up with flowers, beads and feathers and took our photographs. After their dinner, against the light of the camp bonfire and the Jonga searchlights, Angrez Sahib and the beautiful women pulled all the children around them in a semi-circle. They asked us to write our names on a slate with chalk. For every alphabet that was correctly written they would give us a toffee. I was small, while my brothers were big and tall. But I was the only one who could write my name correctly. They asked me to sing Baa-Ba-Black-Sheep along with them. I did that correctly. They were so pleased that they announced a stipend to be given every month to encourage me to study.'

'Oh! So that's why you are so well read,' said Ram.

'But my father Chirag was against education...he felt that it was against the tradition of the Pardhis. My family would go hungry if I did not participate in the family occupation of killing animals.'

'Your own father pulled you out from studies?'

'Well, he tried his best,' Jugnu said. 'But guess who that Angrez Sahib was?'

'You tell me...'

'Feroze Goenka...Goa Sahib.'

'I guessed so...'

'Yes... My God. Goa Sahib tried to reason with Chirag who kept saying that a Pardhi who went to school was disrespectful to Bhawanee and no longer a true Pardhi. But Goa Sahib insisted that for every day I attended school, he would give money to my father. That's how I studied upto the eighth standard. In the holidays, Goa Sahib used to summon me to Katni and hired a special tutor who taught me English, General Knowledge and Geography. He even took me with him to Nepal. Now you understand why he is God for me?'

'Indeed,' Ram said thoughtfully. He had to try and get Jugnu to introduce him to this great fellow Goenka. Perhaps his path to release and to a few beautiful women lay that way. He held Jugnu's shoulders and looked at him earnestly before asking, 'Jugnu can you introduce me to this great Goa Sahib?'

Jugnu was silent initially. But when Ram continued to plead, he smiled affectionately. 'Ram Sir, you are my friend too,' said Jugnu. 'There is something special about you. I will surely introduce you to Goa Sahib. He will be keen to meet you. You will be an instant hit with him. He is the only one who can get you out of jail and convert your nightmare into a dream...he is your miracle man.'

'But Jugnu,' said Ram. 'There is one problem. I have no knowledge of mining, wildlife or guns.'

'Don't worry! Goa Sahib will assess you in one glance,' said Jugnu. 'Such is his greatness.'

'Really?' asked Ram. 'I am looking forward to meeting him. I certainly don't want to stay in this wretched jail all my life.'

'Sir, you have wasted precious time,' said Jugnu, admonishingly. 'By now, a man with your global exposure should have become the owner of a resort or a tiger park, instead of rotting in a jail like this. But never mind, Goa Sahib is coming tomorrow.'

'Jugnu, great man, tell me about your trip to Indonesia...oops, Indo-Asia,' said Ram.

'Sure,' said Jugnu, lighting up a Marlboro, ever ready to reminisce, 'I'll tell you about my expedition to Sumatra in Indo-Asia.' Ram listened attentively, his spine tingling with excitement.

The excitement was palpable that particular day, in Jugnu's tribal village of Supkhar on the lower fringe of the Kanha Tiger Reserve and National Park. This was where the thick forest of sal dried down to its thinnest. The earth was manually tilled and sown with lesser crops, the low-yielding millets—kodon and kutki, the coarser grains that scarcely needed water and nutrients to grow. But this mysterious mantle of the forest also provided sustenance to their chief rivals—the wild animals. Thus the battle of extirpation between the farmer of the forest and the fang of the forest continued unabated.

With a skin as thick as vulcanized rubber, Chirag wore a bright red turban and sat on a sisal charpoy, under the shade of an ageing tamarind tree. Jugnu and the other young men and women of his tribe had gathered around a huge karma tree that stood like an obelisk on the ground. The little children, a motley mixture of healthy and deformed, their skins lurid with rashes and palsy patches, were all playing around happily. They ran in circles playing hide and seek or seven tiles with pebbles, oblivious to the reason for excitement, but ecstatic that there was going to be special food today and enough to go around. A cool breeze blew down from the hills, bringing with it the sweet smell of ripe flowers, bursting with colour and essence. It was a lazy, happy afternoon.

A group of elderly women watched the celebrations from a distance, busy with the preparation of the feast. There was wild boar meat—succulent chunks pressed down in large clay containers. Local forest produce, berries of chironji and ber, the seeds of sal, the beans of the Bauhinia creeper and a kind of wild arrowroot and wild yam were also dug out of the earth and mixed with pungent smaller prey—squirrels, birds, snakes and field rats, caught by the Pardhi children and pickled by the expert mothers.

Chirag summoned Jugnu.

There was complete silence as Jugnu walked up to the raised area where Chirag was sitting and bent down to his father. Chirag lifted him and draped a red gamcha around his neck, and announced, 'Jugnu has done the Pardhi tradition proud. This is his second big success in just a few weeks. I congratulate him. May our Goddess Bhawanee continue to bestow divine powers upon him!'

Everybody clapped for Jugnu who looked embarrassed as he glanced sideways at his pretty wife. She was a petite girl who stood discreetly, dressed in a short green-coloured cotton sari without a blouse. She held their boy, a naked child with tousled hair, who suckled her firm, well formed breasts, as his tiny hands rested on them. She smiled with pride.

'Like me, may you have many able sons, and may your fame remain eternal.' An Emperor was anointing his successor.

'And may Bhawanee help my sons to go to school and be educated,' Jugnu said forcefully with a hint of arrogant defiance so that everybody could hear him.

There was a loud snort of disapproval from Chirag while the women fell silent, hiding their gasps in their clothes. Jugnu's dream was to educate his son and send him to college so that his son would not have to follow the Pardhi tradition. Perhaps his son could become a Laat Sahib—the Sahib who bore the lathi, the mace of authority, carried by the Forest Guard, who could smash his house and send the entire village scurrying for cover. Then he, Jugnu, would sit here like Chirag and talk about the usefulness of padhai and direct that all his fellow Pardhis should send their children to school. Perhaps they could finally break free from the curse of Bhawanee.

He recalled how difficult it had been to execute the special assignment that required his services abroad, across Saat Samundra—the fabled Seven Oceans, in another world. Though he had been unsure, Chirag was firm, 'Once a supari contract is executed with advance payment, it is against Pardhi tradition to refuse a task involving animals.'

🐾

'Juggernaut Partie is your new name for your passport,' Goa Sahib's travel officer had said, cautioning him, 'Do not lose your passport, and do not forget your new name. You will not allow yourself to be caught, and you will never reveal who sent you here.'

Jugnu was guided at every step. He was issued a black Reebok rucksack, a bag of dried fruits, and a plane ticket and picked up from his hotel in Paharganj to be ferried to the airport. His escort was responsible for checking him onto a flight to Sumatra, a city in the 'Indo-Asia'. Jugnu loved plane journeys, whiskey and Marlboro cigarettes in that order. 'You will fly to Jakarta, and then board a bus that will take twenty hours to the city of Jhambi, in North Sumatra,' he had been instructed.

He put on a brave face and desisted from asking questions about the task—it was not expected of a Pardhi to ask questions. He was a born specialist, an expert who had centuries of tradition to uphold. He was simply informed that he would be busy for the next few weeks.

In Sumatra, he was lodged in a small house near the Taman Rimba Jhambi Zoo. He was shown Candi Muara, an ancient Buddhist temple and the other local tourist spots by a local resident, Idris, an Anak-Suku Dalam tribal, now a convert to Islam, who was attached to him as an escort. Idris, an athletic lad with a goatee beard, was very much like Jugnu, loving his Ray Ban sports glasses and tight fitting Levi's jeans and Wrangler tee-shirts.

Jugnu was asked to buy a ticket and visit the zoo everyday till he had understood and memorized its topography and identified all shortcomings in the security system by noting the movements of the beat guards. He soon mastered places to hide and routes for escape in the one hundred and twenty five acre zoo. There were enormous groves of tropical meranti, damar and banyan, interspersed with the fruity and strong-smelling durian and the prickly rambutan and the juicy mango and the leafy banana. Very soon, even in the dark, Jugnu could spot a tree and figure out blindly exactly where he was within the zoo.

On the eighth day, just before the operation, Idris burst in excitedly.

'Boss is coming.'

The Boss turned out to be a local from the South Sumatra capital of Palembang. No one seemed to know his real name. Only that he was an enormously good pay master. He was taller and smarter than the white Sahibs who sometimes visited Kanha. Even though his face was concealed by anti-sun paint, and he wore fancy sun glasses, he looked formidable. Dressed in khaki breeches and a white polo shirt with a khaki hat, he had the imperious curtness of the Forest Sahibs of Kanha.

The Boss beckoned to them, and rested one arm on Jugnu's shoulders. He had a deep voice that could cast a spell on anybody.

'Jugnu and Idris,' he said, his eyes resting on Jugnu, discounting any reservation or anxiety, 'The appointed day is near. The assignment is at hand. Rita, a Sumatran tiger inside the zoo has to be smuggled out in full. Every part is urgently needed. I know you can do it.'

Jugnu looked at the Boss, hypnotized by him. 'Yes,' he mumbled automatically. There was something odd about the Boss; how did he know that Juggernaut was actually Jugnu? How did he pronounce an Indian name so correctly? But there was no time to ask.

Jugnu had been inside a zoo several times, but this promised to be the real challenge of his life. The methodology of the act was explained to him and Jugnu did not take more than a few moments to master the plan. Only that this was not the jungle.

Here they could not work in the day. The zoo housed about two thousand animals of more than a hundred species and was very popular amongst children. Approximately five thousand people visited the Taman Rimba Zoo every day. So they would have to do the job late in the night.

The Boss took out two thick wads of Indonesian rupiah and handed one to both of them. Jugnu looked at the notes excitedly; he loved collecting foreign currency notes. As the Boss vanished, Jugnu stuffed a few notes into his wallet and kept them safely alongside the dollar bills, wondering if the meeting had been a dream.

Jugnu and Idris stood outside the zoo that evening, smoking cigarettes and chatting, waiting patiently for the visitors to leave. They were joined by another local whom Idris introduced as Samba. He had a batik-printed bag around his shoulders with a digital video camera and an IR lamp system in it because the Boss wanted to film the incident minutely. Jugnu asked no further questions since it had the approval of the Boss.

It was a normal day. They had concealed their bags in a thick clump of acacia bushes near the point where they planned to scale the zoo wall. As he pulled himself up Jugnu looked around. He saw a little spider-hunter sucking nectar from a wild banana flower. A proboscis monkey was scratching itself in the trees. Nearby was a beautiful rafflesia emitting an odour from it like that of a decomposing dead rat. As Jugnu stuffed his nose in his handkerchief, Idris said, 'Juggernaut, this is actually a sign of good luck. We call this the bunga bangkai, the corpse plant. Now we will be definitely successful in our mission.'

A mild drizzle began to play spoilsport, but thankfully ceased soon and darkness fell bringing a nip in the air and the muffled glow from an old-fashioned sodium vapour lamp. They kept their entry point close to the tiger enclosure, ensuring that the CCTV cameras were dead as they had been informed. The vaulting over the wall had been easy, and within moments Jugnu, Idris and the local help Samba landed on the soft carpet grass inside the zoo, diagonally opposite the cage, but a safe five hundred meters from the zoo-keeper's office.

There were dim lights in the keeper's office. The subdued sound of popular discotheque music floated across the air. Rules were strictly enforced to switch off most lights at night, so that the animals were not disturbed in their activities by anthropogenic influence. The trio knew that the keeper did not take rounds. After the zoo closed for the day, he just had to give the last feed to the animals at 6 p.m. But this evening, while the keeper's old car stood inside the zoo compound, a pink-coloured scooter with flowers painted on it rested outside the gate. This meant the keeper had a guest. Perhaps, they were playing cards and drinking beer.

The three young men moved with caution, carrying empty Jumbo bags. These strong bags, each capable of carrying a hundred kilograms of weight, were made of unbreakable technical textile, called flexible intermediate bulk containers, or FIBC. They were used for export of fertilizer and other sensitive chemicals. All of them had strung empty Jumbos to their bodies, along with assorted knives strung as a belt beneath their loose batik shirts.

They approached the tiger cage where Rita was housed. A shallow moat surrounded it except for a narrow connecting bridge. Next to the moat was a dry gutter. Artificial rocks with creepers and ferns had been built around the cage, to create an authentic jungle appearance. It had a wall that was about five meters high on three sides and an iron fence on the fourth. The floor of the cage was shaped like a bowl, sloping inwards like a grotto, so that the tiger had the natural feel of a cave, but could not leap out and alarm or hurt visitors as had happened in a zoo in California in the USA. Rita, the only Sumatran tiger at Jhambi Zoo, had been brought in from the wild and was a part of a conservation program run by the Zoological Society of London to save the Sumatran tiger, a subspecies deemed critically endangered. She was also a centerpiece for Jhambi Zoo to teach visitors about conservation.

They could see that Rita was awake and strolling inside the enclosure, as she had done in the past months since she had been brought from the forests of Borneo. They had taken care to start their operation only after the keeper had fed the cat, so that they would remain undisturbed for the next hour. As Rita turned towards them Idris said, 'A few days ago, my brother Irfan had gone with a group of tree fellers to cut trees in the night in the forests of Sungai Gelam. They were almost through, when their truck was stuck in the marshy soil. Suddenly a tiger attacked my brother. He was badly mauled and died. My mother has not stopped crying since then. Time to settle scores!'

'Food,' said Jugnu.

Idris opened the bag containing the cow meat. 'It is already mixed with Trilafon, a concentrated tranquillizer,' he said. Rita's next feed was only at 6 a.m. the next morning. They were wearing thick rubber gloves that made them immune to the electric current that could be flowing through the iron fence. Yet they had to be careful. After all, there had been an instance where an animal had reached through the bars of the cage and grabbed a zookeeper, biting his hands, causing deep lacerations. They could ill-afford such a situation.

A powerful smell of the animal dominated as it prowled irritatedly in the caged precincts. Idris slipped the large chunks of meat into the cage, beating the ground to attract Rita's attention. Rita stood silently, sniffing the raw meat, before it moved the meat into a corner with its paws, as if it did not matter. A moment later, it began circling and then tearing into the meat, quickly devouring it. Within a few minutes of eating the meat, it began pacing the cage. A restless whimper followed and Rita made one valiant effort to hold on, her body shaking. The next moment she collapsed with a thud.

They wiped the sweat from their faces and looked around furtively. In the distance, the keeper's office lights were out now. Was he doing the rounds? The music seemed to have stopped too; and they hadn't noticed. Would they be caught?

'Samba run up and see if the keeper is coming this way,' whispered Jugnu, as he and Idris hid in the gutter.

Samba came back speedily, 'Relax. He is also an animal.'

'Animal?'

'Naked like a dog…humping a bitch.'

So the rider on the scooter was probably a woman friend whom the keeper had invited for a cozy evening. It meant that they were especially lucky; he would soon be fast asleep.

They slipped the key into the lock and opened the bolt with a jarring sound and tip-toed into the cage. Rita was lying unconscious on the ground. They tied a lasso around her neck with a thick plastic rope of the kind used for pulling containers in a shipyard, and dragged her slowly, one of them pulling from the front and the other lifting the body to ensure it did not get stuck. The most difficult part was the negotiation past the steel foot-bridge and across the moat, ensuring she did not fall into it. Finally, with one massive heave and thrust they pulled and pushed the carcass till it landed into the stony portion of the open gutter. Idris went back and locked the cage.

Jugnu opened a canvas bag and took out his equipment. Before he set to work, they pulled the noose around Rita in both directions with all their strength, expelling out the oxygen. The Sumatran tiger, Rita, sputtered silently and was dead.

He extracted a large, sharp knife from the bag, almost like a saw. Together with Idris he turned over the body of the tigress till the white-striped lower body was clearly visible in the light from the neighboring lamppost. With one expert stroke, blended with the searing lust of a kill, he jabbed deep at the bottom and slit the ventral hide slowly and carefully and carved out a long slot, about two feet long. It was a difficult task and even his years of expertise were not good enough given the circumstances. But the slit was neat and straight. He took care not to let the knife poke or slash the topskin anywhere. He knew the skin had to be intact and unblemished to make a wonderful pelt.

'Hold this,' Jugnu said to Idris, asking him to straighten out a translucent bag and to hold it at a particular angle. Jugnu needed to drain the fountain of blood into the bag that Idris was carrying. He had been told, much to his surprise, and contrary to whatever he had seen, that even the blood was precious and 'not a drop was to be lost'.

'Eek Sampah.' Idris had a distasteful look on his face, and suddenly spat out—unfortunately the phlegm landed on Jugnu.

Jugnu froze. He dug his hands into his pocket and took out a yellow handkerchief and unfolded it; one end had a coin embedded into it. He took out the miniature steel replica of the pickaxe from his pocket and touched it to his forehead and closed his eyes in silent and respectful prayer.

'What is that?' asked Idris, baffled.

'Paying respects to Bhawanee, my Goddess!' Jugnu whispered, 'That is the tooth of Kali and this is the peela ruhmal, the hem of the Goddess's apparel, once my Thug ancestors' most important tool to deal with the enemy!' He gnashed his teeth and pulled himself close to Idris who seemed hypnotized. In one swift move, he lunged with the yellow-scarf for Idris's neck, the side with the coin beneath his left thumb, holding the right-end in his right hand.

Idris trembled and jumped back instinctively, screaming at the sight of the garrote and fell into the moat. Jugnu watched him amusedly as he tried to pull himself out, shocked beyond belief. Idris finally managed to pull himself out and perched disbelievingly at the edge of the moat.

Jugnu looked up at the moon peeping through the clouds, lit a cigarette and laughed.

'Hurry,' said Samba.

It took about twenty minutes to do the two most important things—clear the skin from the flesh of the tiger and remove the intestines from the mass of flesh. Jugnu was using two different kinds of knives, one a long blade to make the deep cuts, the other a stouter one, to shred the flesh from the bones and the skin.

'You do that with perfect ease and precision.'

'It is experience acquired over a dozen years and over a hundred kills.'

The skin, cleared of the meat, was then stuffed into one of the FIBC bags and the flesh into another along with the carefully protected fangs and claws. The third bag contained the tiger's blood. While Jugnu dirtied his hands, Samba had been discreetly shooting a full length film with his video-camera.

Samba, a meat-eater and a devout Muslim, had witnessed the ceremonial slaying of many lambs. He never realized that the chanting of prayers and the rituals attached helped to camouflage the brutality. Now there were splotches of blood all over his clothes and the tiger's fur had rubbed off on them like they were inside a factory for stuffed toys. Rita's flesh was loose and sticky like jelly, and he was horrified to see Jugnu scoop it in his hands as if it were water. Already there was an overwhelming stench from the dirty gutter. The blood-spattered knives and the bagful of gore were a horrifying sight and made him long to retch.

Jugnu pulled out the long and sinuous intestines with aplomb, brandished them in the air with the flourish of a snake charmer holding a python around his arms before he swung himself like a discus thrower and chucked them into the gutter. There was a splash, but a thick and gooey mess landed smack on Idris's face, smothering him in gore. He fell back into the drain.

Jugnu laughed hysterically along with Samba. The sound of their laughter reverberated eerily in the deafening silence of the night inside the Jhambi zoo.

'Bajingan Juggernaut! Ngentot lu,' Idris screamed.

The Jail Superintendent welcomed Ram into his room with a courtesy previously unseen. It was like being ushered into the Principal's office in the company of your parents, but in a unique situation – say if they were on the Board of Directors of the Trust that governed the school. And his school friends, Jugnu and Khandar and the others watched enviously from a distance. The Superintendent no longer addressed him as Qaidi Number 2699, but politely as 'Mr Ram.' Tea was served along with glucose biscuits.

Feroze Goenka stood up gracefully and held Ram's hands firmly in his own thick hands. He was dressed in a white suit and a pink shirt without a tie. He wore a beatific smile as he said, 'I am delighted to meet you Ramachandra Prasad Sahib. I was very sorry to learn about all that has happened to you. Law is meant to be fair, not unfair.'

'Likewise, I have heard a lot of good things about you from Jugnu. He respects, no, he loves you. He thinks you are God.'

Goenka beamed proudly. 'It is divine ordinance that I was able to rescue a prodigy. Jugnu was a poor and hungry baby when I took him under my wing, Today I feel proud that he is daring, loyal and intelligent. Tigers too can be trained.'

'Jugnu said you might need some help in your huge business.

Perhaps I can be of use to you,' Ram whispered. He had to sell himself effectively.

'My expanding business requires diversity of backgrounds... and fresh minds and inputs,' Goenka said crisply.

'Yes, I have heard of your interests,' Ram said.

'Global business requires global brain power. Wealth without intelligence is like a woman without breasts...' He carved out a profile of a well-endowed woman with his hands and let his lips pout. His wicked wink made Ram smile.

'Grave injustice has been done to me.'

Goenka interrupted Ram, 'I am familiar with your case. A tigress vanished and you were accused of killing it. Nobody knows how she was killed...or what happened to her. Wildlife Protection Act matters take years to settle.' He continued, 'Your American firm is in trouble...I sympathize with you.'

'I have heard you are like God. Surely you can speak to the government authorities and get me bail. This place is hell.'

'Government authorities can only give false hopes but cannot help,' Goenka said, before adding with a twinkle, 'I can help you... but what do I get in return?'

'The day my matters are settled, I will repay your gratitude and all legal expenses you may incur on my behalf,' Ram said.

Goenka laughed. 'I have enough money. I seek intangibles—loyalty, consistency, commitment. Performance is contextual.'

Ram wondered if he was crossing the limit. 'Loyalty is one thing I have in abundance,' Ram said boldly. 'It runs in my blood. I have been with the same company for the last several years.'

'And that company has let you down! But not us! Also, henceforth your problems will be my problems,' Goenka stretched out his hands, and Ram held them carefully, feeling their velvet-like warmth and the power that exuded from them.

'Thank you,' said Ram. 'I would be grateful.'

'We will manage,' said Goenka. Even as Ram gaped he continued, 'For every not-so-clever man there is one clever lawyer, and for every clever lawyer there is one not-so-clever Judge.'

'I will always remain obliged. Just get me out of this hell!' Ram pleaded. 'I can't take this madness any longer.'

'Tomorrow I will discuss your case with our legal team. Sometimes a petty crime requires complex judicial engineering.'

What crime had he committed? But that was a question to which he had not been able to find an answer for many days now. He lowered his head in submission and Goenka put his hand over his head as if he were anointing him.

'I will be in your eternal debt,' Ram promised, 'Unflinching and absolute.'

'God bless,' said Goenka, patting him.

Goenka was debonair, with rich taste in attire. His laughter was reassuring. Ram peered out through the grilled windows. A black Land Rover purred outside. A private security guard in dark sunglasses, with his hands inside his pockets—possibly armed heavily, stood outside observantly. Within moments, Goenka had driven away, leaving behind him a cloud of dust.

'Perhaps Goa Sahib will put you in the China team; perhaps that English bitch will fall at your feet too,' Jugnu said sharing his chillum with Ram, a little jealously.

Ram was thrilled. What was the China team?

'That is the top—the elite corps,' said Jugnu. 'It has offices in Kathmandu and Mandalay. It is the lifeline for WCC.'

'WCC?'

'The Wildlife Cold-Chain,' Jugnu said sharing his chillum with Ram. 'It starts in Jabalpur where consignments are begun to be sorted and dispatched to the Kathmandu or Burma team for Kunming and beyond. We manage the chain upto Katni. But I think you will have a larger canvas...'

Ram looked at the chillum. He was no longer coughing. The effect of the weed was pleasant and numbing; even the jail looked friendly now.

'Thanks for introducing me to your mentor,' said Ram. 'He is a noble man. I hope to be able to live up to his expectations.'

Jugnu was beatific, 'Bhawanee has blessed us too. We will have our own man in Goa Sahib's charmed circle of confidantes.'

'Wait till our government is formed,' said Narad cryptically.

'Hello, Mr Ramachandran?'

'You?'

'Need to pick your head again,' said Sherry apologetically. 'I've made you some cucumber sandwiches and cold coffee...I think you'll like them.'

'How very thoughtful, I'm sure I'll love them,' Ram said, smiling a little but wondering if she would try to ferret out new secrets from him. He too had to use her to crack the Wilson and the missing Van Ingen skin mysteries. 'But how did you get past the Superintendent?'

'My limitless nuisance value,' said Sherry confidently. 'I told him I wanted to do a story on the way dogs are tortured and hanged in this jail, and how undertrials are being murdered in gang wars. He pleaded with me to do anything but that; luckily for me, he takes anything that affects his job seriously.'

Ram nodded understandingly.

'Try them,' she opened a box with neatly wrapped sandwiches. A dollop of cole slaw and a sachet of tomato sauce accompanied them. She passed the plastic tiffin-box to Ram who accepted it with unparalleled joy. But then he hesitated before beginning to eat. Sherry too observed Ram carefully as he ate. He seemed more composed. His lips widened playfully like they were synchronized swimmers, and his eyes were bright. He sparkled as though a new beginning was being made. She smiled in silent appreciation and passed him the flask of coffee.

'You're looking better. Good rest? Good company?'

'Yes,' said Ram, taking a long swig of the coffee. 'The coffee and the sandwiches are like you…just wonderful.'

It was Sherry's turn to smile.

He paused before speaking again, 'Life here is proving to be decent. Thankfully that person arrested along with me has turned out to be protective. He even got his mentor to meet me.'

'Really?' Sherry was certain she knew the people being referred to. 'And who is that?'

'Jugnu Pardhi,' said Ram.

'Hmmm,' Sherry knew about Jugnu Pardhi and his poaching history. He had been in this area when Burree Maada had gone missing. 'Did Jugnu tell you where he got the money from? Not everybody goes around with hundred dollar bills stuffed in their wallets in poor Jabalpur. Even five hundred rupee notes are rare for common folk in this town,' said Sherry.

'I never thought of asking him that,' said Ram, deliberately untruthful. 'But he seems well padded thanks to his mentors… Feroze Goenka and Abhimanyu Singh.'

'The wildlife enthusiasts,' remarked Sherry, sounding equally evasive.

Ram ate voraciously and looked at her with satisfaction. He was happy to see that she was in no hurry and the jail authorities did not seem to be standing over him to time-out the meeting. It intrigued him that this angelic creature was wasting her life on wildlife, when frustrating such endeavour was so commonplace for people like Jugnu. He had an instinctive urge to needle her, see her flustered.

He decided to change tack, 'Sherry, humour me…why are you

so obsessed with the topic of hunting? It has happened through the ages, and will continue in the future too. All the pre-independence English writing I have laid my hands on in the jail library seems to highlight the importance of wildlife hunting as a fun sport in poor, tropical climes.'

Just as he had expected, his remark had the effect of a red flag on a bull. She was provoked; and she looked her prettiest when provoked. Needling her intellect seemed to be the closest he could get to hugging her.

Sherry fumed silently before retorting, 'Wildlife is Game. Big Game.'

Ram closed the sandwich box and handed it back to her. He wiped his hands and drank the last bit of coffee from the flask, allowing that simple pleasure to suffuse his spirit for a while. He resumed the attack, 'Big game is natural to opens and outback.'

Her face turned crimson as she inhaled deeply and then retorted. 'Bernard Shaw had put it aptly—when the tiger attacks man, he calls it an attack, but when man murders a tiger, he calls it sport. Do you know, apart from wolves, tigers are the only other large carnivores that breed faster than their prey? So a tiger can have, in congenial conditions, a new litter every year. And yet you have a situation where they are almost extinct!' Sherry handed a newspaper report to Ram. The heading mentioned wildlife with a picture of hunted animals.

'Wildlife abuse…'

'Gang-rape would be a better description!'

Ram read the report cursorily. It detailed the death of two tiger cubs in Ranthambore Tiger Reserve. 'They could have been attacked by another tiger,' he conjectured.

'No! Read further. The water source nearby was poisoned.'

'Macabre!'

'Macabre business!'

'I think you are stretching it too far,' said Ram irritatedly. 'Hunting is sport. At best macabre sport, okay?'

'Ram, money makes the Mayor go round,' said Sherry. 'Let me turn the question around,' said Sherry. 'Why are urbane guys like Abhimanyu and Goenka into wildlife?'

'Because I think they are naturally fond of the outdoors,' said Ram. 'Why else?' Actually, this was a question that even he had sought an answer to. It would be interesting to have Sherry's take on it, however biased.

'There is a market for endangered species. From the lowly butterfly to the jumbo-sized elephant…'

Her voice dropped theatrically as she brushed her fingers against his.

Her touch was electric; Ram perked up as if it were a magic wand. He thought of the Raja brothers and their Chinese partners. 'Perhaps you are right.'

'Ram, wildlife was business, and will always remain business,' said Sherry. 'The interconnections and stakes are huge. As one who has some English blood, I should hate to admit it. But the fact is that hunting was the underlying incentive for the biggest conquest in the recent history of mankind.'

Ram's brows arched as he looked up quizzically. 'Attila, the Hun? Alexander the Great? Or, was it Genghis Khan?'

Sherry turned to look outside, beyond the prison, before she announced, with a sneer: 'The conquest of India!'

'1498…Da Gama knocked…at India's gate,' Ram recited the rhyme.

'No! The East India Company—the biggest multinational of its time,' Sherry said. 'Why did it come to India?'

'Spices…silks?'

Sherry remained silent.

'Tea…pearls?'

'No! It brought blood thirsty hunters to Indian shores, masquerading as a cohort of traders. Do you really think the gentle fragrance of exotic Indian spices lured them? No! It was the tantalizing thrill of the chase, the romance of a free hunting zone, where the sun would never set on whatever anyone from the British Empire did! Lots of Camparis and Sundowners to drink with perfumed women in laced gowns and fancy hats! Bimbettes, all wide-eyed at these outdoor adventures and dying to be laid by randy hunters! The scent of the game! The ultimate turn-on!'

In the jail library, along with the Sleeman history he had read political reports of the scenario after the revolution of 1857 in the *Imperial Gazetteers*. Immediately after that was suppressed the East India Company got the full imprimatur of the British Empire. 'Game hunting has perhaps had a place in governance...'

'Macho-imperialism! It just emphasized their superiority over the locals. Perhaps that's why you see photographs of British Viceroys and officers standing ramrod erect, with the carcass of the hunted animal at their feet, like they'd had a triple dose of Viagra!'

'Perhaps...'

Sherry's voice had risen sharply. And then, just as suddenly, her voice dropped to a whisper, 'Wars in Europe are not even half the atonement, Ram. Indians would be justified in asking for reparations, but for the fact that their own rulers were no less trigger-happy.'

She looked like a rabid feminist urging a jury that a rapist be publicly castrated. For a moment she looked cold-blooded and murderous, ready to go any length for her cause. He was beginning to feel slightly scared of her. She saw his look and quickly flashed a smile; once again a harmless diva.

Ram fell silent as he remembered reading about the Nawab of Tonk who had shot six hundred tigers. The Maharajas of Sarguja, Udaipur and Gauripur had shot hundred tigers each. Whether it was Bikaner or Jaipur or Rewa, all the major royals had shot a huge number of tigers in their lifetime. Earlier, even the grand Moghuls had been no different.

'I was shocked to read Emperor Jehangir. He has himself chronicled graphically in his Tuzuk-i-Jahangiri about how he, the Guardian of Planet Earth, had protected this planet by hunting more than ten thousand animals in the wild including over eighty tigers,' Ram parroted from memory to make her happy.

Sherry asked, 'And you would have read about Mehru-Nissa or Nur-Jehan, Jehangir's vivacious and voluptuous Empress, the Eternal Light of this World…how do you think she lightened Mother Earth's burdens?'

'How?'

'With shikar, what else! She bagged four tigers in one hunting session alone. Not to lighten Mother Earth, but to retain her slippery foothold in the coveted royal harem…it seemed to be the mandatory test to win the Emperor's favours.'

Ram nodded and said, 'I've also seen some prints of Jehangir's shikar miniatures.'

'Did you know he maintained a full-fledged department for hunting called the Diwan-i-Shikari?' Sherry asked. 'And this continued all through history. An Italian traveler to Shah Jehan's court recorded His Royal Highness's ordinary amusement! Any guess what it was?'

'Finding sexy new concubines to stack his harem?'

'No! Tiger hunting!'

'Killing tigers…like a school kid would read Harry Potter?'

'Or play a Ninja game,' she added, chuckling. 'And let us not overlook the contribution to this noble cause by another native hero! This one from Mysore in South India, where your beloved bosses, the Raja brothers hail,' said Sherry.

'Perumalan?'

'Tipu Sultan, the Raja of Mysore in the second half of the eighteenth century. The only exception was that he excelled in combating tigers bare handed.'

'But guns had come in by then...'

'Right! But he had to demonstrate his masculinity to the English; as if the size of his huge bloody organ...oops, his huge harem, wasn't good enough for that!'

They laughed aloud. Ram was absorbed by Sherry, mesmerized by her intensity. Why did all discussions have to end up around a tiger? He fell on his knees, lowered his voice and whispered, 'I get this creepy feeling there is something sinister about the tiger. The tiger seems to be everywhere.' He recalled his own brush with the cat crossing his path, the silver tiger of Zentigris and the Van Ingen and Van Ingen tiger rug that had landed him in jail. And what of the crouching tiger that had been flagged in his father's premonition. Would he ever get to the bottom of this tiger mystery?

'I agree. The tiger is more than a tragedy...it has to have something tantric about it. Tipu used tiger stripes or babri as decorations for his throne, in the uniform of his soldiers, on his flags and coat-of-arms and coins. Historically some dictatorial African chieftains decorate their thrones with tiger skins.'

'Tibetans too like to adorn their chubas with tiger trims,' said Ram. 'I wonder if there is symbolism to bare handed hunting. I recall seeing a finely carved statue of a tiger mauling an English soldier in the V&A Museum in London,' said Ram.

Sherry laughed. 'The famous Tipu's Tiger! It lets out blood-curdling cries if wound like a toy! Tipu just wanted to chronicle his individual superiority over the English for posterity,' said Sherry. 'The English retaliated promptly with the Seringapatam medal for those who fought in the 1799 Battle of Seringapatam in which they defeated Tipu Sultan. It depicted the British lion overpowering Tipu's tiger.'

Ram laughed. 'Tipu must have been brave! Nobody would think of going into a jungle bare handed, without guns today.'

'We're in the twentieth century,' said Sherry. 'Modern high-velocity hunting rifles have far greater range and accuracy than muzzle-loading muskets which were heavy and cumbersome.'

'Guns would've tipped the balance?'

'Yes, hunting became more comfortable. Like sitting in Wimbledon or Lords, or a concert soiree in the Opera House—you hunted at leisure, sipped your drinks in the cool comfort of machans and elephant-howdahs. George Yule, the Englishman who boasted of having shot four hundred tigers certainly, didn't go out on foot.'

'Bloody hell!'

'The last few decades have been no different. The Chitwan National Park in Nepal witnessed the killing of 125 tigers in just two months in the 1930s. During his visit to Nepal, The Prince of Wales bagged seventeen tigers and nine rhinos amongst other game in just seven days.'

'And Spielberg makes films about the persecution of Jews in Nazi Germany!'

'There was no Schindler. And there is no holocaust museum for tigers!'

'Terrible! What happened to the voice of reason in England?' asked Ram.

'They cleverly invented fiction around hunting,' said Sherry. 'Outdoor sport was better than indulgences like gambling, homosexuality and other indoor forms of debauchery. And at the end of the road was the reward that hunting imparted—chic belts and furs—a glorious tradition, which our distinguished fashion houses have, I daresay, so assiduously upheld till today.'

'Thankfully, with all this Rio and Kyoto things have changed,' said Ram.

'Hardly true at the micro-level! There are money-bags who have Spanish villas with lots of space...you should know; like your erstwhile bosses, the Raja brothers in sun-drenched Frisco.'

'Yes, they are big time collectors,' said Ram.

'What's on display,' said Sherry, 'is not need but sheer acquisitive greed.'

Greed? Or need? Ram laughed. He had walked past an Amsterdam brothel which had posted that profoundly intellectual question on a signboard.

'It is fashionable to acquire something that is rare—call it scarcity fetish,' Sherry continued. 'The tiger and the leopard are the Everest and Kanchenjunga of wildlife—the loftier symbols of a malaise that is cancerous!' Once again Sherry was breathless—her lips pouted, turned pink. She looked straight out of a Marilyn Monroe poster. Ram smiled encouragingly and put his hands on hers, but she gently moved hers away.

'I have never understood why guys go after little butterflies... you find them in every bush anyway,' he said.

'Have you read Saki's story about Mrs Packletide who is obsessed about bagging a tiger? Keeping up with the Joneses! A Palos Verde or a Duke of Burgundy can fetch thousands of dollars in the international market. There are filthy-rich brats and freaky connoisseurs who want to present these things to their girlfriends and mistresses to convey their undying love. Mobile, modern day equivalents of Taj Mahals. Valentine's Day and all that crap!'

'How do these egoistic twits procure them?' asked Ram.

'They are advertised by word of mouth,' said Sherry. 'It's hush-hush. Show me the money!'

Ram felt drained. He wiped the sweat from his forehead. Sherry could go on forever; but for him, it was like going through a launderette with no scope to be squeezed any further. He stared at Sherry, pained by her doggedness. Attracted by the smooth contours of her sculpted arms, he touched them gently, feeling the softness on the inside of her arms, reaching for her elegant elbows and her warm and comforting palms. Her fingers were long and elegant—they had to be prised open. Her unpainted nails were shapely—sheer art form, he thought. As his hands met hers, for a moment he felt she responded affirmatively to his touch and returned his squeeze. He could almost smell her breath and her natural fragrance. Suddenly, he had an overpowering desire to embrace her and kiss her passionately. And then he reflected on her past demeanour and restrained himself. But even that slightest touch had made his entire body tingle with immeasurable delight.

Sherry looked at him understandingly, her eyes widening, as she smiled at him. She asked, 'Ram, will you please do me a favour?'

Her look was more than engaging. It was hypnotic. Ram jumped at the opportunity. 'Is there something I could do for you from here?'

'You can if you want to...'

'Certainly,' replied Ram, more than willing to oblige... anything to satisfy her...anything to win her favour. 'What?' He looked longingly at her, leaving his hands on her, delighting in her indulgence.

'Just find out from Jugnu Pardhi and his mentors,' said Sherry zeroing in for the kill, 'where they have hidden Burree Maada!'

Sherry pulled away from him gently. She gazed at the distant sky and sighed despondently. Ganga and Ram had both, in different ways provoked her to look at her past, and her family's past. She knew that she had all the urges of a normal woman in her late twenties. Her body clock was ticking away at a furious pace; she needed to settle down. She needed somebody with whom she could share her sorrows and joys. But one question wrenched her soul and bothered her time and again. It had left her uncertain about the world, anguished in private. Why was it not possible for her to have a successful and lasting relationship with a man?

🐾

She was still reflecting on herself when the call came from Lalaji, the grocer who supplied daily provisions to the Jabalpur Central Jail, her cultivated source there. He was breathless, 'Madam, that NRI, Ramchandra Prasad, is being released. Everybody knows Feroze Goenka is taking him out.' The news hit her like a sledgehammer.

She drove furiously to the jail and confronted Ram. It was her duty to warn him of the implications of getting close to the Goenkas. In case Ram turned her down, at least her question about the whereabouts of Burree Maada would weigh sufficiently on him to find an answer.

'Ram, why can't you understand that, things are already bad for you? You must understand the implications of what you may be getting into,' she said. 'Jail is actually, given your circumstances, a refuge for you.'

'It is easy for you to say that, Sherry,' said Ram, not quite able to look her in the eye. 'I am a drowning man. Jugnu's Goa Sahib is my only lifeline.' He lowered his head.

'I should have figured this out when Feroze Goenka visited you in jail,' Sherry said.

'I had no idea he would be so helpful.'

'Appearances are deceptive,' Sherry said. 'He is going to use you! I heard he has already made an announcement about your release?'

'It was a tall order considering I have a criminal case against me,' said Ram. 'I had no idea he could change fortunes. He is like God...he can shape destiny.'

'Then I don't think you understand destiny,' Sherry said sardonically.

Ram's mind drifted back to a course he had taken in MIT, 'Frankly, even I don't believe in it! I am convinced that there is only chaos in the universe—a continuum of stochastic processes.'

'It is strange how life can be so complex and unpredictable,' Sherry softened. 'You know just as I was about to leave my home, I saw this report on CNN about this woman from the States. She fought to change her flight at the last minute somewhere in South America when it was being delayed due to technical failure. And guess what? Her flight crashed but the technically defective flight she skipped taking landed safely an hour later. Who can predict what is going to happen the next moment?'

'Where did that happen?' Ram's head swam and his heart throbbed a hundred times faster.

'The plane went missing off the coast of some South American country...Mexico perhaps,' said Sherry. 'The marines are trying to find it. It was the national airline of some small country.'

Ram's face turned ashen. Jaya had gone on this extensive South American tour—to find commonalities in the sun-worship rituals of the ancient Incas, Mayans and Aztecs. He was already in a cage. Surely no more distress could be coming his way!

'The woman in the plane...was there a name?' Ram asked frantically, his body trembling.

'Indian name,' Sherry paused, thinking. 'Same name as my maid's daughter. Let me see...Jaya something. Reputed artist! Heritage photographer and her companion, a Professor.'

'Oh my God!' Ram moaned. 'Jaya is my wife. I had asked her to come with me to India!' He buried his face in his hands.

Sherry stared at Ram, dumbstruck. Perhaps things couldn't get worse for this man. He had lost his father. He had lost his belongings. He was in jail for no evident crime. And to top it all was the shattering news about the loss of his wife. She did not know what to say. The only sane thing to do seemed to be just to leave him alone with his grief. Let him go to Goenka and carve out his own trajectory. She could do nothing else for him.

'I am sure the news is false,' she said, trying to cheer him. 'There could be an error in the report.'

She held Ram's hand to steady him, as his head dropped onto her shoulder. They remained motionless for a long time.

'What kind of destiny is this? I seem to be bearing the cross for somebody else's crime.'

He was distraught. She continued to hold his hands and after some time, gently freed herself and left quietly. He began to cry piteously.

Ram had spent the whole night in tears. But his face lit up the instant he saw Sherry. She had hastened to him; he needed consolation. She only had a personal goal to pursue; he had lost everything. In the ultimate analysis Burree Maada could die. It was yet another tiger death in a subcontinent that had experienced tiger genocide for centuries. She fully expected to see Ram devastated, but was relieved to see him looking normal.

Dressed in a white cotton skirt and shirt she looked very fresh. She removed her sunglasses and smiled encouragingly at him, her natural poise and fragrance balm to Ram's grief.

Sherry had done a double check on the feature about the wildlife photographer and though there was no specific mention of the woman heritage-photographer, it was abundantly clear that all the passengers in the small twenty-seater plane had perished.

'I had no idea that coming to India...going to the Forest Department to deposit my father's skin was a fatal trap,' said Ram. 'I feel so lost...I am totally devastated.'

When it is our turn to decide, we don't realize... 'I wish I could help you, but only you can come to terms with your grief,' Sherry said, mustering the dryness of a clinical surgeon inside an ICU.

'I feel like the Greek hero Theseus, or maybe that is a bad

analogy...like somebody who is participating in a dangerous pre-ordained game, an actor with a pre-written script, let loose by watchers, only to be stalked and hunted down ,' Ram said recalling the DVD he had watched in Abhimanyu's apartment.

Sherry remained silent for a long time before she said, 'Ram, you are lucky! At least you have the intellectual capacity to understand and analyze. Think of the poor animals that are trapped.'

'I wish that I too could have my sense of feeling blocked or dulled,' said Ram. 'Lobotomy...like an animal, I would not feel any pain.'

'When it is our turn to decide, we don't realize that we cause so much pain to animals...we've lost our essence as superior beings.'

'Given a choice I would prefer the life of an animal,' said Ram.

'We human beings also cause each other so much pain. Take the case of this senior Forest Department officer, Gangavardhan Bishnoi—his nickname is Ganga. Superbly committed! Hounded out of Kanha for trying to do his job. He was completely shattered, even though he refused to admit it.'

'I know of Gangavardhan, though we've never met. His Uncle is Guruji, my father's neighbor in Amarkantak. I'm sorry to learn he is being persecuted. Clearly we share a common past.'

'What a coincidence! By the way, anything on Burree Maada?'

'No, I haven't found the right moment to ask,' Ram replied cautiously. He had decided not to pursue the matter with Jugnu, lest it jeopardize his relationship with his potential benefactor Feroze Goenka. But he was surprised at how easily he was opening up to Sherry, even though it was barely a day since he had learnt of Jaya's tragedy. Was it because he was attracted to her? Was it an opportune moment to tell her about his uneasy relationship with Jaya?

'Please keep trying. I am depending on you,' she said.

'Sure, I will keep my eyes and ears open.'

'And let me reiterate...I still cannot imagine you in this

wretched place,' said Sherry.

'I truly appreciate your empathy for my situation,' said Ram. 'Perhaps I should tell you all that happened.'

He narrated his tale and she listened attentively, holding his hands gently, conveying a sense of togetherness, coaxing him to get it out of his system. When he told her about his father's premonition and how it had come true, she was speechless.

'Even those of us who are non-believers because of our western education are being forced to agree that we are all products of our destiny,' she said.

'Products of our destiny! Those were the exact words of Guruji! How do you say that?'

'Some years ago, if I had been told that I would be living in India and that too in Jabalpur, I would have scoffed at the thought—not that I mind Jabalpur. It is a charming place! But that is how I felt then!'

'Why? Where were you headed?' It was Ram's turn to be curious.

'Harvard,' said Sherry. 'I had started on my doctorate.'

'And then?' asked Ram. Here was a fellow traveller, someone who had brought a spark of joy into his life, who had also faced hardship. There was something in common between them. He wanted to give her compassion and receive her love in return. But he needed to get out out of this jail...only then he could solve the pending mysteries and get closer to her.

'Apocalypse!'

'Why?'

'Suddenly, the whole world ripped apart for me!'

'Tell me what happened...if you would like to,' said Ram, haltingly. Here was a kindred spirit. He leaned towards her, curious to know more about her past, but careful not to upset her.

'Sometimes I feel I am the victim of some curse,' she said and trembled. Her strong emotions only served to make her look more radiant and lovely. She seemed to be extracting strength from the deepest reservoirs of her persona. And just when Ram thought she would begin, she said, 'It won't do us any good Ram. The shrapnel is too deeply embedded.'

🐾

'That sexy English witch seems to have cast a spell over you!' Jugnu said to Ram. He had been smoking a Marlboro, watching Ram as he trudged back to his cell. It was almost as if he had overheard Ram's conversation with Sherry and was weighing the implications craftily. Was Jugnu simply curious, or was he jealous? Suddenly he asked suspiciously, 'Why is she spending so much time with you?'

'She wanted to know something about my American company for her paper.'

'She must be interested in knowing about Burree Maada. Don't tell her anything we discussed. By the way, the other day when I was talking to him Goa Sahib conveyed that he has serious doubts about your loyalty. He feels that maybe you cannot be trusted.' He held Ram by the shoulder and shook him. 'Have you also fallen in love with this jail?'

Ram protested loudly. 'No! No! I want to get out! I can't live this life... I am going mad! I am ready to do everything that I would have hated doing earlier. But I want to get the hell out of this rotten place.'

'What are you willing to do for Goa Sahib?' Jugnu's eyes were blood-shot as he glared at Ram, his eyes burning holes into him. It was just like the time he had lost his temper with Phukat.

'Get buggered by him! Poach more Burree Maadas! I am ready to change my religion and garrote strangers! For God's sake, for Bhawanee's sake, get me out of this fucking hell! Please Jugnu...please. I cannot take this torture anymore, get me out!' He started crying.

SOFT GOLD

'Lucky bastard!' Jugnu congratulated Ram loudly, slapping him vigorously on the back. Ram winced. Perhaps Jugnu was jealous of him. Now he knew what it felt like to win the Nobel Prize without deserving it.

The order for discharge had come like lightning. He had been mopping the wet floor after lunch, when a terse message from the jail superintendent was served for 2699 to report to him.

Even the jail superintendent had been impressed. He made Ram sit before him in the manner of an equal and with a crooked smile he whispered conspiratorially, 'You are a smart bastard! The Court of the Chief Judicial Magistrate of Jabalpur has just granted you bail.' And then, as Ram bowed in thankfulness, he said, 'But remember, it is Goenka Sahib who is to be thanked. He is Farishta. It is his blessing to you.'

'Jugnu, it will take some time for me to believe that I am free!'

'I told you that you would be released, my brother. Goa Sahib will now turn you into 24 karat gold.'

24 karat gold or 24 karat coal was yet to be seen. But he was to be freed. At least he could try and communicate more constructively with Sherry now. But would her disapproval of Goenka come in the way? He asked Jugnu, 'How did he manage this? I did not go to court or make out any application!'

'When Goa Sahib sets his mind on something, he achieves it. Besides, he has mastered this art over thirty years.'

'But how?'

Jugnu pondered, perhaps over how much to disclose. Finally he spoke when he was convinced that no one was within earshot. Then, in the manner of revealing a closely guarded national secret, he whispered, 'Networking…'

'How?' Ram asked, still foggy about the method.

'The Bench is made of human beings,' said Jugnu. AG Sahib helped.'

'AG?'

'He is the highest government legal man and a relative of Darbar, the Maharaja of Baikunthpur. Before he started practising in the High Court, he was Goa Sahib's family counsel. Recently, his son Mrityunjaya bought a ranch in Nepal. Goa Sahib arranged the deal.'

'Why should he buy property in Nepal?'

'The AG's son is a real man, unlike the father who is big phusss,' Jugnu pursed his lips and made a sound like the hiss of a failed firecracker. 'He is fond of horses, wildlife, tribal virgins and the monsoonal lowlands of the Chitwan National Park. The other Goenka brother takes care of him there. A few days ago, Darbar and Mritunjaya had gone to shoot wild boar and ended up with a leopard near Taala, a few miles from Bandhavgarh. While driving back they hit a tiger which died. He called Goa Sahib at midnight and he managed to quash the adverse publicity.'

Ram was now a perfect mix of fright and curiosity. He had never having heard anything like this before. 'So how did the AG help?'

'AG being positive conveys the sense that the government concurs with the case of the accused. That imparts legitimacy and protects everybody—the accused, the lower judge and the higher judge. Goa Sahib's approach is very simple. If a judge has a reputation that he can be influenced, the price is immaterial.'

'You must be kidding.'

'Goa Sahib is pro-judiciary,' said Jugnu. 'He says a judge in one pocket equals whole bureaucracy in other pocket.'

Jugnu laughed derisively even as Ram remained unbelieving. 'How does he keep track of so many people?'

'He maintains a Facebook of important people. Name a

politician, officer or judge. His information is constantly updated. Any relevant news item anywhere gets scanned, aggregated and archived into the digital dossiers. For instance, he knows that one of the top Judges has a particular fondness for young female lawyers, another for foreign cigars…'

'Basic instinct!'

'Is that the name of the disease? Anyway, his aim is simple—earn goodwill and win hearts. Katni Junction has three hundred trains passing through it everyday. Every important person who passes Katni by train gets a tiffin box with food prepared with organic ingredients drawn from Goa Sahib's own vegetable gardens. Initially they are reluctant to accept it. But no hungry man on a lonely journey ever forgets a hot meal.'

Goenka seemed to be a legal trapeze artist. Clearly, Ram thought, his offer was an opportunity, hardly a threat.

As he walked out of jail everything seemed crisp and defined. It was like seeing a 3-D film with stereoscopic glasses and high-precision headphones. The air on the other side of the jail wall smelt different, even fragrant. Perhaps it was simply the oxygen of freedom. Suddenly the jamun and eucalyptus trees in front of him began to sway and mynahs began to chirp.

He had barely stepped into the waiting vehicle that Goenka had sent for him when he noticed something ahead and cursed his luck. It was Sherry, dressed in a green fruit-patterned skirt and lemon shirt that revealed her smooth skin and sexily toned body. For once she was not wearing her trademark running shoes but had switched to heeled shoes. Her hair was left open to cascade over her shoulders bewitchingly; her eyes blazed penetratingly, seducing him like a Transylvanian waif on an icy-cold wintry night, luring him into bloody debauchery. But he had already sold himself to Goenka, the God of Freedom, who waited to feast upon him with carnal rapacity. What if he just ran away? His union with Sherry would be short-lived as he would most certainly be pursued, captured and impaled to a stake. Sherry was voluptuous, she would be delicious in bed, but she could only offer, at best, instant redemption. She shouted something inaudible. He cared far too much for her, but if he stopped now the word would reach Goenka and he would be a lost cause.

Ram avoided her, pretending not to have seen her, and slammed the door with vigour, urging the driver to move on. The man at the wheel observed the drama silently. An ice-box with chilled beer awaited Ram's pleasure. He opened a bottle, and drank long, thirsty sips, remembering the famous jingle: 'Happy days are here again'.

They drove at top speed, past the huge residences with their sloping roofs covered with red Mangalore tiles. They passed the Collectorate, the historic City Hall and the famous crossings named after Englishmen—Laadganj, which was Lordganj in an earlier era, after Lord William Bentinck, the then Governor-General who had visited Jabalpur in 1833 just after the elimination of Thuggee, Panty-Naka, the point named after M.S. Penty, the dealer of automobiles, Uprenganj and Mukadamganj named after Majors O'Brien and MacAdam and several other important crossings. They zipped past Sihora and Sleemanabad—the police outpost named after Colonel Sleeman. Then, into Jhinjri, famous for its rocks with prehistoric carvings, dating back to the Paleolithic age. Finally they were on the outskirts of Katni, cruising into a huge pristine white bungalow, with the national flag flying on the roof and elegant ivy-covered walls. A crest featuring a golden hawk was emblazoned on the black wrought iron gates. They drove along the long and cobbled granite driveway to stop inside the main portico.

Feroze Goenka was waiting on the platform above the steps. He looked cheerful and debonair, dressed smartly in Polo khakis and a tee-shirt with suede Ferragamo monk straps. His left hand was in his trousers and a mobile rested in the right, close to his ears. As Ram alighted, Goenka rushed down the steps and opened the door for him, welcoming him warmly. He seemed younger and fitter now.

'I don't know how to thank you for what you have done for me, I am deeply grateful.' Ram sounded apologetic, though he was trying to convey his happiness.

'Nah…it is my good fortune to be of help to good people,' Goenka said. 'At least I have you now for myself.' He saw that his words had rattled Ram and suddenly started punching a number on his phone. 'We have a common friend who is very keen to speak with you,' he said, handing his phone to Ram. The sound was that of a long distance call.

'Congratulations Mr NRI.' The deep voice was familiar. 'It was nice meeting you at the airport…Hail Feroze Goenka who was able to get you out!'

Abhimanyu Singh, the Maharaja of Baikunthpur!

'All hail to him! Otherwise, I would have been languishing in jail.'

'Give him some time and he will get you out of jail permanently,' said Abhimanyu emphatically.

Ram nodded disbelievingly. The phone felt unusually heavy. He read the name—Iridium. He gasped silently—why, this was a satellite phone! Surprisingly, even the Raja brothers carried one. He perceived a movement in the shadows to his left and looked sideaways. An elderly man, presumably of Far-Eastern descent, stood there, dressed in white cottons and a linen khaki jacket with a white hat. He looked like a tourist.

'Meet His Excellency Mr Wang, an old family friend of mine,' said Goenka. 'He is helping with our international affairs…he has worked for the United Nations.'

'Where?'

'He is an expert on KITES,' said Feroze. 'The Import-Export Policy for Tigers. It is of great importance to us.'

'CITES,' corrected Ram as he extended his hand to Mr Wang who frowned condescendingly before taking the offered hand. He seemed unwilling to talk any further and turned away to disappear behind the pillars into the depths of the house.

Goenka led Ram down an aisle into a large rectangular dining hall with a huge table that had a crisp white tablecloth and an abundance of crystal, silverware and roses. Ram pointed to the black and white photographs of a tall man with a flowing moustache and khaki breeches holding a rifle, presumably a hunter.

'Who is this gentleman?' Ram asked.

Feroze explained, 'That is our beloved father, Sahdev Damodar Goenka. What a legend! A shrewd bania brain but with a bold kshatriya heart! Of course, he was not as great a shot as Darbar, His Highness Maharaja of Baikunthpur, but he handled all shikar provisions for the Palace—the guns, the cartridges, the haaquas and the food to be imported for the partying. He was therefore given the honorific of Mir Shikar by His Highness. Every royal shikar had his inimitable stamp.'

Ram stared at Feroze. His supple skin and neat looks reminded him of a middle-aged Italian fashion designer who appreciated his afternoon wine and siesta. He seemed to read Ram's mind as he said, 'I am not much of an outdoor type anymore. However, my older brother Nowsher was born different. My father was on shikar with the present Darbar's grandfather, when His Highness hunted and killed nine tigers. My brother's birth coincided with this great event and he was named Nau-sher-wan, the killer of nine tigers, to commemorate this. He lives up to his name!'

'I was also told of your interest in other kinds of game.'

Feroze Goenka chuckled mysteriously, 'I am not a high-flier

anymore. I prefer my rice and dal. I sleep on a simple bed. I only scout for bright birds that can be trained to hunt higher. But brother Nowsher is aroused only when he lies down on a tiger or leopard skin. I have to keep sending him a fresh supply, for all the new women who enter his life.'

They laughed, walking towards a marble verandah overlooking manicured lawns to have tea. Ram knew that the only way he could stay out of jail was with Goenka's help and he could not afford to let him think otherwise. He bowed and said, 'Forever yours.'

'Just one year! After that I bet that you will wish to continue working with us.'

'All right, so where do I start?'

'I will show you around my office tomorrow. Also Nowsher needs you immediately,' said Goenka matter-of-factly, his face suddenly grim. 'He handles our East Asia operations from abroad. You will join him.'

'I am ready to go anywhere, and do anything for you,' Ram met Goenka's eyes. 'But what if I slip away to the States or anywhere else in the world?'

Goenka turned to a large painting on the wall. A white dove was being torn apart mid-air by a larger and more predatory bird—possibly a hawk. Ram shivered at the ruthless clarity of the message.

Goenka laughed wickedly, 'you are intelligent, my friend. All right, your first trip is to Kathmandu. You will be Nowsher's guest.'

Ram glanced at the papers on the study table. One envelope contained bits and pieces of neatly cut papers. It was his passport—he could see his name and address and his photograph shredded to pieces. His heart beat faster. It had been destroyed forever. Goenka was right. He was like a bird whose wings had been torn.

Another envelope contained a plane ticket and money along with a passport under the name of Ram Prasad, of India, living in Wright Town, Jabalpur. He glanced at the photograph. It was him all right, slightly morphed.

He wondered why a visa stamp was necessary when visits to Nepal by an Indian citizen did not require a travel visa.

Back in Grey Goose, Sherry flopped onto a cane rocking chair facing the back lawn. It was still early, just before lunch. Her old Vaio notebook resting on her lap was the object of her undivided attention.

As she plodded through the pending mails in her inbox and replied to them, she sipped a tall glass of chilled nimbu paani. Just then she saw that her latest feature based on her interview with Ram had made the front page. The headline read: 'Zentigris Founders Go for the Kill'.

Sherry had not expected her report to be printed so quickly. She had suggested, 'Wilder Side of Zentigris Promoters', as the title. But it was the Editor's prerogative to decide the title based on what would attract attention.

She began reading her article slowly:

'Leo and Taurus are names that conjure up the zodiac images of a lion and a bull, and the waxing and waning of fortunes subject to celestial movements. True to that image, two slick businessmen with the aforesaid pet names, were were once rated as two of the most powerful Indians abroad. These gentlemen had wheeled and dealed inside the Beltway and soared high with their unique blend of power, pelf and chutzpah. But today they find their once soaring personal fortunes subjected to the most turbulent astral volatility conceivable.

'From running a hugely successful software business to recruiting thousands of Indian technologists (see box on the Global Tsars of Technology, HT January 2004), they seemed to have had a bull run on almost everything else they put their minds to, from running upscale eco-spas to leisure journals.

'It is almost unbelievable that this powerful duo that had etched their success on the NASDAQ and the NYSE should now be cooling their heels in a federal lock-up for an oversight that appears piffling in comparison with the scams of the recent past that are still fresh in memory. Meanwhile, HT has tried to uncover little known facts about this amazing duo which should interest the sagacious reader who is bored with details about their more spectacular financial record.

'Leo and Taurus, nicknames for Narasimhan and Taruneswar Raja, two brothers who were born a year apart, hail from the princely city of Mysore in Karnataka, Southern India, also famous for the patriotic king Tipu Sultan who lost to the first Duke of Wellington in the famous Battle of Seringapatam in 1799. Mysore is also known for its resplendent silks and the Dussehra festival in autumn, which culminates with Vijay Dashmi. It is a celebration of the victory of good over evil and caparisoned elephants come out in procession along with other floats before cheering audiences.

'After finishing their graduation in computer science in the late 70s (it was actually a branch of Electronics Science in those days), the two decided to give their entrepreneurial spirit a free hand by borrowing a few thousand rupees from their father to set up a small laboratory for assembling electronic gadgets under the brand name of Cub, with a tiger cub inside an oval circle as their brand logo. Some years later, as their business prospered, they set up a small software firm (with the support of the then Mayor of Mysore, C. Perumalan, who is currently the Chief Minister of Karnataka), in Bangalore. As they grew, they acquired real estate and inaugurated ZenInfo Towers. At this stage, the brand name was changed to Zentigris, and the logo transformed from a cub into a silver-coloured Royal Bengal tigress inside a yin-yang symbol.

The tiger has always been a source of inspiration for us because of its natural ferocity, speed, prowess and sense of balance. But why do the Rajas have this quirky obsession with the tiger?

Their childhood friends remember them not for their academic genius—but for their penchant for mischief, for which they were almost expelled from school. As small boys, they shocked everybody when they managed to smuggle a stuffed and mounted tiger and then installed it in the school lobby. Wildlife has always been more than a passing interest for them. It is a quest. Only a close-knit circle of friends know that they have one of the world's best collections of jungle antiques and stuffed wildlife trophies which adorn their luxurious villa in San Francisco. Much of it has been bagged in personal shikar.

'Their interest in wildlife dates back to their childhood, when their father used to work as a chemical analyst with that famous firm of taxidermists, Van Ingen and Van Ingen in Mysore. The firm, established in 1890 by an Englishman of Dutch origin, Eugene Van Ingen and run until 1999 by his four sons, was renowned globally for being the official taxidermist to the Queen of England, the Maharajas of India and several kingdoms of Europe. Its work of tigers and leopards was outstanding and remains a familiar and distinctive sight in auction sales and in museums even today. It had a stupendous turnover of over five hundred tigers and six hundred leopards a year and processed more than fifty thousand tiger and a hundred thousand leopard trophies during the hundred years of its operations! This prodigious feat earned the Van Ingens the sobriquet: Artists in Taxidermy.

'As kids the Raja Brothers had been awestruck seeing Englishmen and Maharajas go in and out of the Van Ingen factory and had heard endless romantic stories of tiger chase, elephant hunts and week-long shikar adventures. Thus, the elephant and the tiger became both symbols of power and of wealth for them—

attributes and assets that they began to keenly cherish and lust for.

'It is mere coincidence that Ramchandra Prasad, one of their senior executives, is currently in the confines of the Jabalpur Central Jail on charges of buying a skin belonging to the tigress Burree Maada, allegedly killed by poachers inside the high security Kanha National Park. Prasad's version, on the contrary, is that, he had gone to Jabalpur to surrender a tiger skin, that belonged to his dead father, to the Forest Museum and that the skin was not of Burree Maada. The authorities have, however, not bought this story. And, coincidentally, as per Prasad's story, that decades-old, but fresh looking tiger skin was also taxidermied by none other than Van Ingen and Van Ingen, the taxidermy firm in which the Rajas' father had worked in Mysore.

'What binds the Raja brothers to the tiger? Is it just their association with the legendary taxidermy firm in Mysore? With the introduction of the Wildlife Protection Act, hunting is now prohibited in India. And so it seems that they cannot legitimately indulge in their wild pursuits in India anymore, their proximity to various erstwhile royal households notwithstanding. It is learnt that they have been regularly hunting in Southern Africa, Southeast Asia and parts of Europe where conservation laws are more lax. Tour operators in Rawalpindi in Pakistan have known them as 'Bade and Chhote Nawab,' a term used to describe Royalty from the Sub-continent, as they have become celebrated regulars for hunting of the Himalayan ibex and the Blandford urial in Baluchistan.

'It is learnt that their partners from Kunming, China, in the recent, much-celebrated technology joint venture are, quite uncannily, equally fond of wildlife. That may explain what has got these disparate promoters together.

'(To be concluded, Sherry Pinto).'

Just as she finished reading the feature, her Editor called her. He waxed eloquent, 'That was one helluva wicked feature...I loved it. I got many phone calls from Mumbai and as far away as New York. You seem to have the makings of a mystery writer. Readers want to know more about the Chinese promoters. Why don't you go to Kunming?'

'Forbidden City,' Sherry responded cryptically, her face flushed with excitement, wondering what it would be like to go again to China.

'You could throw in a small holiday in between,' the Editor coaxed. 'If you go to Phuket and stay at the Laguna, you have a choice of some of the best spas—I know the Australian Manager of Banyan Tree. The resorts are inter-connected by a lake, so you can swim or row from one resort to the other. Go for it! Fix an interview with Yin and Yang or whatever they are called.'

'That is very kind of you,' said Sherry, inwardly not wanting to let the opportunity pass. 'I'd love to go to China…but the visa…'

'A similar feature about the Chinese guys will make a fantastic coup. Nobody has thought of scraping below the belly button.'

'Or the kundalini,' Sherry said softly.

'Plan your trip and get going…'

Sherry sighed ecstatically. What luck! It had been ages since she had enjoyed a good massage. The last time was when she had travelled north into Chiang Mai and then onwards to Mytkina and the Hukaung Valley, leading a select band of young volunteers. The prospect of a strong male masseur in an open-to-the-sky rose-and-patchouli-scented canvas enclosure with clambering orchids and ferns massaging her parched skin with luxuriant sloshes of spicy geranium oil, kneading purposefully into her naked back with sharp elbows and going beyond her midriff and pressing lower… it sent her spine tingling with excitement. It was the closest thing to heaven!

In Kathmandu, Ram was on the highway, the chauffeur negotiating expertly past crowded narrow lanes with blaring music and garish political posters. Soon they passed the Pasupatinath Temple and travelled along the Bagmati River. The guide-cum-chauffeur announced to Ram, 'We are now passing famous temple of the Lord of the Animals.'

The road was bumpier now and then they could see the tree-encircled Gokarn forest area, in the village of Thali, well out of Kathmandu. Just short of the forest, the van tumbled onto an obscure pot holed avenue and screeched to a halt outside the stupendous iron gates of Bagh Mahal.

'Bagh Mahal was originally with King Birendra before I bought it,' said Nowsher, who welcomed him warmly. Ram could spot a Rolls Royce, a Bentley, and a customized BMW veteran, along with a four-horse carriage with silver and gold plating.

Inside the drawing room, the splendour was equally spell-binding with a chandelier that probably weighed several tonnes. Amongst the mounted photographs was one of Lord Hardinge standing along with the Nepal King's grandfather and two dead tigers at their feet with their lengths mentioned in the photo as nine feet and ten feet respectively. Another plaque described an eleven-foot long white tiger from Govindgarh in Rewa, shot by HH on his maiden visit as a guest of the Maharaja of Baikunthpur. An Iranian rug was mounted on the wall with names of famous Nepalese kings and deities.

Nowsher started fidgeting visibly after tea, almost like a ship changing course. He looked somber as he placed his hands on Ram's shoulders in a protective way, 'My friend, matters of great concern have arisen.'

'Yes, you do look concerned,' Ram said earnestly. 'You can confide in me. I am entirely at your disposal. All your concerns are now mine.'

'I want you to travel north.'

'Europe?' Ram asked breathlessly. Since miracles seemed to be the order of the day, why not expect the impossible?

Nowsher laughed, 'I would love to send you to Zurich to settle pending financial issues. But let's begin the journey of a thousand miles with the first step.'

'Where?' Ram tried hard to conceal the disappointment.

'Tibet, specifically Lhasa and Amdo.'

Ram recalled seeing *Seven Years in Tibet* starring Brad Pitt, which depicted the snowy mountains of Tibet. 'Do you want me to steal Sakyamuni's tooth from the Potala Palace?'

Nowsher guffawed heartily before he said, 'Not quite! But allow me to compliment your sense of geography.'

'I was good in school,' said Ram.

'Please listen carefully. We have been traditional suppliers of rare animal skins—mostly tiger and leopard, to the once huge Tibetan and the neighbouring Greater China market for the last forty years. But recently, an unwarranted event has occurred.'

'What?'

'There has been a forced change in the mindset of ethnic Buddhists in Tibet.'

'Why?'

'You have heard of Dalai Lama?'

'Of course I have!'

'He has recently called upon Tibetans in the course of the Kalchakra Conference of Buddhists to destroy all animal skins. As a result, even those Tibetans that had formerly procured skins at a huge expense are now burning them.'

'So my father's Van Ingen skin and the one from Burree Maada will also be destroyed?'

'In Tibet they would have to,' Nowsher said sullenly, displeased by Ram's deviation from the main point.

Ram recalled the Chinese partners' comments about the Dalai Lama. The wolf in monk's clothes! He asked, 'Where do I come in?'

'I have been assured of your astute business skills. You have to assess, evaluate and advise us about how to undo the damage to our business of supplying animal skins.'

'Would it not be better for someone who understands Tibet to undertake this mission?'

'No', said Nowsher, 'We need to identify the key protagonists of this conspiracy that is ruining our business. Hence a fresh and unrecognized face.'

'Surely you can do that, given your reach,' Ram said.

Nowsher lashed out angrily. 'We could,' he said. 'But we don't want to be directly involved. There is a group of shadowy fanatics on this new thing called the Internet. They could be located anywhere—Tibet, India, Thailand and England. They are school drop outs, misguided vagabonds—spouting the animal cause because it appears offbeat and fashionable. They have given themselves silly names like Love Tiger or Blood Tiger, something like that. It has frightened our distributors. It is imperative that we neutralize their game.' He took out a set of photographs and handed them carefully to Ram, his body shaking.

The photos were of poor quality—they had been taken in low light from a distance with an indifferent camera. One was of a bleeding man whose naked body had been split open ventrally with a sharp object. It reminded him of meat in a butcher's shop. Another was of a skinhead holding a rod, presiding over a kangaroo court—before him was a man whose leg had been caught in a metal trap, like an animal trapped by poachers in a jungle. The trapped man was surrounded by young boys and girls with sticks and was pleading for pardon with folded hands, 'Two of our best skin dealers!'

'Macabre,' Ram said, inwardly laughing at the irony. So these chaps had somebody to scare them too!

Nowsher continued, 'Most unfortunate! These heartless vandals have even lit bonfires in Tibet. Two precious consignments worth millions of dollars were seized as we tried to move them to Kathmandu and the crew of the vehicles murdered gruesomely and burnt along with the skins.'

'What is the local government doing about the killings?' Ram asked.

'The region is in tumult,' said Nowsher. 'There are wheels within wheels in the Tibetan Autonomous Region and the mainland attitude is not fathomable. They are not in love with the Dalai Lama and yet they do not openly support us. So my friend, you will pose as a scholar of Buddhist leanings who is researching Buddhist and Gandhara art in Asia, including Tibet. With your shaven head and fair skin you can easily pass of as a monk or scholar. You will meet the young people, the priests around Potala and the myriad monasteries and also our traditional skin-dealers. You will collect precious information to help devise a strategy. The supply chain must stay alive!'

'Indeed! But won't I need local inputs?' Ram asked, his stomach churning violently. Suddenly Jabalpur Central Jail seemed like paradise in contrast to the unfathomable hazards that lay ahead.

'One of the researchers in the Tibet Field Office of the World Wildlife Fund China is our friend. Elizabeth will personally assist you.'

Nowsher came to him the next morning, dressed in a cream-coloured silk robe, holding a thick sheaf of newspapers in one hand and a slim mobile phone in the other. Ram shivered.

'Will I have to eat yak meat in Tibet?' Ram asked, with all the emphasis he could muster on 'eat.'

Nowsher seemed to give the matter due thought. And then, he first pursed his lips, raised his head and then spoke, 'That was the original plan. But the situation seems to have worsened there—more immolations and violence. A curfew-like situation in Tibet is not conducive to your visit. Instead, I now want you to come with me to Myanmar.'

Ram's head spun. He had become a patsy, an expendable—a mercenary whose services were being bartered every minute for temporary freedom. 'And what am I expected to do in Myanmar? Assassinate Aung San Suu-Kyi?'

'Rubbish!' Nowsher laughed outright, looking him closely in the eye. 'No such distinction for you! I'll be introducing you to one of my close friends, a top General in the ruling party in Myanmar. The present assignment is a matter of charity. Milk and medicines have to be sent urgently for the welfare of the cyclone-hit people in the southeast. Feroze has it all planned out. It is his mission and he will be briefing you in Kolkata.'

Ram stared at him, dazed. He didn't know whether to feel relieved or not as yet.

'Until then, my friend, allow my pet Maya to make your visit to Kathmandu memorable,' Nowsher said putting his arms around him affectionately and winking wickedly. He clapped his hands with the aplomb of a medieval sultan and chuckled. 'Maya teaches yoga in the day and bhoga at night. Depending on your mood, you can choose between Patanjali and Vatsayan.'

Maya's skilful ministrations in the famous Tiger Room had brought back that memorable evening in Bangkok.

There had been a sudden call from Borneo, causing Leo Raja to leave suddenly—perhaps for an impromptu shikar expedition. He had moved into Leo's elaborate Joseph Conrad suite in his favourite hotel, the luxurious Mandarin Oriental and retained the bookings his boss had made with a reputed escort company. In that secured luxury, when the world outside was busy shopping and transacting business, he had enjoyed the sensuous comfort of two nubile Thai masseurs. That subtle art of darkness had been an experience of a lifetime—to be painted and rubbed with a bouquet of scented, exotic massage oils, to be pummelled like wet dough simultaneously by the warm, naked bodies of two beautiful young women…looking out languidly at the vibrant Chao-Phraya River with its shimmering floating markets and the several ancient temples gleaming in the drifting moonlight.

Maya needed no preamble. With a beautiful body that could put a Victoria's Secret model to shame, she entered his life wearing practically nothing but a pink and green Valentino fur collar and floral bouquet, gushing and lovely, more than enough to light his fire. She ripped off his clothes and pushed him against a velvety pelt on the ground and wrapped the collar across his neck playfully. She rubbed her taut and naked body against his for an eternity, her silken hair across him like vines. The sustained skittering and rubbing aroused him. The overall effect of a sizzling nude against him on a feline rug as the session progressed, transformed his appetite for carnal pleasure from a stifled snarl to a ravenous roar.

After leading him assiduously through many blissful endings, and fulfilling his innermost cravings, she patted his bottom and tugged him along with her fingers to the jacuzzi with the candidness of a naked mother descending into a bathtub with her little baby. After a prolonged soak she dried him with a combination of towel and tongue until he had screamed with satiation and found instant sleep.

His mind kept drifting beyond Maya—it hadn't taken much effort to vanquish or be vanquished by her. Perhaps, in an abstract way he had now begun to fantasize about Sherry. Every private interlude with Maya had become one with Sherry in his mind. Suddenly in a moment of personal nirvana he felt he could comprehend Sherry's passionate or perhaps perverted interest in the tiger…or, the tigress—Burree Maada.

He wiped the sweat from his face and reflected on Nowsher. Unlike Feroze, he was more fun-loving and widely travelled. He had perfect command of the English language and a subtle sense of humour, acquired by his association with foreign diplomats and international press. The Kathmandu social circuit seemed to be revolving around him, with lots of cocktail parties happening all the time. With his hair dyed brown and jovial demeanour restored, Ram too was once again the debonair man he used to be in the States. Nowsher introduced him as a visiting business associate and school friend from India and made him the toast of Kathmandu high society. What puzzled Ram was that nobody was keen to learn more about his antecedents.

As he was driven furiously from Imphal to the international border in a Toyota Innova, Ram contrasted this with the relaxed breakfast with Feroze at the Oberoi Grand in Chowringhee. Feroze had personally briefed him about his dual assignment—to escort a truckload of medicines and milk powder for the cyclone-ravaged people of South Myanmar and to make an assessment for the Indian Government about the quality of the Indo-Myanmar border infrastructure. The latter was necessary to facilitate further trade through the land route to help the economic development of northeast India that the Goenkas were pushing for. The truck would be available at Moreh on the Indian side of the border. His Innova bore a red beacon light and a siren and as both the driver and the escort were in military olives, even when they were stopped for routine checks at the Assam Rifles check points, they were not detained unnecessarily. On the way he stopped at a few places at the suggestion of his driver to take photographs of the beautiful lakes.

Finally, after traversing more than a hundred kilometres from Imphal he reached the border town of Moreh. 'Moreh is sleepy and dusty and adjoins Tamu, its Myanmar counterpart,' Feroze had said. 'But remember, it is an international border town.'

His driver seemed to be a regular on this route and knew the lay of the land. 'Let me call your contact point,' he said, quickly dialling a number on his mobile.

Within moments, a fashionable man emerged dramatically and announced as he extended his neatly manicured, effeminate hands, 'Hello Sir, Yumcoccho Bineetkumar, also called Coco, your guide and escort into Myanmar.' He looked like a Bangkok ladyboy with polish on two of his finger nails. There was a hint in the way he tilted his head, of the famous Indian actor Dev Anand, immortalized in the all-time great film, *Guide*.

'Hello handsome, nice name!' Ram greeted him with a big smile and shook hands.

Coco took off his aviators to reveal eyebrows that had been sharpened neatly. He was dressed in a smart suit without a tie and carried a copy of Peter Mathieson's *The Snow Leopard*. He spoke English with a slight Oriental accent. 'My services have been hired by Mr Feroze Goenka of Katni. I will be your escort into Mandalay.' Coco noticed the uncomfortable look on Ram's face and explained, 'I am also the Liaison Officer for the Indian Border Roads Organization for their project from Tamu to Kale.' He showed Ram his Manipur Government Security Pass.

'So how and when do we drive across?' Ram asked.

'First things first,' said Coco. 'An army marches on its stomach and it is now time for our lunch. And then we leave around 2 p.m. We will be joined by two others once we approach the border. You have your papers?'

'Yes,' Ram nodded and looked again at his identity card and the set of papers handed to him by Feroze Goenka. He was all set to cross the Moreh-Tamu portion of the international India-Myanmar border as arranged, posing as an office bearer of the CHEMEXCIL, the Basic Chemicals, and Pharmaceuticals & Cosmetics Export Promotion Council under the aegis of the Commerce Ministry of India. He carried a letter from CHEMEXCIL on its official letterhead stating that as per the directions of the Union Ministry of Commerce, he would be leading a delegation comprising of himself—Ramchandra Prasad of the Chemexcil's Kolkata Regional Office, Yumcoccho Bineetkumar of the Manipur Government Department of Border Roads and Public Works, and Desmond Ingti, a representative of the Reserve Bank of India. Their objective was to investigate major infrastructure bottlenecks, and report back to the Director of the East Asia Division of the Commerce Ministry about the actual difficulties encountered in conducting business across the territorial border. A copy of the order had been endorsed to the Indian Embassy in Yangon for seeking facilitation from the Myanmar Government.

Coco had been scrutinizing the tension written large on Ram's face. 'Don't worry Sir,' he said, 'you are safe in my company.'

Ram could see dozens of villagers crossing the border on both sides complacently. Some were goatherds with grazing goats, dressed in customary village outfits, while others wore modern clothes. People carried cloth and jute bags full of vegetables and other small things. 'Amidst this chaotic free-for-all, the atmosphere is rather happy,' observed Ram lightly.

'Most of them have nothing even vaguely resembling a permit, let alone a passport,' said Coco. And then as if his stomach reminded him, he said firmly, 'Let us eat.'

The tiny restaurant-cum-hotel proudly announced: 'Hotel

Maitree—Indian Hostage Western Laxary'.

Coco laughed readily, joining in with Ram. The short-stapled extra-boiled rice that was served with the barbecued buffalo hind and Churachandpur pork with a distinct Burmese-Thai accent to the cooking was an instant hit with Ram. When they returned to the Innova, he asked Coco, 'So is there any worthwhile Indo-Burma trade?'

'Despite the Indo-Myanmar Border Trade Treaty of 1995, it is subdued because of the poor border infrastructure.'

'I'm glad we are taking medicines for the poor on the other side,' said Ram.

Coco laughed and squinted in astonishment. His eyelashes batted fast, like a bird's wings as his eyes rolled over. He jerked his right hand in a disdainful gesture, as if he had been handed a dumb doll, and pointed to the heavily-loaded truck behind them. It was a light-blue Tata truck with a huge Red Cross painted on it, loaded upto the top with a tarpaulin that had been tied in with coloured plastic ropes. He asked, 'Do you know what our Mother India carries?'

'Medicines and toys for children!'

Coco screamed with laughter, till his eyes brimmed over with tears, 'Toys! Toys for children!' He stopped laughing and said, 'But, of course! My friend, we have a tiger in our tank!'

'What?' Ram stared at him in disbelief. He had gone to jail because of a tiger skin and now he was being told that he was carrying a tiger. He remembered the old Exxon advertisement: 'We put a tiger in your tank'. It used to be displayed along with a tiger mascot. This was absolutely unbelievable, utterly crazy! The damned tiger was chasing him all the way to Myanmar! He remembered Burree Maada and how he had suffered because of her. But before he could speak, Coco lifted up a warning hand to silence him.

A man who had been concealed by the bright glare of the sun on the polished asphalt darted out suddenly. He was dressed in a light grey linen coat and a hat. He stood on the road, just short of the border, waving to them to stop. 'Is he asking for a lift?' Ram looked at Coco.

'No, stop, stop!' Coco instructed the driver. 'Hop aboard Desmond, you bloody ass hole. As usual you made it just in time!' Desmond Ingti, a banker of Naga descent with an oval face and soft features, wore dark Oakley glasses. His very stylized English accent could not take away from the fact that he reeked of rum. The ever-smiling Desmond had worked with the State Bank of India at their Imphal branch. Coco announced, 'This makes our delegation to the Myanmarese border complete—Commerce Ministry, State Government and Finance Ministry.'

'I have to be very alert now,' shouted an excited Coco at the check-post. He hopped off like a monkey and shot photographs of the incomplete warehouse and the abandoned Facilitation Office of the Commerce Ministry that was meant to house the Customs, the Container Corporation, the Directorate General of Foreign Trade, the Export Inspection Council, the representatives of various export promotion councils, the Reserve Bank and a few other banks. Ram and Coco, and the drivers and conductor of the truck signed in a register while Coco entered details and a declaration about the cargo they were carrying. An armed guard of the Assam Rifles peered inside before they were saluted and the barriers lifted manually. First their Innova, and then Mother India trundled uphill on the narrow but bituminized road to Myanmar.

They crossed a bridge, painted half in white for India and half in red for Myanmar, over the winding Mahuya stream with teak trees and ferns on both sides. A short distance and several bumps later, they arrived at the formal Myanmar checkpost. Once again Coco stepped out with a sheaf of papers to do the paperwork.

A considerable amount of time had passed, and Ram looked out anxiously but there was no sign of Coco. His heart began to beat faster. Suddenly two armed guards came running towards the Innova as if they had been directed to arrest Ram. He froze. Was Coco already under arrest or was this a ploy to fix him? The guards opened all the doors and directed him to get out and stand in a corner. Next, they moved to take a closer look at Mother India. They went around it slowly, peering and deliberating amongst themselves. But they did not ask for the hold to be opened. There was pin-drop silence; the only sound Ram could hear was that of his own heartbeat growing louder each second and the sweat trickling down his cheeks. He did not want to be arrested yet again. Would they find growing louder each second and the sweat trickling down his cheeks contraband? Why was Coco absconding?

After what seemed like an eternity of silent snooping, the guards retreated as if ordered to do so by some remote command. Ram observed their physical attributes; they seemed so small and vulnerable. The wooden barrier was lifted and the vehicles passed through imperceptibly before halting on the other side.

Coco came along at full speed and pulled himself into the Innova. He sat down beside Ram with a grin and wiped the sweat from his face with a lavender-coloured handkerchief heavily scented with concentrated Dior Opium. Only after he had smoked a cigarette did he relax.

'Coco, what the hell is happening? Can you please brief me about trade now so that I'm prepared for our meeting with the Myanmar officials,' Ram requested.

'My Indian friend,' said Coco, condescendingly, 'today the composition of the trade basket has altered radically from the days when Myanmar was Burma, and Yangon was Rangoon; when it was of interest to British writers and romanticists like George Orwell. It is now a hub for trade and should have caught the attention of Indian political analysts and economic planners. Alas, much as usual, you Indians are dumb and sleeping; the Chinese, on the contrary, are far more alive to the strategic importance of Myanmar and have offered to build their infrastructure.'

Ram winced at the mention of the word Indian with such indifference. It was almost as if Coco belonged to some third country.

Coco took out a bunch of toffees from a bag labeled Passion Fruit Candy and handed one to Ram. They were made in Thailand with the shape of a heart on the wrapper. Ram loved the taste. 'There is more depth to the trade basket now. Special products, like what we are carrying—bone dust, peels, organics and herbals, are packaged along with medicines and baby milk.' He seemed surprised by the shocked look on Ram's face.

Coco lit another cigarette and offered one to Ram who took a deep drag and relaxed. He fished out a packet of coloured tablets from his shirt pocket and offered one to Ram. It was a small crimson pill in the shape of a rabbit.

'What is this?' Ram asked skeptically, 'First tell me about the tiger in the tank.'

'Come on. This is a Playboy bunny. Make love, not war! Hare Rama, hare Krishna,' Coco said encouragingly.

Ram picked up the tablet hesitantly and popped it into his mouth.

The effect of the bunny was evident very soon. Ram's lassitude wore off, much like the shedding of soiled clothes. He was filled with energy; able to view his situation more tolerantly. The green and yellow countryside zipped past, now seeming like Fifth Avenue at Christmas time. Even the music in the car sounded better.

Coco spoke authoritatively and endlessly about everything under the sun. 'We are now in Tamu, in the Kabaw valley. You can see there is more piety all around.' He pointed to a procession led by Buddhist monks in burgundy robes who trudged silently along the road on foot followed by a man on an elephant. In the distance, healthy oxen and buffaloes ploughed the paddy fields. The local economy appeared to be doing reasonably well. They passed a restaurant nestled against a grove of leafy palm trees, past small pagodas with brass spires and tiny churches with steel crosses.

Coco spotted a Burmese signboard and directed the driver into a narrow lane bordered with banana plantains, branching off from the main highway. They drove for about a hundred meters to arrive at a two-storied building decorated with the signage of the Government of Myanmar and a national flag fluttering in the mild breeze. A group of military guards in olive uniform peered in and surveyed the passengers. Ram's heart began to beat faster. They were armed with rifles and looked menacing. But the examination was cursory as Ram and his companions were soon invited out and asked to walk down a gravel path lined with plantains and ferns.

At the end of the path was a small meeting room with wooden floors. The tables had already been set with refreshments wrapped in cellophane along with small water bottles. Two officers dressed in green cotton lungis with silk borders and white embroidered half-kurtas and sandals on their feet appeared, swaying gently. Accompanying them was a young girl in a purple sarong with a slit, probably a secretary, since she had a notepad in her hands. She had an innocent face with sandalwood thanaka paste smeared on her forehead like an Indian tilak.

The officers invited Ram and the others to sit down, a sing-song lilt to their tones. The senior of the two introduced himself as Colonel U Nyunt and his junior as Major Sein. Five younger officers already seated in a corner were introduced as customs and military interns to learn about import-export procedures. A notepad and an old-fashioned ball-point pen lay on the table before each chair. No computers were in sight. A note with some statistics on border trade and the number of vehicles that had passed since trade had commenced had been typed using some ancient World War II typewriter. While the first page for Ram was in original, the others were reproduced using dark-blue carbon paper. The write-up could well have been in Tamil or Teleugu, given the doughnut script.

Coco was the most comfortable, alternating between English and Burmese with panache. 'India is concerned about the large number of Chinese goods that are coming in, causing the Indian small industries to raise protests. The toy and the plastic industry in Gujarat is practically wiped out.' The Burmese nodded their heads several times; they seemed familiar with his style of speaking.

Desmond interjected, 'Indian exporters face problems because of the unrealistic rate at which the kyat is pegged, forcing most traders to adopt the informal route.'

'There is need to expand the trade basket and strengthen our relations keeping in view the inherent complementaries in the two great nations,' said Ram, even as the hosts looked pensive and nodded their heads understandingly.

The discussions went on for about thirty minutes after which gifts were exchanged. Ram smiled appreciatively upon receiving a small elephant carved out of wood. Coco opened his bag to take out their gifts. They were handed courteously to the senior officers, who unwrapped them carefully and admired the gold-plated Tanjore paintings. The other officials were handed raw-silk wraps from Mysore.

'So what is your route now?' asked the leader, Colonel Nyunt.

'Tamu to Kalewa and then Shwebo to Mandalay with stops,' said Coco in chaste Burmese. 'We shall be grateful if we could have untroubled passage through your beautiful and auspicious country.'

'And may I take this opportunity to reciprocate your warm hospitality by inviting you,' said Ram, 'to visit Bodh Gaya where Buddha attained enlightenment and Kushinagar near Gorakhpore where he attained salvation and his remains are kept.'

'Thank you,' bowed Colonel Nyunt. 'We will be in touch by wireless all through your visit.'

'Wah! We have managed to enter Myanmar without a blemish,' exulted Coco stretching himself, quite overjoyed. He hugged Ram warmly, as they sat down to drink tea at a wayside restaurant in Kale. 'Our credentials are perfect! Mother India and Big Mama have been treated with great respect.'

'Big Mama?' Coco had referred to the truck as Mother India, but this was a new entity.

'I told you, we got a tiger in our tank! You no believe!' Coco laughed and began to sing. 'There was a lady from Niger, who went out for a ride on a tiger, they came back from the ride, with the lady inside, and a smile on the face of the tiger...But this time Mother India has Big Mama inside. Yes Sir!'

'I still don't believe it, you naughty boy,' said Ram, astounded, but amused by Coco's light-heartedness.

'Indeed, Mother India has Big Mama in its belly, or under-belly.'

'What good is a dead tiger?' asked Ram.

'Who told you it is dead?'

'You cannot just transport a live tiger like that!'

'Why else would there be such urgency?' retorted Coco.

Ram remembered Jugnu telling him that they had smuggled Burree Maada out of Kanha. This could be the biggest revelation of his life! It would radically alter the complexion of the judicial proceedings against him!

'Is it Burree Maada?'

'I dunno what the name is,' said Coco indifferently. 'Big Mama or Big Pussy? What's in a name? A tiger by any name will roar as loudly!'

'But why on earth are we transporting a tiger?'

'It has to be taken across for making photo-copies, carbon-copies or some such duplicate or Boys from Brazil thing,' Coco said, flashing his literary awareness. 'And now there will be no hurdles. That is the beauty of a military regime. Total discipline! Not like your India where every ass hole is a big mouth and every big mouth is an ass hole.'

'I still can't believe it,' said Ram. He was taken aback at the thought of smuggling tigers across international borders.

'Come on man, take it easy and enjoy. Good money justifies it all,' Coco said.

'You guys can escort the truck while I fly to Yangon. This road journey is too much,' Ram complained, holding his back and pretending it was paining. This was totally beyond him.

'I think you should not,' Coco glared at him sinisterly. 'It is your choice to fly out of course, but Mr Goenka will be more pleased if you explore and enjoy this countryside first and its special Shwedagon happy endings before anything else.'

Ram read the underlying message clearly—run and be damned!

They resumed driving, enjoying the lilting Burmese music in the background. Suddenly, Coco's phone rang. He ignored it momentarily before hurriedly stepping aside to answer it. Rapid conversation gave way to arguments with somebody very important; even though he protested strongly, the language was not abusive. Ram pretended not to be interested in the conversation and engaged in talking to Desmond.

Coco returned flustered. 'Bloody hell! How irresponsible can they get! Boss has said that now we must return to Manipur from here itself with this No. 4.'

'What is No. 4?' Ram asked.

'He says it is an important cargo of short-grained sticky rice for Japanese and Thai diplomats and restaurants in Delhi,' said Coco.

'It might even contain something stickier,' speculated Ram, growing in wisdom.

'You are so clever!' Coco grinned. 'Mother India is to be switched with an identical truck, code-named No. 4 carrying this special rice. Mother India will probably proceed north to Mytkina with its cargo, in a new name or shape, and perhaps head further north.'

Ram trembled. He had smuggled a tiger out of India so far. Would he be smuggling contraband into India now? Even a battle-hardened Coco seemed to be arguing and shivering for a change?

He decided to change tack. 'That is a strange name. I wonder why it is named No.4. Personally, I prefer names like yours, short and intelligent!'

Coco beamed, temper restored, 'Yes, rightfully my name should be No. 5. The Goenka brothers called me Channel because I was a good channel partner. My favourite perfume is Chanel No. 5, and one day I saw a film on the great Coco Chanel and asked them to call me Coco instead. No. 4 is the colloquial name for heroin, processed to the fourth stage of purification.'

Ram reeled with shock. 'And what else were we carrying in Mother India?'

'Herbals and organics from all parts of India,' said Coco. 'Red sandalwood from South India. From Central India—tiger bone powder and animal peels—tiger, leopard and deer skins. There is an ever-growing demand for exotic things in the larger Chinese region: Hong Kong, Macau, Shanghai, Taiwan, thanks to the neo-rich in the hinterland.'

'What if the tiger had woken up and started roaring?'

'Telazol injections,' said Coco. 'Everytime we stopped I would inspect. Remember those snooping customs guards at Tamu? I think they could smell the tiger. I had to get them summoned back quickly.'

'How much does this No. 4 cargo cost?' Ram asked.

'Plenty! The money is mainly for the risk handling and conveyance, which is the real value addition,' explained Coco. 'It is many times more than the original price of the raw material. A bagload of heroin buys a scooter in Mytkina, a car in Kunming, and a chopper in New York.'

'The risks must be huge!'

'Goodwill and power apart from the moolah,' Coco said. 'You can put that kind of money into a Swiss account, or you buy arms and play power games and topple governments. Money! Money! Money! Must be funny in a rich man's world. Ahaha, ahaha... Nowsher and his friend Ruby are building a fabulous new Venetian in Macau!'

'So how long have you been in this game?'

Coco pointed towards a milestone and laughed. 'We are only the road maps of the game,' he said. 'Though the government across the bamboo curtain has clearly proclaimed that they will shoot anybody caught with white powder, we are cleverer!'

'Are you protected?'

'I always carry protection!' he laughed. 'The Goenka name is as powerful as it gets. Nowsher is a celebrity in Mandalay—rich, a patron of arts and a philanthropist to boot. The brothers have mastered the art of winning friends and influencing people.'

Coco took out a leather snatch from his bag and handed it to Ram with a smile.

'By the way, Boss asked me to give this to you. Five thousand dollars and your ticket, all the way to Yangon. Nowsher is there, waiting for you. Remember the Rudyard Kipling verse about Mandalay:

Ship me somewheres east of Suez, where the best is like the worst,

Where there ain't no Ten Commandments an' a man can raise a thirst.

'So dude, have fun. Only one advice: Carry enough dollars and condoms at all times in your pocket. Cheers!'

He spotted the tiny, bespectacled man with a white gaung baung the moment he walked out of the customs at Yangon Airport. His starched white shirt had a buckramed collar-band buttoned at the top and his blue lungi was draped tightly around his hips and gathered at the waist in one simple, unknotted hitch. He swayed gracefully, flashing a white smile and swiftly ushered Ram into a Mercedes coupe whose air conditioner was already running. Ram leaned back against the softly padded seats as they drove into Yangon city.

The historic city that was earlier called Rangoon seemed to have a timeless feel about it. At the far end of the road were crude billboards commending amusement shows and visits to the Shwe-Dagon Pagoda and hundreds of other famous temples. And just beyond the tar-macadamed road were verdant slopes and manicured lawns with simple but colourful tropical flowers. The freshly painted road markings and the fluttering flags stood out vividly—much like a school sports day inside an army cantonment—proper, subdued.

The liveried chaufffeur of the Mercedes Coupe was taciturn. As they progressed, Ram noticed that this was the only luxury car around, clearly announcing the distinctive style and the status of the Goenkas. Several golfers had disembarked along with him and they passed them now in their open jeeps stuffed with golf bags. He noticed that even though the road was narrow, it was in superb condition. There was a sense of order everywhere, unlike Katni or Kathmandu. No encroachments, no vendors and tea shops on the sides. In fact, the military spit-and-polish cleanliness was visible in most parts. It even reflected in the well-preserved colonial buildings and the gleaming spires of the Kabar Aye Pagoda.

At first sight, the Inya Lake Hotel looked ordinary. The building was unimaginative, like government hotels in India, straight lines and rectangular blocks. Ram guessed that the hotel must have been built in the sixties since the style had a socialist frugality about it. But it was the compound that took his breath away—it was dominated by the iconic presence of mammoth trees, each at least a century old—fig, banyan, teak and rain trees, stately mahoganies and Burmese rosewoods. Though the reception area had a slightly rundown look, it was airy with numerous potted plants with squeaky-clean teak flooring. The staff appeared abundant, all extremely alert and responsive.

Ram was booked into a large executive suite comprising of two rooms, each the size of a suite in a normal five-star, overlooking the huge Inya Lake. Although not chic, and perhaps not really five-star, it felt clean and sanitized, with a startling sense of space. He tried calling Sherry, but her phone was always out of range.

Just as he began to wonder about Nowsher, the strains of old English songs being played on a piano wafted in from beyond the corridor as the door opened.

'Mr Ramchandra! How nice to meet you again!' Nowsher rushed in and embraced Ram in a bear hug. His supple skin glowed as if he had emerged out of a luxurious spa session. His voice seemed to have gathered a Burmese lilt to it. Dressed in a cream lungi and matching shirt, looking the archetypal Burmese, there was no trace of the debonair western diplomat that Ram had met in Kathmandu. 'Welcome to Myanmar.'

'I am delighted to be in your service Sir.'

'This is home territory for us. You must relax and absorb the pure and unblemished beauty of the Burmese countryside and see this historic city. Although I live in Mandalay, I have grown to love every part of this great country. I have chosen to stay in this hotel with you so that we can talk at leisure. Fortunately this hotel is huge, and therefore inconvenient for eavesdropping.' With a guffaw he said, 'I used to come as a young man in the seventies and stay here for weeks with the Russians for small contracts in Thailand and Burma and Vietnam'.

'I like this place,' said Ram. 'It exudes warmth, very much like home.'

'This great hotel was a personal gift of the Russian President Nikita Khruschev to Burma. He took personal interest in its design. At its peak, it was the most modern hotel in Southeast Asia, much, much before the Shangri-Las, Dusits and Mandarins.'

'What a huge lake? Is it exclusive to this hotel?'

'Yes, it is an artificial lake, a masterpiece of soil and water conservation. It was created by the British to supply water to Yangon by joining the various hills that formed little creeks during the monsoons. We will go to the Lake View Bar later this evening. Khun Sam, the bartender, makes the best Sundowners and Singapore Slings apart from other amazing martinis. My personal favourite is the Bay of Bengal, with a subtle hint of coconut juice.'

'That would be lovely,' beamed Ram in anticipation. He remembered glancing at advertisements about this property. 'I believe Dusit is managing this place?'

'Their lease runs out shortly,' Nowsher smiled, pleased with Ram's alertness to business details. 'But, I have a special dispensation as I book this suite for the whole year and may even bid for this property. We'll meet for dinner and plan the week ahead, in an hour's time. Tomorrow we are invited for tea to the house of one of the most powerful persons in Myanmar, Brigadier-General Khin Min, Head of Special Intelligence for the Myanmar Police. He has no friends in Yangon—part of his job is to keep tabs on everyone, so nobody likes him. But he treats me like his brother—we are very close. Our friendship dates back to University days, to the time when he used to drive a broken scooter and I rode pillion.'

'Surely there is no place for me in such exalted company?'

'Oh! You are the most, the real special guest,' Nowsher exclaimed.

'Why?'

'He wants his son to meet you.'

'What use can I be to his son?'

'The General rarely discusses his intimate problems,' Nowsher explained. 'I happened to mention that you are a family friend who has come from the States to be with us for a while and he opened up to confide in me that he is keen to fulfill the stupid dream of his younger son to go to the States for a higher degree. But his son needs references and help with the application. That is when I suggested that you could help.'

Ram nodded. This was certainly less exacting than carting truckloads of narcotic drugs and tigers across international borders. He had forgotten the intricacies of GMAT and GRE, but it would not be impossible to recapitulate things. He looked at Nowsher and said, 'sure, I can handle that.'

Nowsher hugged him appreciatively.

They were seated at a corner table in the Lakeside Bar of the Inya Lake Hotel, with the manager standing obsequiously close, ready to cater to their slightest whim. Old songs from the sixties were being reeled out by talented Burmese singers who seemed to have had little opportunity to display their competence outside their country.

'I love old film themes and romantic songs,' said Nowsher, beginning to write down some popular names on the back of a napkin. 'My heart and my women are still in the 60s and 70s. I am sure you will like them too—Lara's Theme from Dr Zhivago, Harry Lime from The Third Man and Romeo and Juliet.'

'I love them too,' said Ram, as he sipped his Bay of Bengal appreciatively.

He asked Nowsher, 'Do you also have Burmese citizenship?'

'Yes I have, for the past two decades now,' said Nowsher. 'I have a Burmese name too—U Vinayaka—the man of wisdom. The Ganesha! But for friends like you, I remain Nowsher.'

'And what business do you conduct from here?'

'The family interests in Southeast Asia—Mekong Delta countries and beyond,' Nowsher said. 'It is heavy responsibility—palm oil, mining, entertainment and so on...'

'Organics and herbals?'

'Aha! Quick on the uptake, aren't you? I knew you would ask,' responded Nowsher with a grin. 'We promoted a captive farm for tigers in China. Luckily, that is the only sunken investment so far.'

'Nowsher, is it really true that I was escorting a tranquilized tiger to Mandalay?'

'My friend,' said Nowsher. 'You are one of the lucky...after all, how many people can lift a tiger without being devoured by it?'

'I'm shocked that I was not told about it!' Ram pursued the topic indignantly.

He could have been speaking to a wall. 'My friend,' said Nowsher, 'You have done yeoman service to the cause of tiger conservation. It will be used by scientists attached to our farm—they call it hand-made cloning—sophisticated yet customized—to create tigers with specifications that attract tourists.'

'I wish I could see such a farm,' Ram said.

A pretty Burmese waitress in a purple sarong had come to refill their glasses. She smiled at Nowsher who flashed a bigger smile, patted Ram's hand and said, 'Sure, my friend. But you must set your mind to stay here for a length of time. Perhaps even marry again. Let me share a secret: Burmese girls are loyal and obedient souls who adjust themselves to your habits like a glove…your former President Narayanan had also married one. I can personally vouch for them—it is amazing how much love and serenity they can bring into a barren life.'

Ram wondered if the Goenkas, with their elaborate man-management techniques, had already managed to research his private life as well.

'U Vinayaka! My elephant god.' General Min welcomed Nowshers' hands tightly. Nowsher seemed to wince for a moment before he submitted to the intensity of the greeting. He introduced Ram.

'Excellency, thank you for coming all the way from Naypyidaw,' said Nowsher. 'This is my friend, who is visiting from the States. He is an MBA from the Massachusetts Institute of Technology and a product of IIT in India. He has risen to the top in the States.'

The General extended his hands to Ram, 'Welcome to Shway Pyi Daw.'

Nowsher translated swiftly, 'Burma, the golden land. And Naypyidaw is the new capital of Myanmar…one day it will be as grand as Putrajaya in Malaysia.'

The General gestured warmly. They sat down.

General Min was no more than five feet tall; his droopy colourless face and heavily-wrinkled skin reminded Ram of an aging bulldog. For a man who had been trained by the FSB in Moscow, perhaps it could be said that he had the subtle gravitas of a pugnacious apparatchik about him.

'Myanmar is so clean and orderly Sir,' said Ram flatteringly. 'I would like to send details of how to improve civic management in order to help my friends who are administrators in India.'

The General beamed from one large ear to the other as his head swayed with pride; much like the elephant palms that dotted his visitors' room. Behind the drawn curtains an illuminated Sang Dragon tree, the Burmese rosewood, was in full bloom, its yellow flowers forming a resplendent canopy. In the horizon, a huge pagoda gleamed in the rays of the full moon.

'Discipline is our first priority, whether on the roads or in the houses,' General Min said. 'We have zero tolerance for drug abuse, gambling, prostitution and alcohol. We do not have the perversions of the USA—students going on rampage and shooting in their own schools or colleges. No such nonsense!'

Ram nodded in appreciation while Nowsher was a picture of attention. His ears unfolded like retractable antenna as he leaned forward listening as if the holy gospel was being broadcast for the first and last time. 'Fabulous control of crime by you Sir,' Nowsher said, nudging Ram to respond accordingly.

General Min continued to pontificate, 'We haul up and punish the kwe-ma-tha, the filthy dog-bitch-sons and push them into Insein jail. Yes, we even shoot them. See this report that has appeared in the *Straits Times* published from Singapore.'

Min lifted the front page of a newspaper lying on the table and handed it to Ram who read: Whang Fengshui, head of the Chinese Ministry of Public Security's Narcotics Control Bureau praised Myanmar's efforts to fight drugs and wildlife poachers, lauding the actions of a military government often criticized in the United States and Europe for not doing enough to tackle the problem.

Decorum and discipline! It seemed to be General Min's battle cry as he flashed a broad smile, his white teeth shining. He looked up quizzically when an orderly saluted before darting forward with an official-looking envelope on a silver salver. General Min tore the envelope impatiently and glanced at the note typed on light-yellow paper. His eyes enlarged as he quickly folded the note and commanded it to be put away. Was he counting his fingers? Ram nudged Nowsher.

'Shhh...,' whispered Nowsher. 'The joke amongst his colleagues is that he does not trust anybody, not even his hands and consequently takes count of his fingers too. The knives are out but he has learnt to survive. You don't remain Head of Intelligence for two decades just like that.'

General Min went out briefly and returned, practically holding the ears of a chimp of a boy with supple yellow skin. He was dressed in mustard-yellow Nautica Bermudas and an orange tee-shirt with Santa Barbara splayed across it, and sported sky-blue Nike floaters. He could well have been preparing to shoot for a Baywatch episode, except that he had no surfboard with him and he was squirming like a sulky schoolboy.

Nowsher leapt up instantly and opening his arms, smiled broadly, 'Mr Jade! I am delighted to see you!' He was clearly acting a role.

Ram got up and said, 'Hello.'

Nowsher announced, 'Honorable General Min has two brilliant sons—Ahko Tun, Mr Ruby is a big businessman. But Mr Jade is a wizard at electronics. He can be future Bill Gates of Myanmar.' Ram wondered how a duffer could possibly be transformed into a whiz kid.

General Min's chest heaved with pride. He looked at Ram and murmured, 'He must quickly go to the States.'

'Don't worry, Mr Ram will guide him appropriately,' said Nowsher, nudging Ram.

Jade scowled; he did not bother to conceal his disdain for both

Nowsher and the General.

'Ram, perhaps you should go into Jade's room to discuss his future,' Nowsher urged.

'Not my room for a foreigner, we can sit right here and work,' Jade protested indignantly, getting up to leave.

The General looked thunderstruck. But he recovered quickly and said, 'No, no, this is important work, you can go into my Home Office so that you are undisturbed. Follow!' He marched and led Ram down the corridor.

The General's office was suffused with the smell of lemon grass and the all-pervasive teak panelling that exuded a sense of colonial grandeur. Amongst the oils-on-canvas of what Burma had looked like in earlier times was a sepia photograph of the General on elephant-back with a tiger in the foreground amidst thick teak and bamboo undergrowth. The mantelpiece had silver figurines of oriental gods and goddesses with intricate filigree work. On the main table, three hand-held telephones in different colours were assembled along a side rack. Jade pushed the heavy door disrespectfully with his feet as soon as the General's back was turned till it slammed shut. It closed like the door of a vault.

'I'm entering this unholy Home Office for the first time in two years,' said Jade contemptuously. He perked up suddenly, 'I can now read what the old man hides in here.'

Within moments there was a polite knock. A liveried bearer, with gold tassels hanging from his cap, came in with a lemonade beaker topped with ice, and beef satay threaded onto bamboo skewers in a heavy silver salver.

Jade warmed up unexpectedly. He assessed Ram's attire and concluded, 'Some people are naturally friendly. By the way I am not the tech or business-type my father expects me to be. My interest is in environment. Give me a minute. I'll get my papers.' He walked out briskly.

Ram absorbed the subdued elegance and the sense of power that exuded from the General's office. Within moments Jade was back with a laptop stuffed in a duffel bag that also contained several books. Contrary to Ram's initial assessment, he seemed a confident young man. 'I have an LLB degree. But I'm not at all desperate to go to the States for higher studies.'

Ram cut in brusquely, 'Why not work, or practice for two or three years?'

'There are no private law firms worth the name, as the judicial system is very rigid. You cannot write freely or express your views. No foreign investment is encouraged. Only the Chinese have free access, making economic inroads and laughing all the way to the bank!'

'I know people back home working for Discovery, National Geographic and other heritage and environment related bodies.'

'Yes, that's exactly what I want!' Jade smiled, before asking him, 'Is he a relative of yours?' He pointed towards the drawing room.

'Who?' Ram asked, knowing the answer full well.

'The so-called Elephant God!' Jade answered, suddenly seeming a decade older.

'You mean Nowsher Goenka?' Ram asked, uneasy about where the conversation was going.

'Yes, yes!' Jade said. 'How can you stand the bastard?'

'Sometimes you make friends providentially,' Ram said diplomatically.

'Sure he isn't a relative of yours or something?'

'No. He is a friend, of recent origin.' He could not be sure of Jade yet.

'Do you know the implications of being involved with that green serpent in the grass?' Jade peered microscopically at Ram as if he was afflicted by some peculiar disease, ready to snuff him out. Why did he sound like Sherry?

'It has been a recent development,' said Ram, forced to recall how badly he had been trapped. 'He has been kind and helpful to me to get out of deep trouble.'

'Given a chance I would feed him to tigers!'

Ram perceived some sound outside as the door opened a crack. He raised his voice, 'Enough! Let us look at the application forms.' The sound receded as the door closed carefully.

As they discussed various strategies for cracking the American non-profit job market, Ram observed that unlike his father, Jade was a good listener. The study door opened imperceptibly once again and this time Nowsher peeped in like the villain in a Hitchcock thriller. But he did not seem to have the courage to step inside the room. 'Hello, just came by to see if things are going well!' Nowsher's smile was as large as an Oriental umbrella. 'Nyi Jade, please take down notes, otherwise you will forget and my busy friend will return to the States.' A contemptuous look from Jade made him retreat hastily.

As Nowsher closed the door behind him, Jade searched for writing paper inside his bag. 'Shit, as usual I have no blank paper.' He looked for a printer in the office, but there was none. Ram scanned the General's desk. A few manuals and some office files marked, 'SECRET' were piled up neatly, one on top of the other, but no blank paper was to be seen. 'No paper here,' he said.

Jade gnashed his teeth and growled, 'There is urgent need to break the eggs of my father's secretary. How can there be no writing paper in a study.' He opened the drawers of his father's imposing mahogany study table and pulled out a sheaf of papers. They appeared blank. He tossed them to Ram.

Ram turned over the papers to ensure that nothing had been written upon them. Jade was wrong. There were neatly typed notes on cream-coloured paper—precisely the kind that the General had received in the drawing room, with an envelope stapled below. On the top right-hand corner was a warning in English: TOP SECRET. The writing was Burmese, in unmistakable Pali Bhasa script, with circular letters and diacritics.

Jade, not being a witness to the scene in the drawing room, nudged Ram to write on the plain side, which he refused hastily, saying, 'These are secret papers!'

Jade snatched the papers irritatedly. 'Big deal!' he said, before instinctively casting a glance at them. He mumbled some bits in English: Intelligence Report on Operation Jin, and the implications for Burmese Kya. His eyes widened in astonishment.

'Jin...kya?' Ram asked, petrified by the sudden change in Jade's mood and his ebbing decibel level.

'Kya is Burmese for tiger. You must have heard of Burree Maada, the tigress missing from Kanha, India's Hukaung,' Jade said breathlessly, pointing to a picture of his father on an elephant with a tiger barely visible in the thick grass. He glanced at the first paragraph of the report once again, probably an executive summary since it was in bold letters.

'What does it say?' Ram was equally breathless and excited.

'Our Intelligence people have been tracking a Chinese businessman who has made multiple trips to Hukaung Valley.'

Ram recalled the foreign businessman he had met in Katni at Feroze Goenka's house. Could it be the same person? 'Where is Hukaung?'

'To the north, in upper Chindwin. The area around the historic Ledo-Stilwell War road,' said Jade.

'A war road?' said Ram. 'Like the Bridge on the River Kwai.'

'Built by the Americans to move supplies from Assam to Chiang-kai-Shek's besieged army in Kunming which was fighting the Japanese,' added Jade quickly. 'Hukaung is the largest tiger reserve in the world today, stretching across an area of twenty-five thousand square kilometers, more than ten times that of your Kanha Tiger Reserve. So you can imagine the stakes.'

'I don't get it,' said Ram. 'Who has been tracked by your father's people?'

'An advisor to a conglomerate that desires to convert Hukaung into a corporate agricultural farm. He was assaulted yesterday by activists who oppose commercial exploitation of Hukaung Valley. Incidentally, your friend the Elephant God is also closely connected with one such business group.'

'And these activists have the wherewithal to take on such big interests?'

'Kachin Development Networking Group.' Jade looked pensive as he added gently, 'Besides others who passionately love the tiger.'

'Why should the Chinese businessman be interested in wild tigers in the forest of Myanmar?'

'I am both surprised and impressed by our Intel oafs,' said Jade gravely. 'They have correctly deduced that there is a plot to eliminate our wild tigers and focus world attention on our inability to protect them. The plotters want to use that ploy to legitimize farm-breeding of tigers and trade in tiger parts. Other multinationals want the huge area of Hukaung to be free of tigers so that it is available for mega-mining projects. There is a convergence of interest between these diverse private interest groups. My fear is that both your friend and my old man are toeing their line.'

Suddenly Jade grinned wickedly and clicked his tongue.

'Why, what's funny?'

'Nothing,' he said dismissively, continuing to chuckle, looking away. 'I didn't expect such detailed reporting.'

'It must be something very funny,' Ram persisted, amused to see Jade happy and grinning. 'Tell me, I'm curious.'

'Well, the person who wrote this report has a sense of humour not quite in keeping with the Intelligence rank and file. He has stated that the businessman's bank account was deleted!'

'He was robbed?' When there was no affirmative nod from Jade, Ram continued, 'It is a common sign of insurgents and extremist groups. They amputate the hands.'

'Nope.'

'His eyes were gouged by a predatory vulture?'

'No!'

'The nose…the tongue?'

'You aim too high!'

'Legs?'

'His bloody dick!'

'Bizarre and primitive!' The assassins must be demented to mutilate the man like this. 'But how are you so sure it means that?'

Jade finished reading the report quickly before he continued, 'The bank account was found. It was lying encrypted nearby, like a burrito, wrapped tidily in a banana leaf.'

'I repeat! Very criminal besides being primitive and macabre!'

'Remember Planet of the Apes?'

'Yes.'

'Planet of the Tigers…'

Planet of the Tigers! In a flash Ram remembered leafing through the Materia Medica that was brought in by the Chinese partners and the vivid descriptions of alternative cures derived from ancient Chinese texts using herbs, minerals and animals.

Meanwhile Jade continued, 'Some years ago a dozen elephants were found killed near our border at Kanchanburi in Thailand. Their huge penises had been lobbed off for a similar reason.'

Suddenly it made sense to Ram.

'Jin?' he asked.

'Mandarin for gold,' said Jade.

'You know Mandarin?' Ram asked.

'Yes, I have lived in Beijing and New Delhi besides London. Thanks to the Internet I have friends all over—Tibet, South Africa, India…'

Ram recalled Nowsher talking about a group of misguided young people who were against the skins business. Love Tiger or Blood Tiger. Sherry had also talked of the trans-boundary conspiracy and trade in endangered species. What kind of people in Yangon would associate themselves with such dangerous activities?

'Shame! Shame!' Jade shouted as he paced the room angrily. 'Horrendous! Instead of supporting the activists, our guys are launching a man hunt for the Love Tigers who are reportedly behind this assasination. They forget that in the last two months we have lost six tigers from Hukaung—four carcasses have not even been found!'

Nowsher stepped in. He stared coldly at them. Suddenly he looked haggard, far more subdued than he had ever appeared. As if somebody had shaken him up.

Nowsher's mood changed only after his mobile rang. 'Helloo… Vin-aya-ka,' he intoned in a typically Burmese drawl. Then, as he looked at the screen and recognized the caller, indifference changed to expectation. He gulped, stood up and exclaimed respectfully, 'Min-ga-la-ba!'

There was a pause before the caller on the other side started speaking, causing Nowsher to smile and bow repeatedly, as if honored by the call. He placed down the phone carefully and spoke with a flourish,

'General Min is full of praise for you and says you are taw-thaw.'

Though Ram was delighted, he said modestly, 'But I didn't do anything exceptional.'

'General Min is appreciative of your motivational skills with difficult people. He says you can make chimps into champions. It seems Jade spoke well of you, something he seldom does.'

Ram stared at him, not knowing if this was a charade or if he had actually struck the right chord with the General. 'I don't know why you all find Jade difficult,' he said, testing waters.

'General Min is truly concerned about Jade... He is kyet-uh-pot, a bad egg. When Ruby's mother died young, the General married again. The sexy and cunning Thai music instructor was first married to a flamboyant Thai diplomat. She is the one who decided to give Jade a liberal English education and made the mistake to let him travel freely.'

'Jade is not a fool.'

Nowsher led Ram aside and whispered, 'One day, with great reluctance, the General confided in me that,' he stopped to let his eyes rove across the hall to ensure that nobody was listening. 'He knows that Jade sympathizes with the pro-democracy and pro-environment activists and makes the General's enemies within the government take potshots at him. At one stage he was so desperate that he almost had Jade assasinated!'

'Then?'

'I motivated Jade and told the General that it was best to send Jade to the States. After all son is son. Out of sight is out of mind. I volunteered to fix it somehow!'

Ram mulled over this information. 'What is the General's other son like?' he asked, trying to recollect the photographs of the General's family standing on his lawns. While Jade had been dressed in faded blue jeans and a colourful tee-shirt, looking like a nerd, the other son was clean-shaven and clad in crisply ironed trousers and a smart jacket.

'Ruby is a poodle,' said Nowsher. 'The opposite of Jade! He has only one weakness, and that is vintage cars, apart from a girlfriend in Kunming, Very shrewdly, I inducted him as a partner in the Myanmar part of the business as soon as he graduated. You do know, he has the General's ear. I can reach the General in minutes even though he does not carry a mobile phone.'

'Go see Scotts Bazaar and play golf. Become part of the 4-ball of the General and Ruby,' Nowsher recommended strongly, almost pleading with him.

'Playing golf with the General will be a challenge,' Ram said. 'I believe he places huge bets. But I've read up about Scotts. It seems like a great idea.'

'Yes. I've persuaded the government to lease out decrepit colonial buildings in Mandalay and Yangon to convert them into heritage-hotel-cum-shopping complexes, like Chimes in Singapore and Heritage 1881 in Hong Kong. Retain the facade and the history, but make the interiors swanky and get the best brands in the world. They are now warming up to the idea of public-private partnerships.'

'You'll be the Donald Trump of Southeast Asia if you can pull that off,' said Ram.

'Only, if I have smart people like you around me,' grinned Nowsher, punching him playfully.

Ram nodded appreciatively. He remembered fun-filled Faneuil Hall in Boston and the Frisco Chinatown. It was in 1881 Heritage that he had bought Jaya the Vacheron Constantin watch that had never left her wrist since. Had she gone down wearing that beautiful present from him?

'Okay, a bit of fun now,' Nowsher drawled playfully. 'Would you like to sin, with Elinor Glynn, on a tiger skin?'

'Yes, I do, I do!'

'Great!' Nowsher clapped his hands. 'I'll locate my new

Eurasian acquisition called Helen. Tomorrow we finalize the list for my exclusive reception for the Tatmadaw, the Military. The Governor's Residence will be recreated to colonial glory.'

'You've managed to get his official residence for your do?'

'It is a hotel of Rudyard Kipling-era romance. I will be announcing a new flank to the Military Hospital from my side and will be honored by the Chief himself. The military band has already begun rehearsing the music to be played.'

Even as they were talking, Ram noticed that Nowsher had already contacted Feroze. He spoke smoothly, persuasively, 'We must penetrate deep. Fast, even faster; otherwise the Chinese will gobble us up.'

Nowsher's prodding persuaded Ram to go across to the Yangon Golf Club to play golf with the General. He was ready early, much before the honk of the silver Mercedes Cabriolet, a refurbished 1960s classic that took one's breath away and from which music played loudly. Ruby, diminutive as a midget, leapt out easily. He examined Ram, sized him up quickly.

'I've managed to buy cars from every seller in Myanmar and even in Thailand,' he said. 'I'm also a mechanical freak and have retro-fitted them to perfection. I have an Atlantic 29 in Mandalay. It is much smoother than a Merc.'

'I believe you promote music?' Ram asked.

'I am the President of the Myanmar Jazz Society.'

A chatter box who only needed company, he began by telling Ram about the history of the club, 'Nowsher contributed generously to reconstruct the Club House, which was originally made with pure Burma teak and was gutted in the massive fire that occurred after the war.'

They were just short of the club when a military policeman

on a motorcycle zipped past them and asked them to stop. He saluted Ruby and handed him a slip of paper that said:

'The General has been called for an emergency meeting with the Head of Military Security Affairs and cannot join. Please call Jade as less than a three-ball will not be allowed.'

Ruby apologized on his father's behalf and called for Jade.

Ram admired the Golf Club. It was, like the rest of Myanmar, a paradise with swathes of green and rich tropical foliage all around.

They got into action the moment Jade arrived and played twelve holes before it started drizzling and they got a little drenched. The game was abandoned with Ruby leading decisively ahead of Ram and then they rushed into the clubhouse. They ordered beer inside the bar which had several government officials reclining on chairs and rattan sofas. Ruby kept waving every now and then and appeared to know everybody.

Ram loved the wildly boisterous charm of Scotts Bazaar, now called the Bogyoke (meaning General, after the political leader Aung San, father of Aung San Su Kyi) Market. Inaugurated in 1926, it retains its old facade and has many wooden shops on stilts with people milling all around. For a moment he winced when the shops reminded him of the tea stall in Jabalpur where Jugnu and he had been arrested for the James Wilson tiger skin that belonged to his father. But without doubt, this was the best place to study Burmese culture.

A kaleidoscope of colours, the market was full of vegetables, fruits, clothes, slippers and sandals, wooden artifacts and handicrafts. He loved the multi-dimensional visual appeal of the place and felt naturally drawn towards the art area. There were hundreds of stalls, each with hundreds of paintings made by local painters, selling for as little as a dollar. They were mostly simple landscapes of the mountains and the countryside with Buddhist themes as backdrops; oils were more expensive than water colours. They were displayed all over, on the wooden walls of the stalls, hanging on strings between stalls and around the shops, in stacks on the ground and hand-held by helper boys. Every inch of space was utilized to display art. He had never seen anything as vibrant in his life. The Burmese must be the most artistic people in the world!

At the end of the aisle was a crafts shop selling wooden and lacquer statuettes and art works. Ram could hear a girl loudly negotiating the price of a statue of Buddha. The owner was adamant, defending the price he had quoted even as he spoke English like many others of his tribe, 'Ma Daw, this is a rare Buddha from Bagan. This piece is made from one single piece of original Burmese teak and is called Buddha Calling the Earth to Witness. I agree that the original gold leaf is a little worn off, but you can see the rich red underpainting in cinnabar, the natural ore from which mercury is extracted. It is over a hundred years old. You can buy it but you will need a license to carry this out of the country. Our laws are very rigid when it comes to heritage and art works related to history.'

'I like the piece, but reduce the price,' the girl urged.

Ram walked across slowly, trying to see the statue for himself. It was a beautiful wooden figurine of Buddha seated in a meditative mood. The sculptor punched some figures on his calculator, turned it towards the girl, who had her back to Ram and continued to explain, 'Sakyamuni is in the earth-touching mudra, calling on the earth to witness his triumph over Mara, who personifies temptation. On his lap he holds a patra, or alms bowl. See, his face is round and almost boyish, with a small nose and slightly pursed lips. You will not find such a rare piece anywhere in the world.'

'750 too high! My price 250 dollars. Final price!'

'Okay final price—350 dollars.' The sculptor raised his hands over his head in anguish and pretended that his throat was being cut, frustrated by her firmness. Ram wished the spirited girl who was striking such a bargain would turn around. She was hidden from his view by a huge canvas that the painter's assistant was holding, resting it vertically on the edge. Her head was covered by a silk scarf.

The girl was walking on when Ram sensed something familiar about her. He rushed closer and spotted her long and sinuous hands. Instantly he recognized her and shouted, 'Madam, can I please see what you have bought?'

Sherry wheeled around and confronted him, shocked, 'Ram! What a small world! I can't believe its you!'

'And I never imagined I would meet you here. When did you come?'

'I'm returning from Kunming.'

'Kunming? China!' Ram recalled the secret papers in General Min's Home Office.

'To interview the partners of your former bosses, the Raja brothers,' said Sherry. 'They have promoted tiger farms in China and live there.'

'Wow! Phemomenal! How did you go?'

'By road. I stopped at all the exotic places, including the Hukaung Valley.'

'I've heard of that tiger reserve. Just the other day somebody mentioned the gruesome killing of a Chinese businessman.'

Sherry shivered visibly, 'How do you know?'

'I keep informed company,' said Ram. 'Wonder what their motive was?'

'What could it be? I suspect it is pro-something.'

'Pro-democracy,' Ram said, relieved that she did not know what he knew.

'No!' She laughed at his naiveté. Her teeth flashed daintily, pleased to catch him on the wrong foot.

'What then?'

'Pro-tigers...intriguingly, today that almost means anti-China!'

Sherry pointed towards the flower and fruit market where tons of flowers were displayed. A small girl served tea in a tiny shop with fragile rattan chairs. They sat down.

'What did you order?'

'Yay nway gyan,' said Sherry. 'Burmese green tea and Burmese semolina cake with raisins, walnuts and poppy seeds.'

'I tried calling you. I finally have some information to fuel a question that has plagued you for long,' said Ram. 'Why should a tiger be exported alive out of India?'

Sherry stood up in amazement. 'Repeat that!' she commanded, her face flushed. 'You got some dope on Burree Maada?'

'Only that an Indian tiger was part of a recent export consignment to Myanmar.'

'Did it have a limp? Burree Maada had to be trapped to be taken! If it had a limp then that tiger has to be her. It has to be Burree Maada!

'Maybe, maybe not.'

'Just as I suspected—she has been smuggled out of Kanha to...'

'Perhaps a safer sanctuary.'

'A laboratory across the border!'

The hustle and bustle of the bazaar drowned their conversation. Ram reached out for Sherry's hands and leaned closer. Her mint-green silk longyi and flowered batik blouse highlighted her soft contours, complementing her skin which glowed like Venetian marble. He was pleasantly surprised to see how fabulous she looked even without any make-up. He felt a tug at his hands as she urged him to get up and walk in the quieter by-lanes.

'I hope you are making the most to enjoy this exotic trip of yours,' commented Ram.

'Ram, I feel played, gamed!' moaned Sherry, beating her hands in frustration. 'I have been reporting about tiger deaths consistently. But, I seem to have become a cipher, a conduit, unwittingly. The more I publicized the fact that tigers are being poached because of the global demand for tiger parts, I seem to have furthered the goal of those whose objective is to prove that tigers just cannot be naturally conserved in the wild. The Chinese partners are not only fond of shikar, they have invested heavily in captive tiger farms. They are now within striking distance of getting CITES to allow trade in tiger parts from tiger farms by proving that such farm grown tigers can successfully be introduced into the wild. But that is something I dispute. The biological diversity of the natural gene pool is vitiated in a captive farm. It damns the natural evolution of the species!'

She continued, 'There's a lot been happening. A meeting took place in Kunming in the mansion of a powerful shogun. Despite his being over seventy, he has been respected for his family's fanatical loyalty and devotion to the ruling regime for more than a hundred years. A secret deal was struck in the mansion between some top business families across Southeast Asia and Africa.' She paused, 'Beyond frontiers, these are people who can manipulate governments in this region with their money power. The Goenkas are but tiny specks in that dazzling mosaic!'

'Frankly, I can't complain. The Goenkas have been good to me...have you heard of Jin?'

'Huangjin is Mandarin for soft gold. Like black gold for petroleum, or green gold for tea. It advocates tiger farms as the only safe haven for tigers. And, in order to show to the world that Dalai Lama's beacon call to eschew animal skins has been repudiated by his own people.'

'Are there other interested parties in India, apart from the Goenkas?'

'Bang on! The insurgent groups in the northeastern states of India need arms. Royal Thai Army weapons are smuggled out by road to Myanmar and reach the Reds in India along with party drugs in exchange for red sandalwood, raw cannabis, tigers, rhinos and other such exotica. The Goenkas have projected themselves as safe conduits both ways.'

'Don't the Naxalites want to help the tribals by conserving wildlife?'

When he had researched the Naxalites he had read that they were committed to giving the tribals their natural rights in the forests.

'On the contrary, it is now evident that the Naxalites would be happy if tiger reserves and other wildlife parks are permanently rid of endangered species and tourists. It would mean an end to government intervention and policing. Then their Red Corridor would be seamlessly connected and become exclusively theirs. A third of India is already under the Red flag. Comrade Mao's Red Book is their Bible!'

'That would be devastating!'

'Yes, Ram,' said Sherry, her mouth twisting. 'Trade in endangered species, smuggling of drugs, arms, counterfeit currency and timber are all closely interlinked and converge across the Sino-Myanmar-Nepal-India border.' She paused before announcing with a dramatic flourish, 'And you, a civilized corporate executive from Silicon Valley, have willfully allowed yourself to be brutally criminalized. Sadly, you have become part of this reprehensible global racket!'

'Sherry, don't blame me. I too have been gamed by destiny,' said Ram, covering his face with his hands.

'Another favor. Ask Nowsher Goenka the exact whereabouts of Burree Maada and why he is in the tiger farm business when he has so much more.'

He felt lonely and lost. Sherry had hardly been thankful for the information about Burree Maada and had posed yet another question. He wondered what her game plan was.

He felt dejected and bid her goodbye. He walked back towards the parking lot, his head swirling with the thought of deceit.

He was just about to sit in the car when he was accosted by a familiar and friendly voice.

It was cheerful and friendly Ruby. He had raised himself on his toes and leaned against the window. 'Hello…my dear golf partner. Where have you been?'

'I met someone who has just returned from Kunming and thinks it is heavenly. That even Thailand is no patch on it.'

'I was there for an important conference on the future of tigers recently, hosted by an aristocratic old friend at his beautiful villa near Lake Dian. Had I known you were interested I would have asked you to accompany me. I too have bought a property there on a hill overlooking the lovely valley and Dragon Grotto. Restaurants there serve terrific cuisine—like caterpillar fungus-yatsa gunbu. Then you can have an everlasting chain of happy endings!'

Sherry's findings were clouding Ram's mind. He was to leave for India the next day. He finally picked up the courage to confront Nowsher to ask as diplomatically as he could, 'Why are you all promoting tiger farms?'

Nowsher met Ram's eye squarely, though he seemed taken aback. He walked over to the ornate shelves in an alcove beside the bar and picked out an issue of the *Time Magazine* with 'An Inconvenient Truth' written boldly against a globe, with an image of Al Gore seeming to explain the problem. He handed it to Ram, studying him penetratingly, as if sizing up his appetite for the subject. Finally he responded, 'We were keen to protect the tiger line; it is only with that altruistic motive that we invested heavily in captive farms on assurances by the international community that trading in tiger parts would soon be opened up. But, though we kept running up huge expenditures, the other end of the bargain has not been kept.'

Ram was not surprised to hear that. He had read that the governments of China and India were locked in a classic game-theory type of dialectic on the subject of environmental conservation and abatement to make steep unilateral announcements for reducing carbon emissions. The strategy was to force the other side to match their proclaimed goals before secretly encouraging them to pull back. The objective was to hold the high moral ground publicly before quietly following suit. 'But,' asked Ram, 'Why tiger farms, when the tiger can be conserved naturally.'

'My friend, it is expensive to save the tiger naturally. The governments of India and China need to follow a policy of rapid urbanization to find value-added jobs for their hungry millions in the service sector in the cities, not in forests and low-return agriculture that is best left to Africa. Countries like Germany and Switzerland run jails in partnership with the private sector, so why not tiger ranching. We have already undertaken rewilding experiments in South Africa. This will be Public-Private Partnership, PPP in the environment sector.'

'I'm surprised there is no talk about all this in the States,' said Ram.

'The USA already has private tiger breeding,' said Nowsher. 'But then USA is the United States of America. It can afford to have double standards and thumb its nose at the world. Do you know the premium on white tiger cubs which are sold like pugs there?'

'No idea,' said Ram, shrugging his shoulders.

'A white tiger cub sells for as much as twenty thousand dollars.'

'I thought tiger trafficking was banned in the States!'

'It is kept under wraps,' said Nowsher. 'Haven't you seen exotic animals in that city with the casinos, like our Macau...Las Vegas?'

Ram recalled his trip to Vegas for his bachelor party with an assorted group of friends, mostly from MIT. They had spent some very exciting moments and guzzled champagne by the gallons. A very attractive stripper who resembled Sharon Stone had entertained each of the men, kneeling down pretending to unzip them individually. But in Ram's case she had actually done so, and he had turned crimson with embarrassment when he noticed that a few women friends had entered quietly to surprise the men.

The second time he had visited Vegas was with Jaya. They had gone to the Secret Garden in the Mirage Casino and Hotel, the creation of magicians and illusionists Siegfried and Roy. The stars, apart from dolphins, were the striped white tigers with pink paws and ice-blue eyes, snow white and all-gold tigers and snow white lions, and similarly recreated panthers and leopards. He had found them quite bizarre.

'You're convinced that tiger parks serve a public interest?' Ram asked.

'Of course!' Nowsher said confidently, thumping the table. 'Well, to begin with, you are allowing many more people to become aware of the joys of tiger management, without causing biotic disturbance.' He pulled out an album that had photographs of hordes of people watching tigers in what looked like a huge open zoo. School buses were parked in large numbers. 'Harbin is the capital city of the northeast Heilongjiang Province. A huge number of tigers inhabit our Tiger Park there. Children and adults queue in long lines to feed cattle and sheep to the tigers. Here we have taken over the commercial risk from the government. After all, at the end of the day, what is it that you want? More tigers alive; fewer tigers poached. You get all that, and more. Conservation need not be a zero-sum game.'

'Are you saying it can actually be a win-win situation?'

'China, unlike India, is focused,' said Nowsher. 'It has had an Ilaohu Policy, meaning Love Thy Tiger. It has banned production and sale of Chinese medicine containing tiger bone.'

'That's probably to show off environmental sensitivity to the world, prior to the Olympics. But if it is not the government, then who is driving the farms?'

'We, the Tiger Breeding Farmers Association! We are trying, but yes, we have failed so far to effectively lobby for the government to ignore Resolution 12. 5 of CITES. Our contention is that the trade ban has not worked as demonstrated by the fact that tiger poaching continues unabated in countries like Indonesia, Myanmar and India. Fortunately now, the opposition is dying out and we hope to get the Chinese Government to support our cause. Ram, it is historic! We are just a hair's breadth away from success!'

'I still can't believe you have more than a few tigers in your non-jungle park.'

'We have several hundred. But that's not so much! The States has as many if not more. In France the Parc des Felins is a tourist site. And yet anything we do attracts adverse western media attention!'

'So who really opposes you in CITES?'

'India! It lives in a previous century. What a waste of Asian talent! Why can't India and China strategize together on all important issues—Climate Change, Genetics, CITES, etc. I felt so happy when Pan Therapeuticals and Zentigris agreed to set up a joint venture at my behest.'

'I guess you know the promoters of Zentigris, the Raja brothers. What about their Chinese partners, Choo and Fung?'

'I have known the Pan family for many years. We have supplied them with the DNA of wild tigers from different jungles of India and Myanmar for their early research on tiger genetics before all of us decided to collectively invest in tiger captive farms and expand further.'

'I've never seen a tiger farm,' said Ram, pretending to look forlorn. Perhaps he could get some clue as to the whereabouts of Burree Maada.

'Why don't you go,' said Nowsher, handing Ram the brochures he had pulled out.

'Where should I go?'

'Go see for yourself. For instance, our Rainbow Tiger and Panda Park outside Harbin, the St Petersburg of the East, close to North Korea. It was started in partnership with an investment of just a few million dollars that has become rather big now. You'll see how popular it is. It is one of our bigger farms, run professionally. I will ask our people to make suitable arrangements for your trip.'

'That sounds great.'

'I have a brilliant idea! We could utilize your speaking skills and send you to represent our case in international conferences like CITES. Lack of advocacy and PR has been our shortcoming. We need to go about branding these farms as genetic lifeboats that will keep the tiger alive. I assume that you shall leave immediately!'

'We have more than hundred pregnancies in a year!' Suzie, the pretty girl-guide in the lavender jeans and pink parka-collar boasted at the entrance of the Rainbow Tiger and Panda Park, shaped like a tiger's jaw with painted cement fang, each a few feet long. 'This captive park has been chosen as a pilot-project and granted funds as a breeding centre for tiger reintroduction.'

It was a long and rocky path across the village which was spread out against a snow-capped hill. Healthy plants and creepers bearing vegetables—ginger, garlic, broccoli, cauliflower and cabbage adorned the little patches between the houses while small children cocooned in colourful reds, greens and yellows, played outside. Local stations played full blast with melodious songs pulsating out of each cottage. The air was fresh with the smell of freshly boiled egg soup and ginseng tea.

Ram passed an overbridge across a moat that ran all around a grassy enclosure bound by two layers of chain-link fence. Dozens of sleek, healthy-looking tigers lazed around. 'In Rainbow alone, we have more than two hundred of these magnificent animals. The whole village is one large zoo,' Suzie explained. 'Each tiger has been given a name by schoolchildren and they are counseled to take care of them.'

Suzie navigated him to a tea booth from where he had a good overview. She placed an order. A fat waitress came out with a plate of oily french fries with an assortment of vegetables.

'I have never seen such huge fries,' said Ram. 'These must be done in some special animal fat.'

'Stir fried tiger with ginger and hill vegetables.'

Though hunger pangs had been teasing him for a while, he picked up a piece reluctantly. He chewed it. After all, he told himself, he had begun to relish beef; this could not be very different. He picked a fry and dipped it into the dark red sauce that looked like a cross between kimchee and soy sauce. He winced. The batter was a mere brush on the meat which was bland and tough. He had to be a cannibal or an Olympic athlete to digest it!

'We also serve tiger soup, tiger wine and spicy red curry made with tenderized strips of tiger, served with scented rice,' suggested the waitress. 'No problem...good for man.'

'No, thanks, I don't need any enhancement for my manliness.'

She blushed.

A doddering old man hobbled up the path and sat by wooden table and ordered a bowl of soup. On seeing Ram he mumbled something. Ram looked at him curiously, trying to make sense of the gibberish. The old man repeated, 'India.'

'India,' Ram nodded, smiling courteously.

'India...very good!'

The old man clutched Ram's arm and spoke quaveringly to Suzie who began to translate for him.

While he had retired from the Forestry and Wildlife Department in Fujian, his son had worked as a veterinary assistant with this facility. Tragically, his son had been mauled by a tiger in the Park. Ram nodded sympathetically. The old forester clung to Ram and led him to the nearest enclosure so that he could observe the tigers closely. As they stood there, a dead cow was dropped into the enclosure and several tigers pounced upon it.

Ram asked him, 'What is the difference between these tigers and those in the wild?'

The old man did not mince words. He knotted his hands in front of his crotch and bumped his buttocks forward, caricaturing a copulating man. 'No hunting! Only Fug, fug, fug... Many tigers cannot even hunt cow.' Apparently a few days ago the keepers had to step in finally and put a cow out of its misery by killing it.

Ram looked at the tigers. Outwardly they looked just like the tigers he had seen earlier in his life—in the wildlife park at Achanakmar, in zoos and fancy parks like the Secret Garden and in pictures and films. Curiosity got the better of him and he asked the old forester, 'Sir, can you explain the basic difference between these captive tigers and the ones in the wild?'

'Today, not much,' the old man said. 'But, tomorrow, too, too much.'

Ram remembered reading about white tigers and gene mutations. There were unpredictable deficiencies that emerged because of strange mutations in the DNA in communities that encouraged inbreeding in the absence of genetic diversity. An entire race could vanish that way.

'Look, look!' The old man pointed towards two tigers in adjoining enclosures. One stood in a corner of the large grassy park to the left while the other was in a smaller enclosure to the right. He pointed to the one on the left that had just whimpered and said, 'China tiger weak.' Then he flexed his arm and pointed to the one on the right, 'India tiger strong.'

'India?'

'India DNA good,' drooled the old man, as he continued to point towards the tiger in the small enclosure.

Ram's heart pounded as he stared at the tiger in the smaller enclosure. Its movement was regal. Suddenly it stretched and roared deafeningly. Was this Burree Maada, the missing tigress of Kanha? He had smuggled her out of India! How majestic she looked! Just when it began to stride slowly, Ram stared transfixed. Yes, there was a distinct limp!

'Look! Look!' the old man commanded once again, pointing with his fingers towards the two tigers.

Both the tigers were now in front of him. Ram stared keenly. The colours, the dazzling gold and intense black stripes, the curves, the essential movements, everything seemed about the same. Perhaps on intense scrutiny one could say that the local tiger seemed a shade paler. What was the one distinguishing feature about inbred tigers that made them recognizably different?

'Eyes! Look at the eyes!' the old man pointed emphatically with shaking fingers to the paler specimen on the left in the larger enclosure.

And then Ram got it! the eyes of the inbred tiger were misaligned. It was cock-eyed!

The old man grunted, 'Inbreeding disease, Strab-is-mus! My beloved son had reported this condition to the management just days before his sudden death!'

THE GAME

It was well past midnight when Ram reached Baikunthpur. Suddenly, a gigantic lizard fell from space in one composite movement, and something long and fleshy grabbed his feet. Ram shuddered, frightened out of his wits. Thankfully, it was only Jugnu. Ram pulled him up and hugged him asking, 'Jugnu, when did you get out?'

'Yesterday,' said Jugnu. 'I salute Goa Sahib and you.'

'Thank you, Jugnu. How are my other friends in the jail? Khandar, Narad, Balli and Firanghee?'

'Khandar is almost out...just a matter of a day or two. Narad is already on the road. It happened suddenly.'

'So where is Narad?'

'Bastar or maybe Ghadchiroli or Balaghat with his Reds,' said Jugnu. 'I learnt that you have had a very interesting time in Nepal and Burma.'

'Nothing special,' said Ram.

'Come on, I saw a picture of a lovely woman in bed with you in Kathmandu,' said Jugnu flashing a mischievous smile.

Ram froze. 'But...'

'I even know her name. Maya the enchantress, the celestial deception.'

Ram's heart stopped briefly. Nowsher had led him on and videotaped his intimate encounters!

'Like virginity, it is hard to retain your royalty in current times,' admitted Abhimanyu, frustratedly. They were ascending the long and winding ramp to Baikunthpur Palace. 'Every mother-fucking bastard thinks he can take a shot at you.'

The view from the ramparts lifted Ram's spirits. He could see the brilliant countryside—blazing-yellow, glossy-green and rusty-ochre swaths of mustard and soybean growing in irrigated fields, silhouetted lushly against soft and undulating hills. The sky was a clear blue except for white streaks of cirrus clouds through which the sun shone brightly. Wild flowers clung to the walls in resplendent hues.

An old elephant lay chained to an iron post, lavished with buckets of water from a hydrant. A gust of breeze had the pennant of Baikunthpur State, with the distinctive crest displaying two elephants and a peacock, fluttering lazily. Ram spotted a vintage blood-red Rolls Royce and a silver Bentley being cleaned and polished.

'Wow! That's a lovely car, well maintained!' Ram pointed to the Rolls. Royal status may have been snuffed by the Constitution, but the aura of royalty still held good for Baikunthpur.

'My grandfather's Uḍan Khatola, his abracadabra, his magic carpet, his Tiger Car,' announced Abhimanyu proudly. 'It's a Rolls-Royce Phantom III Tourer. The old man visited the Rolls factory in Derby after seeing a similar one with the royalty in Monaco. He got after the makers to customize it for him. The outfitting was specially done by Barker and Co of London, the famous English coachbuilders. Even today the engine is worth its weight in gold. I try and keep the Tiger Cat roadworthy by driving it around once in a while. It must have crept through the bush as elegantly as a cheetah.'

'So do you take it out for vintage car races in Delhi and Bangalore?'

'Nah!' said Abhimanyu. 'I am seldom here, less still after my father expired. But when I bring my foreign friends, they seldom fail to be awed by it. We have one of the first 1941 editions of the Willys Jeep and vintage motor cycles, including a Royal Enfield of

1948, an older Triumph and a valve-driven Harley-Davidson of the 1930s. We always have a local rally of about thirty-forty vehicles on Republic Day. It is like a flag march for us, and it keeps the district administration happy!'

Inside the lounge, under the light of the huge chandeliers, were huge framed portraits of the royal family. Against the fading draperies of taffeta and velvet, black-and-white photographs of various tiger shoots were arranged symmetrically on the walls. Above the portraits and the photographs were mounted trophies of just about every conceivable animal in the world. In two corners of the huge lounge were stuffed white tigers in glass cases, each more than ten feet in length. Tiny lights assisted in making them look sinister.

'I am thrilled to be here.' Ram could not help but admire the cool and commanding manner in which Abhimanyu Singh went about his estate. The quintessential Maharaja—tall and handsome with an unmistakable patina of outdoor robustness. Ram smiled appreciatively and asked, 'Were you in Oxford or Cambridge?'

'Nah, Delhi!'

'But your English accent?'

'I wear many hats…I was heavily into drama. I was the captain of the University squash team, and led an expedition to successfully climb Kanchenjunga. I was shortlisted for Rhodes, and would have made it if my academic record were just a little better.'

'What firm did you join after college?'

'I joined Mother Earth. I spent a full year doing what I am best at—discovering the world. I travelled on my Harley and have a Guiness record for circumnavigating the globe in the shortest time.'

Ram compared Abhimanyu with the man in the portrait above him. That man looked every inch a despotic dictator who must have ruled with an iron hand. It was the portrait of a Maharaja, who with his iron look and haughty moustache would put any feudal lord to shame. It occupied a large portion of the wall, and had the name Kipling inscribed in a corner. 'I thought Rudyard Kipling was only a writer of the Jungle Books and other stories,' Ram said.

Abhimanyu responded, 'Actually, this portrait of my great-grandfather was done by Kipling's father. He was the principal of Bombay's J.J. School of Art. My old man patronized him and would often invite him over for long holidays.'

Ram looked at Abhimanyu closely and asked, 'How come you don't sport a moustache?'

'I knew you'd ask that,' Abhimanyu said with a smile. 'Actually, it doesn't go with my adventurous lifestyle. If my father had his way, I would have had one like in those Fevicol ads...strong enough to tug an elephant.'

They passed through the lounge into the huge drawing room. Ram noticed the massive antiques that adorned the showcases, along with huge ivory sculptures. Pickings from all over Southeast Asia and Africa adorned the walls alongwith a bewildering assembly of paintings. Abhimanyu noted his interest.

'The compelling ones are the Tagores and Jamini Roys on that wall and William and Thomas Daniells along the other. They are priceless. A particularly imposing painting by Johann Zoffany that I have relocated depicts a tiger shoot by Claude Martin, the maverick French founder of the La Martiniere School in Lucknow, with the standing lions of Constantia in the background.'

'Lovely rug,' said Ram.

'Authentic Aubusson,' Abhimanyu stated matter-of-factly. A fearsome German shepherd came over and sat next to Abhimanyu who stroked him affectionately.

'You must be travelling abroad quite a bit, to pick up such phenomenal art. How do you manage it?'

'Indians privately hold a lot of art that has not been brought into the market. Besides, nature photography takes me to exotic and unexplored locales and it also helps to keep the cash register ringing. I have small pads in Bangkok and Hong Kong where I have kept some of the older pieces from my art collection. In India, nobody knows the difference between an original and a clever reprint. But then, why only in India,' he broke off abruptly.

One corner of the drawing room was graced by a huge wooden chair with silver inlay work which looked as if it needed polishing, and jeweled embellishments. It looked like a cross between a medieval throne and a modern rocking chair. Ram sank into it. Abhimanyu explained, 'That is our Vyagrasana…Vyagra, as in tiger.'

Ram instantly leapt up and looked at the black-and-white photographs in undusted wooden frames. One which caught his attention was of several tigers lying dead at the feet of a couple of hunters, with three elephants in the backdrop. It bore the caption: 'Lord Reading on a tiger hunt in Nepal, 1911'. Ram counted; there were eight tigers lying on the ground. Eight tigers! Unbelievable! It must have been a hunt that lasted for a full day if not several days. What a hunt!

An adjoining picture displayed seven dead tigers, along with the carcasses of two rhinos and two bears. The caption read: 'King George's shoot in December 1911'. Yet another was of King George on an elephant, with the line, 'A total of two thousand elephants comprised the retinue. There were a total of thirty-nine tigers and eighteen rhinos killed during this eleven-day hunt. George V stands in his howdah in the centre; the Maharaja of Nepal is in his howdah on the left.'

'Why didn't your forefathers protest against the English hunting in your backyard?'

'On the contrary we encouraged it! Shikar kept them hooked to us,' Abhimanyu said. 'Land of snakes and snake charmers was the euphemism for the land of big game!'

'Did they include you all or were they snooty?' Ram asked.

'Whenever high royalty was visiting India, our support would be sought to lend the esoteric native flavor,' Abhimanyu said. 'See this picture.' Abhimanyu pointed to a photograph that chronicled the Duke of Edinburgh on a hunt with the Maharaja and Maharani of Jaipur during his visit to India with Queen Elizabeth II in 1961. 'My grandfather had been specially invited to personally escort them from Jaipur in his Rolls Royce. But due to a last minute hitch, their visit to Baikunthpur didn't materialize. What a pity!'

Ram's eyes fell on a huge black-and-white photograph of a royal with an enormous moustache, a rifle by his side, the barrel pressing down the game. He looked confident, his features resembling the ruler in the Kipling portrait near the entrance. He was attired in khaki breeches and wore a hunting hat. At his feet were two dead tigers of varying lengths. Standing next to him, perhaps less haughtily and completely devoid of any facial expression was an Englishman, holding his hat in one hand. Abhimanyu explained, 'That was my grandfather, His Highness Akhandvir Pratap Singh, the Maharaja of Baikunthpur. He was on a shoot sometime in the early 1940s with the British Resident stationed at Jabalpur.'

'Shooting two tigers must have been quite an achievement. But, didn't it conflict with your religious reverence for the tiger as the carrier of your kul-devi?'

'You're dead right,' said Abhimanyu, taken aback momentarily. 'But we have a belief that if the vehicle of the lord becomes errant, it must be eliminated and rebuilt. So all shikar was on the premise that the beast had become a threat to order. Frankly, the benefits of shikar were too compelling to ignore. Plus, that shoot helped to upgrade us.'

'Upgrade? But you all were already Kings!'

'To 17-guns!'

'You mean you all could keep 17 guns in the arsenal?'

'That was the protocol privilege, the qualification for royalty, granted by the British. We were a mere 9-guns until then. The British Resident was related to the Viceroy and Baikunthpur therefore became the favourite destination for shikar. See that photo of the visit of the Marquess of Willingdon, the then Viceroy of India, to Baikunthpur. That is Darbar himself driving him for shikar. We became entitled to have a 17-gun salaami at all State functions. When the Princes Conference took place, only 21-gunners like Hyderabad, Kashmir, Mysore, Udaipur and Baroda could sit in the front row. Later, Baikunthpur was also accomodated. My mother was Baroda's daughter. It was a game-changer.'

To the right was a sepia-toned photograph of a youthful figure, probably an understudy Prince standing next to a diffident looking man, perhaps only slightly older than him. His Highness Akhandvir Pratap Singh stood close to them with his rifle, the muzzle end in his hand. Behind them was the dazzling red Rolls Royce Tourer that Ram had seen in the courtyard of the Palace. At their feet were two dead animals. A motley group of villagers and liveried servants stood respectfully to one side. In the horizon were charcoal grey hills and tall teak trees. Ram looked inquiringly at the photograph and commented, 'These animals are not tigers. They look dappled... So very different!'

'Look closely,' urged Abhimanyu.

'Decidedly sleeker than a leopard, more than a tiger.'

'They are cheetahs! My grandfather shot them. A historical moment in 1948!'

Ram looked with amazement at the dead cheetahs. They looked so artistic even in death.

'And who is that thin young royal standing next to His Highness?'

'That is my father, His Highness Ajatshatruvir Pratap Singh also a great shikari,' said Abhimanyu proudly. 'He continued to be a fighter till he surrendered to prostate cancer a few months ago. That timid boy was my grandfather's secretary. I don't remember his name, but I believe he was a good kid. He was well-educated, Allahabad University and spoke good English and all that. Though he was a greenhorn when he arrived at my grandfather's door, he was a good shikari by the time he left. Do you know, Darbar shot the two cheetahs with a single bullet, so good a marksman was he.'

'But I thought India never had cheetahs,' said Ram. He recalled when he had contacted the Chinese partners for exotic trophies. Tong Choo had been emphatic that cheetahs had been extinct in India for many decades.

Abhimanyu seemed flummoxed by Ram's observation. He pondered for some time before answering, 'Actually, it was around the time that cheetahs had just been declared extinct in India. Though initially hesitant, my grandfather gave in to a quirk and just went ahead with the shoot. And the likes of Jaipur, Hyderabad, Rewa, Kolhapur, Bikaner and Baroda, all famous shikaris of their time were so jealous of my grandfather.'

'How cool that the Maharajas took their staff along with them for shikar!' Ram pointed to the young secretary in the picture. He looked pallid and overawed—as if he was about to faint with fright.

Suddenly Abhimanyu turned and looking closely at Ram, winked, 'Buddy, what a resemblance you have with that kid! Look alikes of Robin Williams! That could well have been you in your younger days!'

Ram looked at the photograph once again. The Maharaja's Secretary must have been very young, not more than twenty—a fresh cadet in the presence of a battle-hardy Field Marshal!

'Thank heavens the secretary did not last long. My stupid old man willed a priceless Tagore etching to him.'

'Tagore? The Nobel Laureate?'

'Yes, Rabindra Nath, the Da Vinci of India. He had been

invited by my grandfather to inaugurate the refurbished library in the Palace. It was an unrecorded visit. He spent a few days at Baikunthpur just before he became bedridden.'

🐾

They were sipping cognac in the Baikunthpur Library when Ram asked, 'How did you get interested in hunting and wildlife?'

'It's a long story,' said Abhimanyu. 'It was my dream to become a Forest Officer and enjoy hunting as a perk of service.'

'But isn't protecting forests a perk of service as well?'

'There was a time when a forest officer was not fit for his charge if he could not shoot straight. In fact, if he shot and killed a tiger, he was eligible for an out-of-turn promotion.' He searched for an old book from the beautiful wooden book rack and opened a page that had been marked with a flag. 'Read what Sainthill Wilmot, former Inspector General of Forests of India wrote: "Game laws now add to the duties of the forester, that of gamekeeper, and deprive him of one of the most popular incentives to a forester's career—hunting".'

'Those were the days my friend.' Ram recalled what Sherry and Narad had said, 'And we thought they'd never end!'

'Hunting was the raison d'etre for establishing game parks and they had protocols and systems,' said Abhimanyu. 'That is how wildlife was protected, by regulating it. Yet we've had lunatics... Perry predicted there wouldn't be tigers alive by the turn of the century. Another self-proclaimed expert McDougal cried hoarse that by the year 2000 tigers would only be in cages. It just psyched everyone out. Now these Cassandras have been proved grossly inaccurate but new ones are being born!'

'Conflicting interests have to be balanced for sustenance,' said Ram. He thought of Sherry and wondered how she would have responded.

'But who the fuck cares in India? Unrealistic doctrines have become the fad.' Abhimanyu started stacking books on the table in the manner of a senior lawyer preparing for his defense strategy. 'Sadly India is losing out on the greenbacks! Do you know how much foreign exchange is earned at the Selous Game Reserve of Tanzania? Or the Kruger of South Africa? Or the Skadarsko Reserve of Montenegro? If only we had been more practical we could have easily solved our current account deficit!'

A sharp prod shook Ram out of his reverie on the huge rocking chair. His own sense of helplessness had made Abhimanyu's pontification unendurable after a while. He looked up dazed. Abhimanyu, though tipsy, looked as elegant as ever, a cigar in hand. He winked mischievously at Ram, 'I'm curious about your tenacity...there's something you're after.'

'I'm more the hunted than the hunter.'

Abhimanyu laughed and caricatured a woman. 'Nah...I refer to prey of the other kind.'

'Sadly nothing comes to mind.'

'Who has the hots for Sherry Lara Pinto?'

Ram squirmed uneasily, embarrassed. Yes, he did fantasize about Sherry, but it was a very private and entirely unrequited endeavour. 'Hardly know her.'

'Liar!'

'But you do!'

'Frankly, I can't blame you for being attracted to her. She is amazingly attractive, no?' Abhimanyu asked reflectively.

'Tragically, I've only been a spectator,' said Ram. 'I thought I'd get some insight from you.'

'And I thought you'd have conquered the Himalayas by now.'

'No luck...not even a decent peek.'

'Above the snowy peaks.' He caricatured female breasts. 'Sagarmatha rising.'

Sagarmatha, the Nepalese name for Everest. Ram remembered Sherry sitting beside him in the jail. Was it a pink or purple tiara above her cleavage? He had dismissed it as a subtle piece of jewellery, at best a tattoo. 'Yes, I remember.'

'She has the most tantalizing birthmarks! An exquisite one below the navel—waterfall, fern or flower, call it what you will! And the one just above her...actually, her entire body is one fantastic canvas of natural tattoos.'

Ram cursed himself for not getting close to Sherry. But how could he have, as an imprisoned undertrial? 'But you seem to have successfully hoisted your flag?'

Abhimanyu smiled a full smile. 'When I nailed her the first time a few blocks from the Smithsonian, she was so warm and affectionate...flower or nymph, I couldn't say.' Abhimanyu continued, 'Initially, I had bracketed her as cold and lofty. But when she came around, she was like beaten snow. She just melted into me!'

'Lucky man! Tell me more!'

'Where shall I begin?' Abhimanyu reminisced dreamily.

'She is undoubtedly unique,' said Ram.

He was certain it took more than just brains and brawn to keep Sherry in the zone. She could be so emotionally involved, like she was with her diatribe against shikar. And yet, she could be entirely logical and dispassionate, as she was when analyzing the Raja brothers and the Goenkas.

'Strangely, there is more to her...'

'Frigid? I always got that impression. But then you have first-hand experience,' said Ram.

The thought had sprung to his mind as he watched Abhimanyu contorting. Some women liked to experiment and watch male sexual response. Provoke and titillate, keeping an arm's length. Stoke the fire, remaining cool yourself. It was a sadistic streak in women who liked to dominate men. He could imagine Sherry like that.

Abimanyu coughed and seemed to slip into a private reverie before answering, 'Strange, you know. When she moved into the Palace, she wouldn't sleep with me in the master bedroom because it had mounted animal trophies. She had all the carpets and animal rugs thrown out and the place fumigated, including a priceless Moghul miniature of Emperor Babur's leopard hunt. It was completely spoilt in the process. She said it gave her the creeps. We began to sleep in another room stripped bare as a cave…it felt like a hermitage. Hardly the canvas to keep anybody turned on.'

'So how did you get by?'

Abhimanyu looked up at the painted ceiling, as he began to recount, the story of his first love. 'I can never forget that day, in the middle of March, when the orange-red palash flowers were in full bloom. We had returned after a ride through the yellow and green orchards in the early evening. A bottle of Dom Perignon was polished off before we started on vodka accompanied by the finest Baltic caviar and Appenzeller. We were very much high, very much upon each other. I had signalled off the retainers, sensing her mood. We started singing old college songs…I had pulled out my old Mustang bass guitar which Bill Wyman had personally autographed…she loves singing, you know…we were enjoying ourselves like crazy.'

Ram forced himself to smile, while he listened carefully, his mouth dry with jealousy.

'Really?'

'We grabbed hold of each other and began rolling on the carpet in the library,' said Abhimanyu. 'She has a powerful tongue that she uses like a percussionist, to create the most memorable sensations. I was initially tender with her till she teased me on to be different. I can be quite rough, you know, but she proved to be several shades stronger, enjoying everything I did, begging me to "take her higher". Suddenly she was straddling me, rocking atop me like I were her pet pony.'

His voice had dropped, transported to another time and Ram could almost hear his heart.

'It was building up to an exquisite crescendo, while I lay holding her boobs, pushing and pressing against her, holding her delightfully narrow waist,' Abhimanyu narrated breathlessly. 'As we trotted along oblivious of all else, her whole body seemed to throb and respond like nothing I have ever seen or felt being articulated by a woman. It was ecstasy to hear her ask for more, her full-throated cries resounding in my ears. I have had so many, so many women in my life, but this one was special. Most women close their eyes and bite their lips, but her mouth and eyes were wide open, egging me on, revving up my pleasure...'

'Hmmm...'

'In fact, she commanded me to vary the rhythm every few moments, something even I had never experienced beyond a point. I actually started counting backwards to ensure that I should stay on, because my head was dying to explode and my brains were knocked-out. We must have been in the act for ages, like stars in a porn flick, as we were both drenched in sweat. I had never quite felt the need to hold on for so long. It was excruciating... just extending this great, this titanic moment of pleasure, trying to do the unbelievable...'

Abhimanyu paused to catch his breath as he wiped the sweat from his forehead. He spoke slowly now, his voice choked with emotion.

'And then?'

'And then, as we finally bit our lips and clawed into each other, and she moaned and screamed like she would bring the Palace down…as we fought to climb higher one last time,' Abhimanyu stopped.

'What happened?'

After an agonizing pause he continued in a whisper, 'It was like some bastard had shot an arrow between us. We were on this amazing roller coaster trip to the highest heaven and I had her attention exclusively…we could see the shrine, a few yards from us. Within moments we would have rung the bells together.'

'Wow!'

'And then suddenly out of the blue, her eyes moved away from me…'

'To?'

'A tiny photograph.'

'Photograph?'

'Yes.'

'What was so special about it?'

'It was an old photo of me as a teenager. It just fucking slipped out of a book kept on a side table that we had knocked off. I had my foot on a tiger cub.'

'But she must have known your passion for wildlife!'

'Of course she did,' said Abhimanyu. 'But the problem was something else,' he paused and then said slowly, 'It was a dead tiger cub.'

'Couldn't you have pretended it was somebody else, your grandfather or his secretary or the driver, or some other European…it could have worked!'

'She just paused at that climactic moment and asked me bluntly, "Abe, that's your shikar, isn't it?"'

'You should have flatly denied it!'

'My friend,' said Abhimanyu softly with his lips twisted in a smile, 'when you are micro-seconds away from the greatest orgasm ever in the history of humankind, you can't differentiate between fact and fiction. Besides, when Sherry looks at you penetratingly, you can't fool her anyways. In any case, like a fucking ass, I had myself scribbled with a sketch pen across the photograph: "My first shikar".'

'Awww…'

'She fucking rolled off, saying she was done; I was left hard and dry.'

'Don't say.'

'I felt so humiliated, so cheated!'

'But you'd already explored the alluring vistas. You must have had another day?'

'I couldn't fathom her. She apologized the next day for being so unmindful…gave some crap about the curse of the she-elephant. But things weren't quite the same ever again. She began to look suspiciously at everything—talking to the servants, sniffing into the cellars, insisting they be opened for her.'

'Never mind,' said Ram. 'She's not so far away.'

'I should've factored in family history. Her Aunt Lara was another horny loose cannon.'

'Ignore her,' Ram said, patting his arm affectionately, like a jockey would his favourite race horse. Abhimanyu needed reassurance; his pride had been hit badly. 'So many beautiful women would be willing to die for you.'

'I've had so many lovely women in different cities; film-stars, celebrities! They worship me, for adventure…not just jewels, art and yachts! They yield voluntarily.'

'Forget her man…'

'A woman is just a woman, an event. But,' Abhimanyu paused. After a long silence he sighed, 'Sherry's scent…'

'Really?'

'It's her mysterious inner core that both intrigues and excites me.'

'Good to be desired, but why be so different.'

Abhimanyu's hands twitched as his breath roughened. He spoke angrily now, 'I think I know why she is so pitiably indifferent to reality. That's why she has no fucking respect for tradition or authority.'

'Why?'

'Because she has never been properly walloped as a kid...'

'Maharaja, leave her for lesser mortals like yours truly,' Ram soothed.

'I wish I could, my friend,' said Abhimanyu, his voice resounding chillingly against the stone walls. 'Unfortunately it has become an obsession. I feel compelled...it's an animal craving.' He was like a predator, robbed of its rightful kill. 'The scent haunts me day and night. It forces me to track her relentlessly.'

'Abhimanyu!'

'Someday...very soon now...'

'No...'

'I just want to seduce her to our tykhana. I want to see her naked again. I want to tease and rub her body another time and make her scream and beg for more. I will lay her on a tiger rug, and put this scarf around her neck.' He pulled out a yellow handkerchief from his pocket. 'I won't give her another chance to scoff me. I will complete the unfinished symphony.'

'Abe...'

Ram gasped in surprise as Abhimanyu dug into his pocket and dabbed the sweat on his forehead with his handkerchief. A tiny pickaxe lay in his hand—it shone like steel or silver; it looked just like the kind that Jugnu and the thugs kept hidden with them—the historic symbol of Thugee. He had morphed—his eyes were bloodshot, the look on his otherwise handsome face like that of a modern-day vampire. Had he lived in that decade, he could have replaced Christopher Lee in The Horror of Dracula.

Abhimanyu's obsession with Sherry teased Ram. It made his blood tingle, and he wanted her ever more. He tried calling her. But her phone was always out of range. There was no way he could get near her presently. Shikar—with its sense of chase, the adventure, and the thrill of being able to do something forbidden seemed the next best relief.

'I have never been for shikar, although we lived close to Achanakmar, which we used to visit over the weekends for nature retreats and picnics. My father was paranoid about my handling a gun.'

'Was he your father or an ogre?' Abhimanyu asked. 'Guns give you self-confidence!'

'I saw Hatari starring John Wayne as a kid. I'm ready for some lusty and dirty shikar.'

'Why not recreate royalty…a paean to the Maharaja?'

'It would be truly memorable!'

'I need to relax my senses too,' said Abhimanyu, sighing deeply. 'I've been perpetually on the move the last few weeks.'

'You've been travelling?'

'Been a couple of weeks now,' said Abhimanyu. 'I was in the company of royalty from a European principality. After the Monaco Grand Prix we went leopard and steinbok hunting in the Mkomazi Game Reserve in Tanzania.'

'You mean you know some of the European royalty personally?'

'Yes, we have known most of them over the years. Prince Bernhard of Netherlands used to be very fond of my grandfather. We planned expeditions together.'

'And you continue the tradition?'

'I help to make it memorable by drawing on my personal

contacts across the world. There was a pleasurable upside this time,' Abhimanyu grinned slyly. 'I got to snog the Queen's sexy sister studying in Edinburgh. She thought I was Italian...'

'There you are! So you've been gaming around?'

Abhimanyu laughed aloud. 'Of course! But frankly, at the end of the day, you crave your dal tadka and rice. I prefer India and its homely offerings to any other European or African destination.'

Ram cleared his throat and bowed, 'When can this pitiable commoner be introduced to this royal sport?'

Abhimanyu patted him, smiling indulgently, 'You're not new to this sport.'

'I am.'

'What of the clouded leopard chase with Narasimha Raja?'

'Kalimantan?'

'That turkey almost got done by a leopard.'

'How do you know?' Ram stared at him in disbelief. He had presumed that apart from him, nobody in the world other than the Raja brothers and their Chinese partners knew about that fiasco.

Abhimanyu laughed, 'There is a video recording.'

'You mean somebody finds value in such incidents?'

'Yes.'

Ram stared at him, 'I just don't believe that a video exists.'

'This friend is working on a series that will show real-life hunting and real-time field dressing of the Scimitar Oryx and the Nubian Ibex on high-definition 3-D. He has already procured special cameras to this end. This series will be to hunt-lovers what Titanic is for romantics.'

'And the clientele?

'It's a very niche clientele. Guys who wish to hunt but are scared of losing their reputation as responsible corporates. Or war veterans brutalized by war, in need of another combat high...its very much like crack cocaine or morphine injection to an addict.

A guy wants gnu-spear hunting films. Another one from Arizona wants gerenuk bow-and-arrow hunting.' Abhimanyu warmed up to his passion, 'The detailed tracking, the sounds of the drum-beaters and the forest, the deadly chase and shikar, and the wailing and howling sounds of a hunted animal, the butchery, the visuals, the bloodsport, all of them can be sensationally erotic.'

'Really?'

'A wild bear or leopard being beaten to death in a primeval, aboriginal way, with sticks and wooden clubs...to some it may be ingloriously repulsive...to others such cruelty is more natural and sensual than sex.'

'Tell me, do you truly enjoy hunting?'

Abhimanyu answered reluctantly, 'I am only an opportunist hunter.'

'Meaning?'

'If you're entertaining women, sex comes along... Likewise with safaris, game opportunities present themselves.'

'You know I might have been a terrific hunter myself, but...'

Abhimanyu whispered softly, 'Shikar is an athletic activity. It tests your hand-eye coordination, reflexes and timing. Animals are naturally deceitful to survive predation. One wrong move signals the end! It is this challenge that is so seductive!'

Ram wheeled around, anguish tearing at him. He badly needed to touch, to feel a woman. To squeeze and crunch. He thought of the elusive Sherry and beat his fists in the air. Only an exciting shikar expedition could douse this fire of deprivation. He imagined himself perched on a machan with a rifle in his hands, power coursing through his veins. 'I'd love to be a Maharaja, just for one night...'

Abhimanyu remained silent for a few moments before raising his hands and clapping them against Ram's. 'Great! Let us whet your sense of sport! We will go to Achanakmar Sanctuary. We could easily go into the forests of Baikunthpur. But why fuck around in your own backyard?'

'Tomorrow?'

'The day after! We travel via Amarkantak to the Lamni Forest Guest House. It was built by the British at the turn of the previous century as a hunting lodge. Feroze will join us. This time we will have a special guest too.'

'A Bollywood film-star?'

'You will see,' said Abhimanyu cryptically.

'By the way Abhimanyu, considering our distinguished company, how do we ensure that the bloody Forest guys don't catch us?'

Abhimanyu fished out a folded newspaper cutting and handed it to Ram. It read:

> Man-eater of Achanakmar
>
> Villagers in and around Chhaparwara are living in constant fear of a tiger which had snatched two goats from the village on Friday and has since been continuing to wreak havoc. Yesterday it pounced on an octagenarian tribal woman who had gone to answer the call of nature in the early hours of the morning and dragged her carcass far away. Villagers have begun to keep a round the clock vigil and have even performed prayers through the local ojha to exorcise the village of this grave peril. The headman of the village has written to the Forest Department and the local MLA and MP to urgently help track and kill the man-eater tiger before it claims more innocent lives. The Forest Department is reportedly seized of the matter and has formed a special team to catch the big cat and a shoot-at-sight order has been issued. Villagers are also trying to track down the beast.

'Hell! We should just call it all off...'

'Nah! This is verbatim; just as I had penned it.'

The cool lemon-scented breeze drove away the evening smoke in zig-zag charcoal brush strokes above the low-lying houses and jackfruit trees. His jeep had screeched to a halt outside his father's house, the searchlights brightening up the dark quarters and scaring away a dog that had been feeding on a heap of organic waste in the fading light.

Ram stared at the row of houses for a few moments with a tinge of trepidation before he walked across to Guruji's house He had barely a few minutes at hand as he had to join the waiting hunting party in Amarkantak, next door. This was his grand chance to be a Maharaja. Or James Wilson? A feeble yellow light burned within. His timid knock was greeted only by silence. He paused briefly before knocking again, a little harder this time.

In response he heard the urgent ringing of a small hand-held bell. It was being rung even faster now, as the final mantras were recited. A rusty iron bolt was undone from inside with a clanging sound.

A tall, sepulchral figure emerged, draped in a clinging white toga with the aroma of incense and mystery.

Guruji's eyebrows rose as he asked caustically, 'So released from the cage?'

'Actually, I'm going on prison-related work to Achanakmar. I dropped by to see you.'

'Are you allowed to travel?'

'Only as a model prisoner. I was in Nepal and Burma recently. Tibet was also on the cards, but that trip is postponed.'

'How coincidental!'

'How?'

'The Oriental trail! Da had always wanted to take the Alexandra David Neel trail to Tibet. And later when he heard that Vipassana, the lost art of meditation, dating back to Gautam Buddha's time, was still alive in the remote villages of Burma, he wanted to go there too.'

Ram wondered at the convergence of his father's thoughts with his own actions. Suddenly, Guruji announced, 'By the way, I have found your father's personal diary.'

'Where did you find it?' asked Ram. A tinge of apprehension suddenly clouded his curiosity.

'It had been buried carefully beneath the mattress.'

Guruji led him into the house. It was infused with the smell of agarbattis and jasmine flowers. Ram held his breath as Guruji opened a cloth bag and fished out a small packet, wrapped in an old, yellow satin cover, tied with thick-brown silk threads with tassels at the ends.

Ram untied the threads anxiously. An old, hardbound, maroon-coloured notebook emerged. The corners were of patched cloth, specially stitched for protection. The pages were pale, parchment-like with age. Though the diary had the musty smell of history, it was well preserved. Ram opened it nervously, not sure what further labour his father would inflict on him. Mandating that the tiger skin be deposited with a museum for conservation had already brought disastrous consequences in its wake.

The first page had the Swasti-chinh, the Hindu tantric symbol for social equilibrium and spiritual peace inscribed on it. Below it, his father had written: 'To my dearest son Ram'.

Ram blinked and began to flip through the diary.

His father had quoted profusely from Ralph Waldo Emerson, chronicling his evolution from science to spiritualism; of nature intertwining its principles deeply into the life process. He visualized his father writing long hours into the night, under the swaying light of the single bulb. He was randomly flipping through the closely-written pages, when he came across a blank page. He turned it over to find that the handwriting was different; each word, a pearl of calligraphy, even though written in his father's hand. The word jungles attracted his attention. His heart pounding, he began reading:

'This episode dates back to the winter of 1948. India had barely recovered from the trauma of partition when it was forced to go to war to defend itself. The terrifying conflict that ensued brought life all over the country to a terrible standstill.

'I will briefly chronicle the times leading up to the event that I wish to narrate. I had just completed my Masters from Allahabad University when I was invited by my mentor Dr R.K. Haksar, the Head of the Mathematics and Philosophy Department to meet an old school friend of his who was visiting him for breakfast. His Highness, Akhandvir Pratap Singh, the Maharaja of Baikunthpur, a kingdom south of the Vindhyas, was in Allahabad for a dip in the Sangam, the confluence of the Ganga and the Yamuna rivers. It was exciting to be meeting royalty. I was smart and dashing, my love for travelling just about taking wing.

'We had barely sat down to breakfast and exchanged some views about western art and literature before the Maharaja made an irresistible offer. He badly needed someone who could be his secretary and executive assistant; I fitted the bill. He tempted me with a handsome salary and a fully-furnished colonial house in the jungle, "festooned with saagon and palash, bihi, sitaphal and jamun trees with an exclusive lake to row and swim in". It was an offer I couldn't resist, considering that the great E.M. Forster too had served as Private Secretary to the Maharaja of Dewas and had described that engagement as the great opportunity of his life.

Professor Haksar agreed to grant me leave for a year. And thus, on a lark, I joined His Highness, the Maharaja of Baikunthpur as his Private Secretary.

'The Maharaja, a liberal-minded dandy, was an expert on jungles besides a big-game hunter. Since he was a widower, he had chosen to put his only son into a boarding school in Ajmer.

'His one single obsession was to impress the English at any expense. In pursuance of that goal, he purchased four acres of cherry orchard and had a water well constructed in an obscure hamlet near London when he learnt that the local orphanage lacked drinking water. It earned him mention in several respectable journals in England, at a time when his own kingdom was going through a drought. Within his State, he created a special resort, complete with luxurious suites, individual pools and spas for his English friends. The Maharaja entertained only with the best of wines, liquors and cigars imported from Europe. But few know that it was "shikar" that kept his English friends coming to him for more.

'His Highness loved music and art. He collected Faberge clocks and fancy European objets d'art. My own object of admiration was his astounding library. The floor of the huge hall was covered with Aubusson rugs, the walls adorned with paintings of Daniells, Hodges and Zoffany that he had procured with great effort. Each book was chosen by him. I don't think he ever found time to read, but he ensured that every book published in England found a place in his collection. I was delighted with the opportunity to read in such luxurious surroundings. Another enjoyable part of my duties was to dine with him at all official parties at the Palace, each meal being an epicurean feast. I too thought my decision to join his service was perhaps one of the happiest accidents of my hitherto uneventful life.

'And now I come to this episode, which dates back to a chilly evening in 1948. It was a still day, well after the monsoons. Leaves had fallen, but the undergrowth had not yet shrunk, making wildlife spotting challenging. The previous week had seen a bunch of ICS officers and some beautiful English women at Baikunthpur with many hedonistic evenings—nights on end in machans, plenty of barbeques and champagne.'

A car honked loudly at the gate, startling Ram. He shut the diary and stuffed it into his Hartmann bag and hugged Guruji who seemed shocked by this abruptness. The honking grew more persistent as Ram dashed out and shouted behind him, 'I will soon return, Guruji.'

'Achanakmar is God's own country,' clapped Jugnu in appreciation.

Ram nodded in agreement, as he soaked in the beauty.

They had stopped at a wayside chai shop, perched precariously on a hillside bend against a clump of custard apple and jackfruit trees. The road was narrow, wet and muddy, bordered by an outgrowth of short sal and teak trees. It presented a breathtaking view of hundreds of acres of pristine natural forest. The sunlight filtered through the dew-clad leaves, imparting them with a magical translucence. The comforting aroma of chai being brewed in a frail aluminium kettle mixed with the invigorating jungle scents of menthol and citronella.

'Yes, amazing.'

Abhimanyu put his arm around Ram affectionately. Despite having driven all through the day from Katni, he looked fresh and fit.

'Actually this is a genetic expressway, part of the much larger Achanakmar-Amarkantak Biosphere Reserve,' pronounced a familiar voice. It was Narad, smoking a bidi, his glasses tilted rakishly.

'Comrade! When did you come in?' Ram asked, sweeping away the thick circles of smoke that blew impudently into his face.

'I was in the jeep that was following you; sleeping in the back while Jugnu and Khandar chattered non-stop up front,' Narad drawled.

'I didn't know you were fond of shikar.' Strangely, Ram felt happy to see Narad.

'I am ideologically against this bloody sport,' said Narad haughtily.

'Then why don't you trek through the forest on foot?' Abhimanyu taunted. 'Alongside the meandering Maniyari, wildlife will have the opportunity to interact with an intellectual creature.' The others burst into laughter as Narad squirmed uncomfortably.

But he revived soon to continue, 'You know, our mandarins claim that India is a poor country. They don't value our diverse forests and wildlife as part of our GDP.'

Jugnu opened a pack of Marlboros, bowing facetiously, 'Meet Narad, accomplished in nature as well.'

Narad continued as if he had not been interrupted, 'There are a hundred and fifty species of birds alone.'

Abhimanyu had the last word, 'However there is confusion over jurisdiction. Boundaries of three districts intersect here—Anooppur and Dindori in Madhya Pradesh and Bilaspur in Chhatisgarh. This lends anonymity to our expedition. It is sort of a no-man's land situation.'

And then looking at the forest he said, 'When the cat is confused, the mice are amused.'

The wind blew dry leaves in their faces. Clad in khaki waterproof trousers and jacket, with matching canvas outback hat, Abhimanyu looked every inch the rugged safari man. He waved a negligent arm towards his SUV and a servant dived on cue to fetch ice-cold Breezers and beer for them.

'We seem to be well fortified,' said Ram, peering into the vehicle as Abhimanyu showed him the interior.

'Yes, we have all the equipment necessary for camping—khoontas for tethering the bait, a stun-gun flashlight and various carving instruments. That crocodile-leather bag carries the guns—the old Holland and Holland and Purdeys. The spear and hunting knives are of the Jehangir era, and those daggers used to be carried by Tipu Sultan!'

They were assembled in Katami, the largest forest village in the Lormi Block of Bilaspur district, in the centre of Achanakmar. 'I am taking you to the Diyabar beat, next to the lake. We have some friendly tribes in the Gond and Korkus who are our tried and tested helpers. They take care of all my needs when I am here. Let us go,' Abhimanyu ordered.

'Somebody is joining us?' asked Ram.

'Feroze. And the special guest.'

'How special?'

'The Holy Pope of these forests!'

The sound of an approaching vehicle suddenly broke the quietness. A haze of dust preceded the customized olive-coloured Jonga which bellowed towards them and came to a screeching halt. For a split second there was silence before Abhimanyu sprang up to receive the special guest.

His guest was dressed in military fatigues with camouflage markings and jumped out of the Jonga like an athlete. He had been followed by a jeepload of armed guards. They leapt out and quickly reassembled in formation. They seemed to be chosen carefully from amongst the Gonds and Korkus and Baigas from Bastar, Mandla and Balaghat—thin and bony, with probing nostrils and dark faces that blended seamlessly with the dark forest. All of them were no older than twenty, and possessed the mean looks of Doberman Pinschers.

Abhimanyu hugged the military man and introduced him to Ram, 'My brother, Panther. The only real man in the jungles of Central India! Panther, not Pink Panther!'

The guest acknowledged Ram indifferently. It was as if he controlled these jungles and the others were interlopers, tourists at best. Abhimanyu explained, 'He runs an agency that trains tribals for jobs in the para-military forces. Panther is revered as a father-figure amongst the tribals for providing them limitless employment opportunities.'

Ram noticed that the men accompanying Panther were watching the meeting silently. All of them seemed trigger-happy, quite ready to blow up anybody or anything remotely menacing.

When Panther finally spoke, his voice was thick and swollen, probably the collective effect of smoking nicotine, chewing tobacco and swallowing jungle dust. 'I am happy to meet you Mr Ram, I have heard about you from Narad.'

Heard about him from Narad? Had Narad been hanging around to greet this special visitor? Ram sensed rather than saw the silent greeting that had passed between the two.

He looked at Panther closely. He was dark and stocky—like the hero of a South-Indian film, with jet-black hair and a thick moustache, his shirt-sleeves rolled up. Abhimanyu bent towards him and whispered, 'This is Paneerselvam Thygarajan, aka Tyagiji, the Naxalite chief who controls Maoist operations in all of Central India.'

It dawned on Ram. Narad was a foot soldier; Panther was his leader.

The machans had been constructed artistically. Strong teak frames were cantilevered into a fork in the main trunk of a huge banyan tree and supported horizontally and vertically by thick sisal ropes.

Wooden planks formed the base which was corralled by a bamboo parapet with a gap overlooking the quarry. A rug had been laid on the floor with folding wooden chairs and a wooden table arranged in one corner. As the evening breeze gained momentum, the machan swayed. On one side was the luxuriant foliage of the forest while the other was a rising slab of sheer rock bounding a silent water body. After having tramped through the thick forest ceremonially on elephant back, perched in wooden howdahs, furnished with embroidered masnads and frills, Ram was relieved to move onto the steadfastness of the machan.

'This is the royal tradition—the foretaste of the shikar, the oeuvre. We need a sundowner,' said Abhimanyu, looking skywards. The sun glowed dimly now, as if its power supply had been switched off. He held out two hip flasks containing vodka and tonic. 'After this, no more alcohol as such smell can be sensed by the beast and they won't come near.'

'Will we be able to take aim from this height?' asked Ram, feeling the wind against his cheeks.

'This is not very high, only about a hundred feet. Our rifles have a range of a thousand yards.'

'How will we know when a tiger has been spotted and is close?' Ram queried next.

'Elaborate instructions have been given to the haquas comprising of the Baiga and Gond tribals under Jugnu's command. They will drive the game towards us. I only wish I had brought my other satphone to give him. This area has several leopards besides three tigers,' Abhimanyu said. 'One of which is injured.'

Perhaps this was an allusion to the man-eating tiger that Abhimanyu had spoken of, thought Ram as he whisked away a wasp. Following Abhimanyu's guidance, they had cotton soles to their boots; these had the advantage of clinging like limpets to the rock and enabling them to move as noiselessly as a cat.

Their dinner of roast chicken and fish with biryani was washed down with the vodka. When Feroze began to belch, Abhimanyu had to ask him to restrain himself.

It was dark now, with only the silver moon to give them light. They had already been up on the machan for almost an hour. A milder breeze blew now and the rustling of the leaves and the imperceptible swaying of the machan caused them to talk more animatedly, though their tones remained muted.

'How long will we have to be on the machan?' Ram asked naivély.

'Never ask such a question if you want to be part of a shikar. The Marquess and Marchioness of Willingdon loved sitting on machans. They could do that for days; it was like a camp for them. Once the Marchioness slipped off the machan accidentally and landed pretty close to a hungry tigress that had been hiding the whole night. Were my grandfather not such a good shot, she may have been killed.'

Panther opened a pouch of paan masala. Ram offered him a Corona he had picked up at Abhimanyu's. He dismissed it contemptuously, saying, 'Can't help blood-sucking multinationals.' Panther was about to light up a bidi when Abhimanyu objected vehemently, 'No smoking please.'

Suddenly there was a stir as Jugnu climbed up the machan hurriedly to offload a canvas bag with two flasks, one containing sugar cane juice, and the other lemon water.

Feroze barked angrily at Jugnu, 'Why are the bloody haquas not being able to drive out the tigers? Will the bastards make us sit here the whole night?'

❖

Even though they had only been in the machan for two hours, it seemed as if they had been up for several days already. Ram looked down to where a cow and a calf had been tethered to a peepal tree near the waterbody, in the open area facing the rocky wall, against a rich backdrop of lantana bushes and bamboo clumps.

'Jugnu and Khandar bought that cow from a neighboring village,' Abhimanyu explained, playing with a dagger. 'I would have preferred to avoid a cow as bait because of the religious feelings connected with it. This cow is suckling, and so it was even more expensive. Luckily the farmer did not guess our purpose, even though he became sentimental, insisting that we keep the calf together with her mother.'

The calf bleated and suckled at her mother's udders.

'Let us hope we spot a leopard at least,' Ram said. 'Maybe we can do shikar of a leopard. Even that will be some redemption.' Even though there was no predator in sight, all the rifles were loaded in preparation and laid against the parapet.

A langur jumped down and stared at them before springing away. Feroze pretended to shoot it. The machan swayed, reminding Ram of the hanging bridge over a gorge in a western film. This was indeed an experience of a lifetime, to be in the jungle with only the sounds of leaves and birds and small animals.

'I refuse to keep hanging here forever. I have urgent work and must leave soon,' Panther said. 'My boys will be getting restless.'

Suddenly the atmosphere became tense as he took out his pistol from its holster, and fidgeted with the trigger. 'I am itching to fire it,' he said. Abhimanyu held his hand, cautioning him to wait.

'You had said there were many tigers. This wait is bugging us,' Feroze whispered on behalf of everybody to an irritated Abhimanyu. In the distance they could hear the tom-tomming of drums.

'Have patience,' commanded Abhimanyu exasperatedly. 'This is not a nautch-girl's dance to start at your pleasure!'

The silver light of the full moon was now powerful enough to make the night appear like day.

They had been up on the machan for several hours by now; talking and feasting from time to time. Dawn was still some hours away, when a cool breeze, with the enticing smell of menthol and bamboo, began to buffet the machan. They tried to converse to keep awake, with Panther and Feroze expressing their dislike for the government and Abhimanyu harping on the attributes of a good shikari by recounting episodes from his earlier adventures. Ram felt completely redundant, out of his depth with the conversation.

And then just as Feroze began to get irritated too, he realized that Abhimanyu was beginning to lose his temper. Suddenly he took a back seat, massaging Abhimanyu's ego, addressing him with the Persian honorific for the chief huntsman, Qarawul Sahib. Abhimanyu smiled, temper restored.

Ram was beginning to feel drowsy. 'It is your turn to keep vigil,' said Abhimanyu just then, nudging Ram. Goenka and Panther had fallen asleep on their chairs and were snoring gently. 'Let me also catch a few winks. Wake me up at the slightest movement. Okay?'

'Yes Boss.'

The snoring of the three men made Ram terribly sleepy but he tried hard to control himself. Suddenly he remembered his father's diary, which he had thrown into his bag. He switched on the torch, pulled out the old diary and resumed reading:

'His Highness and I had set out that evening in the Tiger Car—the red Rolls-Royce Tourer that was specially upholstered and fitted with powerful searchlights and rear-elevated seats in England. A "haqua" group (village scouts, or "beaters" who carried drums and sticks to "beat" a noise to drive out the wild animals from dense hideouts and make them flee into the open), had already preceded us. We were meant to go and sit in one of the many wooden machans that had been specially erected for hunting in a distant village. The haquas would light fires and beat tom-toms to drive the beasts towards us.

'We were headed towards one such machan in Jhumka village and had driven several miles into the forest along the muddy road when the effect of all the wine I had drunk at lunch made my eyes droop. Perhaps His Highness was affected too because I can swear that even his eyes closed momentarily. When I opened my eyes, the car was standing still and I could scarcely see yonder, but for the blazing searchlights. A beautiful peacock with its fan spread wide open stood right in front of us. Another peacock came into view, its tail rustling on the fallen leaves, looking just as stately. His Highness was already admiring them. And then came a tearing sound, as an animal emerged swiftly out of the undergrowth into the clearing right in front of the car. The peacocks bounded away and disappeared from our gaze as the new animal stopped and stood unperturbed, barely twenty meters from the car, staring at us expressionlessly, its eyes unblinking in the powerful lights. I was amazed beyond words, for this handsome animal that stood before us was unlike anything I had ever seen.

'It had a small and perky head, with curious, high-set eyes, slender at the waist with a deep chest and tan fur. Its bushy tail with round black spots that converged into total blackness, gave it a distinctive appeal. Sherpa, our Tibetan driver and an old hunter himself, finally shed light. Stammering with excitement he whispered, "Hukum…cheetah."

"Yes, it looks different from a leopard, but how?"

"Hukum, look at the eyes, like it has applied kaajal."

'Black tear marks ran from the corner of its eyes down the sides of the nose to its mouth, giving it the look of a contemplative Turkish knight with kohl-smudged eyes, resting during a blood-soaked medieval crusade.

'What stood in front of us was a full-grown wild cheetah! I had read somewhere that the cheetah had not been spotted in India for some decades now; so this would be a great discovery to report to nature journals. I was thrilled. I had seen several tigers, but this was the first time I had spotted a cheetah in the wild. I had been informed that the Baikunthpur forests were home to a hundred cheetahs once upon a time. Some of them had been captured as cubs and trained to help in hunts. In fact, there was a whole manual in the royal library on the manner of capturing, training, treating and cultivating cheetahs for shikar.

"This is the most extraordinary sight in recent years," His Highness agreed breathlessly, his hands trembling with excitement.

"What an opportunity!" Sherpa nudged me excitedly.

'The cheetah stared after the peacocks, impervious to all else. And then, it was joined by another similar looking animal.

'Sherpa stared fixedly, with his eyes bulging like peeled almonds, before he said, "Hukum Darbar, that is cheeti. The cheetah and the cheeti are both in mood for masti." I understood instantly that he meant to convey that the two were ready to consummate their affection for each other at the peak of their mating season. Sure enough, the male and female cheetahs began to neck and lick each other lustfully. "The cheetah is the fastest animal in the world. At this unique moment it is a shikar opportunity for just a few seconds...once in a lifetime," Sherpa intoned as he looked at me to support his view. I looked at His Highness who was motionless. He had a complex mind...what was he debating?

'Suddenly, Sherpa handed His Highness his favorite Holland

and Holland rifle. His Highness nodded slowly, his eyes fixed on the animals, and started loading it.

'Within seconds, the two stepped out stealthily, tip toeing towards the cheetahs. Barely fifteen yards from them, Sherpa ducked. He bent at an angle and pushed out his butt, while his shoulders stayed steady. His Highness laid his gun on Sherpa's shoulders. The car's spotlights kept the cheetahs in focus; it was evident that they were fully engrossed with each other, intertwined in the very natural act of procreation. The male cheetah mounted the female one, embedding itself such that they became one composite image. It was a perfect photograpic opportunity, the kind that took pride of place in a nature journal of repute like the National Geographic Society. For an instant it appeared as if the male cheetah had been disturbed and the two men froze. But it quickly resumed its act.

'The elegant rifle with the royal walnut stock, customized and imported directly from the manufacturers must have been enticing as His Highness stroked it seductively. I held my breath wondering what he was going to do next, when he took aim. And then he paused.

'Suddenly, there was a whipcrack followed by a flash with the raised head and body of the mounting cheetah sinking to the ground. It was one smooth slide as he continued to be wrapped over his female consort. A deafening silence ensued as the forests appeared to freeze frighteningly.

'I jumped off the car. We approached the cheetahs in single-file. Sherpa led the way, followed by His Highness, while I brought up the rear. Was it faking death, only to attack us? What about the female cheetah?

'The pair lay sprawled on a bed of leaves and twigs as Sherpa edged closer. He held a fallen branch of leaves and began to swipe the ground around the entangled bodies as His Highness held his gun ready. There was no movement, except for the rustling of leaves. The cheetahs did not stir. I held my breath as he went up even closer, and touched the cheetahs with a shorter stick. Both the animals were still. Sherpa raked the head of the cheetahs one by one as they bobbed lifelessly. They were dead! A single bullet had ripped through the male before striking the female and killing her too.

'The haquas burst upon the scene from different directions and the news of the killed cheetahs spread amongst them like wild fire. They started shouting with joy. "Darbar has hunted two cheetahs with a single bullet," It meant that His Highness would announce remissions of lagaan or land taxes and special baksheesh to those who had participated in this special expedition.

'Although I admit that I was considerably shaken, it did appear an unprecedented victory for His Highness. It was an extraordinary high and the thrill of the fiesta was infectious, rubbing off on me as well. We celebrated for the next few days, uncorking bottle after bottle of champagne, severely depleting the seemingly inexhaustible stock usually available in the royal cellar.

'That was when I saw His Highness's imperious mien at its height. He sent for Ralph Arnold, a young Anglo-American photographer, a child prodigy, who had gained popularity in the subcontinent for his coverage of Indian wildlife, to take a photo of the hunted cheetahs. "What do Rewa, Indore, Kotah and Baroda know about hunting? They have not shot a cheetah in the last two decades. This tale will be the recital from Mysore to Buckingham Palace!"

'However, much to His Highness's chagrin, when the photographs arrived, while His Highness and I looked our normal selves, there was a smudge that looked like a blood-stained shroud in place of the dead cheetahs. Was this some kind of trick-photography? His Highness was livid and insisted on perceiving it as a bad omen. He sent for Ralph Arnold once again. But the photographer could not be traced as he had left India to live in Tibet with the Lamas. I had deemed the matter almost forgotten, when having read an account of the hunting prowess of the Maharaja of Kota, His Highness summoned me, "Ananda I want you to go immediately to the Bombay Natural History Society and report my hunt of the cheetahs. Give them a glorious account so that it is chronicled in my name for posterity."

'Since I had worked on a project for the BNHS to conduct an ornithological survey of Baikunthpur State, I was familiar with their officious style of functioning. I promptly drafted a letter for the Secretary of the Bombay Natural History Society, recounting the shoot:

> Respected Mr Editor,
>
> We thank you for publishing the earlier shoots of His Highness Akhandvir Pratap Singhji, the Maharaja of Baikunthpur, so accurately in your esteemed annals.
> I now wish to draw your kind interest to the result of a unique hunting expedition in which His Highness has, with his enormous hunting skills and prowess, shot a pair of cheetahs on foot, in a rare encounter that lasted for several hours into the night in a game of hide-and-seek. It was a courageous and determined endeavour on the part of the Darbar to shoot the cheetahs and to succeed in killing them single-handed. The hunted cheetahs measured, 6 ft. 3 inches and 6 ft. 2 inches between pegs. Unfortunately, no photograph of the dead cheetahs is available due to technical difficulties. It would indeed be very kind of you to have this shoot chronicled for record in the Bombay Natural History Journal. On behalf of the Royal State of Baikunthpur, I assure you of my highest

consideration and would consider it my honour to provide any other information that you may deem relevant in this endeavour.

I sent the letter by personal messenger. Surprisingly, there was no response from the BNHS and once again, the matter was seemingly forgotten.

'It was later one day, when His Highness chanced upon the smudged photograph that his anger returned with full vigour. By sheer providence, the local Assistant Conservator of Forests, Sita Ram Bishnoi was present, and he reminded us of the photograph that he had taken of the dead cheetahs with His Highness just after Ralph Arnold's session. This photograph was crystal clear! His Highness being of hyper-excitable temperament, promptly directed me to go to Bombay and BNHS once again, now that we were armed with definite photographic record to back our claim.

'So, as directed by His Highness, I travelled to Bombay.

'On the appointed day, I presented myself in a white linen suit and hat, at the offices of BNHS at their quaint 6, Apollo Street location, photograph in hand.

'I entered the office of the BNHS Honorary Secretary, an Englishman by the name of Mr James Wilson, and was welcomed by his assistant who was seated in an open cabin in the passage, below the large oil-on-canvas painting of a huge hornbill, which had become the mascot of BNHS.

'A charming girl by the name of Miss Pinto, she spoke fluently in English and remembered that my letter had indeed been received. She accepted my visiting card with the seal of the Baikunthpur State embossed on it courteously and carried it excitedly into the conference room. After a short length of time, she came out to inform me that Mr Wilson would meet me after his scheduled meetings for the day. Meanwhile, I could spend time in their library. Her entire demeanour suggested that he would be delighted to meet me.

I was on a high; things were going as per plan. The only fly in the ointment seemed to be the radio relaying news bulletins about our triumphs and losses in the Indo-Pakistan War around Kashmir. Miss Pinto fetched me coffee and we chatted light-heartedly as she told me interesting stories about William *The Hornbill* and how it had arrived as a canary before it became part of BNHS folklore. She seemed quite impressed by the mystique of royalty, jungles and wildlife and even agreed to visit me in Baikunthpur the following month. I was thoroughly enjoying this visit to BNHS.

'A little later, having leafed through several magazines and their in-house journal, *The Hornbill*, I walked past the library into the Reference Room. It was furnished with comfortable sofas, probably meant for the Governing Council members. I spotted a fat, leather-bound register labeled: General Observations of the Editorial Board.

'Almost idly, I turned the pages of this register and chanced upon a typewritten note in the form of a draft which mentioned Baikunthpur and the cheetahs. With bated breath, I began glancing through the contents:

> The Editorial Board was shocked to hear about the shameless account of the cheetah killing. They concurred that the cheetah is a timid creature, never known to attack man unprovoked. The spotting of this almost extinct species by the erstwhile Maharaja of Baikunthpur and his party is almost unbelievable.

'Just then I saw Mr Wilson emerging from his meeting and entering the library. Miss Pinto winked mischievously at me and announced his name, indicating that I should stand up. I promptly did so and greeted him respectfully, having worked out in my mind an imaginary account of the cheetah hunt, hoping to be able to defend the actions of His Highness of Baikunthpur. The scholarly Mr Wilson held my card as I stretched out to hand him the photograph, when he jerked away, apologizing perfunctorily that he was busy with other appointments. He seemed uppity. Or was dismissive more appropriate?

'Miss Pinto was flummoxed by this behavior on his part, kept repeating that it was most uncharacteristic of him. In retrospect, I can only say that it was my ingrained exuberance that led me to linger on needlessly.

'After more than an hour, Mr Wilson strode in, waving the photograph of the cheetah hunt, his nostrils flaring. Barely concealing his anger, he barked, "BNHS is nauseated by the account of this senseless slaughter of cheetahs. We have debated amongst ourselves and decided not to even remotely mention this blot upon hunting in any of our published chronicles!"

'The remonstration continued as if I was an errant schoolboy, guilty of vandalizing the school library. He returned the photograph and made me sign an office copy of a complaint that had been dispatched to the Chief Secretary of the Central Provinces. Signed by their President, the BNHS issued a scathing criticism of the incident:

> That a sportsman should be so grossly ignorant of the present status of the cheetah in Asia, and behave so wantonly as to destroy such a rare animal, more so when he had the extraordinary good fortune to run into not one but two—is too shocking to digest. Action should be taken against the Forest Officer in whose jurisdiction this was permitted to occur and Divisional Commissioners and Deputy Commissioners should be, for the future, directed to strictly enforce the rules of the game with the entire rigor that conservation of wildlife so urgently implores!

'I was stunned. Our royal achievement was being berated as irresponsible and uncivil. I was chastised beyond measure. I would have willingly buried myself on the spot.

'I left the BNHS premises, head hanging low, tears running down my face. I did not even look back to bid farewell to Miss Pinto who stood on the steps forlornly. I have never been able to forget that interlude in my life.

'The BNHS episode made me introspect seriously on whether I had been disproportionately over-awed by His Highness's glamorous lifestyle. For once I spied in his pomp, the boast of decadence. While Indians were being killed in war, with Nehruji doing his best to inspire national character, here we were, indulging in the most hedonistic of pleasures. And we were doing this, not for any pressing altruistic cause, but just to adorn our homes with animal trophies. And what did we hope to achieve? Excite the imagination of some flamboyant English officers and their equally indulgent wives!

'When I returned from Bombay, the Assistant Conservator of Forests, Sita Ram Bishnoi—a cousin of our own Atma Ram, came to meet us. His normally cheerful disposition was gone. He was still on probation and the severe reprimand from the Inspector-General of Forests who had recorded the excoriation from BNHS on his personal record, had hit him hard. Sita Ram was a nervous wreck. It was gratifying to learn that his only son, Gangavardhan, a very late issue, had joined the Indian Forest Service and is currently posted somewhere in Madhya Pradesh, rated as a competent officer of the highest rectitude.

'I kept the hurt and embarrassment of the Bombay trip bottled within me till I found His Highness in an amiable frame of mind. It was only then that I related, rather indignantly, the humiliation that I had been subjected to at the BNHS. He laughed it off, advising me not to let it leave a scar on my mind. And then, almost as an afterthought, he admitted that the thought of conserving the cheetahs had indeed arisen in his mind. But, he countered, "He was merely a victim of circumstance and destiny."

"How?" I asked him.

'Thereupon, His Highness narrated in the fashion of a tragic hero, his unusual dialogue, many decades ago, with a wandering astrologer who had predicted that he would enjoy a regal and fulfilling life, in fact, an invincible one. However, he would meet his match one day, and if he did not exercise suitable caution at that juncture, he would be felled by it.

'His Highness had laughed; who would have the temerity to challenge his royal invulnerability?

'The prediction: A wild animal!

"Wild animal!" His Highness had roared in haughty disbelief.

'The astrologer had pondered for a while before stating thoughtfully that it would be a smart animal, nimble and agile, capable of springing out unexpectedly. His Highness had dismissed him as a quack and a trickster and banished him forever.

'And then, the cheetahs had appeared, as if led by destiny, into his life that day! His Highness confessed dramatically that he'd had no intention of killing the cheetah. But in that split second, just when he had deciding against shooting, the prophecy surfaced in his mind, blotting out all thought except the desire to kill.

'It was hard to entirely believe or disbelieve him!

'His Highness often taunted me that I did not have the temperament necessary for a prolonged life in the jungles. Even though I had been issued a rifle from the royal arsenal and I was comfortable handling it, inwardly I was always terrified by the thought of shikar. My constant prayer was to avoid a situation where I would have to prove my manliness. But after the cheetah shoot, I found myself on a roll, eager to prove my competence in the field.

'It was a tiger shoot, some days after the cheetah hunting incident. We waited in Jhumka village all night, watching a fat calf tethered as bait, not far from the machan near which we had spotted the cheetahs. Just when we had practically dozed off, and the first rays of dawn were breaking, the crude squawking of a langur monkey woke us up.

'A mature tiger, at least eight or nine feet long, had attacked the calf and was beginning to tear ravenously at it. Its golden fur and angry eyes gleamed hypnotically in the early light. The Maharaja nudged me sardonically and asked if I would be man enough for the shot. I held the rifle in my hands and was about to take aim, when my hands began to shake like the sails of a ship in a storm.

'The tiger bared its fangs and snarled angrily at us. It was a blood-curdling moment and I can still recall that I was completely paralyzed by fright. The Maharaja laughed at me and snatched my rifle; nudging me aside roughly, he adjusted his sights to take aim. He commanded me to watch carefully.'

There was a gap in the diary. Ram looked up. The others were still dozing. He flipped the pages and continued to read:

'What happened to His Highness the Maharaja of Baikunthpur finally?

'Darbar's passion for shikar continued to the end. I kept receiving exciting letters from him, neatly typed on thick cream-coloured paper and signed affectionately by him in his favourite turquoise ink using his thick-nibbed Caran d'Ache fountain pen. Most of them were full of his heinous shikar adventures, often mentioning the shameful cheetah shoot and spiritedly recalling my days in Baikunthpur. His communication continued even after he suffered a hand injury.

'Many years later, I was informed of an astounding accident

by old Sherpa, the royal chauffeur. After leaving the service of His Highness, Sherpa worked with the taxidermists Van Ingen and Van Ingen in Mysore for some years, before moving back to his native land Tibet. He went on to establish a flourishing business in animal skins in Lhasa and his grandson remained in close contact with His Highness's family. His Highness had always appeared impregnable and immortal to me, given his mammoth energy to hunt and indomitable spirit to live life to the fullest.

'Sherpa's account was also reported by one of the vernacular magazines. After an unexpectedly long and torrential spell of rains, the sun had emerged brightly and His Highness sat in the courtyard, his personal barber administering to him. He had been reading the newspapers while the barber snipped a few recalcitrant locks, and lathered him for a shave. Suddenly, a magnificent gargoyle, fixed high on the Palace walls, broke free from its grouting—perhaps due to the onslaught of the rains to fall on top of His Highness. It landed squarely on his head, killing him instantly.

'Given his age and the painless reprieve, the matter should not have been of much interest to anybody. However, because of the prophecy about his invulnerability, he had chosen to confide in me, it turned out to be a matter of extraordinary curiosity. A strange compulsion prompted me to inquire about the gargoyle that had felled His Highness. I could scarcely believe it! His Highness had indeed been killed by a nimble and agile animal that had sprung out unexpectedly. The gargoyle that caused his death was in the shape of a cheetah!'

Ram took a deep breath. It was a tale out of Ripley's Believe It Or Not. He continued to read. The last entry in the diary appeared after a gap that seemed well-deliberated. Although not as consistent in the steadiness of the handwriting, it seemed to be penned more recently. There were blotches of fresh ink, almost as if they had been written in the last few days of his father's life, and certainly written very carefully.

He read on:

'Ram, my beloved son, I have a confession to make.

'I had called you to expiate my sins, but fate deemed otherwise. You were travelling and the lines were so bad that we could barely hear each other.

'I have always told you that the tiger rug I cherish so much was a present from Mr James Wilson, an English hunter who departed from India. I confess now that this was fiction, which went on to become the story of my life.

'The truth is that the mood of Baikunthpur had overpowered me.

'In the course of my duties at the Palace, I was introduced to Mrs Palmer, a guest of His Highness, and a vivacious American from Dallas, who claimed to be an accomplished hunter. It was after a sumptuous dinner, as we chatted in the library about the war and hunting that I boasted that I was a pretty good shot myself. She promptly challenged me to bag a tiger. She was not only beautiful, but also a very bold woman and offered to include me in her annual all-women hunting expedition to South Africa if I managed to shoot a tiger longer than ten feet. Meanwhile, keen to impress Mrs Palmer, I had already begun to practise shooting secretly, my ambition being to bag big game. So when the bet was cut by His Highness I was very charged, upbeat about my chances.

'And now I recount that fateful day, when we encountered the tiger. His Highness had snatched my rifle, and adjusted his sights to take aim. Suddenly, I remembered Mrs Palmer's challenge and pleaded with His Highness to allow me to take the shot. I begged, no, I tore the rifle back from him. In fact, this fresh machismo made me to throw all inhibition to the winds. I still remember vividly how His Highness had laughed profusely at my new found enthusiasm. I pulled the trigger entirely of my own volition, without any hesitation whatsoever. Though I missed the first shot, I was not entirely off the mark as the tiger staggered and withdrew into the bushes. I pursued it hotfoot, a torch in one hand and my rifle in the other; and when I spotted it writhing in agony, I shot it once again maddened now with the lust of the chase.

'I can only reflect now and say that as soon as I saw the tiger in the cross-wires of my rifle, it infused dark power in my hands and mind. The lust that overtook me was carnal, stripped of any vestige of humanity that I may have possessed.

'Sherpa and the taxidermy experts from Mysore's Van Ingen and Van Ingen who had already been camping here for the past week, jointly conducted the skinning, preserving and drying rituals of the dead tiger and I was surprised how dexterously the bullet hole was sewn in. You can imagine my delight when the Van Ingen representative certified that the tiger measured a full 10. 2 feet from tip of nose to tail. Mrs Palmer refused to believe the news of my fantastic kill initially. It was only after she was told that Van Ingens had certified the length that she began to sing paens of my gallantry. She offered to engage me exclusively as her escort for a trek within the jungles of Nepal, since the Africa-expedition was being deferred for political reasons. In any case we parted; I could not accompany her as I received the news that Professor Haksar had met with a severe accident. Before I left for Allahabad, His Highness presented the pelt to me as a memento. It was deeply moving that the mighty tiger had been reduced to something so everlasting.

'That tiger shoot has haunted me every single day of my life, compelling me to preserve the skin and seek redemption. I invented the fiction of James Wilson, partly because I was traumatized by the reprimand from the Secretary of the BNHS, and partly because

I could not reconcile myself to the fact that I was a murderer. But I do know that all the perfumes of Arabia will not sweeten this little hand.

'And whenever a personal tragedy befalls us, this chapter of my life comes back to haunt me. Perhaps this was why I prevented you from pursuing rifle-shooting as a sport in school. I am not sure if our family can ever atone for this heinous crime.

'Life is a short flight
So breathe light
Undo the scent of the game
And fly, even when the wings are torn.'

A bell rang in Ram's mind. What was the kingdom his father had mentioned in the diary?

He read the name carefully: Baikunthpur.

Baikunthpur? A kingdom south of the Vindhyas!

It came together with a flash. Sherry's former boyfriend and his debonair companion in this hunt in the jungles of Achanakmar was Abhimanyu Pratap Singh, the current Maharaja of Baikunthpur. It meant that Abhimanayu was the descendant of the Maharaja that his father had worked for!

He recalled the picture in Abhimanyu's palace, the one that showed the Maharaja of Baikunthpur with the dead cheetahs. There was another man in the picture. That slim and frightened looking man. The Private Secretary of the Maharaja. That was none other than his own father!

Ram's heart pounded. His mind swam as everything seemed to undergo a tectonic change. Even the world around him seemed to join in, as the machan started swaying roughly in the breeze. The momentum took him unawares and his rifle slipped from its resting position against the bamboo parapet, sliding imperceptibly to the edge of the machan. He lunged forward to retrieve it. But his hands trembled and the rifle was no longer in his command.

Just then there was a rustle of leaves and a snarl. Abhimanyu rose swiftly and poked Feroze who had been snoring loudly. Feroze woke with a start, sputtering and gasping for breath.

'Shhhhh, tiger!' Abhimanyu cautioned. Clearly the predator was lurking behind the bushes.

The tailwind picked momentum and Ram's rifle slid down and fell to the ground with a loud clatter. Abhimanyu cursed him and swore, 'I could distinctly see the tiger as only I can. The rifle's falling will alert it. Idiot! Now bloody fool, you will go down and fetch it.'

Ram looked at him apologetically. Below them, the cow stood still staring at the bushes while the calf lay quietly.

Another twenty minutes passed before they heard the distinctive alarm call of the black-faced langur, accompanied by a snarl from deep inside the jungle. Suddenly, the bells around the cow's neck rang furiously as it attempted to break free from its tether.

Feroze and Panther began to excitedly talk to each other.

'Silence!' Abhimanyu whispered angrily, pointing towards the jungle.

The breaking of dry twigs pointed to a powerful animal nearby. They trained a torch in the direction of the bushes that parted slowly to reveal a flicker of gold. Now they could see the emerald balls, the eyes of a mature tiger, within meters of the cow and her calf, head peering out of the undergrowth and staring in their direction. They waited breathlessly, holding their loaded rifles in their hands. The predator's tawny hide was as yet shrouded in the dark green of the forest, but the gleam was discernible. Abhimanyu began to take aim.

Just as swiftly as it had appeared, the tiger vanished. The rustling stopped and the cow seemed to relax. The calf too was awake now; it was as if there had never been any danger at all.

Feroze and Panther resumed dozing while Abhimanyu and Ram kept watch.

Ram decided to flatter Abhimanyu and said softly, 'I'm impressed by your focus. You have to be born with it. And you don't seem to need much rest.'

Abhimanyu glowed visibly, 'It is an old shikar habit that I have inherited from my forefathers. I have excellent night vision too.'

'Even with acute sleep-deprivation?'

'I can sleep once a week and catch up on all the lost hours later while on horseback. I mean when travelling.' He rested his rifle against the bamboo parapet and began sipping the sugar cane juice. His hands rested on a set of night-vision equipment—infra-red cameras and binoculars used by the military for operations in the jungles.

Moments later, the cow seemed to be restless once again, muzzling its calf protectively. Perhaps it had sensed the proximity of the predator. Abhimanyu shook the other two brusquely and asked them to prepare to shoot. Panther got up with a start and hurriedly took a loaded rifle, kissed it and began to adjust the sights.

The branches of a peepul tree, in the direction of the cow, started swinging as the cow began to moo.

'Should I shoot now?' asked an excited Panther.

'No! Wait. Let the beast attack the cow. It is obviously hungry and is not getting a better prey than this. Then you can take proper aim and shoot.'

Panther swore irritated. 'I can't wait.' He was ready to let loose a volley of high-velocity bullets, when Abhimanyu gestured restraint.

'Look, I can sense some movement!' Feroze exclaimed, pointing to the bushes in the opposite direction. 'I am certain I saw the tiger in that direction. Should we shoot?'

'No, you never shoot until you see the beast, or else you may end up killing a forester,' cautioned Ram, looking up at Abhimanyu who nodded in agreement. Ram gently prised away the rifle that Feroze held. He read the marking on the rifle. It was a well-oiled Holland and Holland with exquisite engraving of the Baikunthpur crest on a gold oval, perhaps customized bespoke by the British manufacturers specially for His Highness.

Once again the tiger took a back seat and the cow settled down.

Feroze sneezed. 'It has become very cold,' he said.

Abhimanyu pulled out a canvas pouch and passed it around. 'Have some almonds. It will deal with your sneezing,' he said. .

Dawn was almost upon them, they could see a little more clearly, perhaps because their eyes had become more attuned to the darkness. This time the bushes parted to reveal a fully grown tiger, at least ten feet in length. It was majestic! Its appearance was so unexpected that the guns were still resting against the bamboo parapet, leaving the hunters totally unprepared. All of them were captivated by its elegance and confidence. It moved in the direction of the cow and calf which were shuffling uncomfortably now, and circumambulated them from a distance as if inspecting the captive prey. The hunters took aim and were about to pull their triggers when the tiger suddenly vanished into the jungle, as suddenly as it had appeared.

'Get the bastard!' Panther screamed impatiently, looking accusingly at Abhimanyu. 'How could you let it go?'

Abhimanyu snapped irritably, 'Panther you should have shot first. I held that kill for you. It was your kill, closest to you. But you were bloody day-dreaming.'

Panther gnashed his teeth angrily at him. 'How was I to know if it was my shot?' He pointed his gun in the direction of the tiger without taking proper aim. Just as he was about to pull the trigger Abhimanyu pressed down the barrel with his hands, forcing him to lower it. But Panther resisted and managed to win the tussle.

He fired. There was sound of the bullet hitting a tree.

'Novices! Fools! Don't you know that if you can't see the beast, you shouldn't shoot? Now the tiger knows a shikari is waiting for it. And if it is injured, as perhaps it is, it won't return. We may as well call off this shikar!' Abhimanyu's face had turned red with anger.

'I apologize on behalf of the group, Darbar,' Feroze said, stroking Abhimanyu's arm, trying to douse the tension, until he seemed pacified.

They waited in grim silence for another thirty minutes. Suddenly, beyond the teak trees, the silhouette of the tiger that must have escaped Panther's bullet reappeared before them. It was now crouching for the kill, readying itself for the final leap. This time the cow turned her head in the direction of the tiger, mentally prepared to put up a fight. The guns were cocked. But the tiger was determined to stay concealed.

'Bastard tiger,' Feroze mumbled irritatedly.

'Son-of-a-bitch tiger,' said Panther.

Abhimanyu was silent, observing and thinking hard. Ram had never seen him so tense. He was upset about the manner in which this shikar had gone so far. Now he seemed to be calculating distance, trajectory and air speed, like a golfer aiming for a hole-in-one, to go in for the final assault. 'That cow fighting to break free must surely excite the tiger. It should be very hungry now. In fact, I am certain it is injured. That should make it more desperate to kill. Perhaps, there is another way to lure the tiger! Let there be blood, the smell of blood should entice the tiger. Then it is certain to attack the cow. You guys give me protection! Coming Ram?' He looked enticingly at Ram.

Ram was stunned. 'Kill somebody?'

'The calf. Even if the smell does not, the bleating cow will attract it as an easy kill. All hungry and injured predators like it easy,' Abhimanyu said. 'It is a smart tiger; it has sensed the danger around it. But it is also an exhausted and desperate one, sufficiently intoxicated with the lust of the game and will not leave this area until it has hunted. However we can't sit here forever. Panther has to go. It is possible that the tiger has cubs that it wants to teach to hunt. I think this hide-and-seek is because of the cubs. Besides, as long as the haquas are out there, it is trapped and cannot retreat into the jungle.'

'I can't wait any longer. I want the bastard. Should I go down?' Panther asked.

'We should do what Darbar says. You don't stand a chance in hell without your army, Panther,' Feroze taunted Panther.

Abhimanyu pulled out an ornate dagger from his cummerbund and handed it to Ram. He looked disgusted, 'Shikar needs strong balls and lots of patience. It needs nerves of steel. A man who is bold and fearless. In the olden days, kings and princes used to spend fortnights on a machan without spotting, let alone shooting a tiger. And yet they never complained!'

'Shut up! You are bugging me!' Panther had a gun pointed at Abhimanyu.

'If Ram succeeds in doing what Darbar recommends I will return his original passport and he will be a free man,' said Feroze.

'How can you? You shredded the passport,' Ram said, horrified by the ease with which he was being expended.

'No, it's in my custody,' said Feroze. 'A dummy was shredded to fool you.'

Ram sighed with relief. He would repay the favor. But Feroze and Abhimanyu continued to look at him steadily, scornfully, clearly doubting his competence and bravery! 'Abhimanyu, you are the perfect shikari,' he said. 'If you can give me close cover, I'll go down alone.'

'We can have some action at last,' Panther said with a smirk.

'You have to be extremely careful. You're encountering a very deceptive tiger,' Abhimanyu cautioned.

Snatching a swig of juice, Ram announced: 'I am braver than you all thought.'

'Yes, but you also need to be super quick, if you wish to outsmart the tiger!'

Ram could feel their eyes bore into him as he began to descend. They had guns in their hands. And then, just as he began to descend, he turned back to look one last time. Abhimanyu's gun had been replaced by a video camera.

The naked ribs of the bamboo scaffold felt part scruffy and part slippery. A langur squawked loudly, announcing the unwelcome human to the animal world. He began to regret his bravado.

The pre-dawn chill and the sharp breeze served to sharpen his acuity. It was unnerving to realize that he was all alone in this wild, wide world. From the lofty and immaculate heights of Cupertino, he had descended into a bottomless abyss. These could well be the last few moments of his life. If he was attacked by the waiting tiger, nobody would ever know where he had disappeared. And yet, if he turned back, he would be mocked forever.

He slithered down the teak and bamboo scaffold for an eternity, his hands bruised and hurting, before seeing ground and landing with a thud on the wet undergrowth. Torchlight hit him on the face. Thank heavens! His fellow hunters were covering him!

The cow and the calf were tethered just a few yards away. The torchlight suddenly swerved on them as if to remind him about his mission. Ram stealthily approached the animals, armed with the dagger, one eye on the jungle, expecting the tiger to pounce on him at any moment. The cow was clearly more familiar with human beings than tigers. She stirred and her tail started swaying. The calf also hobbled up.

He seemed to be confronting the cow as he moved to kill the calf. He cast a quick look around and was relieved that there seemed to be no movement in the bushes. No crouching tiger ready to pounce. He must do his job fast. The cow began to muzzle the calf.

He looked towards the machan. All of them were looking closely at him. Abhimanyu was operating the camera.

Ram stroked the calf. It was white with soft yellow spots in places and thin, slender legs. It was probably three months old. It seemed so much like a human baby. He looked at the cow and felt its velvety smoothness. It appeared to be beckoning him, as if to speak with him. He stroked it gently. Suddenly a stone came hurtling at him, hitting him on the shoulder. It was Abhimanyu. He had to hurry up. Was the tiger in the bushes?

Ram examined the dagger. It had a naked blade that could kill the calf in a few blows. Where should he begin his attack? There was thick skin which needed to be penetrated. Should it be a jab or a slow and long movement of the blade into the flesh? Should he go for the neck or the rump?

Ram had barely readied himself to strike the calf when the cow swished its tail and hit the dagger throwing it off Ram's hand. The dagger fell vertically a few feet away on the ground, its blade penetrating the soft sticky earth. He was about to rush to pick up the dagger and confront the cow when something struck his mind.

He stared at the cow. As he looked into its eyes, Ram saw for the first time in his life, how beautiful they were. They were deep and long pools of feeling with subtle emotions to convey. But there was no fear or anger in them. And yet there was mellowness. They were the eyes of a creature saddened by what was happening, pleading for liberation from her bondage.

Ram lifted the dagger and looked at the jungle. The leaves rustled again. The predator was certainly near, but it had not yet had the courage to attack, sensing human intervention. It was probably preparing the ground for the attack, factoring in the new obstacle. It had experienced several hours of hunger and would not retreat leaving easy prey behind. Besides, the haquas had by now begun to converge towards them as the sound of drums began to grow louder. He looked up again. Abhimanyu was preparing to send another projectile in his direction.

He took one last look at the cow. It continued to look totally submissive. There was also an air of detachment. Like a meditating yogi. Meditating or levitating? His father? Now both the cow and the calf were looking plaintively at Ram. Would he be their savior or their slayer? Would he bring them happiness or sorrow?

Ram's legs trembled and he loosened his grip on the dagger and took a deep breath. Sweat ran down his spine profusely. Did he not possess the physical or mental strength required to kill the animals? Was he going to be proved a failure?

Another missile came hurtling. This time a solid chunk of wood, sharp at the edge, struck him hard on the neck. It cut into his skin and blood trickled down. He saw the cow communicating with him—seeking understanding, imploring him—begging for the calf to live? It was asking to be killed instead.

Ram stood paralyzed. His father's words came back to him! The guilt and remorse that he was forced to live with, having killed a tiger. All the perfumes of Arabia will not sweeten this little hand. He had used Lady Macbeth's words of repentance. Later, he had spurned the service of the Maharaja and the accompanying hedonistic lifestyle. More significantly, he had become a self-abnegating recluse.

What else had his father written?

'Life is a short flight. So breathe Light. Undo the scent of the game.'

What did the old man mean by the game?

Why did he leave such a message? Had he anticipated this situation as well?

Ram reflected on his life in that instant. He had lost everything he held dear. He had lost his job, his credibility and all his material belongings. His wife too was dead. There was no certainty how much longer he would have to spend in jail—perhaps all his life, knowing the way the justice enforcement system worked in India. He had debased himself thoroughly—both physically and mentally. He was bonded in the employment of criminals with the global reach and network to track him anywhere in the world.

Ram looked at the cow. Like him, she too had no escape route. Her situation was no different from his! Was there an escape route? Could he undo the albatross around his neck? Did that old school poem have anything for his situation?

What were those lines?

He prayeth well.

He prayeth well.

Who loveth well.

Both man and bird and beast.

'Bastard! Kill or be killed!' Abhimanyu yelled with anger, shattering whatever stillness remained in the night. Ram trembled to see him coming down the scaffold armed with daggers. Soon the issue would be resolved forever. It was only a matter of moments.

Ram's hands trembled and sweat streamed down his cheeks. He had to fulfill the inner command now. He staggered forward, holding the dagger firmly in his right hand. The tiger roared from the bushes. Was it ready to pounce? Heart pounding, he cut the rope with which the calf was tied. A few more slashes freed the cow too. As Abhimanyu landed jerkily on the ground, the cow and the calf cantered into the forest with the bells around the cow's neck tinkling disturbingly.

'Bastard! What have you done, you foolish bastard? Why did you let them go?' Abhimanyu screamed, looking menacingly towards him. For a moment it seemed that he had transformed into the vampire that Ram had perceived in Baikunthpur Palace when he had revealed his secret desire to lure Sherry into his tykhana. Abhimanyu came rushing at him, his daggers flashing murderously, intent upon a kill.

Just then all hell broke loose. A tiger leaped out of the bushes with a blood-curdling roar and pounced at Ram. It knocked him down with a powerful punch and instantaneously attacked Abhimanyu, who was totally taken aback by the suddenness of the assault. For a split second Abhimanyu tried to dodge, but the tiger pinned him down, forcing his head to the ground. Both remained locked with each other, even though the tiger had the upper hand. Ram, bleeding heavily, collapsed under the shock of the powerful blow and the frightful vision of a killer tiger.

But Abhimanyu was a strong man. With a dagger in his hand which he raised to strike the tiger, he had barely struck once when the tiger knocked the dagger with a powerful punch of its paw, sending it flying in the air.

Meanwhile, up in the machan, Feroze had seen the tiger attacking. He slided down quickly, carrying a long dagger and a rifle slung on his shoulders to support Abhimanyu. When he approached the wrestling man and animal, they were still grappling valiantly, like free-style wrestlers, straining their powerful muscles. Abhimanyu was holding on to the last and as Feroze watched anxiously with bated breath. He was confident that Abhimanyu would fight to win.

Abhimanyu struck the tiger with his dagger several times with his strong hands, but the powerful animal had every advantage. In one swift move it raked his chest with its claws and caught hold of his neck, shaking it like a plastic toy. Blood poured out as it beat his head against the rocky ground and tore at the windpipe until his body went limp in a pool of gore, lifeless.

Feroze, barely a few feet away from the tiger, confronted the beast, shell-shocked and dazed at the way the battle was unfolding before him. He had never been part of a shikar where his escort was mauled. Never before had he been left to face a hungry tiger that had already tasted human blood. He had never imagined Abhimanyu as anything but invincible. The tiger snarled ravenously with its jaws wide open and sprang at Feroze who cowered, paralysed merely by its bloodthirsty eyes and ferocious fangs.

Meanwhile Panther rushed to respond. From the machan he had the tiger squarely in his cross-wires. There was no chance of missing the beast with his modern weapon. He took aim and squeezed the trigger and let loose a volley of bullets. But he missed noticing that the tiger had pounced on Feroze and had pulled him to the ground. The bullets struck target. Both man and animal screamed and roared in pain. The tiger released Feroze's body as it went limp, hit by a bullet. Blood also oozed from his swollen head like an unplugged fissure.

Another shower of bullets followed, missing the target once again. The tiger disengaged itself and tore away, bleeding and limping into the forest.

Panther climbed down from the machan, shaken beyond measure, dripping in sweat. Ram, regained consciousness and just managed to drag himself inside the safety of a bamboo clump. Would Panther search and shoot him now?

Panther's soldiers heard the gunshots and rushed to his help, their guns cocked. They were ready to fire rapidly. Ram held his breath for a moment before losing consciousness once again. He did not hear the sputtering roar of a jeep approaching, or the blaring siren. He also did not hear the familiar voices shouting frantically. There was commotion all around.

Panther shouted his snappy command repeatedly, 'Abort! Abort! Disperse! Disperse!' He covered his face with a gamcha and charged towards his waiting Jonga with military markings.

Within seconds, he had disappeared into the dense jungles towards Chhatisgarh, leaving behind a huge cloud of dust that engulfed the jeep coming furiously from the direction of Balaghat.

🐾

Several days after the tragic events in Achanakmar, Ram and Sherry were seated in the office of the Director of the Tibetan Institute of Culture and Arts. The stone floor and the thick stone beams did little to alleviate the chill outside. Colourful Thangka paintings and appliqué-works, depicting meditational deities, decorated the walls. Tibetan prayer-sutras chanted softly in the background. Ram was turning the pages of the local journal, looking up from time-to-time at the gigantic Dhauladhar Himalayas with their snow-clad vertical slopes flanking the beautiful glacial lakes. Sherry worked steadily on her laptop. Both were lost in thoughts of their own.

The past few days had moved at express speed. They had rushed to Dharamsala to attend the last rites of Sherry's father, whose death, barely hours after they had attended the state funeral of Ganga, had left Sherry grief-struck.

'Ram, see this!' Sherry exclaimed, pointing towards her Vaio.

'Feature on Ganga?'

'No! I've just bumped into this site. It has a huge cache of wildlife artefacts and shikar videos on sale, including a tiger-skin going for twenty-five thousand dollars—the seller says it dates back to when hunting big game was legitimate. Apparently he has all the legal clearances, including a letter of provenance from the previous owner.'

'Show me!'

'Let me run you through,' said Sherry, as she scrolled down

the diverse portfolio of skins and taxidermied mounts and heads that were on sale.

'It seems to be a virtual museum which displays skins and stuffed animals,' Ram observed.

Sherry glanced at the captions and write-ups, 'Each picture also carries a historical profile—a short write-up about the animal that has been preserved. It is well planned and presented. Both expertise and effort have not been spared.'

He looked at the other products for sale. Apart from animal skins, there were manuscripts about shikar and antique guns.

'I'll show you the tiger skin.'

'What site is this?'

'www.antiquetrophies.com.'

'It displays wildlife trophies and artefacts, both for restoration and sale. Another site is: www.legendsofthewild.com. Both sites seem to contain the same material, though they have different physical addresses, professedly in different cities.' Sherry scrolled down the first URL. The last page had a photograph of a tiger skin with a caption below it:

> Preserved by the famous firm of taxidermists of Mysore, India, Van Ingen and Van Ingen, genuine skin of a tiger, length 10.2 feet, shot in India, dating back to the romantic days of the British Raj. Priceless! Quality, as good as new, with half-a-century of mystique and myth attached.

'Van Ingen and Van Ingen!' Ram's pulse raced. 'My father's tiger skin matched these measurements!'

For a full picture click here.

She clicked on it. A fully enlarged image of the tiger-skin filled the screen.

'It can be any skin,' said Sherry. She remembered how he had been punished before for mistaking a skin. 'How can we be sure this is your father's skin?'

'I can recognize my skin a mile away,' said Ram. 'I have erred once—not again!'

'Sure?'

Sherry concentrated on the tag that was a part of the skin. She moved the cursor around the tag. There was a hyperlink. Clearly, the seller knew the value of the tag and the authenticity that it underlined. It could be blown up for a better view. It read:

'Van Ingen and Van Ingen, Mysore, Artists in Taxidermy, January 1949'.

'Besides the length of the skin from tip of head to tail is 10.2 feet,' Ram said, and pointed towards another label that had a star near it. 'This is one of the rare Van Ingens where they have recorded the actual month of issue! Just see if there is something else that is hyperlinked.'

Sherry moved the cursor. It was indeed hyperlinked. She clicked at it and enlarged the caption. The pink, dog-eared tag roared to life:

'To keep this specimen in good order...'

'This is it!' Ram paced up and down excitedly.

'Can we discover who is running this show?' Sherry clicked the contact point.

It was an outline sketch of a face—it could be Caucasian or Asiatic. Below that was a personalized note:

> I am against animal poaching which still continues around the world. I am a member of the Guild of Taxidermy & the British Historical Taxidermy Society.
> I honor CITES & the WWF in their action against the illegal taking of wildlife.
> I donate a percentage of my profit to the WWF from my sales.

> Tiger hunting was a way of life a couple of centuries ago. Around 1900 there were an estimated 100, 000 tigers in the wild. Hunting them became very fashionable as the British Empire grew and was popular with both Indian nobility and high ranking British officers. Even English royalty joined in the sport.
>
> Hopefully my preservation and restoration work will give something to future generations to admire. I believe that if an antique tiger skin can be purchased, it may even prevent another live tiger from being poached.

Sherry said, 'The name reads A.P.S. Tusker. It sounds familiar!'

Ram replied instantly, 'Strange coincidence. The Raja brothers knew a Tusker who was to help their expedition into Central India, with the Chinese partners.'

Sherry had begun to read another column called Big 5 Diary. It had colourful photographs of a hunted African elephant with Loxodonta Africana written in parentheses. Similarly, listed with photographs were a hunted hippopotamus, an African lion and and an African rhino.

'By the way, Mr Tusker also runs personalized, tailor-made safaris and licensed expeditions to hunting concessions for ivory-tuskers, Cape buffalos, and African leopards...South Africa and Namibia, Borneo, Mozambique, Pakistan, Montenegro. There are graphic blogs written by those who have been satisfied with their hunts. For 50, 000 US dollars you can get a fifty-pound tusk elephant hunt, and for as little as 300, 000 US dollars a black rhino trophy hunt.'

Ram recalled the phone call in Borneo when Leo Raja had sidelined all official discussion and taken that one call which had confirmed that, 'The Goddess can be worshipped now.' Leo's joy had rivalled a drug addict promised an early fix.

'Can you spot any photo of this Mr Tusker?'

'It is clearly a BOT—an Internet Robot—simply a digitally generated image. It could be anyone, anywhere. You have to first email Mr Tusker giving your personal details, establishing your interest in wildlife, before he contacts you. The first site has an address in the United Kingdom, the other in Australia. He probably has the wherewithal to figure out if you are worth cultivating or not.'

'No clues about who he could be. Dead end?'

'Not necessarily. Both sites are maintained by the same company which has a help line listed. Let's try and see if somebody answers.' Sherry skyped the international number and raised the volume of the speakerphone. A tape-recorded voice was at the other end, heavy and loud. Ram responded instantly.

'That voice is familiar. It reminds me of the person Leo had spoken to from Borneo—slightly masked, possibly using a voice morphing software. I happened to hear some of the conversation after which Leo went to Kalimantan on his infamous clouded leopard hunt—deliberately heavy and gruff. Leo had called him "Friend". Later when the Chinese partners planned to visit India for shikar he had referred to a Tusker. It seemed to ring a bell!'

'You think Tusker, Friend and the guy at the end of that line are the same person?'

'I certainly suspect so. Let us check out the hyper linked photographs.'

She scrolled down the photographs from historic albums of stuffed trophies and hunted animals.

'Let us go over that link of the image gallery,' said Sherry. 'The one named Emporium. It is both a static and a walk-through. It must have cost a fortune to design it. It says royal collection for sale. Obviously a very good 3-D photographer was hired to do this job.'

A huge hall with all kinds of stuffed trophies on the walls and paintings of royalty sprang up. Each trophy was hyperlinked with a small legend that explained its history.

Sherry looked inquiringly at Ram; his mouth had popped open in surprise.

'See that huge photograph on the wall. It looks just like the picture of the living room in Baikunthpur Palace and that photo on the wall is the one depicting the cheetah shoot. That is the Maharaja in a hunting suit and that shaken young man is my father! Clearly Tusker has a close connection with Baikunthpur.'

'Did I mention that I picked up a satellite phone in Achanakmar?'

'No,' said Ram excitedly. 'Panther must have dropped his phone when he descended in a hurry. I remember he had one on him when we were up on the machan. You brought it along?' He suddenly recalled that Abhimanyu also had a satellite phone on him.

'It was almost buried in the ground, just near that tree where the calf had been tethered,' said Sherry. 'A buzzing sound guided me to it. I was about to answer the call from an unknown number when Ganga snatched it from me. The caller asked for someone whose name Ganga noted.'

'Is there anything else that you can remember, please try,' Ram begged.

She rummaged inside her bag frantically before emptying the contents on the table. Hair clips, hair-bands and handkerchiefs emerged along with scraps of paper and a clatter of coins. She pounced upon a crumpled wisp of paper, the size of a safety pin. A name had been scribbled on it, perhaps in a hurry. She handed it to Ram.

Ram stared at the paper before straightening it and announcing, 'Tusker.'

'Wonder what APS stands for?'

Something else was teasing his memory. When he had spent

the evening at Abhimanyu's flat in Mumbai, he had answered Abhimanyu's phone and spoken to a stranger—a foreign woman. She had asked for Apes. Could it have been APS...

'Yes,' said Ram conclusively. 'It adds up! In all probability antiquetrophies. com is an outfit run by the same person who owned that satellite phone—not somebody from the United Kingdom or Australia or Panther. His Highness Abhimanyu Pratap Singh, erstwhile Maharaja of Baikunthpur. He is, oops, sorry, he was—A.P.S. Tusker!'

'I still cannot fathom what brought Ganga and you to Achanakmar,' said Ram.

'Ganga offered to show me around Pench,' said Sherry, with a sad smile. 'We had planned to visit Kanha and enter from the Mukki side, the South gate of KTR, near Balaghat. I had barely reached when a report in the local papers created havoc in the Vidhan Sabha.'

'Poaching of tigers?'

'No,' said Sherry. 'It was about man-eating tigers that were on the rampage in Dindori and Achanakmar and villagers who were living in constant terror. Ganga was asked by Bhopal to travel through the night and immediately ensure that appropriate measures were taken in consultation with the forest administration of Chhatisgarh. He asked me to cover this operation to catch the man-eating tiger.'

'Do you know that Abhimanyu had put out that report himself so that our shikar could be legitimized?'

'Treachery of the vilest order!' Sherry sneezed. The evening breeze had turned cold. She wrapped a red shawl around herself as Ram got up to partially shut the window. Her fair skin glowed radiantly against the thin sliver of light as her lips flushed pink.

'I still think Ganga was naive to have set off on that suicide run on the Naxals,' said Ram. 'Forest Department people are not Special Police officers.'

Sherry reminisced, 'We found you crumpled on the ground, bleeding and unconscious. Goenka was dead. Abhimanyu's skull was broken. We rushed you to the hospital.'

'I remember when I recovered consciousness in the hospital. It felt as if I had come back from the dead.'

'Within minutes of our return to Balaghat Ganga received a wireless alert that Naxals had stormed the Police Training School and two of Ganga's Forest Department probationers whom he had personally recommended for all-round training, were also trapped inside. You are right, perhaps he could have avoided going himself. But Ganga always defied the composite of the complacent, risk-averse civil-servant. He simply took off in his jeep with whatever staff he had—equipped with World War II muskets and lathis!'

'He was walking into a trap…must have been a sitting duck?'

'The Inspector-General of Police said that he shot a dozen of the Reds before they threw a grenade on his jeep. He went up in flames along with it. Considering that the Naxals had the advantage of a full-fledged surprise offensive, it was creditable that he was able to carry assault into their camp.'

'I guess,' said Ram. 'Panther must have been terribly frustrated after the botched shikar at Achanakmar. Within Red circles he must have wanted a cover for his foolish actions. I could sense that he was trigger-happy and extremely restless on the machan. By the way, what about Ganga's family? I didn't see anyone.'

'His parents are no more,' said Sherry. 'He was the late issue of a Forest Department junior official who had been posted in the Baikunthpur area several decades ago. His father was discharged from the Forest Service and was held responsible for the killing of the last cheetahs spotted there, after they had been declared extinct. They were actually shot…'

'By the Maharaja of Baikunthpur…'

'It seems he couldn't take the dishonour and went over the brink. Ganga was a loner too. He was a cocktail of ebullience, and low spirits. Oscillating between spurts of focused professionalism and unshackled creativity—I guess that is how it is with irreverent bureaucrats. Anyway, isn't death the ultimate liberation?'

'I just wish the government could recognize these unsung heroes.'

'At least in this case they have…'

She handed him a press-clipping.

'Gangavardhan Aranyaprem Bishnoi Award: To be awarded to that Forest or Police Officer who gives his utmost to the protection of wildlife.'

'So when do you return to the States?' Sherry asked Ram who had almost dozed off. It was only when she repeated her question that he opened his eyes.

He recovered with a start. 'Maybe soon,' he said blankly, stretching and staring out of the window.

She nodded understandingly.

And then he said, 'Maybe never.'

She raised her eyebrows in surprise. 'But, now that you are being offered the top job by the new owners of Zentigris and your wife is alive…things are back on track for you.'

'I still can't believe that the Indian government is withdrawing the tiger skin case against me,' said Ram, 'It is all so unexpected.'

'Yes, home run and happiness for you at last.'

'Happiness of choices,' he said. 'And a choice to start afresh.'

'It will be a new beginning for you in the States.'

'Strangely,' said Ram, 'every day that I spend here, I seem to find absolution...this is the fresh start.'

He sat with his back to the window, facing her, as she stared at him, absorbing his words. Against the streaming rays of sunlight and the backdrop of the mountains, he looked bright and cheerful. 'You certainly look restored,' she said.

He nodded and asked, 'And will with each passing day here. What about you? Will you go back to Jabalpur or will you stay here?' He couldn't take his eyes off her. She was glowing; there was something transcendentally pure about her.

'It's a difficult choice for me as well,' she said.

'Why? You have been offered your father's position to fill.'

'What of the blood on my hands?'

'Blood? You are the apostle of peace and non-violence.'

'I have a confession to make.'

'You too...?' Sherry looked beyond hurting anything or anyone. Her gentleness and sensitivity had been infatuating. He looked up wearily. His father's confession had already been devastating enough. Was it Sherry's turn now? He did not have the capacity to bear any more pain.

'Love Tiger...I have disbanded it.'

Ram stared at her, trying to recall where he had heard the name.

Sherry helped him. 'Jade and I were part of it. It turned unexpectedly ugly in Tibet and Hukaung...'

Ram remembered Nowsher telling him about the skin dealers in Lhasa who were being threatened and killed by a shadowy group of young activists, united only through social groups on the Internet. They had been taking law into their own hands. It was Jade who had translated for him from that secret report about the dismembered Chinese businessman in Hukaung.

'It has impacted public opinion,' Ram said.

'Violence isn't the best answer to violence. Thankfully, I have an opportunity now to do things differently,' Sherry said, putting her laptop aside.

Ram seemed to miss a heart beat. Was it jealousy?

'I have an exciting offer from Harvard,' said Sherry. 'I can complete my doctorate and work on a fully-funded project which will permit me to attend CITES meetings on behalf of the sponsors that have observer status. I have taken the call.'

'The call of the snarling tiger?'

Sherry smiled. 'The call of the she-elephant. An entire herd has been massacred at the Bouba N'Djida National Park in Cameroon. Eighty-six elephants including thirty-nine pregnant females…I'll start afresh.'

She crossed her beautifully sculpted hands on the table. He gazed at them motionlessly for a while before reaching to hold them once more. She smiled; a lovely smile. He got up to hug her and she seemed to melt in his arms, clinging to him warmly.

After what felt like an incredible lifetime, Ram walked up to the window, opened it fully and looked out. The mist drifted past in milky swirls and the snow-clad peaks were now hidden from view. The cold breeze hit him on the face, making him alive with excitement.

He looked at Sherry. She was sitting with her face in her hands. His eyes fell on his father's diary; he felt drawn to read and reflect on the last lines yet again:

Life is a short flight
So breathe light
Undo the scent of the game
And fly, even when the wings are torn.